Availa
from
Spe

Once Upon a Wedding
by Stacy Connelly
&
Accidental Princess
by Nancy Robards Thompson

The Midwife's Glass Slipper
by Karen Rose Smith
&
Best For the Baby
by Ann Evans

Seventh Bride, Seventh Brother
by Nicole Foster
&
First Come Twins
by Helen Brenna

In Care of Sam Beaudry
by Kathleen Eagle

A Weaver Wedding
by Allison Leigh

Someone Like Her
by Janice Kay Johnson

A Forever Family
by Jamie Sobrato

ONCE UPON A WEDDING

Connor McClane had stepped to life from the photograph.

From his form-hugging T-shirt to his worn jeans and boots to the sunglasses covering his eyes.

Kelsey tried to swallow. Once, twice. Finally, she gave up and croaked out, "Mr McClane?"

"Yes?" He stopped to look at her, and Kelsey's only thought was that she still didn't know the colour of his eyes. Brown, maybe? To match the mahogany of his hair and tanned skin. Or blue?

A dark eyebrow rose above his mirrored sunglasses. A rush of heat flooded her cheeks. "Uh, Mr McClane –"

"We've already established who I am. Question is who are you?"

"My name's Kelsey Wilson."

He flashed a smile that revved her pulse.

Had she known her aunt was going to assign her this mission, she would have worn something different – like full body armour.

ACCIDENTAL PRINCESS

"Luc, where have you been?" Sophie's voice was barely a whisper. "I've missed you."

His mouth went dry. As he searched for the words, she reached out and ran a gentle finger along his jaw line.

His head tilted into her touch. He wanted to keep her here. Safe.

Her mouth was just a breath from his. Those lips... so tempting…would taste so sweet. A rush of desire urged him to give in to the taste and feel of her while the rest of the world melted away.

There were so many reasons he shouldn't…

…but at the moment, he couldn't seem to remember any of them.

First published in Great Britain 2010
Harlequin Mills & Boon Limited,
Eton House, 18-24 Paradise Road, Richmond, Surrey TW9 1SR

ISBN: 978 0 263 87966 7

23-0510

Harlequin Mills & Boon policy is to use papers that are natural, renewable and recyclable products and made from wood grown in sustainable forests. The logging and manufacturing processes conform to the legal environmental regulations of the country of origin.

Printed and bound in Spain
by Litografia Rosés S.A., Barcelona

ONCE UPON A WEDDING

BY

STACY CONNELLY

ACCIDENTAL PRINCESS

BY

NANCY ROBARDS THOMPSON

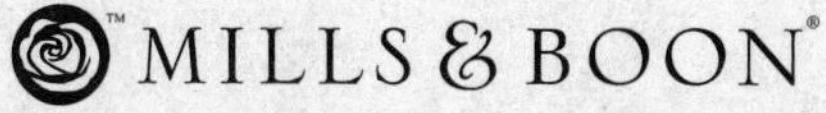

ONCE UPON A WEDDING

BY
STACY CONNELLY

Stacy Connelly has dreamed of publishing books since she was a kid, writing stories about a girl and her horse. Eventually, boys made it onto the page as she discovered a love of romance and the promise of happily ever after.

When she is not lost in the land of make-believe, Stacy lives in Arizona with her two spoiled dogs. She loves to hear from readers and can be contacted at stacyconnelly@cox.net or www.stacyconnelly.com.

To all my friends –
Thanks for being as excited about my dream coming true as I have been.

Chapter One

I can't believe I'm doing this, Kelsey Wilson thought as she hurried through the airport as fast as possible in her straight skirt and low-heeled pumps. Her oversized purse thudded against her side with every step. The shoulder strap caught a lock of red hair that had escaped her sensible bun, and she felt as though someone had reached out and grabbed her. Holding her back from the job she had to do.

The family is counting on you, Kelsey. Her aunt's voice rang in her mind. *You know what can happen when a woman falls for the wrong kind of man.*

Kelsey hadn't needed Aunt Charlene's reminder. She had her mother as an example. Olivia Wilson had thrown away everything for a man who left her with nothing. Olivia had been eighteen when she met Donnie Mardell—Kelsey's father, though she never thought of him in those terms. Donnie had promised Olivia a love of a lifetime, as well as freedom from her too-strict parents, and she fell for every word. When her father made her choose between Donnie and her family, Olivia chose Donnie. But while Olivia may have had stars in her eyes, Donnie had dollar signs in his. When the Wilsons offered him money to leave town, he took it without a glance back at his girlfriend or unborn child.

But Kelsey's cousin Emily hadn't fallen for the wrong man. She was engaged to Todd Dunworthy. The only son of a wealthy Chicago family, he'd come to Scottsdale to start his own company and add to his already considerable fortune. Todd was handsome, charming, and Charlene couldn't have handpicked a better son-in-law.

Kelsey had worked nonstop for the past two months to put together the perfect wedding. The dress, the flowers, the music, the cake, everything wove together like the hand-stitched Irish lace in Emily's veil. But Kelsey knew how delicate that lace was. One wrong pull, and it could all fall apart.

She refused to let that happen.

She *needed* this wedding to be amazing. She'd staked her reputation on the success of the ceremony, certain her cousin's wedding was the spotlight that would make her business shine. She'd been so sure of that she'd put most of her savings into a down payment for a small shop in Glendale. Kelsey had felt confident making the huge step. After all, her aunt and uncle were wealthy, influential people with wealthy, influential friends. Once the guests saw the job she'd done, Weddings Amour would flourish.

Even more important, her aunt and uncle would see that she, too, could succeed, that she was more than the poor relation they'd taken into their home. She'd been sixteen when her mother died, sixteen when Olivia finally admitted she was not an only child as she'd led Kelsey to believe. Olivia had an older brother, a sister-in-law and two nieces…total strangers who became Kelsey's only family.

Hold your head high, Olivia had whispered to Kelsey only days before passing away. Her face pale and gaunt, her blond hair long gone, her mother's eyes still blazed with the pride that empowered her to walk away from her family when she'd been pregnant at eighteen. *You may not have been raised as one of the wealthy Wilsons, but you're going to show them what an amazing young woman you are.*

Tears scalding her throat like acid, Kelsey had promised. She'd had no idea how difficult—how *impossible*—keeping that promise would be.

Finally, though, after eight years, she would have her chance to make good on her word. As a wedding planner, Kelsey had found her niche. She was organized, efficient, detail-oriented. Lessons learned as she scheduled her mother's doctor appointments, oversaw her medications and dealt with the insurance company served her well as she juggled caterers, musicians, photographers and the occasional Bridezilla.

Every wedding that ended in *I do* was a tribute to her mother's memory, and Emily's walk down the aisle would mean more than all the previous weddings. But before Emily could say her vows, Kelsey had to deal with one serious snag.

A sudden attack of nerves cartwheeling through her stomach, Kelsey swung her purse off her shoulder. She unzipped the center pocket and pulled out her day planner where, along with every detail of the wedding, she'd written the flight information. According to the listed arrivals, the plane from Los Angeles was on time.

Connor McClane was back in town.

Kelsey flipped to the front of the day planner and pulled out a photograph. Her aunt had said the picture was ten years old, which could account for the worn edges and creased corner. Kelsey feared there might be another reason. How many times had Emily stared at this photograph and wondered what might have been?

Kelsey had never met her cousin's ex-boyfriend, the bad boy from the wrong side of the tracks, but the snapshot said it all. Connor McClane leaned against a motorcycle, dressed head-to-toe in black—from his boots, to the jeans that clung to his long legs, to the T-shirt that hugged his muscular chest. His arms were crossed, and he glared into the camera. A shock of shaggy dark hair, a shadow of stubble on his stubborn jaw and mirrored sunglasses completed the look.

Kelsey could tell everything she needed to know from that picture except the color of Connor McClane's eyes. The man was trouble, as bad a boy as Donnie Mardell had ever been. Kelsey knew it, just like she knew Connor was better looking in a two-dimensional photo than any living, breathing man she'd ever meet.

Stuffing the picture and her day planner back in her purse, she hurried to the waiting area, where she focused on every man headed her way. He'd be twenty-nine by now, she reminded herself, four years her senior. Kelsey didn't suppose she was lucky enough that he'd aged badly or gone prematurely bald.

A beer belly, she thought, mentally crossing her fingers. A beer belly would be good.

But at the first glimpse of the dark-haired man sauntering down the corridor, her heart flipped within her chest and her hopes crashed. No signs of age, baldness or overhanging waistline…just pure masculine perfection. Her mouth went as dry as the surrounding desert.

Connor McClane had stepped to life from the photograph. From his form-hugging T-shirt, to his worn jeans and boots, to the sunglasses covering his eyes, every detail remained the same. A plane took off from a nearby runway, and the low rumble reverberating in her chest could have easily come from a motorcycle.

Kelsey tried to swallow. Once, twice. Finally she gave up and croaked out, "Mr. McClane?"

"Yes?" He stopped to look at her, and Kelsey's only thought was that she still didn't know the color of his eyes. Brown, maybe? To match the mahogany of his hair and tanned skin. Or blue? A bright, vivid contrast to his coloring.

A dark eyebrow rose above his mirrored sunglasses, a reminder that she had yet to answer him. A rush of heat flooded her cheeks. "Uh, Mr. McClane—"

"We've already established who I am. Question is, who are you?"

"My name's Kelsey Wilson."

He flashed a smile that revved her pulse. His head dipped, and she sensed him taking in the red hair she struggled to control, the freckled skin she tried to cover, and the extra pounds she sought to hide beneath the khaki skirt and boxy shirt. She saw her reflection in his mirrored glasses, a much shorter, much wider version of herself, like a carnival funhouse distortion.

Kelsey didn't feel much like laughing.

Had she known her aunt was going to assign her this mission, she would have worn something different—like full body armor. The image of what Emily might have worn to meet her former boyfriend flashed in Kelsey's mind. She shoved the pointless comparison away. Too much like trying to force Strawberry Shortcake into Barbie's wardrobe.

"Well, what do you know?" Connor stood in the middle of the corridor, mindless of the sea of people parting around him. "The Wilsons sent out a welcoming party. Heck, if I'd known I'd get this kind of reception, I might have come back sooner."

"I doubt that," Kelsey muttered.

Connor McClane had planned his return perfectly, coming back to ruin Emily's wedding. Aunt Charlene was certain of it. Kelsey knew only one thing. Her cousin had nearly thrown her future away once for this man, and she could see how Emily might be tempted to do it again.

"Don't underestimate your appeal," he told her, and though she couldn't see beyond the reflective sunglasses, she had the distinct impression he'd winked at her.

Kelsey straightened her spine to the shattering point. "My appeal isn't in question. I'm here to—"

Keep him away from Emily, Kelsey. I don't care how you do it, but keep that man away from my daughter!

"To do what, Kelsey Wilson?"

His deep voice made her name sound like a seduction, and suddenly she could think of all kinds of things to do that had nothing to do with her aunt's wishes. Or did they? How far would Aunt Charlene expect her to go to keep Connor away from Emily?

"To give you a ride from the airport," she answered with a saccharine smile. "Baggage claim is this way."

Connor patted the duffel bag slung over one shoulder. "Got everything with me."

Eyeing the lumpy bag, Kelsey wondered how dress clothes could survive such careless packing. Maybe he planned to ride his motorcycle up to the church in leather and denim, the same way he'd ridden out of town ten years ago? Unless—

"You didn't bring much with you. You must not plan to stay long."

Something in her voice must have given away her hope, because Connor chuckled. He adjusted the duffel bag and headed down the corridor, his strides so long Kelsey nearly had to jog to keep up.

"Oh, I'll be here as long as it takes," he told her with a sideways glance, "but I won't need more than a few days."

A few days. Did she really want to know? Did she really want to throw down the verbal gauntlet? Kelsey took a deep breath, partly to gather some courage, partly to gather some much needed oxygen. "A few days to what?"

"To stop Emily from marrying the wrong man."

Connor hadn't known what to expect when he stepped off the plane. He'd given Emily his flight information with the hope she might meet him at the airport. He'd wanted a chance to talk to her away from her family and her fiancé. He was realistic enough to know the whole Wilson brigade might be lined up at the gate like some kind of high-fashion firing squad. But he hadn't expected a petite redhead. He'd never imagined the Wilson genes could produce a petite redhead.

"So who are you anyway?" he asked, only to realize the woman was no longer at his side.

He glanced back over his shoulder. Kelsey Wilson stood in the middle of the corridor, her brown eyes wide, her lips adorably parted in shock. She didn't look anything like the other Wilsons, and curiosity stirred inside him. He couldn't picture her at the elegant country-club settings the status-conscious family enjoyed any more than he'd imagined himself there.

A Wilson misfit, he thought, *on the outside looking in.* Their gazes locked, and the momentary connection rocked him. Shaking off the feeling, he circled back around and asked, "You coming?"

The flush of color on her cheeks nearly blotted out her freckles. "You don't actually think you can come back here after ten years and expect to take up where you left off? You weren't right for Emily back then, and you aren't right for her now!"

As far as insults went, the words were pretty tame, especially coming from a Wilson. And it wasn't as if he had any intention of taking up where he and Emily had left off. He'd made his share of mistakes, and some—like thinking he and Emily had a chance—didn't bear repeating. Emily had been looking for someone to rescue her from the life her parents had planned for her, and he'd been young enough to think of himself as a hero.

Connor knew better now. He was nobody's hero.

Still, Kelsey's reminder stirred long-buried resentment. *Worthless. Good for nothing. Troublemaker.* Gordon Wilson had shouted them all when he'd discovered his younger daughter sneaking out to meet Connor. After being knocked around by his old man during his childhood, he knew a thing or two about male aggression and had arrogantly faced down the older man.

But Charlene Wilson's clipped, controlled words had managed to pierce his cocky facade. "From the moment Emily was born, she has had nothing but the best," Charlene told him with ice practically hanging from her words. "We have given her the world. What could *you* possibly give her?"

He'd tried to give her her freedom, the chance to live her life without bowing to her family's expectations. If someone had given his mother that same chance, things would have been different, and maybe, just maybe, she would still be alive. But when Emily made her choice, she didn't choose him. She took the easy way out—and in the end, so did he, Connor thought, guilt from the past and present mixing. But he wasn't going to fail this time. He was here to help Emily, no matter what the redhead standing in front of him like a curvaceous barricade thought.

"Look, whoever you are," he said, since she'd never explained her relationship to the Wilsons, "you didn't know me then, and you don't know me now. You don't have a clue what I'm good for."

He ducked his head and lowered his voice, not wanting to attract attention, but the words came out like a seductive challenge. He stood close enough to catch a hint of cinnamon coming from her skin. The color faded from her complexion, and her freckles stood out clearly enough to play a game of connect-the-dots. He shoved his hands into his pockets rather than give into the urge to trace a five-point star over one cheek. He tried to imagine Kelsey's reaction if he touched her. Would she recoil in shock? Or would he see an answering awareness in her chocolate eyes?

Right now, sparks of annoyance lit her gaze. "I know all I need to know. You're no good for Emily. You never were—What are you doing?" she demanded when Connor leaned around to look over her shoulder.

"Amazing. You can't even see the strings."

"What strings?"

"The ones Charlene Wilson uses to control you."

"Aunt Charlene does not control me."

Aunt Charlene, was it? He didn't remember Emily talking about a cousin, but they hadn't spent time discussing genealogy. "Funny, 'cause you sure sound like her."

"That's because we both want to protect Emily."

Protecting Emily was exactly why he was there. Adjusting the duffel bag on his shoulder, he started toward the parking garage. "So do I."

"Right." Kelsey struggled to keep up with him, and Connor shortened his stride. "Who do you think you have to protect her from?"

"From Charlene. From you." Before Kelsey could voice the protest he read in her stubborn expression, he added, "Mostly from Todd."

"From *Todd?* That's ridiculous. Todd loves Emily."

Yeah, well, Connor had seen what a man could do to a woman in the name of love. Seen it and had been helpless to stop it from happening… Shoving the dark memories of his mother and Cara Mitchell aside, Connor said, "Todd's not the golden boy the Wilsons think he is. The guy's bad news."

"How would you know?" Kelsey challenged as they stepped out the automatic doors and into the midday sunshine. Exhaust and honking horns rode the waves of heat. "My car's this way."

Connor followed Kelsey across the street to the short-term parking, where the fumes and noise faded slightly in the dimly lit garage. "I could tell from the second we met."

She stopped so suddenly he almost crashed into her back. When she turned, he was close enough that her shoulder brushed his chest, and the inane thought that she would fit perfectly in his arms crossed his mind.

Her eyes narrowed in suspicion. "You've never met Todd."

"How do you know?"

"Be-because," she sputtered. "Emily would have told me."

Despite her words, Connor saw the doubt written in her furrowed brow as she walked over to a gray sedan. The car nearly blended into the concrete floor and pylons. Between her plain vehicle and sedate clothes, he had the feeling Kelsey Wilson was a woman who liked to fade into the background.

But he was trained to notice details. He'd bet the brilliant hair she kept coiled at the back of her neck was longer and wilder than it looked, and try as they might, the shapeless clothes did little to hide some amazing curves.

"If Emily tells you everything, then you know she and Dunworthy spent a weekend in San Diego a few weeks ago, right?" At Kelsey's nod, Connor added, "Well, I drove there to meet them, and we had dinner." Keeping his voice deceptively innocent, he asked, "Emily didn't mention that?"

"Um, no," Kelsey grudgingly confessed.

"I wonder why. Don't you?" he pressed.

Not that there was much to tell, although he wasn't about to admit that to Kelsey. When he left town, he never thought he'd see Emily again. But after hearing through the long-distance grapevine that she was getting married, calling to congratulate her seemed like a good way to put the past behind him. The last thing he expected was Emily's invitation to have dinner with her and her fiancé while they were vacationing in California. But he'd agreed, thinking the meeting might ease his guilt. After all, if Emily had found Mr. Right, maybe that would finally justify his reasons for leaving Scottsdale.

But when Connor went to dinner with Emily, he didn't see a woman who'd grown and matured and found her place in life. Instead, he saw in Emily's eyes the same trapped look as when they'd first met—a look he could not, would not ignore.

Kelsey kept both hands on the wheel and her gaze focused on the road, but she was far too aware of Connor McClane to pay much attention to the buildings, billboards and exit signs speeding by. The air-conditioning blew his aftershave toward her heated face, a scent reminiscent of surf, sand and sea. His big body barely fit in the passenger seat. Twice now, his arm brushed against hers, sending her pulse racing, and she nearly swerved out of her lane.

She'd been right in thinking the man was dangerous, and not just to Emily's future or her own peace of mind, but to passing motorists, as well.

"I can't believe how much the city has grown. All these new freeways and houses…" He leaned forward to study a sign. "Hey, take this next exit."

Kelsey followed his directions, wishing she could drop him off at a hotel and call her familial duty done. Unfortunately, playing chauffeur wasn't her real purpose. Connor had flat-out told her he planned to ruin Emily's wedding. If she didn't stop him, her own business would be destroyed in the fallout. Who would trust a wedding planner who couldn't pull off her own cousin's wedding?

Panic tightened her hands on the wheel. "Where are we going?" she asked.

"My friend Javy's family owns a restaurant around here. Best Mexican food you've ever tasted."

"I don't like Mexican food."

He shook his head. "Poor Kelsey. Can't take the heat, huh?"

They stopped at a red light, and she risked a glance at him. He still wore those darn sunglasses, but she didn't need to look into his eyes to read his thoughts. He was here to win back Emily and show the Wilsons and the rest of the world they'd underestimated him all those years ago. But until then, he'd kill some time by flirting with her.

Kelsey didn't know why the thought hurt so much. After all, it wasn't the first time a man had used her to try and get to her beautiful, desirable cousin.

The light turned green, and she hit the gas harder than necessary. "Let's just say I've been burned before."

A heartbeat's silence passed. When Connor spoke again, his voice was friendly, casual and missing the seductive undertone. "You'll like this place." He chuckled. "I can't tell you how many meals I've had there. If it hadn't been for Señora Delgado…"

Kelsey wondered at the warmth and gratitude in his words. Something told her Connor wasn't simply reminiscing about tacos and burritos. An undeniable curiosity built as she pulled into the parking lot. The restaurant looked like an old-time hacienda with its flat roof and arched entryway. The stucco had been painted a welcoming terra-cotta. Strings of outdoor lights scalloped the front porch, and large clay pots housed a variety of heat-tolerant plants: pink and white vinca, yellow gazanias, and clusters of cacti.

Still checking out the exterior, Kelsey remained behind the wheel until Connor circled the car and opened the door for her. Startled by the chivalry, she grabbed her purse and took his hand. As she slid out of the seat, she hoped Connor didn't guess how rare or surprising she found the gesture.

She thought he'd let go, but he kept hold of her hand as he led her along red, green and yellow mosaic stepping stones that cut through the gravel landscape. His palm felt hard and masculine against her own, but without the calluses she'd somehow expected.

When he opened the carved door, he let go of her hand to lay claim to the small of her back. A shiver rocked her entire body. His solicitous touch shouldn't have the power to turn on every nerve ending. And it certainly shouldn't have the inexplicable ability to send her mind reeling with images of his hand stroking down her naked spine…

Full body armor, Kelsey thought once again, uncertain even that extreme could shield her from her own reactions.

Desperate to change her focus, she looked around the restaurant. A dozen round tables stood in the center of the Saltillo-tiled room, and booths lined each wall. The scent of grilled peppers and mouthwatering spices filled the air.

"Man, would you look at this place?" Connor waved a hand at the brightly colored walls, the piñatas dangling from the ceiling and the woven-blanket wall hangings.

He removed his sunglasses to take in the dimly lit restaurant, but Kelsey couldn't see beyond his eyes. Not brown, not blue, but gorgeous, glorious green. A reminder of spring, the short burst of cool days, the promise of dew-kissed grass. Without the glasses to shield his eyes, Connor McClane looked younger, more approachable, a little less badass.

"Has it changed?"

"No, everything's exactly the same. Just like it should be," he added with a determination that made Kelsey wonder. Had someone once threatened to change the restaurant that was so important to his friends?

A young woman wearing a red peasant-style blouse and white three-tiered skirt approached, menus in hand. "*Buenas tardes.* Two for lunch?"

"Sí. Dónde está Señora Delgado?"

Startled, Kelsey listened to Connor converse in fluent Spanish. She couldn't understand a word, so why did his deep voice pour like hot fudge through her veins?

Get a grip! Connor McClane is in town for one reason and one reason only. And that reason was not her.

The hostess led them to a corner booth. Kelsey barely had a chance to slide across the red Naugahyde and glance at the menu when a masculine voice called out, "Look what the cat dragged in!"

A good-looking Hispanic man dressed in a white button-down shirt and khakis walked over. Connor stood and slapped him on the back in a moment of male bonding. "Javy! Good to see you, man!"

"How's life in L.A.?"

"Not bad. How's your mother? The hostess says she's not here today?"

"She's semiretired, which means she's only here to kick my butt half the time," Javy laughed.

"I didn't think you'd ever get Maria to slow down."

"This place means the world to her. I still don't know how to thank you."

"Forget it, man," Connor quickly interrupted. "It was nothing compared to what your family's done for me over the years."

Modesty? Kelsey wondered, though Connor didn't seem

the type. And yet she didn't read even an ounce of pride in his expression. If anything, he looked…guilty.

"I'm not about to forget it, and I *will* find a way to pay you back," Javy insisted. "Hey, do you want to crash at my place while you're here?"

"No, thanks. I've got a hotel room."

Finally Connor turned back to Kelsey. "Javy, there's someone I'd like you to meet. Javier Delgado, Kelsey Wilson."

Javy did a double take at Kelsey's last name, then slanted Connor a warning look. "Man, some people never learn."

Still, his dark eyes glittered and a dimple flashed in one cheek as he said, "Pleasure to meet you, *señorita.* Take care of this one, will you? He's not as tough as he thinks he is."

"Get outta here." Connor shoved his friend's shoulder before sliding into the booth across from Kelsey. "And bring us some food. I've been dying for your mother's enchiladas." He handed back the menu without opening it. "What about you, Kelsey?"

"I'm, um, not sure." The menu was written in Spanish on the right and English on the left, but even with the translation, she didn't know what to order.

"She'll have a chicken quesadilla with the guacamole and sour cream on the side. And we'll both have margaritas."

"I'll take mine without alcohol," Kelsey insisted. Bad enough he'd ordered her lunch. She didn't need him ordering a drink for her, especially not one laden with tequila and guaranteed to go right to her head.

"Two margaritas, one virgin," Connor said with a wink that sent a rush of heat to Kelsey's cheeks. With her fair complexion, she figured she could give the red pepper garland strung across the ceiling a run for its money.

"I'll get those orders right up."

As his friend walked toward the kitchen, Connor leaned

back in the booth and gazed around the restaurant. Nostalgia lifted the corners of his mouth in a genuine smile. "Man, I've missed this place."

"So why haven't you come back before now?" Kelsey asked, curious despite sensible warnings to keep her distance.

He shrugged. "Never had reason to, I guess."

"Until now," she added flatly, "when you've come to crash Emily's wedding."

Losing his relaxed pose, he braced his muscled forearms on the table and erased the separation between them. His smile disappeared, nostalgia burned away by determination. "First of all, there isn't going to be a wedding. And second, even if there was a wedding, I wouldn't be crashing. I'd be an invited guest."

"Invited!" Surprise and something she didn't want to label had her pulling back, hoping to create some sanity-saving distance. "Who…" She groaned at the obvious answer, and the confident spark in Connor's emerald eyes. "What on earth was Emily thinking?"

"Actually, she summed up her thoughts pretty well."

Connor reached into his back pocket and pulled out an invitation. He offered it up like a challenge, holding a corner between his first and second fingers. She snatched it away, almost afraid to read what her cousin had written. Emily's girlish script flowered across the cream-colored vellum.

Please say you'll come. I can't imagine my wedding day without you.

Good Lord, it was worse than she'd thought! The words practically sounded like a proposal. Was Emily hoping Connor would stop her wedding? That he'd speak now rather than hold his peace?

"Okay," she said with the hope of defusing the situation, "so Emily invited you."

"That's not an invitation. It's a cry for help."

"It's—it's closure," she said, knowing she was grasping at straws. "Emily has moved on with her life, and she's hoping you'll do the same."

He frowned. "What makes you think I haven't?"

"Are you married? Engaged? In a serious relationship?" Kelsey pressed. Each shake of his head proved Kelsey's point. He wasn't over Emily.

Kelsey couldn't blame him. Her cousin was beautiful, inside and out. And experience had taught Kelsey how far a man would go to be a part of Emily's life.

Connor slid the invitation from her hand in what felt like a caress. "There's no reason for me not to be here, Kelsey."

Here, in Arizona, to stop the wedding, she had to remind herself as she snatched her hand back and laced her fingers together beneath the table. Not *here* with her.

The waitress's arrival with their drinks spared Kelsey from having to come up with a response. Connor lifted his margarita. "To new friends."

Rising to the challenge this time, she tapped her glass against his. "And old lovers?"

If she'd hoped to somehow put him in his place, she failed miserably. With a low chuckle, he amended, "Let's make that old friends…and new lovers."

His vibrant gaze held her captive as he raised his glass. Ignoring the straw, he took a drink. A hum of pleasure escaped him. The sound seemed to vibrate straight from his body and into hers, a low-frequency awareness that shook her to the core.

He lowered the glass and licked the tequila, salt and lime from his upper lip. "You don't know what you're missing."

Oh, she knew. The taste of a man's kiss, the scent of his aftershave on her clothes, the feel of his hard body moving against her own. How long had it been since a man had stolen her breath, her sanity? How many weeks, months? She'd probably be better converting the time into years—fewer numbers to count.

Odd how Kelsey hadn't missed any of those things until the moment Connor McClane walked down the airport corridor. No, she had to admit, she'd suffered the first twinge of—loneliness? Lust? She didn't know exactly *what* it was, but she'd first felt it the moment she'd looked at Connor's picture.

"Aren't you having any?"

Her gaze dropped to his mouth, and for one second, she imagined leaning over the table and tasting the tequila straight from Connor's lips.

"Kelsey, your drink?" he all but growled. The heat in his gaze made it clear he knew her sudden thirst had nothing to do with margaritas.

Maybe if she downed the whole thing in one swallow, the brain freeze might be enough to cool her body. She sucked in a quick strawful of the tart, icy mixture with little effect. Frozen nonalcoholic drinks had nothing on Connor McClane.

Still, she set the glass down with a decisive clunk. "You can't come back here and decide what's best for Emily. It doesn't matter if *you* don't like Todd. You're not the one marrying him. Emily is, and her opinion is the only one that matters."

Connor let out a bark of laughter. "Right! How much weight do you think her *opinion* carried when we were dating?"

"That was different."

"Yeah, because I was a nobody from the wrong side of the tracks instead of some old-money entrepreneur with the Wilson stamp of approval on my backside."

A nobody from the wrong side of the tracks. Kelsey schooled her expression not to reveal how closely those words struck home. What would Connor McClane think if he learned she had more in common with *him* than with her wealthy cousins?

Kelsey shook off the feeling. It didn't matter what they did or didn't have in common; they were on opposite sides.

"Did you ever consider that Emily's parents thought she was too young? She was barely out of high school, and all she could talk about was running away with you."

"Exactly."

Expecting a vehement denial, Kelsey shook her head. "Huh?"

One corner of his mouth tilted in a smile. "I might have been blind back then, but I've learned a thing or two. Emily was always a good girl, never caused her parents any trouble. She didn't smoke, didn't drink, didn't do drugs. No tattoos or piercings for her."

"Of course not."

From the time Kelsey had moved in with her aunt and uncle, she'd lived in her cousin's shadow. She knew all about how perfect Emily was—her fling with Connor the sole imperfection that proved she was actually human.

"Emily didn't have to do those things. She had me. I was her ultimate act of rebellion."

Kelsey listened for the arrogant ring in his words, but the cocky tone was absent. In its place, she heard a faint bitterness. "No one likes being used," she murmured, thoughts of her ex-boyfriend coming to mind.

Matt Moran had her completely fooled during the six months they dated. With his shy personality and awkward social skills, she couldn't say he swept her off her feet. But he'd seemed sweet, caring, and truly interested in her.

And she'd never once suspected he was secretly in love with her cousin or that he'd been using her to get closer to Emily. So Kelsey knew how Connor felt, and somehow knowing that was like knowing *him.* Her gaze locked with his in a moment of emotional recognition she didn't dare acknowledge.

The question was written in his eyes, but she didn't want

to answer, didn't want him seeing inside her soul. "What was Emily rebelling against?"

Connor hesitated, and for a second Kelsey feared he might not let the change of subject slide. Finally, though, he responded, "It had to do with her choice of college. She hated that exclusive prep school, but Charlene insisted on only the best. I suppose that's where you went, too."

"Not me," she protested. "I had the finest education taxpayers could provide." One of Connor's dark eyebrows rose, and Kelsey hurried on before he could ask why her childhood had differed from her cousins'. "So after Emily survived prep school…"

He picked up where she left off, but Kelsey had the feeling he'd filed away her evasion for another time. "After graduation, Gordon wanted Emily to enroll at an Ivy League school. She didn't want to, but her parents held all the cards—until I came along. I was the ace up her sleeve. Guess I still am."

The bad-boy grin and teasing light were absent from his expression, and Kelsey felt a flicker of unease tumbling helplessly through her stomach. Did Connor know something about Todd that would stop the wedding? Something that would tear apart all Kelsey's dreams for success and her chance to prove herself in her family's eyes?

"Emily invited me because her parents are pushing her into this marriage. She's pushing back the only way she knows how. She *wants* me to stop the wedding."

"That's crazy! Do you realize Emily is having her dress fitting right now? And we're going to the hotel tomorrow evening to make final arrangements for the reception? She loves Todd and wants to spend the rest of her life with him."

Leaning forward, he challenged, "If you're right, if Emily's so crazy about this guy, then why are you worried I'm here?"

A knowing light glowed in his green eyes, and history told

Kelsey she had every reason to worry. After all, on the night of her senior prom, after spending the day having her hair artfully styled and her makeup expertly applied, and wearing the perfect dress, Emily had stood up her parents' handpicked date…to ride off with Connor on the back of his motorcycle.

Having met Connor, Kelsey could see how easily he must have seduced her cousin. With his looks, charm, his flat-out masculine appeal, how was a woman supposed to resist?

And Kelsey wondered if maybe Emily wasn't the only one she should be worried about.

Chapter Two

"Honestly, Kelsey, why are you ringing the doorbell like some stranger?" Aileen Wilson-Kirkland demanded as she opened the front door. She latched on to Kelsey's arm and nearly dragged her inside her aunt and uncle's travertine-tiled foyer.

"Well, it's not like I still live here," Kelsey reminded her cousin.

Aileen rolled her eyes. "You probably rang the doorbell even when this *was* your home."

"I did not," Kelsey protested, even as heat bloomed in her cheeks. Her cousin might have been teasing, but the comment wasn't far off. She'd never felt comfortable living in her aunt and uncle's gorgeous Scottsdale house, with its country-club lifestyle and golf-course views. Before moving in with her relatives, *home* had been a series of low-rent apartments. And, oh, how she'd missed those small, cozy places she'd shared with her mother.

"I didn't want to barge in," she added.

"You're kidding, right? Like I haven't been dying to hear how things went! Did you pick up Connor? Does he look the same? Do you think—"

Ignoring the rapid-fire questions, Kelsey asked, "Where are Emily and Aunt Charlene?"

"Emily's still having her dress fitted."

"Oh, I'd love to see it." A designer friend of Kelsey's had made the dress for her cousin, but so far Kelsey had seen only drawings and fabric swatches.

For such a gorgeous woman, Aileen gave a decidedly inelegant snort as they walked down the hall. "Nice try. Do you really think you can escape without going over every detail from the first second you saw Connor right up to when you left him—" Emily's older sister frowned. "Where *did* you leave him?"

"At a restaurant."

"By himself?"

"What else could I do, Aileen? Follow him to his hotel and ask for an invitation inside?"

"Well, that would make it easier to keep an eye on him."

"Aileen!"

Waving aside Kelsey's indignation, Aileen said, "I'm just kidding. Besides, he doesn't have a car, right?"

"Like that's going to slow him down! Don't you remember the time Connor got busted for joyriding in a 'borrowed' car?" She hadn't been around then, but her aunt had remarked on Connor's misdeeds long after he'd left town. In fact, Connor's name had come up any time Emily threatened to disobey her parents. Like some kind of bogeyman Aunt Charlene evoked to keep her younger daughter in line.

Her cousin's perfectly shaped brows rose. "You don't think he's still involved in illegal activities, do you?"

"I have no idea," Kelsey said, ignoring the internal voice yelling *no.* Her automatic desire to rush to Connor's defense worried her. She was supposed to stop him, not champion him.

"You should find out," Aileen said as she led the way into the study. The bookshelf-lined room, with its leather and mahogany furniture, was her uncle's masculine domain, but even this room had been taken over by wedding preparations. Stacks of photo albums cluttered the coffee table.

"Why me?" Kelsey groaned.

"You want to help Emily, don't you?"

"Of course I do!" she insisted, even if she had to admit her motives weren't completely altruistic.

"And you want the wedding to be perfect, right?" Her cousin already knew the answer and didn't wait for Kelsey's response.

"I know Mother exaggerates, but not when it comes to Connor McClane. I wouldn't be surprised if he tried kidnapping Emily again," Aileen added.

Kelsey fought to keep from rolling her eyes. "She took off with Connor on prom night and didn't come back until the next day. I think your parents overreacted."

"Maybe, but I guarantee he'll try to stop the wedding somehow." Aileen pointed an older-therefore-wiser finger in Kelsey's direction. "But don't let him fool you."

He hadn't bothered to try to fool her. Was Connor so confident he could stop the wedding that he didn't care who knew about his plan?

Walking over to the coffee table, Aileen picked up a stack of photos. "Here are the pictures Mother wants to show during the reception."

"Thanks." Kelsey flipped through images of her cousin's life. Not a bad-hair day or an acne breakout in the bunch. Even in pigtails and braces Emily had been adorable. As

Kelsey tucked them into her purse, she noticed a stray photo had fallen to the Oriental area rug. "Did you want to include this one?"

Her voice trailed off as she had a better look at the picture. At first glance, the young woman could have been Emily, but the feathered hair and ruffled prom dress were wrong. "Oh, wow."

From the time Kelsey had come to live with her aunt and uncle, she'd heard how much Emily looked like Kelsey's mother, Olivia. Kelsey had seen similarities in the blond hair and blue eyes, but from this picture of a teenage Olivia dressed for a high school dance, she and Emily could have passed for sisters.

Reading her thoughts, Aileen said, "Amazing, isn't it?"

"It is. Everyone always said—" Kelsey shook her head. "I never noticed."

"Really? But they look so much alike!"

"My mother, she didn't—" Laugh? Smile? Ever look as *alive* as she looked in that photo? Uncertain what to say, Kelsey weakly finished, "I don't remember her looking like this."

"Oh, Kelse. I'm sorry." Concern darkened Aileen's eyes. "I should have realized with your mother being so sick and having to go through chemo. Of course, she didn't look the same."

Accepting her cousin's condolences with a touch of guilt, Kelsey silently admitted Olivia Wilson had lost any resemblance to the girl in the picture long before being diagnosed with cancer. What would it have been like had her mother retained some of that carefree, joyful spirit? Kelsey immediately thrust the disloyal thought aside.

Olivia had given up everything—including the wealth and family that now surrounded Kelsey—to raise her daughter. Emily's wedding was Kelsey's chance to live up to her promise. To hold her head high and finally show the Wilsons how amazing she could be.

With a final look at the picture, Kelsey slid the photo of her mother back into one of the albums. "It's okay," she told Aileen. "Let's go see if Emily's done with the fitting."

"All right. But be warned," Aileen said as she led the way down the hall toward Emily's bedroom. "The photographer's in there."

"Really?" Kelsey frowned. "I don't remember pictures of the fitting being included. Was that something Emily requested?"

She had long accepted that her ideas and her cousins' differed greatly, but a seamstress fretting over her measurements would have been a nightmare for Kelsey, not a photo op.

Aileen shrugged and opened the door just a crack. "The photographer said it was all part of the package."

A quick glance inside, and Kelsey immediately saw what "package" the photographer was interested in. Emily stood in the middle of the bedroom, with its girlish four-poster bed and French provincial furniture. Her sheer, lace-covered arms were held out straight at her sides while the seamstress pinned the beaded bodice to fit her willowy curves. Dewy makeup highlighted her wide blue eyes, flawless cheekbones and smiling lips.

"What do you think, Mother? Will Todd like it?" Emily leaned forward to examine the skirt, testing the limits of a dozen stickpins.

The photographer, a man in his midtwenties, started snapping shots as fast as his index finger could fly. It wasn't the first time Kelsey had seen slack-jawed amazement on a man's face. Too bad she saw the expression only when her cousin was around.

"Of course he will. Audra is an amazing designer, and she created that dress just for you. It's perfect," Aunt Charlene insisted, keeping a narrow-eyed glare on the photographer.

Charlene Wilson didn't share her daughters' beauty, but she

was a tall, striking woman. She could instantly command a room with her timeless sense of style and demand for perfection from herself and those around her. Today she wore a beige silk suit that wouldn't dare wrinkle and her brown hair in an elegant twist at the nape of her neck.

Glancing down at her own clothes, a map of creases that spelled fashion disaster, Kelsey knew her aunt would be horrified by the sight. Fortunately, Charlene was far too busy to notice. Kelsey slid the door shut and walked back down the hallway with Aileen.

"I know all brides are supposed to be beautiful," Aileen said with a mixture of sisterly affection and envy, "but that's ridiculous."

"Please, I've seen pictures of your wedding. You were just as gorgeous."

Aileen gave a theatrical sigh. "True. Of course, I wasn't lucky enough to have you to plan everything. I ran myself ragged, and you make it look so easy."

Kelsey laughed even as her cheeks heated with embarrassed pleasure. "That's because I'm only planning the wedding. It's far more stressful to be the bride."

"Still, you're doing an amazing job. Mother thinks so, too, even if she hasn't told you. This wedding will make your company."

That was just what she was counting on, Kelsey thought, excitement filling her once again. "I know." Taking a deep breath, she confessed, "I put down first and last month's rent on that shop in Glendale."

Aileen made a sound of delight and threw her arms around Kelsey in a hug that ended before she could lift her stiff arms in response. After eight years, Kelsey should have anticipated the enthusiastic embrace, but somehow, both her cousins' easy affection always caught her off guard.

"That is so exciting, and it's about time! You should have opened a shop a long time ago instead of working out of your home."

"I couldn't afford it until now."

"You could have if you'd taken my father up on his loan," Aileen said.

Kelsey swallowed. "I couldn't," she said, knowing Aileen wouldn't understand any more than her uncle Gordon had. Starting her business was something she had to do for herself and for her mother's memory.

Wilson women against the world... Her mother's voice rang in her head. Opening the shop wouldn't have the same meaning with her uncle's money behind the success.

Aileen shook her head. "Honestly, Kelsey, you are so stubborn." A slight frown pulled her eyebrows together. "But something tells me you're going to need every bit of that determination—"

Kelsey jumped in. "To keep Connor McClane away from Emily. I know, Aileen. But if Emily's so crazy about Todd, what difference does it make that Connor's in town?"

Ever since he'd posed that question, Kelsey couldn't get his words out of her mind. Okay, so in her opinion, Todd Dunworthy didn't hold even a teeny, tiny, flickering match to Connor McClane. But if her cousin truly loved Todd, shouldn't he outshine every other man—including an old flame like Connor?

"Kelsey, we're talking about Connor McClane. I know you've sworn off men since Matt, but please tell me that idiot didn't rob you of every female hormone in your body!"

Even after two years, the thought of her ex-boyfriend made Kelsey cringe. Not because of the heartbreak but because of the humiliation. Still, she argued, "I'm not discounting Connor's appeal." If anything, she'd been mentally recounting every attractive feature, from his quick wit to his sexy smile and killer bod. "But if I were a week away from getting married and madly in love with my fiancé, none of that would matter."

Aileen sighed and slanted Kelsey a look filled with worldly wisdom. "It's cold feet. Every engaged woman goes through it. I called things off with Tom three times before we finally made it to the altar. You'll see what I mean when you get engaged."

The idea of Kelsey getting engaged was in serious question, but if that time ever did come, she was sure she'd be so in love she'd never harbor any doubts. "Okay, so you called off your engagement. Did you run off with another man?"

"You know I didn't."

"Well, that's my point. If Emily and Todd are right for each other, Connor's presence shouldn't matter."

"It shouldn't, but it does. You weren't here when Emily and Connor were together. He's the kind of man who makes a woman want to live for the moment and never think of tomorrow. When Emily was around him, she'd get completely caught up in the here and now of Connor McClane. But her relationship with Todd is something that can last." Aileen flashed a bright smile. "Look, you've handled prewedding problems before. All you have to do is keep Connor away. You can do that, can't you, Kelsey?"

What else could she do but say yes?

Connor scrolled through his laptop's files, going over the information he'd compiled on Todd Dunworthy. He had to have missed something.

Swearing, he rolled away from the desk in his hotel suite and pushed out of the chair. He paced the length of the room, but even with the extra money he'd paid for a suite, he couldn't go far. From the closet, past the bathroom, between the desk and footboard, to the window and back. He supposed he should consider himself lucky not to have

Kelsey Wilson shadowing his every step. An unwanted smile tugged at his lips at the thought of the woman he'd met the day before.

He'd finally convinced her to leave him at the restaurant, telling her he had years to catch up with his friend, Javy. The words were true enough, but he'd seen the suspicion in her brown eyes. He chuckled at the thought of the atypical Wilson relative. She was nothing like Emily, that was for sure. Compared to Kelsey's fiery red hair, deep brown eyes, and womanly curves, Emily suddenly seemed like a blond-haired, blue-eyed paper doll.

But no matter how much curiosity Kelsey Wilson provoked, Connor couldn't let himself be distracted.

After his relationship with Emily ended, Connor had drifted around Southern California. Different state, but he'd hung out with the same crowd. Busting up a fight in a club had gotten him his first job as a bouncer. He'd worked security for several years before taking a chance and opening a P.I. business.

Up until three months ago, he would have said he was good at his job, one of the best. That he had a feel for people, an instinct that told him when someone was lying. Listening to his gut had saved his skin more than once. Not listening had nearly gotten a woman killed.

From the first moment he'd met Todd Dunworthy, Connor had that same hit-below-the-belt feeling. And this time he was damn sure gonna listen. So far, though, his background check had merely revealed Dunworthy was the youngest son of a wealthy Chicago family. Numerous newspaper photos showed him at the opera, a benefit for the symphony, a gallery opening. And while the events and locales changed, he always had a different woman—tall, blond and beautiful—on his arm.

No doubt about it, Emily was definitely Todd's type.

"You sure you don't hate the guy just 'cause the Wilsons

love him?" Javy had pressed on the ride from the restaurant to the hotel.

Connor couldn't blame his friend for asking. And, okay, so maybe he would dislike anyone who met with the Wilsons' approval, but that didn't change his opinion. Todd Dunworthy was not the man they thought he was.

He'd spoken to several of the Dunworthy family employees and none of them were talking. It wasn't that they wouldn't say anything bad about their employers; Connor expected that. But these people refused to say a word, which told him one important thing. As well paid as they might be to do their jobs, they were even better compensated to keep quiet.

Most were lifers—employees who had been with the family for decades. But there was one woman he hadn't been able to reach. A former maid named Sophia Pirelli. She'd worked for the family for two years before suddenly quitting or getting fired—no one would say—two months ago. The silence alone made Connor suspicious, and figuring an ex-employee might be willing to talk, Connor wanted to find her.

A few days ago he'd found a lead on Sophia's whereabouts. As much as he longed to follow that trail and see where it ended, he couldn't be in two places at once. He wanted to stay focused on Todd, so he'd asked his friend and fellow P.I., Jake Cameron, to see if the former maid was staying with friends in St. Louis.

Grabbing his cell phone, he dialed Jake's number. His friend didn't bother with pleasantries. "You were right. She's here."

Finally! A lead that might pan out. "Have you found anything?"

"Not yet. This one's going take some time."

Frustration built inside Connor. Although he trusted Jake and knew the man was a good P.I., Connor wasn't used to relying on someone else. "We don't have a lot of time here."

"Hey, I've got this," Jake said with typical confidence. "I'm just telling you, she's not the type to spill all her secrets on a first date."

Connor shook his head. He shouldn't have worried. His friend had been in St. Louis for all of two days, and he already had a date with the former maid. "Call me when you've got anything."

"Will do."

Snapping the cell phone shut, Connor hoped Jake worked his cases as quickly as he worked with women. But he wasn't going to sit around waiting for Jake; he wanted to find something on Dunworthy, irrefutable proof that the guy wasn't the loving husband-to-be he pretended.

Scowling, he resumed pacing, lengthening his stride to cross the room in four steps instead of eight. Connor had never been one to back down from a fight, but some battles were lost before they'd even begun. Gordon and Charlene Wilson would never take the word of the kid from the wrong side of the tracks over their handpicked golden boy.

Dammit, he needed an insider. He needed someone the Wilsons trusted to break the bad news. He needed one of their own. He needed…Kelsey.

Connor laughed out loud at the idea, but damned if he didn't think it might work. Kelsey hadn't played a part in his past relationship with Emily. She was as unbiased a witness as he could hope to find. She had nothing at stake with Emily's wedding, nothing riding on her cousin saying "I do."

No doubt about it, Kelsey was his best shot.

The following evening, Emily twirled around the hotel's atrium, her arms outspread like Sleeping Beauty. "You were right, Kelsey. This is the perfect place for the reception. Don't you think so, Mother?"

She looked so beautiful and happy Kelsey half-expected cartoon animals to surround her at any moment. Smiling at her cousin's unfettered happiness, she breathed a sigh of relief. Connor McClane was wrong, dead wrong. Emily and Todd were meant to be.

"It's lovely," Aunt Charlene commented without looking up from her mother-of-the-bride notebook. "I knew we could count on Kelsey to find the perfect place."

"Um, thank you, Aunt Charlene," Kelsey said, surprised and pleased by the compliment. Even after eight years, Kelsey and Charlene had a tentative, tightrope relationship that had yet to get past a disastrous beginning.

When Kelsey had first come to live with the Wilsons, she'd been overwhelmed by their obvious wealth, and her cousins' beauty and grace had left her feeling outclassed. Especially when Charlene took one look at her and declared, "Someone must take this girl shopping."

Looking back now, Kelsey realized her aunt had been trying to relate to her the same way she did to her own daughters, who loved nothing more than a day spent raiding Scottsdale boutiques. But back then, as an intimidated, awkward teenager, Kelsey had suffered the pain of being seen as an embarrassment by her new family.

She'd survived the multiple fittings and outfit changes—a living, breathing, *silent* mannequin—as her aunt and a shopkeeper went back and forth over which colors, styles and accessories best suited Kelsey. But when she stood with her aunt at the register, when she saw the *hundreds* of dollars a single item cost, a sick sense of disbelief hit her stomach.

How many weeks' rent would that pair of shoes have paid for when she and her mother were living in tiny one-room apartments? How many months of food? How much better might her mother's medical have been with that kind of money?

In a quiet, cold voice, Kelsey had told the saleswoman to put every item back, before marching out of the store.

Later, once Kelsey had calmed down and realized how ungrateful her actions must have seemed, she tried to apologize to her aunt. Charlene had declared the matter over and forgotten, but never again did she offer to take Kelsey shopping.

Their relationship had yet to recover from that day. By asking Kelsey to coordinate the wedding, Charlene had helped breach the gap, but Kelsey knew this opportunity didn't come with second chances. This was her one shot.

"I've always thought this was an amazing place for a reception," Kelsey said, hearing the dreamy wistfulness in her own voice. The glass ceiling and towering plants gave the illusion of being in a tropical paradise, and from the first time she'd seen the hotel, Kelsey had known it was perfect.

Perfect for Emily, she reminded herself.

Although between having so many of her friends working the wedding and Emily's willingness to let Kelsey make so many of the decisions, the entire event was feeling more like *Kelsey's* dream wedding.

Except the choice of groom...

The insidious thought wove through her mind along with images of Connor McClane... His rebellious saunter, his too confident grin, his...*everything.*

"I hope Todd likes it." Emily lowered her arms, a small frown tugging at her eyebrows. "Do you think he will?"

"It's a five-star hotel, one of the finest in the state," Charlene said imperiously.

"I know, but Todd's family is from Chicago. They have all those historic buildings and...Todd can be particular."

Kelsey's hand tightened on her day planner at her cousin's hesitant tone. Suspicions planted by Connor's too-pointed comments threatened to sprout into tangled choking weeds, but

Kelsey ground them down. Finger by finger, she eased her grip before she left permanent indentations on the leather book.

Her cousin was a people pleaser. Of course she worried what Todd would think. "He agreed to let you make all the decisions about the wedding," Kelsey reminded Emily, who had in turn, left most of the decisions up to her. "So he must trust your choices."

"I know, but…" Emily took a look around the atrium without the excitement she'd shown moments ago. Trying to see it through Todd's particular eyes?

"But what?" Kelsey prompted gently.

"It's—it's nothing." Emily shook her head with a laugh. "I just want everything to be perfect. You understand, don't you, Kelsey?"

Yes, she knew all about trying and failing again and again. But not this time—not with Emily's wedding. "Of course I do. And your wedding will be perfect," she insisted, before an already familiar masculine voice filled the atrium and sent shivers up and down her spine.

"Hey, Em! How's the blushing bride?"

"Oh, my gosh! Connor!" Emily squealed her former boyfriend's name and ran to meet him. A broad smile on his handsome face, he caught her in his arms and spun her around. "What are you doing here?" she asked.

Keeping an arm around Emily's shoulders, Connor glanced at Kelsey. "When Kelsey said you'd be here, I had to see you."

Heat rushed to Kelsey's face. Bad enough Connor had outmaneuvered her. Did he have to rub it in in front of her aunt?

Connor McClane had been in town less than twenty-four hours, and she could already feel the familiar undertow of failure dragging her under.

"You told him we'd be here?" The words barely escaped the frozen smile on her aunt's face. Charlene would never make a scene in public. Even if it meant smiling at the man out to ruin her daughter's future.

"No! I didn't." Except she *had* told Connor Emily was making final arrangements for the reception that evening, and he would know where the reception was being held. After all, he'd been invited. "I didn't mean to," she almost groaned.

Charlene straightened her razor-sharp shoulders, taking charge of a situation that had gotten out of control. Out of *Kelsey's* control. Interrupting Emily and Connor's conversation, she said, "Mr. McClane, you'll have to excuse us. Emily has a wedding to plan."

"Mother!" her daughter protested. "Connor's come all this way to see me. We have so much to talk about. Can't this wait?"

"This is *your* wedding we're talking about, Emily! The most important day of your life."

The most important day of your life. Kelsey understood the sentiment. Every bride wanted her wedding day to be perfect, and she was doing everything in her power to see that this affair was the type every girl dreamed about, but Emily was only twenty-eight years old. Shouldn't she have something to look forward to?

Why Kelsey chose that moment to meet Connor's glance, she didn't know. He flashed her a half smile as if he could not only read her thoughts but agreed one hundred percent.

"You're right, of course, Mother." Emily turned to Connor with a smile. "I'm sorry, Connor. We don't have much time before the wedding, and there's still so much to do."

"Don't worry, Em. We'll have plenty of time to talk before then. I'm in Room 415."

"You're staying here?" Kelsey blurted the words in horror. At the hotel where not only the reception was taking place, but also the rehearsal dinner.

Connor's grin was maddening—and disturbingly enticing. "Thought it would be convenient."

"Convenient. Right." That way he could *conveniently* intrude on every event she had planned for the location and drive her insane!

"Kelsey, Emily and I can take things from here. You have…other matters to attend to now."

Her aunt's pointed look spoke volumes. Charlene could handle the final wedding details. Kelsey's job was to handle Connor McClane. She desperately clutched her day planner to her chest like a leather-bound shield. There were some things in life she could not control, but everything else made it onto a list. A methodical, point-by-point inventory of what she needed to accomplish, making even the impossible seem manageable. Nothing beat the satisfaction of marking off a completed task.

And although Kelsey certainly hadn't counted on Connor when she prioritized her checklist for Emily's wedding, as long as she kept him occupied for the next week and a half, Kelsey would be able to cross him off once and for all.

Catching a touch of her aunt's righteous indignation, she straightened her own shoulders and nodded imperceptibly. Satisfied, Charlene marched Emily out of the atrium.

Emily cast a last, longing glance over her shoulder, and the uncertainty Kelsey saw in her cousin's gaze strengthened her resolve. Aileen was right. Emily was suffering from cold feet. Her worries about her future as a wife and eventually a mother had her looking back to simpler times. Back when she could lose herself in Connor's live-for-the-day attitude.

But her cousin would only regret it if she threw away her future for a man of the moment like Connor McClane. And Kelsey could not allow Emily to make the same mistake her own mother had.

Chapter Three

"You know, Kelsey, I've never been *attended to* before."

Even with her back turned, as she watched Emily and Charlene walk away, Connor sensed the determination rolling off Kelsey in waves. Shoulders straight and head held high, she looked ready for battle. And yet when he took a closer step, his gaze locked on a curl of hair that had escaped the confining bun. The urge to tuck that curl behind her ear and taste her creamy skin nearly overwhelmed him. He sucked in what was supposed to be a steadying breath, but the air—scented with cinnamon and spice and *Kelsey*—only added to the desire burning through his veins.

Struggling to hide behind the cocky facade that had served him so well in his youth, Connor murmured, "Gotta say I'm looking forward to it."

"I don't know what you mean," she said stiffly.

"You think I don't know I'm those 'other matters' your aunt was talking about?"

Kelsey opened her mouth, looking ready to spout another unbelievable denial, only to do them both the favor of telling the truth. "You're right, Connor. My aunt wants me to keep you away from Emily."

"Charlene wants me gone and Emily happily married. There's just one problem."

"That would be you," Kelsey pointed out. "A problem easily solved if you were actually gone."

"If I leave, Emily's problems will have just begun."

"That's your unbiased opinion?"

"Yeah, it is," he agreed. "And not one your aunt and uncle are gonna listen to."

"Can you blame them?" Kelsey demanded.

No, and that was the hell of it. Connor knew *he* was the only one to blame. He knew what the Wilsons thought of him and he knew why. He could still see the look in Gordon Wilson's eyes when he offered Connor money to break up with Emily. Not a hint of doubt flashed in the older man's gaze. He'd been so sure Connor—a dirt-poor loser from the wrong side of town—would take the money.

Connor had longed to shove the money and his fist into the smug SOB's face. But he hadn't. He *couldn't.* And the pride he'd had to swallow that day still lingered, a bitter taste on his tongue.

He'd let Emily down, although from what he'd gathered during their recent conversations, she didn't know anything about the payoff. She thought their breakup had been her idea…just as she thought marrying Todd Dunworthy was her idea. But Connor knew better, and this time he wasn't going to be bought off.

"The Wilsons aren't going to listen to anything I have to say," he acknowledged. "That's where you come in."

Kelsey frowned. "I *am* a Wilson."

He hadn't forgotten…exactly. "You're different."

Drawing herself up to her five-foot-nothing height, shoulders so straight Connor thought they just might snap, Kelsey said, "Right. Different." Hurt flashed in her chocolate-brown eyes as if he'd just insulted her, when nothing could be further from the truth.

"Hey, wait a minute." Pulling her into a nearby alcove, out of the way of nearby guests, Connor insisted, "That was *not* a put-down. Your aunt and uncle turned their noses up so high when they met me, if it rained, they would have drowned. I was trailer trash, and no way was I good enough for their little girl. So when I say you're nothing like them, you can say 'thank you,' because it's a compliment."

There were a dozen words he could have said, compliments he could have used, but the stubborn tilt of Kelsey's chin told him she wouldn't have listened to a single one. Someone—her family, some guy from her past—had done a number on her.

No, words wouldn't do it, but actions… How far would he have to go to show Kelsey how attractive he found her? A touch? A kiss? The undeniable proof of his body pressed tight to hers?

"In case you've forgotten," Kelsey pointed out, her voice husky enough to let him know she'd picked up on some of his thoughts and wasn't as immune as she'd like him to believe, "according to my aunt and uncle you *kidnapped* their daughter."

"It was not kidnapping," he argued, though he'd had a hell of a time convincing the police. Fortunately Emily had backed his story, insisting that she'd left willingly. Eventually the charges had been dropped; Emily had been eighteen and legally an adult, able to make her own choices. Not that her parents had seen it that way. "But that's my point. Your aunt and uncle won't listen to anything I have to say. Which is where you come in."

"Me?"

"Right. We'll be partners."

"Partners?"

"Sure. After all, we're on the same side."

"Are you crazy? We are not on the same side!" Kelsey argued.

"I want Emily to be happy," he interjected, shaking her thoughts as easily as his sexy grin weakened her composure. "What do *you* want?"

Challenge rose in the lift of his eyebrow, but Kelsey couldn't see a way out. The trap was set, and all she could do was jump in with both feet. "Of course I want her to be happy."

"That's what I thought. Kelsey, this guy won't make her happy. He's not what he seems, and I want to prove it. The Wilsons won't believe *me,* but with you to back me up, they'll have to at least listen."

Kelsey longed to refuse. She didn't trust him. Not for a second. Oh, sure, his story sounded good, but finding dirt on Todd wasn't just a matter of looking out for Emily—it played perfectly into Connor's interests, as well.

If Connor did find some deep, dark secret to convince Emily to call off the wedding, not only would he be the hero who saved her from a horrible marriage, he'd also be there to help pick up the pieces. But if Connor couldn't find anything in Todd's past, what was to keep him from making something up? Working together, he wouldn't be able to lie. Not to mention, he'd given her a way to keep an eye on him.

Connor held out his hand. "Deal?"

Sighing, she reached out. "Deal."

Connor's lean fingers closed around her hand. Heat shot up her arm, and a warm shiver shook her whole body. Like stepping from ice-cold air-conditioning into the warmth of a sunny day.

"All right, partner."

"Not so fast." She hadn't lived with her businessman uncle for as long as she had without learning a thing or two about negotiation. "You might want to hear my terms first."

"Terms?"

Kelsey nodded. As long as Connor thought he needed her, maybe she could get a few concessions.

Instead of balking, Connor grinned. "Let's hear 'em."

"First, we're equal partners. I want to be in on this every step of the way. No hearing about anything you've found on Todd after the fact."

"No problem. From this point on, we're joined at the hip. 'Course, that will make for some interesting sleeping arrangements."

"Second, this is strictly business," Kelsey interrupted, as if cutting off his words might somehow short-circuit the thoughts in her head. But they were already there: sexy, seductive images of hot kisses and naked limbs slipping through satin sheets in her mind. She could only hope Connor couldn't read them so clearly by the heat coloring her face.

"And third?"

"Thi-third," she said, clearing her throat, "you stay away from Emily. *If* we get any dirt on Todd, *I'll* break the news to her. Until then, I don't want you filling her head with your 'bad feelings.'"

Expecting an argument, Kelsey was surprised when Connor nodded. "I'll keep my distance."

"Okay, then, we're partners." She should have experienced a moment of triumph, but all Kelsey could think was that she'd just made a deal with the devil.

Certainly, when Connor smiled, he looked like sheer temptation.

"Got to hand it to you, Kelsey, you're one hell of a negotiator. Two outta three ain't bad."

It wasn't until Connor strode away that Kelsey realized he'd never agreed to her second condition.

As Kelsey stepped into the florist shop the next morning, cool, floral-scented air washed over her. She breathed deeply, enjoying the feeling of a refreshing spa treatment without the outrageous prices. She wasn't a big believer in aromatherapy, but the stress of dealing with Connor might drive her to alternative measures. Anything to stop her pulse from jumping each time she saw him—and to keep her hormones under wraps and in control for the next ten days.

Why couldn't life be easy? Why couldn't she plan an elegant, trouble-free wedding? The kind where the biggest worry was the ice sculpture melting too quickly in the summer heat. Instead, she got Connor McClane, a man guaranteed to make women melt with nothing more than a look.

"Kelsey! Thanks so much for coming!" Lisa Remming, Kelsey's friend and the owner of In Bloom, circled the checkout counter to greet her with a hug. As always, Lisa dressed in clothes inspired by her favorite flower—bird of paradise. Her long brown hair and blue eyes were complemented by a sleeveless fiery-orange blouse and swirling olive-green skirt. "I feel so bad for calling you."

"Don't be silly." Kelsey waved off her friend's apology and pulled out her checkbook from her purse. "It's no problem."

"I still can't believe I'm doing flowers for Emily Wilson's wedding! There isn't a florist around who wouldn't kill for this job."

Hiding a smile, Kelsey teased, "Wow, who knew florists were so bloodthirsty?"

Lisa made a face, then gave Kelsey another hug. "I totally have you to thank for this."

The two women had gone to high school together, and

Lisa was one of the few people in whom Kelsey confided. By the time she'd moved in with her aunt and uncle, Kelsey had gotten accustomed to blending in and going through her teen years unnoticed. Telling her fellow students she was a long-lost member of the wealthy Wilson family would have shoved her under a microscope.

The only worse fate would have been the exclusive prep school her aunt had suggested she attend.

"I really hate asking you to do this," Lisa said as she reached behind the counter for an invoice.

"A deposit is standard practice."

"I know, but— We're talking about the Wilsons. It's not like they're going to leave me holding the bill. But with the flowers for the church and the bouquets and the boutonnieres, I have to pay my suppliers and—"

"And that's why you need the money up front." Kelsey tore off a check. The amount for the deposit alone would have depleted her own meager bank account, but Aunt Charlene had given her access to the special account established for Emily's wedding.

"Thanks." Lisa breathed a sigh of relief as she noted the deposit on the invoice. "This wedding is going to mean the world to my business." She laughed as she pressed a button on the cash register and slid the check inside. "Like I need to tell *you* that, right? You'll be flooded with calls after Emily's friends see the amazing job you're doing. Have you thought anymore about getting your own place?"

Excitement pulsing through her veins, Kelsey nodded. "I've put down first and last month's rent on the space in downtown Glendale, near the antique shops."

Lisa gave a squeal. "And you didn't even say anything! When are you moving in?"

"As soon as the current renters move out. The landlord's supposed to give me a call."

"You must be so excited! I know I was when I first opened this place. Do you have all the furniture and office equipment you'll need? Have you thought about hiring a support staff and—"

"Whoa, Lisa! Don't get carried away," Kelsey said with a laugh that sounded far too shaky.

"I'm not. Don't tell me you of all people—with your day planner and your endless lists—haven't thought of these things."

In fact, she *had,* and only days ago she'd been riding high on her plans. Now, with Connor back in town, she feared she'd put the honeymoon before the wedding, and her stomach roiled at the thought of losing control. "I don't want to get too far ahead of myself."

"What are you talking about?" Lisa challenged. "Emily's wedding is only a week and half away. You aren't too far ahead. If anything, you're behind!"

"Well, thank you for giving me that combination vote of confidence and total panic attack."

"I'm sorry. But I know how much effort you've put into this, and I want to see it pay off for you."

I want Emily to be happy. What do you *want?*

With Connor's words ringing in her head, Kelsey insisted, "Emily's happiness comes first."

"Honey, Emily's happiness *always* come first," Lisa deadpanned.

"That's not fair, Lisa," Kelsey insisted quietly.

Emily and Aileen could have turned their backs when their unknown and potentially unwanted cousin showed up to live with them. Instead, they'd done everything possible to include Kelsey. It certainly wasn't their fault she'd never fit in.

"I know." Lisa's sigh expressed an unspoken apology. "But

I also know you've played second fiddle to both your cousins for as long as I've known you. I don't want you to be so focused on Emily's wedding that you lose track of your dream."

"I haven't and I won't."

Despite her determined vow, a touch of guilt squirmed through Kelsey. She'd kept silent about renting the shop for exactly the reasons Lisa mentioned. Her aunt wouldn't want her attention on anything other than the wedding. But the shop was nothing compared to Connor McClane. The man was a living, breathing distraction.

"Emily's wedding *is* my dream," Kelsey added. "A high-profile event with an extravagant budget and built-in publicity thanks to my uncle's business contacts and my aunt's country-club friends—it's guaranteed to put my business on the map."

"I agree, and I can't believe you pulled it off in only two months!"

"It *was* short notice, wasn't it?" Kelsey asked, fiddling with the zipper on her purse.

"Yes, but you did it!"

Kelsey nodded. Thanks to working almost nonstop, she'd pulled off planning the event in a fraction of the time it normally took, but Emily had insisted on a June wedding… hadn't she?

Sudden doubts buzzed through her mind like annoying insects, unrelenting and unavoidable. Had Emily pushed for the summer wedding? Or was the idea Charlene's…or Todd's? Kelsey had been so focused on getting everything done on time, she hadn't stopped to wonder about the short engagement. Until now…until Connor had stirred up the hornet's nest of doubt.

Connor hung up the phone after ordering breakfast and ran his hands over his face. He hoped the distraction of food would wipe the nightmare from his memory. It wasn't the first time disturbing images had invaded his sleep.

The beginning of the dream was always the same. Connor watched his client, Doug Mitchell, arrive at his wife's apartment through the tunnel-eye view of a telephoto lens; only when he tried to stop the man from attacking his estranged wife, did the dream shift and alter, keeping him off balance, unsure, helpless. Sometimes he froze in place, unable to move a muscle, unable to shout a warning. Other times, he ran through air thick as quicksand, each move bogged down by guilt and regret.

But no matter how the dream changed, one thing remained the same: Connor never arrived in time to stop Doug.

A sudden knock at the door jarred the memories from Connor's thoughts. Undoubtedly the Wilsons had picked the best hotel around for Emily's reception, but no one's room service was *that* fast. Besides, he had an idea who might be on the other side of the door, and it wasn't the maid with fresh towels.

Opening the door, he summoned a smile for the woman standing in the corridor. "Morning."

Emily Wilson beamed at him, looking like a Hollywood fashion plate of old in a yellow sundress layered beneath a lightweight sweater and a scarf knotted at her neck. "Connor! I'm so glad you're here. I know I should have called first, but—"

He waved off her not-quite-an-apology and held the door open. "Come on in."

As she breezed into the hotel room and set her handbag next to his laptop, Connor was glad to see the computer logo flashing across the screen. Last thing he needed was for Emily to see the dossier on her fiancé.

Emily took her time looking around the suite's miniature living area: a cluster of armchairs and end tables encircling the entertainment center. The added touches of a stone fireplace, balcony overlooking the pool and hot tub spoke of the hotel's five-star accommodations, but Connor doubted she was impressed. After all, she'd grown up surrounded by luxury and wealth.

"What are you doing here, Em?"

"I wanted to see you." She blushed as prettily now as she had at eighteen, but somehow for Connor the effect wasn't the same.

An image of Kelsey flashed in his mind, and he couldn't help making the comparison between Emily and her cousin. It was the difference between a sepia photograph—all soft, dreamy hues—and a full-color, HD image that instantly caught the eye.

As a hotheaded teen, Emily had been his unattainable fantasy. But now it was Kelsey and her down-to-earth reality who kept intruding into his thoughts.

Like yesterday evening, when he'd stood on the balcony and watched to see if the Arizona sunsets were still as amazing as he remembered. As he watched the blazing light slowly fade on the horizon, it wasn't past evenings that came to mind. Instead he thought of the way sunshine caught the fire in Kelsey's auburn curls…

"I snuck out like when we were kids."

Emily's words jarred Kelsey from his mind. He told himself the swift kick in the gut was remembered pain and not anything current or life threatening. But, dammit, he didn't need the reminder that as far as the Wilsons were concerned, he'd never be good enough. And while Kelsey might not look like her blond-haired, blue-eyed cousins, she was still a Wilson, and some things never changed.

Judging by Emily's impish grin, she'd enjoyed reliving her youthful rebellion and the walk down memory lane. Too bad the trip wasn't so pleasant for him. Feeling his smile take a sardonic twist, he asked, "Still can't risk being seen with me in public, huh, Em?"

Her eyes widened in what looked like genuine dismay. "No, Connor! It's not like that." She reached out and grasped his arm, and the frantic expression did take him back in time, filling his thoughts with memories of the girl so desperate to make everyone else happy, she'd made herself miserable.

Relenting slightly, he leaned one hip against the arm of the sofa and reminded her, "We're not kids anymore, and we're too old to be sneaking around."

"I know." Fidgeting with her engagement ring, she added, "But I wanted to see you, and I didn't want…anyone to get upset."

"You mean Todd?" Connor asked pointedly.

"You have to understand, he's very protective of me. I'm sorry the two of you didn't hit it off when we met for dinner in San Diego last month."

Connor held back a snort of derisive laughter at the irony. No, he and Todd hadn't hit it off. In fact, at the end of the night they'd nearly come to blows. Connor could admit he hadn't walked into the restaurant with a totally open mind. It was entirely possible Connor would dislike any man who met with the Wilsons' approval on principle alone. But within fifteen minutes of meeting Todd Dunworthy, Connor had stopped thinking about the past and started worrying about Emily.

In that short span of time, Dunworthy bragged about his Scottsdale loft apartment, his top-of-the-line SUV, his various summer homes in exotic ports of call, all of which would have been little more than annoying except for one thing.

He talked about Emily the same way. She was new and bright and shiny just like the fancy Lexus he drove, and Connor hadn't been able to shake the feeling that Dunworthy wouldn't have thought twice about tossing her aside for a newer model.

And the bad feeling roiling through Connor's gut like acid

ever since he'd been hired by Doug Mitchell got so much worse. Outwardly, Doug and Todd Dunworthy had as little in common as, well, as Connor and Todd did. But from the moment he met Doug, the cold look in the man's eyes and the way he spoke about his wife set Connor's teeth on edge, too reminiscent of the way his father had talked about his mother, the bitter blame he'd placed on her for dying and saddling him with an unwanted kid to raise.

But Connor had set aside his personal feelings and taken the job. *Taken the money,* his conscience accused. If only he'd listened to his gut then…

Taking a deep breath, Connor looked out the window, hoping the daylight might dispel his dark thoughts. Only, it wasn't the sunshine that broke through the shadows, but memories of the sunset, memories of Kelsey, that eased the weight on his chest.

The spark in her dark eyes, the stubborn jut of her chin, her determination to stand up to him…even if she barely stood up to the height of his shoulder. He didn't doubt for one second she'd be a formidable opponent, and he was glad to have her on his side.

Turning his focus back to Emily, he said, "I'm sorry, too, Em." And he was. He wanted her to be happy, and he was sorry Dunworthy wasn't the man she—or more important, he suspected, her parents—thought him to be.

Something in his tone must have given his suspicions away, because Emily's already perfect posture straightened to a regal, Charlene-like stature. "Todd is a wonderful man," she insisted. "I love him. I really do, and I can't wait to be his wife."

How many times had Emily repeated that statement before she started believing it was true? The words had a mantralike sound to them. Or maybe more like the punishment meted out by a second-grade teacher: *I will not chew gum in class. I will not chew gum in class.*

"I should go," she murmured.

"Emily, wait." A knock on the door broke the tension. "Look, that's room service. I ordered way too much food. Stay and have breakfast with me."

Without waiting for her response, he stepped around her and opened the door. The waiter wheeled in the cart, filling the room with the scent of bacon and eggs. He pulled the covers off the steaming plates and revealed a meal large enough for two.

"I shouldn't," she protested, eyeing the food with a look of longing. "I need to watch what I eat or I won't be able to fit into my dress."

Connor tried to smile; dieting before a big occasion was undoubtedly a prerequisite for most women, but he didn't think it was the dress Emily had in mind. He'd shared only a single meal with Dunworthy, but he could still see the smug smile on the bastard's face as he waved the waiter and the dessert tray away with a laugh. "Gotta keep my bride-to-be looking as beautiful as ever!"

"Come on," Connor cajoled. "You're not going to make me eat alone, are you?"

Sighing, she slid onto the chair and confessed, "This smells amazing."

"Dig in," he encouraged. "Nothing like carbs and cholesterol to start the day right."

The spark in her eyes reminded him of the old Emily, and she grabbed a fork with an almost defiant toss to her head. "Thank you, Connor."

"Anytime, Em," he vowed, knowing her gratitude was for much more than a simple offer to share breakfast.

He picked up his own fork, ready to dig into the eggs,

when a hint of spice seemed to sneak into his senses. Normally sides like toast or muffins were an afterthought, something to eat only if the main meal wasn't filling enough. But the powder-sprinkled muffin on the edge of his plate suddenly had his mouth watering.

He broke off an edge and popped it into his mouth. The moist confection melted on his tongue, tempting his senses with sugar, cinnamon and...*Kelsey.*

The hint of sweet and spicy had filled his head when he stood close to her, urging him to discover if the cinnamon scent was thanks to a shampoo she used on the red-gold curls she tried to tame or a lotion she smoothed over her pale skin.

If he kissed her, was that how she'd taste?

"What's Kelsey doing today?"

The question popped out before Connor ever thought to ask it, revealing a curiosity he couldn't deny yet didn't want to admit. He set the muffin aside and shoved a forkful of eggs into his mouth in case any other questions decided to circumvent his thought process.

After taking a drink of juice, Emily said, "Oh, she's likely running herself ragged with wedding preparations, making sure everything's going to go according to plan."

Her words sent suspicion slithering down his spine. At a small, low-key wedding, the bride's cousin might be the one behind the scenes, making sure everything went *according to plan.* But not at the Wilson-Dunworthy wedding, where professionals would handle those kind of details.

"What, exactly," he asked, "does Kelsey have to do with the wedding preparations?"

Emily frowned. "Didn't she tell you she's my wedding coordinator?"

"No," he said, setting his fork aside and leaning back in the chair, "no, she didn't."

"I'm lucky to have her working on the wedding. She's amazing when it comes to organization, and she's taking care of everything."

Everything, Connor thought wryly, including him.

Chapter Four

So much for unbiased. So much for impartial. So much for finding his insider in the Wilson camp, Connor thought. Kelsey was involved in this wedding right up to her gorgeous red head.

"She started her business over a year ago," Emily was saying. "My father offered to finance the company, but she wouldn't take the loan. She's always been weird about money."

Ignoring his grudging respect for Kelsey's decision and the curiosity about her *weirdness* when it came to her family's money, Connor focused on what she was getting from the Wilson family name. "So this wedding's a big deal to Kelsey, huh?"

"Oh, it's huge! She's counting on my wedding being the launching pad for Weddings Amour. The business is totally her baby, and she loves it. Says it makes her feel like a fairy godmother, starting couples out on their own happily-ever-after."

Connor let out a snort of disbelief. He hadn't read any

fairy tales since he was six and figured it had been nearly as long since he'd believed in happily-ever-after.

"What?" Emily demanded.

"It's—nothing." He stabbed at his eggs. "The whole thing is crazy. Fairy godmothers, everlasting love, all of it—"

It was impossible. He'd seen far too many marriage vows broken from behind the telescopic lens of his camera. Those couples had likely had dream weddings, too, but the dream couldn't survive reality. And sometimes—like with Cara Mitchell—happily-ever-after turned into a living nightmare.

"Well, don't tell Kelsey her business is a joke. She takes it very seriously."

"I bet she does."

Seriously enough that Charlene Wilson had put Kelsey in charge of "attending to him." He'd overheard the comment yesterday but hadn't realized he'd be in the hands of a professional.

"Why all the questions about Kelsey?"

"Just curious." When Emily's eyes narrowed thoughtfully, he added, "I don't remember you talking about her when we were going out, that's all."

She shrugged. "I didn't know her then."

"Didn't *know* her? She's your cousin, right?"

"I, uh, I meant I didn't know her well."

"Uh-huh." Emily was a horrible liar and not much better at keeping secrets. He could have pressed. A few pointed questions, and Emily would have told him everything.

Connor refused to ask. Even as curiosity stacked one row of questions upon the next, he wouldn't ask. Not about why Emily hadn't known her own relative, not about why Kelsey had gone to public school instead of the exclusive prep schools her cousins had attended, not about why she was *weird* when it came to the family fortune.

He wasn't back in Arizona to find out about Kelsey Wilson.

Returning his focus to that goal, he asked, "What's Todd up to today? He must have a lot of free time on his hands while you and your mother and Kelsey take care of all the wedding details."

"Oh, no. He has a meeting this morning. He'll be at his office most of the day."

"Really?" Now, this could be something. Connor forced himself to take a few bites of waffle before he asked, "What kind of meeting?"

"I'm not sure." A tiny frown tugged her eyebrows. "Todd doesn't tell me much about his work." Laughter chased the frown away. "Just as well. I'd be bored silly."

"I doubt that. You're smart, Emily. Smarter than you give yourself credit for."

"Thank you, Connor," she said softly.

"How'd you two meet anyway? I don't think you've said."

"At a department store." She smiled. "We were both shopping for Christmas presents for our mothers, but he didn't have a clue. Finally he asked me for help. It was really cute."

"Hmm. Almost as cute as when we met."

"Oh, you mean in that sleazy bar where you had to fight off those bikers who were hitting on me?"

"A bar you weren't old enough to be at in the first place," Connor pointed out.

"Luckily you were there to rescue me," she said, lifting her glass in a teasing toast.

"Yeah, lucky," Connor agreed as he tapped his own glass against hers.

Emily might not know it, but he was here to save her again.

The tiny butterflies taking flight in Kelsey's stomach as she drove toward the hotel turned into radioactive monsters by the time she stepped into the lobby. She'd been crazy to make a deal with Connor McClane. Somewhere along the way she was going to lose her soul.

Although they hadn't made plans to meet this morning, the best way to keep an eye on Connor was to embrace their partnership. As she walked by the three-tiered fountain toward the elevators, the doors slid open. Kelsey gasped and ducked into an alcove—the same alcove to which Connor had pulled her aside the day before—and watched in disbelief as her cousin walked by.

What was Emily doing at Connor's hotel?

Her cousin rarely left the house before noon, and it was barely nine o'clock. What was Emily doing up so early? Or had she stayed out too late? Kelsey's stomach churned at the thought. She hated to think her cousin would be so susceptible to Connor's charms. *And what about you?* her conscience mocked. *How easily did you agree to work with Connor in this very spot?*

But that was different! That was about business and keeping an eye on Connor and keeping him away from Emily…not that Kelsey had done a bang-up job at either so far.

Emily slipped on a pair of sunglasses and smiled at a bellboy, who nearly tripped over his feet as she walked by. She didn't look as if she'd rolled out of bed with her ex-lover, but then again, Kelsey had never seen Emily look less than perfect. Ever.

Kelsey stayed hidden as her cousin sashayed across the lobby and out the automatic doors, then made a beeline for the elevator. "So much for his promises," she muttered as she jabbed the Up button.

"But why am I even surprised?"

She stomped out of the elevator on the fourth floor. Had she really believed Connor would keep his word?

Maybe she had. Which only went to prove how some

people never learned. Rapping on Connor's door hard enough to bruise her knuckles, she thought she'd be better off banging her head against the wood.

"Kelsey." Opening the door, Connor greeted her with an assessing look and not an ounce of shame. Bracing one arm on the doorjamb, he said, "I'm surprised to see you here."

"Are you?" Determined to ignore the masculine pose that could have come straight from some sexy man-of-the-month calendar, she ducked beneath his arm and made her way inside. She refused to have an argument in the hall where any guest, bellhop or room-service waiter might walk by. "If I'd shown up a few minutes earlier, it would have been a regular family reunion."

"You saw Emily?"

"So much for your promise to keep your distance!"

Connor frowned. "I said I'd stay away. I can't help it if she comes to see me."

"Right. And I'm sure she forced her way inside your hotel room. Probably tied you up and had her way with you, too."

Connor pushed away from the door and stalked toward her with that challenging expression still in his eyes. "That would really mess up your plans, wouldn't it?"

"She's engaged, Connor. Doesn't that mean anything to you?"

"Yeah. It means she's about to make a mistake."

Connor stepped closer, and the only mistake Kelsey could concentrate on was her own in thinking she could confront Connor face-to-face and not be overwhelmed by his masculine sensuality. He hadn't shaved and the morning stubble only made him that much more appealing. Worse, she could practically feel the erotic scrape of whisker-rough skin against her cheeks, her neck, her breasts—

Afraid he could read her every thought by the glow in her cheeks, Kelsey ducked her head. Her gaze landed on the nearby breakfast tray, on a white coffee cup and a pink bow-shaped smudge left by Emily's lipstick. The mark may have been left on Connor's cup, not on the man himself, but the reminder that Emily had been there first doused Kelsey like a bucket of ice water. "Emily's only mistake was inviting *you*."

"Yeah, I bet that's tough on you, isn't it? When you told me yesterday working together would be strictly business, I didn't realize that meant you were getting paid."

"So I'm coordinating Emily's wedding. Don't act all offended like it was some big secret. I thought you already knew."

"Yeah, well, I didn't. If I had—"

"You would have what?"

Scowling at her, he said, "Look, if you want to work together, I need to know you care more about your cousin than you do about your business."

If she wanted to work together! Just yesterday, she thought agreeing to work with Connor was possibly the most foolish thing she'd ever done. And now she had to fight to keep the opportunity?

Yes! a voice inside her head argued. *Because it's the only one you'll get. How else will you keep an eye on him? How else will you keep him from stopping the wedding?*

"Of course I care about Emily."

A sardonic twist of a smile lifted one corner of Connor's mouth. Darn him for making even sarcasm look sexy! "I know you care about her. The question is, do you care enough to put her first over everything else you want?"

The intensity in his eyes transformed the question from a challenge about her loyalty to Emily into something more personal. Something dark and revealing about his past. *Prove that you care…*

It was a test Emily had failed. She hadn't cared enough, or

she'd cared about her family's approval more. Was Emily the only woman who hadn't passed, Kelsey wondered, or were there other women who hadn't given Connor the proof he needed?

"You can't prove you care about someone," she stated flatly. "Not in words. Actions show how you truly feel."

Like Connor showing up for Emily's wedding…and Emily showing up at Connor's hotel room. Trying not to think what those actions meant, Kelsey continued, "I'm here. That alone should prove—"

"That you're a clever businesswoman? I already knew that."

Tightening her grip on her purse strap, Kelsey fought for control. She couldn't pretend she didn't have a lot riding on Emily's wedding.

As she racked her brain for a way to prove her loyalty, Kelsey realized nothing she said would be enough. Meeting his gaze, she stated, "I can't prove it to you, Connor. Because love and caring aren't about proof. They're about faith. So, if I'm supposed to trust your gut when you tell me Todd isn't right for Emily, you're going to have to trust me when I tell you Emily's happiness matters most."

With his gaze locked on hers, Connor stayed silent long enough for Kelsey to anticipate half a dozen responses. Would he laugh in her face? Turn away in cynical disgust?

Seconds ticked by, and she held her ground by pulling off a decent imitation of her aunt. She kept her back straight, her head held high, and still managed to look down her nose at a much taller Connor.

He ruined the hard-won effect with a single touch, tracing a finger over her cheek. The steel in her spine melted into a puddle of desire.

"Good to have you back on the team," he said softly. "We have work to do."

* * *

Connor knew he'd crossed the line when Kelsey's eyes widened to a deer-caught-in-the-headlights look. He needed to back off. If he pushed, she'd bolt. But it was the urge to ignore his own boundaries that had him pulling back even further.

If anyone could make him *want* to trust again, Kelsey might. And that sure as hell wasn't the kind of thought a man wanted to have while sober. Especially not a man like him about a woman like her.

Kelsey was a Wilson, and he'd already learned his lesson when it came to how Wilson-McClane relationships ended. He knew better than to make the same mistake twice… Didn't he? Just because he'd indulged in a minor fantasy—discovering the five freckles on Kelsey's cheek *did* combine to make a perfect star—didn't mean he was losing his grip on the situation. He had everything under control, even if that star-shaped outline made him wonder what other patterns he might find on Kelsey's body….

Far too aware of the bed only a few feet away and Kelsey's teasing scent, that alluring combination of cinnamon and spice, Connor redirected his focus. "Are you hungry? I could order more room service."

"No, thank you." Her words were too polite, bordering on stiff, and they matched her posture.

"All right," he said, thinking it just as well they get out of the hotel room before he ended up doing something as stupid as touching Kelsey…and not stopping. "But you really don't want to go on a stakeout on an empty stomach." Connor didn't know if his sudden announcement loosened anything, but Kelsey definitely looked shaken.

"Stakeout?" Echoing the word, her brown eyes widened.

"Don't worry. We'll stop for staples along the way." He grabbed her hand, pulled her from the room and out into the hall.

She protested every step of the way and all throughout the elevator ride down to the lobby. "Are you insane? I am *not* going on a stakeout."

Her voice dropped to a hiss as the elevator door opened, and she even managed a smile at the elderly couple waiting in the lobby.

"You agreed to this, remember? Equal partners?"

As he strode across the lobby, Connor realized Kelsey was practically running to keep up with his long strides, and he slowed his steps.

Jeez, it'd be faster if he picked her up and carried her. A corner of his mouth lifted at the thought of Kelsey's reaction if he tried. "You really are tiny, aren't you?"

"I— What?"

She bumped into him when Connor paused for the automatic doors to open. He had the quick impression of soft breasts against his back before Kelsey jumped away.

Tiny, he decided as he looked over his shoulder with an appreciative glance, but curved in all the right places.

Something in his expression must have given his thoughts away. Kelsey glared at him. "I am not going on a stakeout."

"How are we going to find anything out about Todd if we don't watch him?"

"I thought you'd hire someone!"

"Right. Because the Wilsons would believe whatever some guy I *paid* has to say about their golden boy."

Score one for the away team, Connor thought, when Kelsey stopped arguing. Pressing his advantage, he guided her outside. "Besides," he added, "staking people out is what I do."

"You—you're a cop?"

He couldn't blame her for the shock in her voice and gave a scoffing laugh. "No. I'm a private investigator. Turns out we're both professionals," he said. "And if it makes you feel any better, I do have a friend working another lead. But he's in St. Louis."

"What's in St. Louis?"

"A maid who used to work for the Dunworthy family. She either quit or was let go a few months ago."

"So?"

"She pretty much disappeared after that, and I want to hear what she has to say about her former employers."

Midmorning sunlight glinted off the line of luxury cars brought around by the valets: Lexus, BMW, Mercedes. He'd come a long way from his bike days. Too bad. He would have enjoyed getting Kelsey on a Harley. Once she loosened up a bit, she'd love the freedom of hugging the curves, wind whipping through her hair, speed pouring through her veins. He could almost feel her arms around his waist…

Kelsey waved toward the visitor's lot. "We can take my car."

It didn't look like loosening up would happen anytime soon. "Sorry, sweetheart, but I'll bet Dunworthy has already seen your car."

Connor signaled a valet, and within minutes a vintage black Mustang pulled up to the curb. Seeing the question in Kelsey's eyes, he explained, "It's Javy's. Something less flashy would be better for surveillance, but borrowers can't be choosers."

He tipped the valet and opened the passenger door for Kelsey. When she looked ready to argue, he said, "Todd has a big meeting at his office." He'd looked up the address after Emily left. "I'm curious to find out who it's with. How 'bout you?"

As she slid into the passenger seat, Kelsey muttered something he couldn't quite make out.

Connor figured it was just as well.

* * *

"I cannot believe I'm doing this," Kelsey muttered from her slumped-down position in the passenger seat.

"You've mentioned that," Connor replied.

They were parked in a lot across the street from Todd's office. The row of two-story suites lined a busy side street off Scottsdale Road, the black glass and concrete a sharp contrast to the gold and russet rock landscape, with its clusters of purple sage, flowering bougainvillea and cacti. Connor had circled the building when they first arrived, noting all the building's entrances and confirming Todd's car wasn't in the lot.

"What if someone sees us?"

"What are they going to see?" he retorted.

She supposed from a distance the car did blend in. Thanks to heavily tinted windows, it was unlikely anyone could see inside. Tilting the vents to try to get a bit more air to blow in her direction, Kelsey admitted, "This is a bit more boring than I expected."

"Boring is good," Connor insisted. Despite his words, he drummed his fingers against the steering wheel in an impatient rhythm, clearly ready for action.

"I'm surprised Emily didn't tell me more about your job."

"Why would she?"

"Because to anyone not sitting in this car, being a P.I. sounds exciting." When Connor stayed silent, she asked, "Do you like it?"

"Yeah. Most of the time."

The tapping on the steering wheel increased like the sudden peaks on a lie detector, and Kelsey sensed he was telling her not what he thought she wanted to hear, but what he *wanted* to believe. Something had happened to change his mind about the job she suspected he'd once loved. "It must be difficult. Seeing so much of the darker side of life."

"It can be. Sometimes human nature is dark, but at least my job is about discovering the truth."

Was it only her imagination, or had he emphasized that pronoun? Subtly saying that while he pursued truth and justice, she— "You think *my* job is about telling lies?"

"Selling lies," he clarified.

"I promise a beautiful wedding and give the bride and groom what they're looking for. That's not a lie."

"Okay," he conceded, "maybe not the beautiful wedding part, but the sentiment behind it? Happily-ever-after? Love of a lifetime? Till death do us part? Come on!"

"Not every marriage ends with the bride and groom riding off into the sunset. Real life comes with real problems, but if two people love each other, they work it out."

He snorted. "Not from my side of the video camera, they don't."

Irritation crackled inside her like radio static—annoying, incessant and almost loud enough to drown out a vague and misplaced feeling of disillusionment. All these years, she'd heard about Connor and Emily as a modern-day Romeo and Juliet, but the story of star-crossed lovers lost all meaning if one of the players didn't believe in love.

And while Kelsey's faith might have been shaken by what happened with Matt, she still longed for those happily-ever-after and love-of-a-lifetime dreams Connor cynically mocked.

"My aunt and uncle never believed you loved Emily," she said, disappointed. "Everything you've said proves them right."

"Your aunt and uncle weren't right about me—no matter what they think."

Dead certainty ricocheted in his voice, and Kelsey regretted the tack she'd taken. Too late to back down and far too curious about what made Connor tick, she pressed, "Either you believe in love or you don't. You can't have it both ways."

"I just don't want to see Emily get hurt. That's why I'm here."

She opened her mouth, ready to push further, when Connor pulled the handle on the driver's-side door. "I'll be right back."

Kelsey grabbed his arm. "Wait! Where are you going?"

"To check the rear lot. Todd might have pulled in back there while we've been watching the front." With one foot already on the asphalt and refusing to meet her gaze, Connor seemed more interested in escaping her questions.

"I'm coming with you." She scrambled to unlock the passenger door. When she sensed an oncoming protest, she said, "Partners, remember? You're the one who dragged me along. You aren't leaving me now."

"Forget it! He'll recognize you."

"Todd knows what you look like, too," she argued as she turned back toward him.

"Fine," he bit out as he dropped back into the seat, "but there's something you have to do first."

Thanks to her questions, a noticeable tension vibrated through Connor, evident in his clenched jaw and the taut muscles in the arm he'd braced against the wheel. But the tension gradually changed, not easing, but instead focusing to a fine, definitive point—one that seemed wholly centered on her.

His intense gaze traveled over her hair, her face, her mouth… The gold flecks in his green eyes glowed, and Kelsey's skin tingled as if warmed by his touch. Surely he wouldn't try to kiss her. Not here, not now! Time raced by with each rapid beat of her heart, a single question echoing in her veins.

Why *didn't* he kiss her? Right here, right now—

Her pulse pounded in her ears, drowning out the sound of passing traffic. The heat shimmering on her skin could put the mirage hovering above the asphalt to shame. Shifting his body in the driver's seat, Connor eased closer. The scent of his aftershave, a clean fragrance that called to mind ocean breezes and sun-kissed sand, drew her in. Like waves rushing to the shore, helpless to resist the undeniable pull, she reached for him….

But instead of a roll on the beach, Kelsey crashed against the shoals, her pride battered against the rocks when Connor suddenly turned away. He twisted his upper body between the seats and reached into the back. "Here, take this."

Kelsey stared dumbly at the baseball hat he held.

"See if you can cover your hair."

Her hand was still raised in an attempt to reach out and capture a passion obviously only she felt. An admission of her willingness to make a fool of herself.

Kelsey jerked the hat from Connor, eager to grab hold of anything to save face. "Do you really think this will make a difference?"

"A huge one." Almost reluctantly he added, "Your hair is unforgettable."

But he'd forget all about her and her hair once Emily was a free woman again. Unforgettable. Yeah, right.

Kelsey didn't realize she'd spoken the words until Connor murmured, "It's the kind of hair a man fantasizes about. Trust me."

But she couldn't. She'd nearly made a fool of herself seconds ago, and in case she ever forgot, she had the living, breathing epitome of Connor's perfect woman as her cousin. Kelsey couldn't compare; she never had.

Jerking back toward the door to put as much room as possible between them, she shook back her hair and pulled it away from her face with sharp, almost painful movements. Unable to hide behind her long locks, she felt exposed, vulnerable. Even more so when Connor's gaze remained locked on her features.

"How's that?" she asked, as she twisted her hair into a bun and shoved the bright red Diamondbacks cap into place. When

Connor continued to stare, Kelsey fisted her hands in her lap to keep from yanking off the ridiculous hat. Finally, she demanded, "What?"

Shaking his head, Connor seemed to snap out of his stupor. "I hadn't realized how much you look like Emily."

His words hit like a punch in the stomach. Look like Emily? Not a chance. She'd seen the disappointment in the Wilsons' faces when they first saw her. If Emily and Aileen were beautiful Barbie dolls, then Kelsey was clearly supposed to be Skipper, a younger, blonder version. But she looked *nothing* like her cousins, a point driven home at every Wilson function, with every meeting of their friends and associates. The surprise—if not flat-out disbelief—when Kelsey was introduced as one of the Wilsons.

I hope they had her DNA tested, Kelsey had heard one uninformed, high-society snob whisper. *It wouldn't surprise me if that girl ended up being a con artist out for the family fortune.*

Kelsey had struggled to hold her head high and hold back the tears when she'd wanted to lash out at the woman. She was every bit her mother's daughter, *not* her father's, and inside she was as much a Wilson as Gordon, Aileen and Emily. But outside—where it counted—she couldn't be more different.

"Give me a break!" She tried to laugh off the remark, but the fake sound stuck in her throat. "Emily and I look nothing alike! She's tall and thin and blond and—beautiful!"

Her voice broke on the last word, and Kelsey had never been so close to hitting anyone. Giving in to the impulse, she socked Connor in the shoulder. She had a quick impression of dense muscle and bone, but he caught her hand before she could fool herself into thinking she could do more damage.

"Hey!" A quick tug of her arm had her falling against him. "So are you!"

"Tall? Blond?" Kelsey shot back sarcastically.

"Beautiful!" he retorted.

"But I'm not—"

"Not Emily?" he interjected softly. He brushed an escaping strand of hair—her unforgettable hair—back from her face, and the touch she'd only imagined became reality as he traced his index finger over her eyebrow, across her cheekbone, and skimmed the corner of her mouth. Heat and hunger combined with a tenderness that snuck beneath her defenses. "There's more than one ideal for beauty, Kelsey."

Still pressed against his muscular chest, she knew Connor was the epitome of masculine beauty for her, and she had the devastating feeling that would never change, even years from now. He was the best of the best, and she was a long shot, the dark horse.

"Stop it," she whispered furiously.

"You don't have to be Emily. You can just be yourself."

The deep murmur of his voice reached inside and touched that vulnerable place, but this time instead of opening old wounds, his words offered a healing balm. And meeting his gaze, Kelsey realized he understood her vulnerability in a way no one else could because he'd felt the same way. He'd never been good enough to date the daughter of the wealthy Wilsons, and she had never felt good enough to *be* one of the wealthy Wilsons.

"Connor…" Just one word, his name spoken in a hushed whisper, broke the connection. He blinked, or maybe Kelsey did, because when she looked again, his sexy smile was back in place, all sense of vulnerability gone. "Except for right now. Right now you have to be someone Todd won't recognize."

"Right." Kelsey pulled back, and Connor let her go. She might not have a sexy smile to hide behind, but she could be businesslike and professional…or as businesslike and professional as a wedding coordinator spying on a future groom could be.

"Come on," she muttered as she tugged the brim lower. She didn't know if she'd need the hat to hide her identity from Todd, but maybe she could use it to hide her emotions from Connor. "Let's do this."

She climbed from the car and was headed straight for the building by the time Connor caught up with her. Grabbing her hand, he said, "This way."

With Connor leading the way, they walked half a block before crossing the street and doubling back behind Todd's building. But the lot was empty except for some abandoned crates and an overflowing Dumpster.

"Let's go. Todd's meeting must have been canceled," Kelsey said. She walked around to the front of the building without bothering to take the circular route that got them there, her low heels striking the steaming pavement.

Connor caught up to her as she reached the front of the building. "Look, I admit this was a dud, but—" He cut off with a curse.

Kelsey didn't have time to take a breath before he shoved her into a recessed doorway and nearly smothered her with his body. Her vehement protest came out a puny squeak.

"Don't move." The husky whisper and warm breath against her ear guaranteed she couldn't take a single step without falling flat on her face. "Todd's pulling into the parking lot."

No, no, no! This could not be happening! Swallowing against a lump of horror, Kelsey fisted her hands in his T-shirt and tugged. "Let's go," she hissed.

"Can't. He'll see us if we move. Just…relax."

Despite the advice, every muscle in his body was tense, primed and ready for action. But it was Kelsey who jumped when the car door slammed. "He'll see us."

"No, he won't. He's heading for his office."

She had to take Connor's word for it. With his body

blocking every bit of daylight, she couldn't see beyond his broad shoulders. Too bad the rest of her senses weren't so completely cut off. Instead, the scent of his sea-breeze aftershave combined with potent warm male, and the masculine heat of Connor's chest burned into her skin where he made contact with her. Kelsey locked her knees to keep from sinking right into him.

Heart pounding in her ears, she whispered, "Where is he now?"

"Unlocking the door."

She felt as much as heard his low murmur and hissed, "We should go." Right now, before the heat went straight to her head and she did something unforgivably stupid, like melt into a puddle of desire at Connor's feet.

Chapter Five

"I am not meant for a life of crime."

Seated in a restaurant not far from Dunworthy's business, Connor pressed a beer into Kelsey's hand. That she took it without complaint told him how much the incident at Todd's office had shaken her.

Their near miss had lasted only seconds. Connor had pulled Kelsey toward the car immediately after Todd entered the suite; she'd barely ducked inside the Mustang's ovenlike interior when he came back outside. Connor might have suspected the other man sensed something wrong if not for the way he sauntered out to his top-of-the-line SUV without checking his surroundings. If he had, it was a good bet he would have caught sight of Connor sliding into the driver's seat only a few yards away.

Connor had wanted to follow him, but with Kelsey along, the risk wasn't worth it. Not that it was her fault they'd nearly been spotted. No, Connor took full blame. He'd let Kelsey distract him. He could have driven her back to the hotel and her waiting car but had instead veered off to the restaurant, which had a bar. He figured she could use a drink. After standing in the doorway with the Arizona sun roasting his back, Connor could use a cold shower, but a cold beer was the next best thing.

Liar, a mocking voice jeered. The hundred-plus temperature was a killer, but it was the feeling of Kelsey's body pressed to his that heated his blood.

"Hate to tell you, but we didn't break any laws."

She took a long pull on the bottle, then set it back on the bar with an audible clunk. "We were trespassing."

Hiding his smile behind the beer bottle, he bit back a burst of laughter. "The parking lot is public property. We had every right to be there."

"Oh." Kelsey stared thoughtfully at the bottle. He couldn't tell if she was relieved or disappointed. Finally, she looked up, her expression resolute. "Okay, so maybe what we did wasn't illegal, but—but it was unethical. It isn't right to go around spying on people. Especially when they aren't doing anything wrong. And I don't have time to waste chasing Todd or any of your ghosts around town." She slid out of the booth.

Connor frowned. "Hey, this doesn't have anything to do with me."

"Bull. You're out to prove to Aunt Charlene and Uncle Gordon you're much better for Emily than their handpicked golden boy."

Connor recoiled against the padded booth. Was Kelsey right? Did coming back to Arizona have more to do with salvaging his ego than protecting Emily?

No. No way. He wasn't nearly that pathetic. Unfortunately,

Kelsey had almost reached the door by the time he came to that conclusion. "Kelsey, wait!"

"Hey!" The bartender called after him. "Those beers weren't free, you know."

Swearing, Connor dug out his wallet, threw a handful of bills on the bar, and raced after Kelsey. The sunlight threatened to sear his corneas after the dimly lit bar, and he shaded his eyes against the glare. "Kelsey!"

The rush of nearby traffic nearly drowned out his voice, but Connor doubted that was why she didn't stop. Jogging after her, he caught her as she reached the car. It took a second longer to realize he had the keys, and she couldn't go anywhere without him.

Dammit, what was it about Kelsey that made him so crazy? He hadn't felt like this since—since Emily.

You're a fool, boy. Just like your old man. His father's voice rang in his head. *The both of us always want to hold on to what we can't have.*

Thrusting the comparisons aside, he said, "Look, I know this afternoon was a bust, but this isn't about me."

"Really?" Disbelief colored her words, and Connor fought a flare of irritation mixed with admiration. Had to respect a woman who wasn't easily snowed.

Taking a deep breath, he forced the irritation aside. He couldn't risk losing Kelsey as a partner. That was the reason he didn't want her to leave. It had nothing to do with wanting to spend more time with the woman who had him so fascinated.

Yeah, right, his conscience mocked. Back at Todd's office, he'd been tempted to forget all about the other man and prove to Kelsey just how beautiful she was. But he refused to make out with a woman in a parked car. Especially *not* Javy's car, the same vintage automobile he'd borrowed to take Emily out on dates all those years ago.

He wasn't that same punk kid anymore, even if he was once again lusting after one of the wealthy Wilsons.

"Let me buy you lunch, and I'll tell you what I *do* know about Todd."

Back in the restaurant, under the bartender's watchful eye, Connor and Kelsey placed their orders. As soon as the waitress walked away, Kelsey leaned forward and prompted, "Okay, let's hear it."

"First, did Emily ever tell you how we met?"

Kelsey's gaze dropped as she fiddled with her napkin. "She might have."

"Well, just so you have the whole story, Emily went to a bar. She was underage and in over her head. Some guys started hitting on her. She tried to shrug it off, but she was afraid to tell them to go take a hike. Because that wouldn't have been *nice.* But I could see the panic in her eyes. She was waiting for someone to step in and save her."

"And so you did."

"And so I did." Leaning across the table, he covered Kelsey's hand, intent on claiming her complete attention. Only when her eyes widened perceptibly did Connor realize he'd nearly erased the two-foot distance separating them. He was close enough to count the freckles dotting her upturned nose, to catch hold of her cinnamon scent. Her startled gaze flew to meet his, and as the spark of attraction he saw in her brown eyes flared to life inside him, Connor was the one having a hard time staying focused.

"The, uh, thing is—when I look at Emily now, I see that same panic. She's in over her head, letting herself get pushed along because she's too *nice* to stand up for herself."

"So you rode back into town, ready to play the hero."

"I'm no hero," Connor stated flatly, leaning back in the booth and pulling his hands from Kelsey's. The softness of her skin threatened to slip beneath his defenses, making him weak. The passion in her eyes when she spoke about everlasting love and dreams coming true made him want to believe though he knew better.

Even if he didn't have countless professional examples of love gone wrong to draw from, he also had his parents' as proof of love's fallibility. During their short-lived marriage, his parents drifted so far apart that in the end, neither his father nor Connor had been able to pull his mother back to safety.

If only she'd listened— Helplessness roiled in his gut, but he'd learned his lesson.

It would take more than words to keep Emily safe; he had to have proof. But right now, words were all he had to convince Kelsey. The only way to do that would be to open up and be completely honest. "I didn't expect to like Todd when I met him. I walked into that restaurant in San Diego knowing he's the Wilsons' golden boy and everything I'm not."

"Now who needs the lesson about being himself?" Kelsey murmured.

"Nothing like having my own words shoved back in my face," he said with a smile, which fell away as he realized how much they did have in common, how easily Kelsey understood him. Their gazes caught and held, the spark of desire running on a supercharged emotional current.

A touch of pink—sunset pink—highlighted Kelsey's cheeks, and she dropped her gaze. "Not shoving, exactly. More like gently tossing."

The waitress arrived with their food, breaking the moment and giving Connor a chance to refocus on what he wanted to say. "This is about more than disliking Dunworthy on sight. It's about the way he treats people he thinks are beneath him."

"Like who?"

"Like the valet he was pushing around after we left the restaurant."

"What?"

"I was pulling out of the lot when I saw Todd grab the kid and shove his face an inch from the bumper to show where he'd *dented* the car." Leaning forward, Connor added, "It was a rental, Kelsey. You can't tell me he had any clue whether that scratch was there before or not. But he's the type of guy who likes to intimidate people, especially people who can't or won't fight back."

"What did you do?"

"Jumped out of my car and pulled him off."

"And Todd actually grabbed this kid in front of Emily?"

Connor snorted. "No. She'd left her sweater in the restaurant and had gone back for it. By the time she came out, Todd was wearing a crocodile grin and the valet had pocketed a tip the size of his monthly paycheck."

Something else Dunworthy had in common with the Wilsons—thinking money could make anything or anyone disappear. Not that he blamed the kid for taking the cash. How could he when he'd done the same thing ten years ago?

"You don't think Todd would hurt Emily, do you?" Kelsey asked, disbelief and worry mingling in her expression.

"I don't know," he said. "All I know is that he thinks he can do whatever he damn well wants as long as he pays for the privilege."

"Kelsey! Where have you been all day?" Emily rose from the table in the middle of the Italian restaurant. "I've been calling you since first thing this morning."

Kelsey braced herself against Emily's exuberant greeting, hesitantly patting her cousin's slender shoulder blades. First thing this morning, Emily had been with Connor. Kelsey seriously doubted she'd been on her cousin's mind. "I've, um, been busy."

"What have you been doing?" Emily demanded as Kelsey slipped into a seat next to her and across from Aileen and her husband.

"I was—" Kelsey's mind blanked as she met her cousin's curious gaze, and she couldn't think of a single excuse.

I was with Connor. We spent the day spying on your fiancé, which was possibly the craziest thing I've ever done, right up to the time I thought Connor might kiss me.

"Kelsey!"

She jumped at the sound of her aunt's voice, terrified for a split second that she'd said the unbelievable words out loud. "What?"

Charlene frowned with a question in her eyes. "You paid the florist, didn't you?"

"Yes! Yes, I did." As if the forty-minute errand explained her absence during most of the day.

"Good. I hope it wasn't a mistake going with such a small shop. As worried as that woman sounded, you'd think she was down to her last dollar."

Irritation buzzed like a rash under Kelsey's skin. "Her name is Lisa Remming, and she's an amazing florist. A deposit is standard policy. We signed a contract stating she could cancel the order if it wasn't paid on time," she added, knowing her friend would never have considered canceling such an important order.

"All right, Kelsey. You've made your point," Charlene said. Kelsey thought she might have caught a hint of respect in her aunt's expression.

But Emily's eyes widened, and she grabbed Kelsey's hand. "Lisa wouldn't do that, would she?"

"No, of course not," she reassured her cousin, feeling like

a jerk for worrying her cousin just to make a point with Charlene. "The flowers are going to be beautiful."

Emily smiled, relieved someone else had solved the problem. "Thank goodness. I can't imagine getting married without the right bouquet."

Kelsey, personally, couldn't imagine getting married without the right groom. She *wanted* to believe Todd was that man for her cousin, but ever since Connor had rolled into town, doubts had swirled through her mind like a desert dust devil.

"Emily, darling!" a masculine voice called out. Dressed in designer slacks and a slate-blue silk shirt, Todd Dunworthy approached, his perfectly groomed blond hair glinting, and his teeth flashing in a blinding smile.

Sheep's clothing, Kelsey thought suddenly. Expensive, designer-crafted sheep's clothing…if she believed Connor. But that was the question. *Did* she believe him?

"Sorry I'm late," Todd apologized without looking away from his fiancée. "My meeting ran late."

"Your meeting?" Kelsey didn't realize she'd spoken the words out loud until all eyes turned her way. Tempted to blurt out that he'd spent less than five minutes at the office, she choked back the words. She couldn't say that without revealing her own presence. And, as she'd told Connor, Todd's meeting could have changed locations. Hoping Todd would reveal that was the case, she pressed, "I mean, what meeting, Todd?"

He waved his hand carelessly, and his sleeve pulled back to show a hint of the gold watch he wore. "Just business. You wouldn't be interested," he said, flashing a wink that was more condescending than charming.

"Oh, but I am," Kelsey interjected, when Todd would have changed the subject. He shot her a look clearly meant to back her down—*to put her in her place*—but Kelsey stood her ground. She could almost feel Connor at her back, giving her the strength to do the right thing. "You'll be family soon, and I hardly know anything about what you do."

"Honestly, Kelsey, enough about work," Emily interrupted, despite the fact that Todd had remained completely—suspiciously?—silent. "We have more important things to discuss."

Ever the peacemaker, Emily turned the conversation to the wedding and her honeymoon. She smoothed over the tension like a pro until, on the outside at least, everything *looked* perfect.

But as the conversation moved on to drinks and appetizers and who wanted to try the chef's special, Kelsey couldn't help noticing how her cousin's gaze would occasionally drift off in the distance. And she wondered if maybe, just maybe, Emily was waiting for Connor—or *anyone*—to rescue her again.

Connor drummed his fingers against the steering wheel, his gaze locked on the Italian restaurant. Candlelight flickered in the antique sconces, illuminating the rustic red brick, aged pergola, and carved wooden doors.

After taking Kelsey back to the hotel and her car, Connor called Jake Cameron, eager to hear what the man had found. But the conversation hadn't gone as he'd hoped.

"I told you this would take some time," Jake had said, sounding more frustrated and less confident than during the last call.

"Yeah, I know. You also told me you had a date with Sophia Pirelli. You had to have found *something*."

Silence filled the line, and Connor might have thought the call was disconnected, except he could still sense his friend's tension coming across loud and clear. "Jake—"

"Look, I'm seeing her again. I'll call you later."

He'd hung up after that, leaving Connor to battle his own tension and frustration. Unwilling to sit in his hotel room and go over the same information on Dunworthy again, he'd headed for Todd's condo, planning to talk with some of the man's neighbors, when he spotted the familiar SUV leaving the parking garage.

As Connor followed Dunworthy from his Scottsdale loft, careful to stay two car lengths behind, he had plenty of time to make some calls, and discovered the studio-sized units cost well over two million dollars. Knowing the man would pay such an outrageous price for an exclusive address to call home, Connor should have expected what was to come.

He'd already trailed Emily's fiancé from one expensive store to another, growing more and more disgusted as Dunworthy racked up a small fortune in purchases. Wine shops, jewelers, tailors. Connor had held back far enough to keep Dunworthy from spotting him, but not so far that he couldn't see the dollar signs in the salespeople's eyes.

The afternoon had proved a dud just like the meeting that morning, and Connor wished Kelsey had come along. He missed her company—an odd admission for a man who worked alone. He missed her wry comments and witty comebacks, not to mention the tempting thought of kissing her. It was no longer a question of if, but when…

He did have one lead, thanks to a call he'd overheard Todd make on his cell phone, but he would have to wait to follow up.

He sat up straight in the driver's seat as the restaurant's carved doors opened. "'Bout time," he muttered as the elder Wilsons stepped outside along with Aileen and her husband. Todd and Emily followed, and even though Connor had his gaze locked on the other man, it didn't take much to distract him. Just Kelsey.

She stood apart from the rest of the group—not so far she couldn't hear the conversation, just far enough she couldn't be easily drawn in. He'd noticed her do that at the hotel when he'd crashed their little reception planning session. She'd trailed a step or two behind her aunt and cousin, hiding behind the copious notes she took in her day planner. Observing, but not really joining.

Just the way he did. He never would have thought his job as a private eye and Kelsey's job as a wedding coordinator would give them something else in common, but there it was. Still, the Wilsons were more than Kelsey's clients; they were her family. So what was the reason for that distance?

Now wasn't the time to worry about it. Connor jerked his gaze away from Kelsey. He didn't let his attention stray back to her, not even once, surprised by how hard that was.

Todd slapped his future father-in-law on the back, then kissed Charlene's cheek and said something to make the older woman laugh.

I'll be damned, Connor thought, his respect for Dunworthy as an adversary rising a few notches. He'd never seen the woman crack a smile, yet Todd had Emily's mother eating out of his hand.

The group, a silent film of family togetherness, said their goodbyes amid hugs and kisses, with Kelsey drifting just outside the happy circle. They broke into pairs, the elder Wilsons off to the left with Aileen and her husband, Emily and Dunworthy to his car—illegally parked, Connor noted—alongside the restaurant. Kelsey, the odd woman out, headed toward the back of the restaurant, crossing the parking lot…alone.

Todd's SUV engine roared. He should follow, Connor knew. His hand went to the ignition, but he didn't turn the key. A gut feeling, the kind Kelsey had sardonically discounted, held him in place even as Todd backed his vehicle away from the restaurant.

He had to go now if he had any hope of following. Instead, he leaned forward. Kelsey had nearly disappeared around the building. That side of the restaurant wasn't as well lit. Her hair looked brown in the meager light, the shadows dousing its fiery color. Dressed in a denim skirt and lace-trimmed green T-shirt, she looked smaller than usual…younger and more vulnerable.

Connor had already pushed the car door open before he caught sight of the dark shape of a man cutting across the parking lot and heading her way. Surprise drew Kelsey up short. Connor was still too far away to hear what she said, but he was close enough to see the guy reach out to grab her.

It was his nightmare brought to life. Close enough to see, too far away to help… For a split second, Connor froze until he realized this was no dream and the woman in danger wasn't Cara Mitchell. It was *Kelsey.*

Adrenaline pounded through his veins. A short burst of speed, the rhythmic thumping of feet against pavement, and he was there. Muscles flexing, he had the guy's arm twisted behind his back, his face shoved against the side of the restaurant.

"You okay?" he demanded of Kelsey, surprised by the breathless gasp fueling the words. His heart pounded like he'd run half a mile instead of thirty yards. Trying to outrun the past…

"Kelsey?" He could feel her behind him but didn't risk looking over his shoulder. "Are you okay?"

"Connor, what—" Too stunned by his sudden appearance to get the words out, Kelsey pressed a hand to her pounding heart, surprised the organ was still where it was supposed to be. For a second, she thought it had jumped right out of her chest.

"Did he hurt you?"

She blinked, the question not quite registering, and stared at her ex-boyfriend, who was pressed like a pancake against the restaurant's brick wall. Matt Moran had hurt her. He'd wounded her pride, trashed her self-confidence, hitting her where she was most vulnerable with the reminder she could never compare to her oh-so-beautiful cousin.

Matt made a strangled, high-pitched sound that might have been her name. "Kelsey! Tell him I wouldn't hurt you."

Connor shot her a quick glance. "You know this guy?"

The tension eased from his shoulders, but Kelsey knew he could be back in battle mode in a split second. The masculine display shouldn't have impressed her. She'd never advocated violence as a way to problem-solve. But seeing her former boyfriend pinned to a wall, well, it did her heart some good.

"Yes. You can let him go. He just wanted to talk to me."

Only, Kelsey hadn't wanted to hear anything Matt had to say. She'd already heard it all, ironically enough, from Connor.

He let go of the other man's arm and spun him around. "I take it you don't want to talk to him," Connor said. "Can't blame you there." He gave the other man a hard, intense look, then seemed to sum up Matt's entire character with a single shake of his head. Too bad Connor hadn't been around when Kelsey first met Matt.

Oh, who are you kidding? a mocking inner voice asked. She would never have noticed Matt if Connor had been around. But for all their differences, Connor and Matt had one glaring similarity.

"Kelsey, please," her ex-boyfriend practically whimpered. "You've gotta talk to Emily and tell her she can't marry that guy!"

Even without glancing in Connor's direction, she could feel his gaze. Heat rose to her face. She wanted to ignore both men at the moment, but she focused on Matt who was suddenly, oddly enough, the lesser of two humiliations.

"Emily's in love with Todd, and their wedding is going to be perfect." Determination rang in her voice, but Kelsey wondered who she was hoping to convince.

"You don't understand!" Matt took a single step in her direction, but froze when Connor uncrossed his arms. Keeping a nervous eye on the other man, Matt weakly finished, "I love her."

"Believe me. That is one thing I *do* understand."

He'd offered the same pitiful excuse as an explanation for using her, for taking advantage of her feelings, for making love to her and imagining Emily in her place.

Her ex-boyfriend had the grace to hang his head in shame but not enough sense to know when to give up. "Maybe if I could talk to her—" Matt pressed.

"Oh, for Pete's sake, get over it!"

His eyes widened in surprise, but Kelsey felt a shock when the words sank into her soul, and she realized the real object of her anger. She was tired of feeling like a fool for believing his lies. Of accepting his unacceptable behavior. Of shouldering the blame for the failure of their relationship when Matt was at fault.

"Let it go, Matt, and move on. I have."

Maybe that wasn't entirely true. As far as love was concerned, she certainly wasn't ready to take the plunge again, but might it be worthwhile to test the water?

"The lady asked you to leave." Connor crossed his arms over his broad chest, suddenly seeming to take up twice as much space and ready to literally enforce her advice for Matt to move on.

With a single, pitiful glance at Kelsey, Matt shrank back into the shadows. She didn't know if he'd heard a single word she said, but it didn't matter. *She'd* listened.

"Man, you've had your work cut out for you, haven't you?" Connor asked, once Matt had left. "How many of Emily's exes have you had to deal with?"

Emily's exes. Kelsey crossed her arms over her stomach, some of her earlier pleasure fading. The toe she'd stuck in the deep end felt chilled by frigid water. "So far, you're the only one. Matt isn't one of Emily's ex-boyfriends. He's mine."

Kelsey didn't know why she spilled that bit of information.

It wasn't as if she wanted Connor to feel sorry for her. She didn't know *what* she wanted from him.

He kicked at the asphalt and glanced in the direction the other man had disappeared. "Hell, Kelsey, you shoulda told me that before. I wouldn't have been so gentle."

The unexpected comment startled a laugh from her. It bubbled inside, shaky at first but growing stronger until she felt lighter, buoyed by the emotion and perhaps the chance to let go of the past. "How exactly do you throw a man *gently* against a wall?"

"*Gently* means he gets to slink off under his own power. *Not so gently* requires an ambulance."

"I guess Matt doesn't know how lucky he was."

"You're right, Kelsey. Something tells me he has no idea."

Certainty filled Connor's deep voice. Just listening to him made her feel free from the shame and embarrassment that had held her down for so long. Stepping closer, he crooked a finger beneath her chin. "You okay?"

She nodded, feeling his finger slide along the sensitive skin beneath her jaw. "Yes."

Concern gave way to relief and then anger. "You should have had someone walk you to your car. You have no idea what could happen—"

"Connor, I'm okay," Kelsey interrupted, worried by the tension that was evident in the set of his shoulders. A tension that seemed rooted in a different incident from a different time. "I wasn't in any danger."

Exhaling a breath, Connor seemed to release the pressure building inside and shake off whatever memories had caught him in their grasp. "You still need to be more careful."

True, Matt had startled her, coming out of the shadows the way he had, but he'd lost the power to hurt her long ago. And despite Connor's warning that she should be more careful, *he* was the most dangerous threat around. His lethal charm tore through her defenses, and a question that should have come to her much, much sooner sprang to mind. "What are *you* doing here, anyway? How did you even know we'd be having dinner tonight?"

Connor glanced at the front of the restaurant. A frown darkened his expression before he shook his head and blew out a breath. "Well, I *was* following Todd."

"What!"

"That's how I knew he was at the restaurant," he explained slowly, as if she had trouble keeping up. "So, tell me about dinner."

"Not so fast. You first."

"Okay," he said agreeably. "I haven't had dinner yet, and I'm starving!"

"I meant, tell me what you found following Todd."

"I will, but I really am starving. Come on." With a last look at the now-empty spot in front of the restaurant, he caught Kelsey's hand and said, "Let's go."

"Go where?" she demanded even as she followed alongside, far too aware of the tingle that raced up her spine as his fingers entwined with hers. The innocent touch certainly shouldn't have weakened her knees, but Kelsey could barely concentrate beyond the heat of his skin pressed to hers.

"To find someplace to eat."

Despite the extreme heat during the day, the temperature had lowered with the sunset. A gentle breeze carried the scents and sounds of nearby shops: gourmet coffee, decadent chocolate, the rise and fall of laughter and the faint strains of jazz music.

A group of girls walked toward Kelsey and Connor, heading in the other direction. Tall and beautiful, long limbs left bare by short skirts and tank tops, their not-so-subtle glances at Connor quickly turned to confusion as they shifted to Kelsey.

She didn't need a thought bubble over their heads to know what they were thinking: *What is* he *doing with* her? And after the run-in with Matt, Kelsey couldn't stop that question from digging deeper and deeper.

"Hey." Connor tugged at her hand. "You still with me?" he asked, as if he had somehow lost *her* interest.

"I'm here," she said. Now if she could only focus on *why* she was there. "Did you find anything on Todd?"

Connor took his time answering, waiting until he'd found a casual dining restaurant with outdoor seating. Cooling misters hissed overhead, the sound blending with the distant strains of an acoustic guitar being played on an outdoor stage. After giving the waiter his order, Connor leaned back in his chair and said, "If I'd found anything, you'd be the first to know. Unfortunately, all he did was shop."

"All afternoon?"

He laughed at her startled response. "I thought you'd be impressed."

"Surprised is more like it," she muttered, thinking of Todd's excuse. Still, she hesitated before confessing, "Todd was late for dinner. He said it was because of a business meeting."

"What? That five-second trip to his office this morning?" Connor scoffed.

"Maybe he didn't want to tell Emily he'd gone shopping for her."

"Except he was shopping for himself—unless Emily's taken up imported cigars."

"Um, no."

After a waiter dropped off glasses of ice water and Connor's steak sandwich, he said, "What else?"

"It was dinner, Connor, not an inquisition," she said as Connor dug in with both hands.

Truthfully, Kelsey hadn't *wanted* to find anything. She

wanted to believe Todd and Emily would have a beautiful wedding followed by a happy marriage. "It's probably nothing but—" she paused, not believing her own words "—none of Todd's family are coming to the wedding."

"Did he say why?" he asked, sliding his plate of fries her way.

Kelsey shook her head at the offer and said, "His parents already had a trip to Europe planned, and his sister is pregnant and didn't want to travel."

Connor shrugged. "So it could be nothing."

She blinked. Connor had jumped on even the slightest inconsistency in Todd's behavior. She couldn't believe he was letting this one go. "Are you serious? Can you imagine my aunt and uncle *not* showing up to Emily's wedding?"

"Not every family is like yours."

"Okay, fine. Forget the Wilsons. You might be the P.I. expert, but I'm the wedding expert, remember? And families *always* come to weddings!"

Connor's gaze cut away from her as he balled a paper napkin between his fists, and Kelsey knew. This wasn't about Todd's family or her family or families in general. It was about Connor's. A family she knew nothing about, one she couldn't recall Emily ever mentioning.

"You know, I don't think Emily's ever talked about your family."

"Why would she?"

Because, at one time or another, Emily had told Kelsey nearly everything about Connor. So much that Kelsey felt she'd known him long before she first caught sight of him at the airport. But she certainly couldn't tell Connor how she'd listened to those stories the same way a teenager might pore over celebrity magazines for the latest gossip on the current Hollywood heartthrob.

"I don't know. Maybe because if things had worked out like you'd planned, they would have been *her* family, too."

Connor gave a rough bark of laughter. "Emily had enough family to deal with without adding mine to the mix. Besides, my parents died before I met Emily."

The abrupt comment hit Kelsey in the chest, and she felt ashamed for pushing. She ached for his loss, an echo to the pain she still felt over the death of her own mother.

"Oh, Connor." Her defenses crumbled to dust, and with her heart already reaching out, her hands immediately followed. The heat of his hands—strong, rawboned, and masculine—sent an instant jolt up her arms. Her heart skipped a beat at the simple contact, but it was the emotional connection that had her pulse picking up an even greater speed. For a second, as their eyes met, Connor looked as startled as she felt.

Taking a breath deep enough to force her heart back into place, she focused on the reason she'd dared touch him in the first place. "I'm so sorry. I lost my mom when I was sixteen. Do you want—"

"It was a long time ago," he interrupted, jerking his hands out from hers in a pretense of reaching for his wallet to pull out a few bills. "I should get going. I'll walk you back to your car."

Stung by his abrupt withdrawal, Kelsey ducked her head before he could see the embarrassed color burning in her cheeks. Focusing on her purse, she searched for the keys she knew perfectly well were in the outside pocket.

"No need. I'll be fine," she insisted, and started walking. But if she thought she could out-stubborn Connor, he quickly proved her wrong.

"You will be fine," he agreed, his light touch against her lower back a complete contrast to the steely determination in his voice. "Because I'm walking you to your car."

Kelsey didn't argue, even though Matt was probably long gone. Thanks to Connor, he'd learned his lesson. Too bad she had yet to learn hers. Because no matter what Connor said about how beautiful she was, actions spoke louder than words, and all the compliments in the world couldn't erase the hurt of reaching out to Connor only to have him pull away.

Chapter Six

Early the next morning Kelsey stood outside her shop, gripping the key tightly enough to dig grooves into her palm. The unexpected phone call from her landlord couldn't have come at a better time. She still had plenty left to do for Emily's wedding, but she couldn't think of Emily without thinking of Connor. And Kelsey definitely did *not* want to think of him. Last night, she'd felt a connection—that loss and difficult childhoods gave them something in common. But Connor didn't want common.

He didn't want *her*.

With the morning sunlight glinting off the windows, she couldn't see inside, but in her mind's eye she pictured *her* shop. The subtle green and pink colors, the faded rose wallpaper, the shabby-chic-style parlor where she would meet with clients. Romantic without being overblown; classy while still being casual.

It was going to be perfect. Excitement jazzing her veins, Kelsey stuck the key in the lock, opened the door and blinked. With her dream office so firm in her thoughts she could practically smell her favorite peach potpourri, reality hit like a slap to the forehead.

No soft colors, no floral wallpaper… Shabby, yes, but chic?

"Not even close," Kelsey muttered as she flicked on the lights and stepped inside.

The landlord had shown her the space a few weeks ago, when it had been a struggling craft store. Shelves and bins had lined every wall, filled with yarn and cloth, paints and silk flowers. She'd focused on the space, knowing everything else would go when the other store closed. But she never stopped to think about the mess left behind.

Holes from the now-absent shelves marred the walls with peg-board consistency. The carpet had a two-tone hue thanks to the areas exposed to foot traffic, and the bare fluorescent bulbs overhead buzzed like bug zappers in August. No wonder the landlord had left the key hidden outside instead of meeting Kelsey.

But Kelsey hadn't spent her childhood living in sub-par apartments without learning a thing or two from her mother. "Wilson women against the world," she murmured as she pulled the phone from her purse and called the landlord.

If there was one thing Connor hated, it was being wrong. The only thing worse was being wrong and knowing he had to apologize. Meeting his own gaze in the mirror, he knew he owed Kelsey a big apology. He'd seen the hurt in her chocolate eyes at his abrupt withdrawal and he felt like a jerk. She'd reached out to him—physically and emotionally—and he'd pulled away.

He could justify his actions with the same excuse he always used when thoughts of the past intruded. That time was over and done, enough said. And yet, the sympathy and understanding in Kelsey's expression made him *want* to talk about the past. He'd wanted to turn his wrist, take her hand into his and hold on tight. That completely foreign desire had so rattled him, that he'd locked his jaw and put an early end to the evening.

After showering and throwing on some clothes, Connor called Kelsey's cell. The phone rang four times before she answered, sounding breathless and sexy and— "Where the hell are you?" he demanded before he could keep the words from bursting out.

And what was she *doing* to give her voice that husky, bedroom quality?

"I'm…working."

She was *lying.* Before he could remind himself what Kelsey did or who she did it with was none of his business, he heard a loud clatter followed by an abbreviated scream and a thump that sent his heart racing. "Kelsey!" Silence filled the line, giving Connor plenty of time to imagine half a dozen dangerous possibilities. "Kelsey!"

"I'm here. I'm fine," she said after what sounded like a scramble for the phone. "I knocked over a ladder and a bucket of spackle went flying."

Ladder? "Spackle?"

"You know," she said, her voice sounding slightly muffled, and he imagined the phone held against her shoulder. "That compound stuff you use to patch walls."

"I know what spackle is. The big question is, why do *you* know what it is?"

"I'm just handy that way," she said a little too brightly, and Connor flashed back to the hurt in her eyes. Her answer might have been different if he hadn't pulled away the night before. "Kelsey—"

"I've found an office space to rent. That way I'll have more room to sell my lies about happily-ever-after to unsuspecting brides and grooms."

Connor flinched despite her light-hearted tone. Seemed as if he might have even more to apologize for than he'd thought. "What's the address?"

"Why?" she asked, as if she thought he planned to come by and torch the place.

"Because," he said after a deep breath and a ten count for patience, "I owe you an apology." Kelsey didn't respond, and in the silence, Connor knew she wanted more. That need rose up again, pressure building inside him as words he'd held back for years struggled to get out. "I owe you an apology," he repeated, "and an explanation."

"I'm an idiot," Kelsey muttered as she washed spackle from her hands in the tiny bathroom. She would have liked to look herself in the eye as she spoke those words, but the bathroom was missing a mirror, had no hot water, and a questionable-at-best toilet.

Why had she given Connor the address? Why had she invited him to invade her place? The dream office that filled her thoughts so strongly that morning had faded over the past several hours of hard work. The last thing she needed was Connor's presence to overwhelm what was left of her lace-and-roses dream in a deluge of cotton and denim.

Not to mention his cynicism.

Yet she'd been unable to resist the demand in his voice or his promised apology.

The ring of the bell above the front door alerted her to her first visitor and saved her from her own thoughts. "Kelsey?" a familiar female voice called out.

She banged on the faucet handle a few times to turn off the

water and hurried out, shaking her hands to get them dry. "Lisa? What are you doing here?"

Walking through the shop with a bouquet of gerbera daisies in one hand and a bottle of wine in the other, her friend cast a dubious look around. "Not quite what I expected," she said as she met Kelsey at the back of the shop.

"It needs work," Kelsey admitted. "But I called the landlord and talked him into reducing the first month's rent if I handle the repairs."

"And that's why I'm here," her friend announced as she set the wine and flowers on the ladder. "I know you too well. You're always willing to help your friends, but you never ask for help. Of course, I had no idea you'd need this much help, but it's a good thing I called Trey, too." Trey Jamison was another good friend, and she frequently hired him as a DJ for her weddings.

"You didn't have to do that," Kelsey told Lisa.

"Yes, I did because you wouldn't. I knew you'd be here all alone with no one to help you and…"

Lisa turned as the bell announced another arrival, her words trailing away. Kelsey couldn't blame her friend. She felt pretty speechless as Connor stripped off his reflective glasses and locked that green gaze on her from across the shop. "Hey."

"Hey," Kelsey responded, the word far more breathless than she wanted to admit. Her stomach did a slow roll at the sight of him. Just as she'd feared, he shrank the space until it encompassed only the two of them. Thoughts of lace and roses fell away, overwhelmed by Connor's masculine presence. Her senses took in every bit of him—the faded gray T-shirt that stretched across his chest, the jeans that clung to his muscular legs, the low murmur of his voice.

Lisa's silence didn't last nearly as long as Kelsey's. Her friend gripped her arm and whispered, "Who *is* that?"

"Connor McClane," Kelsey murmured back.

"Connor—" Lisa's eyebrows rose. "Emily's ex? What is he doing here?"

Emily's ex. Kelsey's heart cringed at the description. "Good question," she muttered as his promised apology and explanation rang in her mind.

Before she had the chance to ask, Trey pushed through the doorway. With his long hair caught back in a ponytail, and wearing an oversize T-shirt and raggedy cutoffs, he looked ready to work. But after gazing around, he said, "Way to go, Kelse!" Walking over, he spun her in an exuberant hug. "This place is great."

"You think?" she asked, with a laugh at her friend's enthusiasm.

"Well, it will be when you're done with it, right?" He glanced at Lisa and Connor for confirmation, and only then did Kelsey realize she had yet to introduce them.

"Oh, I'm sorry. Trey, Lisa, this is Connor…"

The introduction faded away as she caught sight of the scowl on Connor's face. Instinctively she stepped out of Trey's embrace, which was *crazy.* Because Trey was just a friend and crazier still because Connor could *not* be jealous.

Could he?

Still, Connor was less than friendly as he crossed the shop to greet Trey. The handshake the two men exchanged seemed more like a prelude to battle than a customary introduction. "Good to meet you," Trey said, his smile growing wide even though Kelsey thought she saw him subtly flexing his hand once Connor released it.

"Pleasure," Connor said, the word sounding anything but.

"Okay, let's put all this testosterone to use," Lisa said, bringing a heated blush to Kelsey's face. "Where do we start?"

"Yeah, give us the list," Trey said, holding out his hand.

"You guys don't have to do this. You can't give up your weekend to help me out."

"Like the time you filled in for me when I got snowed in back East and didn't have anyone to open up the flower shop?" Lisa challenged before glancing at Trey expectantly.

Immediately he picked up where she'd left off. "Or the time you shoved chicken soup and hot tea down my throat to get my voice back in time to DJ that last wedding?"

"That's different," Kelsey protested.

"Why? Why are you the only one allowed to help?" Lisa demanded. "When do we get to return the favor? And hey, we're not dummies. We all know helping you helps us."

"Yeah, as long as she doesn't forget her friends when she's off coordinating weddings for the rich and famous," Trey whispered in an aside to Lisa.

Overwhelmed by their generosity, Kelsey blinked back tears. Growing up, it had always been Kelsey and her mom—Wilson women against the world. But maybe that was only because Olivia hadn't had friends as amazing as Lisa and Trey.

"All right! All right! I give in. And I promise to remember all the little people," Kelsey laughed before grabbing the list as well as a handful of paint swatches, wallpaper samples and various store ads from her day planner.

"Trey, here are the paint colors and wallpaper. If you could pick them up from the hardware store along with a carpet steamer, that would be great. Lisa, here's a picture of the drapes I want for the front window. Could you see if they have a large area rug to match? Anything to hide this carpet."

Even as Kelsey split the shopping between her friends, she was aware of Connor's speculative gaze focused on her. What was he thinking? she wondered. That her romantic trappings were literally that—traps for couples foolish enough to believe in love?

"Got it, boss," Trey said, saluting her with the green and pink paint samples. "Want me to pick up lunch while I'm out?"

"No need. Sara's catering our workday. Her word, not mine," Lisa laughed as she grabbed Trey's arm and led him toward the door.

"Man, I wanted pizza and beer. Sara'll probably bring mini quiches and crudités." As the two of them walked outside, the laughter and casual camaraderie went with them, leaving behind a tension that for Kelsey buzzed as loudly as the fluorescent light overhead.

Ready to take the offensive, she turned to Connor. What apology did he want to give? What explanation? Her lips parted on those questions, but he beat her to the punch.

"How many of your friends are working Emily's wedding?"

Just like that, momentum changed, and Connor had her backpedaling and on the defensive. "Lisa and I went to high school together, and I've made friends with some of the other people I've worked with. But I never would have hired them if I didn't think they'd do an awesome job."

She lifted her chin, ready to battle for her friends the same way she had when she hired them for Emily's wedding. But if this was a fight, Connor didn't play fair.

Reaching up, he tucked a loose curl behind one ear. His eyes glowing with a warmth that stole the fight from her spirit and the breath from her lungs, he murmured, "It wasn't a criticism. Only an observation. Your friends obviously care a lot about you. Just like you care about them."

Intensity lit his emerald eyes, and Kelsey could almost believe he wanted her to look out for him, to care about him—but that had to be a delusion due to lack of oxygen from the breath he'd stolen with his nearness. "I do," she managed to murmur.

"So why was it so hard for you to accept their help?"

She started to deny it, but when Connor's eyebrows rose

in challenge, she knew he wouldn't believe anything but the truth. And maybe if she told him, he would understand why Emily's wedding was so important. "Fixing things is what I do. It's what I'm good at. I wasn't brought up as one of the wealthy Wilsons. I was raised by my mother. We didn't have much, but growing up I didn't know that. All I knew was that I had an amazing mother who taught me how to cook delicious meals without spending more than a few dollars and how to clip coupons to make the most of what little money we had."

A memory came to mind, and Kelsey smiled. "Our favorite day was Black Friday, but we didn't just shop for Christmas. We bargain-hunted for the whole year. My mom taught me how to look at secondhand furniture and see beyond the layers of flaking paint or rust. She showed me how to strip away the exterior to the natural beauty beneath."

Her smile faded away. "But then she died, and I came to live with my aunt and uncle. None of the things I knew how to do mattered anymore. Coupons and discount stores and secondhand furniture were as foreign to them as paying hundreds of dollars for a pair of shoes was to me. They had people to shop and clean and fix things." Kelsey gave a short, sad laugh. "The only thing broken in their house was me. I know they cared about me, but…I just didn't fit, no matter how hard I tried."

"Kelsey." The low murmur of Connor's voice mirrored the tenderness in his gaze. This time it was Kelsey's turn to pull away, to try to escape.

"That's why the wedding is so important. It's my chance—" her *only* chance, because if she screwed this up, why would the Wilsons or anyone trust her again? "—to prove that I can do this, that I'm good at *something.* So I really hope your gut's wrong, Connor, and that Todd is everything my family thinks he is. Or all this hard work is going to be for nothing."

"It won't be for nothing because you're going to be a

success with or without Emily's wedding. Maybe if you *were* more like Emily or Aileen, more used to everything going your way, you'd be more likely to give up. But a single setback won't stop you. You're stronger than that." Catching her hands and smiling at the streaks of spackle marring her skin, he said, "You aren't afraid of hard work."

Strong…unafraid… Kelsey liked the sound of that, but she wasn't feeling the least bit of either as Connor stroked his thumbs across the palm of her hands. She felt downright weak and terrified by the desire coursing through her at such a simple touch.

Her fingertips tingled, tempted to chart the planes and angles of his face, the strong column of his throat. The broad shoulders and wide chest covered by cotton as soft as Connor's body was strong. But she curled her hands into fists. She wouldn't—couldn't—reach out to him again. The embarrassment of Connor pulling away was too painfully fresh in her mind, and her heart was too vulnerable to risk rejection a second time.

In the end, she didn't have to reach out; she didn't even have to move. It was Connor who pulled her closer, Connor who lowered his head, Connor who brushed his mouth against hers. Any thought of him pulling away disappeared as he deepened the kiss. He buried one hand in her hair and wrapped the other around her waist, holding her body tight to his, as if she were the one who might back away.

But escape was the last thing Kelsey wanted.

Instead she wanted to capture this moment, bottle it up, save it for a time when memories were all she would have left of Connor. But even that proved impossible, as he slanted his mouth over hers, his lips and tongue stealing her breath, robbing her of her ability to think, and leaving her with no choice but to feel….

Her breasts against the hard wall of his chest, her heart pounding desperately enough to match the rapid beat of his, the firm press of his fingers against her hip. She splayed her fingers across his back, searching out as much contact as possible, the material thin enough, soft enough, heated enough, that she could imagine his naked skin and the play of muscles beneath her hands.

"Connor." His name escaped her on a breathless sigh as he trailed a kiss across her cheek to her jaw, his warm breath setting off a chain reaction of shivers down her spine. She swayed closer, her hips brushing against his solid thigh. The heated contact weakened her knees, and all she wanted was to sink to the floor, pull Connor down with her and feel the weight of his body on top of hers.

She might have done just that if not for the ring of the bell and an embarrassed "Oops. Pretend I was never here."

Kelsey tore away from Connor in time to see her friend Sara backing out of the door with a platter of food in her hands. She wanted to call Sara back, but it was too late, leaving Kelsey with little choice but to face Connor. With his eyes dark with passion, his chest rising and falling, it was all she could do not to dive back into his arms.

Two seconds ago an interruption was the last thing she wanted. But now with passion clearing, she realized it was exactly what she needed. Already Connor was going to her head; it wouldn't take much for him to go straight to her heart. "That, um, was Sara. I should ask her to come back inside."

Her friends were waiting, her dreams were waiting and she didn't dare push them aside. Not even for Connor. No matter how much she wanted to.

Hours later, Connor looked around Kelsey's shop, amazed by the transformation. The scent of paint filled the shop, and the soft pink and green colors highlighted the walls. The carpets had been shampooed, and the new rug and drapes stored in the back would soon complete the new look. Kelsey's self-proclaimed talent for stripping away the layers and revealing the beauty beneath was on magnificent display in all the work she'd done.

How could she possibly doubt her own worth, her own ability? Connor wondered…until he tried to imagine Emily—or heaven forbid, Charlene—dressed in a T-shirt and cutoffs, with their hair covered by a bandana, a streak of pale pink war paint on one cheek and spackle on the other. None of the other Wilson women would be caught dead looking the way Kelsey did right then. Yet seeing her eyes sparkle as she laughed with her friends, celebrated every small success and worked her *ass* off, Connor didn't think he'd ever seen a woman look as vibrant, as alive, as *sexy,* as Kelsey.

As if feeling the heat of his gaze, Kelsey glanced his way. Heat flared in her cheeks, and she ducked her head, taking a sudden interest in flipping through the phone directory, cell phone in hand as she searched for a plumber.

A phone call to her uncle, and her plumbing problems would have been solved. Hell, a single call to Gordon Wilson and *all* her problems would have been solved. Gordon could have easily set up Kelsey in a furnished, upscale Scottsdale or Paradise Valley suite instead of a work-in-progress strip mall in downtown Glendale.

He'd meant every word when he called Kelsey strong and fearless. She'd been only sixteen when she went to live with her aunt and uncle, an age when most kids would have lost themselves in a world filled with wealth and privilege. But not Kelsey. She'd stayed true to herself, to the lessons her mother had taught her. Even now, when her family's money could make her dream an instant success, Kelsey refused to take the easy way out…not like he had.

He'd had his reasons for taking the money Gordon Wilson had offered him to leave town all those years ago, reasons he believed justified his actions, but he couldn't help thinking that had Kelsey faced the same choice, she would have found another way.

She flat-out amazed him. He would have liked to ignore the emotion spilling through him, but Connor had learned his lesson when it came to ignoring feelings…even if this one wasn't hitting his gut as much as it was pulling at his heart.

"Place looks great, doesn't it?"

The sudden question jerked Connor from his thoughts, and he turned to face Lisa. Judging by the woman's sharp gaze, he doubted Kelsey's shop was on the woman's mind. "It does. You, Trey and Sara were a huge help," he added.

Kelsey's friends had thrown themselves into helping, Trey especially. But despite the close eye Connor kept on the other man, he hadn't seen any proof Trey and Kelsey were anything other than friends. And yet Trey's touchy-feely familiarity had set Connor's teeth on edge. A reaction as unfamiliar as it was uncomfortable.

He rarely felt possessive over a woman, and certainly not after a kiss or two. But then again, what a kiss! He could still taste her, could smell the cinnamon and spice he'd come to associate with Kelsey. No too-sweet floral scents for her. Nothing expensive, nothing fancy, just…Kelsey.

"You weren't too bad yourself," Lisa said with enough tongue-in-cheek attitude to make Connor wonder if she'd noticed how he strove to outlift, outwork, out*do* Trey. Turning serious, she said, "We're all glad to help Kelsey. She's the kind of friend who always takes care of everyone else. This is the first chance we've had to pay her back."

"I doubt she expects payment."

"She doesn't. It's in her nature to help." The brunette paused, and Connor sensed her debating over her next words. "I think a lot of it comes from taking care of her mom."

"Kelsey told me her mother died when she was sixteen." But despite what she'd told him, Connor knew he had only part of the story. Why had Kelsey's mother—Gordon Wilson's sister—raised Kelsey on her own? Single mom or not, she should have had the family fortune at her disposal, and yet that clearly hadn't been the case.

What had caused the rift between Kelsey's mother and her family? And what about the father Kelsey never mentioned? Connor didn't ask Lisa those questions. It was up to Kelsey to offer answers…if he asked her.

With a glance at her watch, Lisa told him she had to go, but she left with a few final words he translated into a warning. "Kelsey's a great girl. She deserves the best."

Connor waited for the woman to add that Kelsey deserved better than him, but when she merely gazed at him in expectation, he realized Lisa wasn't telling him Kelsey deserved better *than him;* she was telling him Kelsey deserved the best *from him.*

"Well, I finally found a plumber who can come this week…" Kelsey's voice trailed off as she walked from the back room, cell phone in hand.

Connor stood alone in the middle of the shop. Even with the progress they'd made, bringing her dream closer to reality, he overwhelmed the place. If anything, the shop's increasingly feminine decor only served as a larger reminder of Connor's masculinity. And after that kiss, Kelsey didn't have any doubt whatsoever about his undeniable and—she was beginning to fear—irresistible masculinity.

"Lisa had to take off," he explained.

"Oh. She was probably afraid I'd put her to work again if she didn't sneak away."

"I don't think so. Your friends will obviously do anything for you."

Uncomfortable with the praise, Kelsey countered, "Like Javy would for you."

Connor frowned. "Yeah. He thinks he owes me, but the truth is, his family bailed me out when I was a kid. Nothing I've done would be enough to repay them."

Despite the explanation he'd promised earlier, Connor's voluntary statement caught Kelsey off guard, surprising her almost as much as his kiss. She shook her head and protested, "Just because I spilled my guts doesn't mean you have to—"

"I want to," he interrupted. "I should have told you about my past last night, but I haven't told anyone since Señora Delgado pried it out of me as a kid."

"You—you didn't tell *anyone?*" Kelsey prodded.

You didn't tell Emily?

His penetrating gaze read into the heart of her question, hearing what she *hadn't* asked, and he vowed, "I didn't tell anyone."

And suddenly Kelsey wasn't sure she wanted to know. Listening to what he had to say seemed to take on a greater significance because Connor wanted to tell *her,* to confide in her, something he'd never told Emily.

Without saying another word, Connor stepped forward, his long strides erasing the distance between them. He caught her hand and led her over to the love seat her friends had surprised her with. She'd been overwhelmed by their generosity. The sofa would be the perfect place for her soon-to-be-married couples to sit side by side and decide floral arrangements, wedding invitations, dinner menus.

But as soon as Connor sank down onto the love seat, she

decided it would be the perfect place for her to curl up in his arms, the perfect place to kiss him and never stop. The masculine-feminine contrast sent a slow roll of awareness through her stomach as he settled back against the rose-covered cushions. In faded cotton and rough worn denim, he should have looked out of place; instead, his broad shoulders and wide chest looked far more comfortable and inviting than the floral chintz ever could.

Swallowing, she folded onto the couch beside him, one leg bent and angled toward Connor. He stared straight ahead, keeping his silence, and Kelsey sensed his thoughts drifting back to a past he'd purposely chosen not to face…until now.

Taking a deep breath, he said, "My father was a truck driver. Eighteen-wheeler. He worked hard, drank hard. He was…strict."

The tension in Connor's shoulders and the way his hands tightened into fists gave a clear definition of the word. Her heart ached for the boy he'd been, a boy she could picture so easily. Dark hair that was too long, a body that was too skinny, and a gaze that was too old. She could see him in her mind as if, somehow, he'd been there all along.

Crazy, she thought, but she felt she knew him so well. And now that Connor was willing to give out answers, did she dare ask more questions? Could she risk getting to know him even better?

In the end, no matter the potential danger to her heart, Kelsey had to ask. Not because she needed to hear the story… but because Connor needed to tell it. "And your mother?" she asked softly.

One by one his fingers unclenched then slowly laced together as if cradling something precious. "She was a dreamer. She was always…looking for something. Always hoping for a better life, only she never found it. I was eight when she died.

She'd been taking art lessons, or maybe it was a dance class. I can't remember."

Connor cleared his throat. "Anyway, this place wasn't in the best part of town. I begged her not to go. I knew something bad was going to happen. But she went anyway. No one knows exactly what happened," he added, the tension pulling at his shoulders revealing how much not knowing still troubled him, "but the police figured a mugging went wrong. Either my mom fought back or the guy panicked, and the gun went off."

"Oh, Connor, I'm so sorry." Just as she feared, her heart ached a little more at the telling, and she longed to reach out to him, to comfort him. But she didn't. This time it was her turn to twist her fingers together, strangling the desire to touch him.

Because—despite his kiss—she still feared her touch wasn't the one Connor wanted.

But he never told Emily about his family. He's telling you! Aching or not, her heart had the strength to argue, and Kelsey felt her resistance crumbling.

"The guy stole her purse and wallet," Connor went on as if she hadn't spoken. "It took three days before the police figured out who she was."

"Didn't your dad report her missing?"

"He was on a long-distance drive. He didn't know anything was wrong."

"But when your mother didn't come home, someone must have tried to get hold of him. The people you were staying with—" As soon as she said the words, realization flooded Kelsey and her breath caught. "You were alone, weren't you?"

"My mom thought I was old enough to take care of myself, and it should have only been for a few hours."

Hours that had stretched into days.

"Wasn't there anyone you could call? A friend of the family?"

"Probably, but hell, I was eight. My mom had told me she

was going to be right back. Calling someone would have been like admitting something was wrong, admitting she wasn't coming back. Ever."

Kelsey felt heartsick at the thought of the frightened, abandoned boy Connor had been. "You were so young. How did you get on without her?"

"My dad and I stumbled along, but he always blamed my mom for dying. If she'd been happy with her life, if she hadn't always been out looking for more and expecting something better, she'd still be alive. If she'd just *listened* to me. I could have—"

Saved her. Connor didn't say the words, but they rang in the silence and underscored everything he did. "It's not your fault, Connor," she insisted, and this time she couldn't keep from reaching out and grasping his hands as if she could somehow heal the pain and guilt with her touch. "People make their own decisions, and you aren't responsible for their choices."

"No, only for my own," he agreed darkly, but tension tightened his hands into rock-hard fists.

Her family was so wrong about Connor. He wasn't out to ruin Emily's wedding—he was trying to save her from a past he couldn't possibly change. But Kelsey still wasn't convinced Todd was the threat Connor thought him to be. After all, Connor's *gut reaction* had pinned Matt to the restaurant, mistakenly seeing her ex-boyfriend as a physical threat. Wasn't it possible Todd was as harmless as Matt, and Connor was looking through the eyes of the past and seeing a danger that wasn't there?

"I can't imagine what that must have been like to lose your mother so suddenly." *So violently.* "But don't you think maybe that's colored the way you see people?"

"People like Dunworthy?" he asked with a wry twist to his lips. He pulled his hands out from beneath hers in the pretense of shifting to face her on the love seat. "I know you think I'm wrong about him, but it's because of my past that I'm sure I'm right." As if sensing her doubt, he asked, "Haven't you ever met someone and instantly known the kind of person they are?"

Thoughts of her first impression of Connor assailed Kelsey. The bad boy. The troublemaker. The man out to ruin Emily's wedding and destroy Kelsey's chance to prove herself to her family, to make her mother proud… But he was so much more than that.

"Maybe once or twice."

"Like when you met me?"

One corner of his mouth kicked up with the teasing comment, but the smile lacked full-force charm, his heart not in it. The emotional waters had gotten too deep, and Connor was clearly pulling back to shallower depths. And Kelsey almost wished she had stayed on the surface, wished she could still see Connor the way he wanted to be seen—cocky, self-confident, unbreakable. But she felt herself going under, caught by the pull of this man who was so much more than the rebel he played.

Struggling to break free, she focused on the easy out Connor had taken and followed him to more solid ground. "I knew you were going to be trouble the moment I met you. Does that count?"

"Talk about biased," he murmured. "How many Connor McClane stories have you heard over the years?"

"More than a few."

"More than a few hundred, if your aunt and uncle had anything to say about it." The teasing tone stayed in his voice, but Kelsey could tell her family's poor opinion of him still rankled. He was clearly out to prove the Wilsons wrong, but Kelsey suspected he had as much to prove to himself. "And here I've been a perfect gentleman."

"Well, not perfect," she argued. But who wanted perfect? Perfect was for women like her cousins; Kelsey much preferred the real thing to Ken-like perfection.

"I'm crushed. Señora Delgado will be so disappointed."

"Señora Delgado?"

"Javy's mother."

"How did you and Javy meet?"

"We went to school together. Mrs. Brown's sixth-grade glass."

"And you two became fast friends?"

"Nah, we hated each other. I can't even remember why. Oh, wait, it had something to do with a girl. We thought we were pretty hot stuff on the playground. Both trying to impress Alicia Martin. Unfortunately for us, she had a thing for older men."

"Eighth grader?" Kelsey guessed, playing along to maintain the teasing mood.

"Worse. P.E. teacher. And man, the guy was old. Like twenty-five. Anyway, we bonded over a couple of cafeteria juice boxes, and I started hanging out with him at his mother's restaurant. Before long, I was washing dishes and bussing tables. If the Delgados hadn't fed me through most of junior high and high school, I don't know what I would have done. Probably would have dropped out to work full-time if Maria hadn't stopped me."

Kelsey knew the drop-out rate was horrible, especially in Arizona, but as much as she'd hated school, she never once considered not finishing. "How did she stop you?"

"By telling me I *should,*" Connor said wryly. "She said anyone foolish enough to give up a free education didn't deserve one."

Smiling at the woman's use of reverse psychology, Kelsey said, "I think I'd like to meet her. Not every woman has enough influence to keep a boy in school *and* teach him to clear dishes off a table."

"You're on. Let's go to the Delgados' restaurant. Maybe Maria will be there."

Kelsey swallowed. Was Connor asking her out? On a *date?* She waited for the little voice in her head to tell her this was a bad idea, but she didn't hear it. Possibly because it was drowned out by the *big* voice screaming, "Go for it!"

She knew the voice of reason would be back, loud and clear, and ready to say "I told you so" if she let herself fall for Connor. But that worry, like the voice, seemed far off, and she couldn't resist the chance to spend more time with Connor.

"I'm a mess," she said in weak protest. "I can't go anywhere looking like this."

As Connor's gaze swept over her, Kelsey felt her face heat. She could only imagine what he saw. She had spackle under her nails, drywall dust in her hair, and more splotches of paint than freckles covering her arms. She was sweaty and disheveled, and even though Connor had worked as hard as anyone, he looked—

Gorgeous, she thought with a sigh, taking in the lock of dark hair he'd constantly pushed back from his paint-streaked forehead, the hint of five o'clock shadow shading his jaw, the damp T-shirt that molded to his shoulders and chest.

"I'll pick you up at your place in half an hour," he said as he stood and reached down to pull her to her feet.

Kelsey shook her head, ready to refuse, and yet when she opened her mouth she said, "An hour."

"Forty-five minutes."

"An hour." She laughed as she shoved him toward the door. "And not a minute sooner."

Chapter Seven

Mariachi music greeted Connor as he opened the car door. Judging by the nearly full parking lot, the restaurant was packed. The lunch hour tended to draw patrons from nearby businesses; at night, the place had more of a party atmosphere. The music would play, tables would be pushed aside to create a dance floor, and he was *definitely* looking forward to slow dancing with Kelsey.

He was looking forward to the entire evening with an anticipation that caught him off guard. After spilling his guts the way he had, escape should have been the only thing on his mind. He never talked about his past—*never*—and as little as two days ago, the thought of opening up about a time that still left him feeling lost and vulnerable would have tied his stomach into barbed-wire knots. And the thought of confiding in a Wilson!

Connor shook his head in disbelief, even as he admitted

Kelsey was no ordinary Wilson. She might not fit the Wilsons' model of perfection, but she fit his.

He rounded the car to open Kelsey's door, a split second too late, as it turned out. She already had one shapely leg extended, but he was in time to reach out a hand to help her out. Surprise lit her gaze, as if she hadn't considered his invitation to dinner a *real* date.

And despite the casual, last-minute offer, Connor realized he very much wanted this to be a real date. The kind of date where everyone in the restaurant would know Kelsey was with him. The kind where he never wanted the night to end and where, when the evening finally *did* end, a good-night kiss was not only expected, but breathlessly anticipated.

And when that time came, Connor vowed, he'd make sure there was no doubt in Kelsey's mind.

"You look amazing," he murmured, placing a hand at the small of her back.

Pleasure brightened her eyes and put color in her cheeks despite the less-than-original compliment. But hell, it was more than her looks. It was Kelsey. *She* amazed him.

"Thank you." She smoothed her hands over the embroidered skirt she wore. "I was hoping it wouldn't be too dressy."

"It's perfect." The flared skirt and off-the-shoulder blouse had a Spanish touch that emphasized her curves, and he wondered again how she could be so oblivious to how good she looked.

But that mix of confidence and insecurity was so much a part of Kelsey. He'd watched her divide the workload and make decisions without hesitation this afternoon, giving him an idea of how good a wedding coordinator she must be. Yet that confidence completely deserted her when it came to her personal life.

Living with the Wilsons had done that to her, Connor was

certain of it. They'd stripped her of her confidence, of her faith in her abilities, which they deemed worthless and beneath them.

Same way they'd declared *him* worthless and beneath them.

Connor shook off the dark thoughts as they stepped inside the restaurant. The scent of sizzling fajitas and salsa reminded him Trey hadn't been too far off about Sara's lunch. The caterer had brought delicate sandwiches and a fruit salad that looked more like a table centerpiece than something to eat.

"Man, I'm starving. I had a total slave driver nearly work me to death and only feed me bread and water."

"It was sandwiches, not just bread. And sparkling water, if that makes you feel any better." Kelsey laughed. "Besides, *you* volunteered, remember?"

"Yeah, I did." And he'd gladly do it again. Just looking into her excited brown eyes, listening to her laughter, made him feel—Connor thought for a moment, searching for the right word—happy. At peace. With nothing to prove, nothing to make up for. For the first time in his life, despite spilling the story of his sorry, less-than-sterling past, Connor felt he could be himself and that alone would be enough.

Except you didn't tell Kelsey the whole *story,* his conscience argued, dimming his contentment.

He hadn't told her about the money he'd taken, money he'd given to the Delgados to save the restaurant that pulsed with life around them. The business meant the world to Maria, especially following the dark days after her husband passed away. But Miguel's medical bills and the damage caused by an accidental grease fire had almost ruined the restaurant financially. In an effort to save it, Connor had taken the money from Gordon Wilson instead of throwing the check back in the smug SOB's face.

He knew what the older man thought. That he was nothing more than a gold-digging opportunist. But he was starting to think Kelsey might be the one Wilson, the one woman, to understand.

Was that why he'd invited her here? So she could meet Maria Delgado and see how important the woman was to him? So she could see for herself why he'd taken the money?

"Kelsey—"

"How about this? I'll pay for dinner tonight, compensation for all that slave labor?" she suggested as she stepped forward to talk to the hostess.

"Kelsey, wait." He caught her hand, wanting, *needing* to tell her the whole truth.

The seriousness in his tone made her eyes widen. "Hey, if you want to pay—"

"It's not that. I need to tell you—"

"Connor! *Mijo!*"

Hearing the familiar voice, Connor turned toward the sound with a large dose of relief and only the smallest amount of disappointment. The moment was gone, and he focused on Maria Delgado as she moved among the crowded tables toward him. She hadn't changed from the woman he remembered. Sure, she had a touch more gray in her waist-length hair and a few more wrinkles, but her dark eyes were as warm and welcoming as ever.

"Señora!" Connor bent to wrap his arms around the diminutive woman.

"My son told me you had come home! It is so good for you to be back!"

"It's good to see you, too." Seeing the undisguised interest in the older woman's eyes, he added, "Maria Delgado, this is Kelsey Wilson."

"Pleasure to meet you, Mrs. Delgado. Connor has told me a lot about you and how much your family means to him."

Maria beamed at him like a proud mother. "Connor, he is

family," she said to Kelsey. "And for him to bring you here, you must be very special. Never has he brought a young lady to the restaurant."

The implication that he'd brought Kelsey "home" to meet his family should have sent panic shooting like warning flares through his system, and yet seeing the two women talking and laughing together felt…*right.*

Kelsey also ignored the too-telling observation, but an adorable blush lit her cheeks as she added, "Your restaurant is amazing. I have to admit, I've never cared for Mexican food, but the quesadilla I had the other day was delicious."

"I always say, people who do not like Mexican food have not had *my* food." Maria pressed a hand against her bosom, pride shining in her dark eyes.

As Maria led them through a maze of crowded tables, Connor asked, "Where is Javy tonight?"

The *señora* waved a dismissive hand. "Ah, that boy. He is out with some girl. I tell him he needs to settle down, but does he listen? No. My son, he is too handsome for his own good. He does not have to work to get these girls' attention. Too often he chooses the easy way. He does not realize some things you must work for." She turned to Kelsey in a shared feminine confidence, a twinkle in her dark eyes. "But Connor, he is just handsome enough, no?"

"No. I mean, yes," Kelsey stuttered, flustered by the question. Connor was ready to jump in and rescue her from having to answer when she made her own save. "I think Connor is more than handsome enough," she said in a whisper plenty loud enough for him to overhear, "but he still has his work cut out for him."

Señora Delgado chortled and gave what sounded like a quick prayer beneath her breath. "Come, I will give you the best table in the house."

"I thought all the tables were the best tables," he teased with a wink at Kelsey as he placed his hand on the small of her back.

"Sí," the older woman agreed, "they are all the best."

Kelsey grinned, sharing his humor in the *señora's* unflappable logic.

After showing them to a secluded table in the back, Maria kissed Connor's cheek and went back to work. Kelsey's hand touched the ladder-back chair, but Connor beat her to it. As he pulled it out for her, he leaned close. Close enough to catch the cinnamon scent of her skin. Close enough to see the freckles she'd tried to hide beneath makeup. Close enough to hear her breath catch in reaction to his nearness. "You should know by now, Kelsey," he murmured, "I'm not afraid of a little hard work."

Her eyes widened, but just like she had with Señora Delgado, Kelsey found her own footing and knocked him for a loop when she said, "I'm counting on it."

Time froze as the moment held them in its grip. The restaurant, with its loud music and bright lights, faded away, leaving behind only Kelsey's gorgeous brown eyes and softly parted lips. A burst of laughter from a nearby table broke the moment, and Kelsey sank into the chair he held for her. Connor had little choice but to take his own seat and curse the table separating them.

A waiter came by with menus, but Connor could tell by the frequent glances she sent his way Kelsey's mind wasn't on dinner. Finally she set the menu aside and said, "Is it true what Señora Delgado said before? You never brought anyone here?"

He'd let her get away with the unasked question before, but not this time. "Come on, Kelsey. Are you interested in *anybody* or in Emily?"

At first she looked ready to protest, only to square her

shoulders and meet his gaze head-on. "Okay. Did you ever bring Emily here?"

"No. The Delgados are like family to me, and I wasn't sure Emily would get that." He hadn't been able to picture Emily at the rustic, homey restaurant. He still couldn't…and yet Kelsey fit in so perfectly. He'd never had a doubt about bringing *her.*

Not waiting for her to ask why—or wanting to look too closely for a reason himself—Connor pushed back from the table. Kelsey's eyes widened in surprise as he held out his hand and said, "Come on. Let's dance."

As Kelsey took Connor's hand, it occurred to her that she had no idea how to dance to the Latin-flavored beat pulsing from the speakers. But that didn't stop her from following him onto the tiny dance floor, where the music instantly switched to a ballad.

Connor's smile flashed as he pulled her into his arms. "Couldn't have planned it better myself."

"I'm not so sure you didn't."

"This wasn't me. It must be fate."

Kelsey didn't know about fate, but being held in Connor's arms certainly felt like a dream. She wasn't the only one who had dressed up for the evening. Connor had showered and shaved, brushed his dark hair back from his forehead. A touch of sexy sophistication replaced a bit of his bad-boy image thanks to the white button-down shirt and black slacks he wore instead of his usual T-shirt and jeans. No matter what Maria Delgado said about her son, it was Connor who took Kelsey's breath away. He was the most gorgeous man she'd ever met, and the sheer look of masculine appreciation in his eyes made her feel beautiful. But even as the physical connection robbed her of her breath, the emotional connection threatened to steal her heart.

Listening to him talk about his past and seeing his love for Señora Delgado revealed a different side of Connor. A fiercely loyal and caring side that would be as easy to fall for as his cocky grin and killer body.

Right, her conscience told her. *And the fact that Connor never shared that side of himself with Emily, never told her about his childhood, never brought her to the restaurant, that has* nothing *to do with it.*

Kelsey wanted to shove the goading voice aside, but it was impossible to ignore. Connor had trusted her with the heartbreak of his past and a happier part of his present, and it was almost impossible not to think of the future. Not a forever future, of course, but the immediate future—and how she'd gladly spend what time she and Connor had left in his arms.

For the first time in years, Kelsey didn't feel like she'd come in a distant second to her too-beautiful cousin, an irony her disapproving conscience couldn't overlook, as Connor was the one man in a position to best make comparisons…

"You're too quiet," Connor murmured in her ear. "It makes me nervous."

Kelsey laughed at the thought of *anything* making Connor nervous. "Don't be. I was just thinking."

"Hmm. Those might be the most nerve-racking words a man ever hears. Should I ask *what* you've been thinking?"

Not brave enough to admit the whole truth, Kelsey said, "Only that we don't have much time left."

Connor cocked an eyebrow. "Until the wedding?"

"Until you leave."

"Ready to see me go, huh?"

"Surprisingly, no," Kelsey said, although Connor didn't seem surprised by her admission.

Because it was so obvious how her heart slammed into her chest every time he came near? How her knees turned to jelly with a single look? It wasn't something she wanted to admit to herself, forget giving Connor that kind of ammunition. Because even though telling her about his past and bringing her to meet his surrogate mother might have melted the walls around her heart, nothing said Connor felt the same.

"Good," he said. "Since I'm not ready to leave."

"Because you haven't figured Todd out yet?"

Connor scoffed. "I did that a long time ago. No, it's you I'm still trying to figure out."

This time it was Kelsey's turn to laugh. "I'm no mystery. I've already spilled all my secrets."

"I think there's more to discover. But I've already figured out a few things on my own. Like how you feel in my arms…how you taste when I kiss you…how I can make you blush without even trying."

Feeling her face heat, Kelsey protested, "Like you aren't trying right now."

"Naw," he said with a grin that did more than make her face heat as he lifted a hand and traced a pattern on her cheek. "If I was really trying to make you blush, I'd tell you how much this star on your cheek turns me on—especially when I think about all the other shapes I might find…and where I might find them."

Kelsey swallowed. She'd spent her whole life hating the freckles that marked her pale skin, but in a split second, in a single sentence, Connor had made her forget every teasing comment, every self-conscious thought.

"Connor." The lone word was all she could manage, but every bit of the emotion she felt echoed in her voice.

Making a sound deep in his throat that could have been a groan, he protested, "Don't look at me like that or I'll end up doing something not meant to be done in public."

Kelsey did lower her gaze, from the hunger in his eyes and

past his too-tempting lips, to stare at his throat. Not because of what he'd said, but because she didn't have the courage to look him in the face and say what she wanted to say. "There are…more private places."

Connor's arms flexed, pulling her closer, and his voice was a deep rumble in her ear as he said, "My hotel room."

Seemingly without conscious thought, an image flashed in Kelsey's mind—Emily leaving Connor's room—and she blurted out, "My house."

Bringing their dance to a halt, Connor stepped back slightly and nudged her chin up. "Are you sure?"

Even though he was asking about so much more than a simple destination, Kelsey met his gaze and repeated, "My house."

She felt slightly guilty as Connor pulled her through the restaurant. "Shouldn't we say goodbye?"

"Maria'll understand," Connor insisted without breaking stride.

Deciding she'd rather not think about how much the woman might understand, Kelsey focused on keeping up with Connor's long strides. Her heart pounded wildly in her chest, but the crazed rhythm had less to do with how fast they were going and so much more to do with what would happen once they got back to her place. And Kelsey didn't think Connor could walk fast enough….

And he must have felt the same, she realized when they reached the car. Instead of unlocking the door, Connor turned and pulled her into his arms.

"I've wanted to do this from the moment I saw you."

The husky words would have been easier to believe had Kelsey spoken them, but coming from Connor, they sent a thrill rushing through her as enticing as his kiss. "You wanted to do this at the airport?"

"At the airport. In your car on the way from the airport. The first time we came to the restaurant." His voice dropped to a husky murmur. "My hotel room."

Kelsey shivered, her thoughts instantly turning to the king-size bed where she wouldn't have to imagine the press of Connor's body against her own. His green eyes glowed as if he'd read her thoughts and was right there…in his hotel bed…with her.

Ducking his head, he caught her lips in a kiss that picked up right where the last had left off. The hunger and intensity didn't have to build; passion and desire had shimmered between them all evening like desert heat. Kelsey sank her hands into his dark hair, her fingers sifting through the silky strands. With Connor leaning against the side of the car, Kelsey didn't have to stretch to reach his mouth; they were perfectly aligned—lips to lips, chest to chest, thigh to thigh.

Connor slid his hands down her back, his fingers claiming the soft flesh of her hips as he pulled her tighter into the vee of his body. Kelsey thought if it were possible to pass out from pure pleasure, she might sink to the ground on the spot.

Instead, she broke away from his kiss. Hiding her face against his neck, she murmured, "My house, remember?" And then she gave in to temptation and pressed her mouth to the strong column of his throat, right where his pulse pounded in time with the pulsing Latin beat coming from the restaurant.

His throat jerked as he swallowed, and he pushed away from the car door without breaking their embrace. He reached back for the door handle and fumbled for a second before he broke away with a muffled curse and twisted around to get a better grip. But instead of pulling the door open, Connor paused, hand in the air as if he'd forgotten what he was doing. Seeming to shake off the hesitation, he opened the door for her.

But in that split-second hesitation, the intensity dissipated like smoke from a doused fire. Her heart still pounded from the kiss, and her breath was far from steady, but the mood had definitely changed. He wouldn't meet her gaze, and Kelsey couldn't help wondering… "Connor, what's wrong? Did I do something—"

"No," he bit out. His fierce expression lessened when he saw her flinch, but frustration filled his movements as he ran a hand through his hair. "No, you didn't do anything wrong. It's just—this is crazy. *You* make me crazy! I haven't made out with a girl in a car since Emily, and now here I am with another Wilson—"

His words cut off abruptly, but not before the small thrill Kelsey experienced at the thought of driving Connor McClane crazy was buried by a wave of doubt and insecurity as she imagined Connor and Emily making out in a car.

And—could this really *get* any worse—not just any car. The vintage Mustang belonged to Javy, who'd undoubtedly owned it for years. Back when Connor would have borrowed the hot car to pick up Emily…

Humiliation burning in her cheeks, Kelsey wanted nothing more than to go home, but she dreaded getting in that car. It didn't matter that she and Connor had already driven all over town in it; now, all she could see was Emily in the passenger seat, wind whipping through her blond hair. Emily, searching for a favorite song on the radio. Emily, slipping into the back seat where Connor waited…

"This was a mistake."

"Kelsey—"

"Can we go?" she interrupted. Maybe if she closed her eyes, she could picture herself somewhere else.

"No."

"What?"

Connor's dark frown told her she'd definitely heard right the first time. "No. I'm not gonna let you run off."

"There's nothing else to talk about, Connor. You and Emily—"

"All right. Fine. Let's talk about how there hasn't been a 'me and Emily' for *years.* I can't change my past, and I can't change yours."

"*My* past?"

"How much of this is about me and Emily? And how much of it is about *you* and Emily? How many times have you felt you couldn't live up to your cousins? How many times have the Wilsons made you feel second best?"

How many? Kelsey couldn't count the numerous times she'd tried walking in her cousins' footsteps only to fall in disgrace again and again. "Uncle Gordon and Aunt Charlene treated me *exactly* like they treated Aileen and Emily. But that was the problem. I'm—not like those girls."

"You don't have to be, Kelsey. You're you. That's more than enough."

Honesty and desire glowed in Connor's eyes. But as much as she longed to believe him, as she slid into the passenger seat Kelsey couldn't help feeling like she was trying yet again to fill Emily's place.

Shoving the key into the ignition, Connor started the car, and they were silent throughout the ride back to Kelsey's; the rumble of the engine was the only sound. Only as they pulled into her driveway did she find the courage to ask the question shouting through her thoughts the whole time.

"Why did you stop? If it wasn't about Emily—"

Connor sighed. "We were in the middle of a public parking lot where anyone could walk by. I should have the self-control to keep my hands to myself. But being back here has me acting like a hotheaded kid again. *You* make me feel like a hot-headed kid," he practically growled, not sounding the least bit happy about the idea. "Not Emily. *You.*"

"I want to believe you. But this is all happening so fast, and it isn't easy to change how I feel after a matter of days!"

"I know. But I'm gonna keep trying."

Connor walked her to the front door, where he leaned close, giving her ample time to pull away. If his earlier kiss had struck like a flash of lightning, this was like the slow promise of a sunrise. Kelsey felt the gentle rays first, the touch of warmth against her cheeks as his fingers slid into her hair. And then light blazed behind her eyelids as he kissed her.

Heat poured through her, starting where his mouth brushed against hers then spreading out to all parts of her body, all the way down to her tingling fingertips and toes. Just when he'd left her knees weak and her willpower completely shaken, he eased away, ending the kiss slowly, reluctantly. "I want to see you tomorrow."

"I can't—"

"Kelsey."

"Not because of, well, anything. I'm busy tomorrow."

"With your shop?"

Kelsey shook her head regretfully. "The shop will have to wait a few days. I'm meeting Emily for brunch, and then we're going shopping for bridesmaids' gifts. Assuming that doesn't take all day, I have to meet with a friend who's putting together an audiovisual presentation for the reception."

"What time?"

"In the afternoon."

"Dunworthy has a meeting set up for tomorrow at six. Interested in another stakeout?"

Kelsey forced herself not to look over at the Mustang. The vehicle had somehow turned into so much more than a simple car. It was a physical reminder of Connor's past with Emily. A past Kelsey wasn't sure she could ignore. "Do I even want to know how you came across the information?"

"Nothing illegal. I got it the old-fashioned way. I overheard a conversation he was having on his cell phone." Connor frowned. "Well, I guess the cell phone part isn't old-fashioned, but the eavesdropping was."

"It could be nothing. A dead end like the other day."

"Could be. Wanna find out?" His eyebrows rose in exaggerated challenge, and Kelsey couldn't say no.

"See you tomorrow."

Kelsey knew she should open the door and step inside instead of gazing after Connor like a lovesick teenager, but she couldn't tear her gaze away as he walked down her driveway to the car.

He turned back before she had the chance to duck indoors, seeming unsurprised to find her staring after him. "There's something you should know, Kelsey. I might have kissed your cousin in this car. But I never slept with her."

"In the car?"

His lips kicked up in a smile, but the look in his eyes was completely serious. "Or anywhere else."

Chapter Eight

The next afternoon, standing in her sun-filled kitchen, Kelsey poured steaming black coffee into a thermal mug. She'd tossed and turned most of the night, her sleep plagued by dreams. Even now, she was haunted by images of gliding down an endless, rose-strewn runner toward her groom—toward Connor—only to watch, helpless, as he smiled his devastating smile and walked away with Emily.

"It's just a stupid dream," she muttered, as if speaking the words aloud might give them more strength. "I'm not marrying Connor. I'm not *falling* for Connor."

So she'd had temporary a lapse of judgment, of sanity. She'd been caught in the moment—the restaurant's party atmosphere, the sexy rhythm of the music that had seeped into her soul and pulsed in her veins…

Oh, who are you kidding? an all-too-knowing voice

demanded. She hadn't been caught up in the moment; she'd been caught up in the man.

Maybe she should ask Emily how she'd dated Connor for months *without* sleeping with him. Although Emily never divulged intimate details, Kelsey assumed they had made love. Now that she'd met Connor, it seemed even harder to believe Emily—or any woman—could resist.

Knowing now that Emily *had* resisted made Kelsey wonder if her cousin's feelings for Connor were as strong as she'd once believed, or if Connor was right and Emily had only been using him. What was it he'd said—he was Emily's lone act of rebellion? But even if that were true, it didn't necessarily change his feelings. Maybe coming back wasn't about picking up where they'd left off, but about finally taking that relationship further.

Her stomach felt more than a little sick at the thought, and she thrust the glass pot back into the machine, grabbed the to-go lid and slapped it onto the mug. But her aim must have been slightly off, and the cup tipped, splashing coffee over the countertop.

Gasping, Kelsey dove for a manila envelope lying nearby, snatching it out of the way of the java flood. She clutched the package to her chest with a relieved sigh. Emily's life in pictures filled the envelope, most dating back to the days prior to digital CDs.

Kelsey shuddered at the thought of telling her aunt she'd ruined the photos of Emily's first piano recital, first ballet, first play. She had to get back in control. Her near destruction of the photographs was a small symptom of a larger problem.

She was letting Connor get under her skin.

She'd taken possession of her own shop the day before, the realization of a dream that sometimes seemed as old as she was. Her thoughts should have been consumed by plans for polishing the place until it shined, expanding her nonexistent advertising budget, hiring the support staff Lisa had mentioned.

Instead Connor filled her thoughts and her dreams, and was far too close to edging his way into her heart. Was this how her mother felt when she met her father? Kelsey wondered. Had Donnie Mardell become more important to Olivia than her own hopes and dreams? More important than her own family?

Kelsey forced herself not to panic. Surely she wouldn't make that big a mistake, not with her mother's life as an example. How many times had Olivia warned Kelsey to rely on herself and not to risk leaning on someone who would let her down in the end?

"Wilson women against the world," Kelsey murmured, the familiar motto calming her as she set the envelope safely aside and unrolled a swath of paper towels.

The sudden sound of the doorbell caught her off guard. She didn't have time for unexpected guests any more than she had time for unexpected doubts. Dropping the paper towels over the spilled coffee, she headed toward the front door as the bell pealed again. After a quick glance through the peephole, Kelsey pulled the door open.

As if her thoughts had somehow conjured him out of thin air, Connor leaned against the doorway. How was it that he looked better every time she saw him? Was it because she now knew his shoulders were as strong as they looked? How solid his chest had felt beneath her hands? How his hair had felt like warm silk against her fingers? And how his mouth had worked magic against her own?

"Hey, Kelsey," he said before striding inside.

Trailing after him as if *he* owned the place and she was the uninvited guest, she asked, "What are you doing here?"

He stopped to face her, a frown replacing his cocky smile. "I thought you were coming with me. Todd's meeting, remember?"

"That's not until six," she protested as she walked into the kitchen to the mess she'd left behind.

"What happened in here?"

As much as she would have liked to lay the blame at Connor's feet, she said, "Don't ask." She balled up the soggy paper towels, groaning at the coffee-colored stain left behind on her beige Formica, and tossed them into the trash. She grabbed the envelope of photographs and her purse and brushed by Connor on the way to the door.

"I have to meet my friend about the audio-video presentation for the reception, remember?"

Connor shrugged. "So we go there first and stake out the meeting after."

She should say no. She should keep him far, far away, and not just because of the havoc he might wreak on Emily's wedding. "I'm already running late." As a flat-out denial, the words fell short.

"So let's go."

"Okay, but—" Kelsey straightened her shoulders. "I'll drive." She should have known it wouldn't make any difference how matter-of-factly she made that statement, Connor would see through it.

Judging by the look in his dark eyes, he did see—straight through to her heart. "Sounds like I need to work even harder."

"Connor—"

"It's okay," he interrupted. He stepped closer, and Kelsey tensed, half in preparation to defend her decision and half in anticipation of his approach. But nothing could have readied her for Connor cupping the back of her neck and pulling her into a kiss.

To her dismay, it ended before it even began. A quick press of lips again her own, and then it was over. And Kelsey had to clench her hands into fists to keep from grabbing the front of Connor's T-shirt and demand that he do it again. That he do it *right.*

As he pulled away, he gazed at her flustered—heated—face and smiled. "I never could resist a challenge."

"Are you sure this is right?" Kelsey asked.

Connor's directions to Todd's meeting had brought them to a Scottsdale neighborhood that rivaled her aunt and uncle's when it came to exclusivity, opulence and sheer expense. The winding roads led them past multileveled mansions surrounded by artfully arranged desert landscapes, sparkling water fountains and wrought-iron gates.

They were practically the first words she'd spoken since they'd dropped off Emily's pictures earlier. Kelsey had been grateful to focus on the straightforward directions of right, left, north and south rather than try to traverse the dangerous path her heart was traveling down.

Catching a street sign carved into a boulder, Connor said, "Turn here. This is it."

"Nice place." Irony filled Kelsey's voice at the understated description. The two-story home had a circular entryway, decorative columns, and floor-to-ceiling windows.

When she tapped on the brake, Connor insisted, "Don't stop." With a glance out the back, he said, "Okay. We should be good here. Go ahead and turn around."

Kelsey glanced in the rearview mirror. Thanks to a neighboring oleander hedge, she could barely see the house. Hopefully Todd wouldn't notice the two of them lurking in her car a block away. After turning the car to face the house, she asked, "Now what?"

"Now we wait."

Kelsey sighed. "I don't think I have the patience for being a private eye."

Connor's lips quirked into a smile. "That's okay. I'm not planning on changing careers and becoming a wedding coordinator, either. Besides, it's almost six."

"Todd will be late," Kelsey predicted. "He's always late." Tardiness was one of her aunt's pet peeves. A sign, according to Charlene Wilson, that showed a person believed his time more important than those around him. Somehow, though, she smothered her annoyance when it came to Todd.

"So he isn't perfect after all."

"I never said he was."

Connor made a thoughtful sound but hardly embraced her words. No surprise. *She* wasn't the one Connor wanted to impress. He was determined to prove her aunt and uncle wrong about Todd. But would that really be enough to make Connor let go of the past? Would Connor ever believe he was good enough, or would it take being good enough for Emily for him to see his own worth?

She sighed and sank lower in the seat, not wanting to think too hard on the answer to that question. Seconds later a car rounded the corner, and Kelsey impulsively grabbed Connor's arm. "Look!"

Her heart skipped a beat at the feel of his warm skin and muscle beneath her palm. When he leaned closer for a better look, her pulse quickened.

A woman sat behind the wheel of the luxury car, and Kelsey wondered if Connor might get his proof. Neither of them spoke as they waited for Todd's arrival and the meeting to unfold. Ten minutes later, Todd's SUV pulled up. When he climbed from the vehicle and casually glanced in their direction, Kelsey gasped.

"Relax," Connor advised. "He can't see us."

As she focused on the scene outside, Kelsey frowned in confusion. Todd flashed a smile at the woman as he walked up the driveway, but when he reached out to shake the woman's hand, the gesture was not only platonic but professional.

Connor swore. "I don't believe it. That woman's a Realtor. There's a lockbox on the front door."

Sure enough, the brunette led Todd to the front door, where she opened the small box and pulled out a key. With a flourish she turned the handle and waved Todd inside. Since Emily hadn't mentioned a new home, Kelsey wondered if the place was a wedding gift. Despite her questionable opinion of the man, she couldn't help feeling impressed by the romantic and extravagant gesture.

"We should go."

"Just—wait," Connor ground out.

A few minutes later Todd and the Realtor exited the house. Judging by the smile on the woman's face, Kelsey assumed the meeting had gone well. She shook Todd's hand again, nodded enthusiastically over whatever he said, and waved as he drove off.

"That's that," Kelsey said as she reached for the ignition. Connor stopped her with a touch, closing his hand over hers and slipping the keys out of her grasp before she ever realized his intention. "Connor, what—"

"Come on."

Connor kept a firm grip on Kelsey's hand as they walked toward the house despite her repeated tugs and her sharply whispered protests. As long as he had the keys, she couldn't go anywhere without him. So why exactly was she trying to pull away? The better question: why was he still hanging on?

"Connor! Stop! We're going to get caught!"

"Doing what? You know, I'm really starting to wonder about this guilty conscience of yours."

"You should," she muttered, "considering I didn't *have* one until you came along."

The front door opened, and Kelsey dug in her heels deep enough to leave divots in the grass. The Realtor looked surprised, but only for a moment. Professional smile in place, she asked, "Are you two interested in the property?"

Kelsey's grip tightened on Connor's hand. A quick glance in her direction revealed a panicked look that screamed *busted.* Fortunately, he had a bit more experience when it came to covering his butt, as well as any curvaceous female backside he dragged along for the ride.

Flashing a smile, he said, "My fiancée and I were driving through the neighborhood and noticed the lockbox. We don't have an appointment, but—"

"Oh, I'd love to show you around."

The inside of the house lived up to the exterior's elegant promise. Gorgeous views, a wide-open floor plan and every upgrade imaginable—travertine floors, granite countertops, stainless-steel appliances. The decor matched the surrounding desert with golds and browns and a hint of green.

"The house is beautiful," Kelsey said, once she'd realized the Realtor wasn't going to accuse them of trespassing.

"It's only been on the market a few days," the Realtor said as she concluded the six-bedroom, four-bath, media-room tour back at the front entry. "Another couple is interested in the property for their first place."

"Right. 'Cause this is the perfect starter home," Connor muttered.

Kelsey opened her mouth, ready to insist she didn't need a mansion, only to remember she and Connor weren't engaged. They wouldn't need a starter home or any other kind.

"Out of curiosity," he said, "can you tell how much the other couple is offering?"

The woman's smile was both sympathetic and hopeful. "I don't think money was an issue, but I have several other properties I'd be more than willing to show you." She pulled a card from her pocket and held it out to Connor. "Give me a call, and I can give you a list of houses that might fit your lifestyle."

Connor managed a nod, but as they walked out of the house, he crushed her card in his hand. *"Fit my lifestyle,"* he bit out. "Not to mention my budget."

His body thrummed with frustration, and Kelsey expected him to chuck the card into the street. Finally he shoved it into his pocket and stalked toward her car.

Kelsey didn't bother to ask for her keys back when Connor automatically went to the driver's-side door. Instead, she slid into the passenger seat. Trying for a practical tone, she said, "We already knew Todd has money."

"Yeah, we did," he said with a grim twist to his lips. "I'm starting to think the guy might be perfect after all."

"No one's perfect," Kelsey insisted. "Everyone has their faults and—"

"And the Wilsons certainly saw mine."

"You were a kid," she argued. "You can't believe what happened back then has anything to do with the man you are now."

Muttering what sounded suspiciously like "Don't be so sure," he cranked the engine and peeled away from the house.

Kelsey slapped a hand down on the armrest, but her tight grip slowly loosened. Despite his obvious frustration, Connor kept the car under perfect control. Within minutes they were on the freeway, but the turn he took wouldn't lead to her house.

Streetlights flickered on as daylight faded, marking the way toward an older part of Phoenix. They passed an abandoned drive-in, a boarded-up gas station and liquor store, the only business likely to thrive in such a depressing neighborhood. She could have asked where they were going, but as they drove by houses with peeling paint and duct-taped windows, lawns choked by weeds and neglect, she already knew.

A few minutes later Connor braked to a halt, gravel crunching beneath the wheels. He didn't say anything or make a move to get out of the car. With both hands still gripping the wheel, he stared at the trailer park across the street.

Kelsey had seen plenty of mobile home communities before. Manufactured homes, they were called now. Houses laid out in neat rows, with flower beds and swimming pools like any other nice, little neighborhood.

This was not that kind of place. The dirt lot, with its haphazard trailers and junkyard of vehicles, made the use of the term *park* an irony. The murmur of the engine was the only sound until Connor gave a sudden, harsh bark of laughter. "This is it. Where I came from. Who I am."

"No, it isn't." Unlocking her seat belt, Kelsey shifted on the seat to face him. The fading sunset glowed in the distance, casting his profile in bronze. "This isn't you any more than where I grew up makes me who I am."

"You're a Wilson. You're—"

Connor cut himself off, giving Kelsey the chance to interject, "I *am* a Wilson. But I'm not Emily. I'm not Aileen. And I wasn't raised like them."

"I know. On the outside looking in," he said, as he turned to look at her. Face-to-face, Kelsey could see the gold flecks in his green eyes. "That's what I thought when I first met you. The Wilson outsider."

That insight, pointing how she'd always felt—a part of and yet apart from her family—made Kelsey feel as if Connor knew her better than anyone. His words and the tenderness in his gaze crept inside her chest and wrapped around her heart. Somehow, being on the outside didn't matter so much when he was there with her. "You were right," she said softly.

But if he could somehow see inside her, Kelsey felt she was starting to do the same and getting to know the real Connor. His coming back to Arizona had to do with more than simply disliking Todd or even with proving her family wrong. His return had to do with a guilt *inside* him. As if by stopping the wedding, he could somehow make up for a past he could not change.

"And maybe that's why I can see you so clearly. This isn't who you are, Connor," she repeated. "Maybe it's who you were, but that's all. I've seen who you are now. You're a good friend, a good man—"

A sound rose in Connor's throat, part denial, part despair, and he jerked open the car door as if desperate for escape. Kelsey winced as he slammed it behind him, but she didn't hesitate to follow. He couldn't shut her out that easily!

"Connor, wait!" She scrambled out of the car after him, trying to keep up with the long strides that carried him across the weed-and-trash-strewn lot. She gasped as her foot hit an uneven spot on the heaved asphalt. She took a tottering step, arms windmilling for balance, but gravity won the battle, and she hit the ground.

"Kelsey!" Connor swore beneath his breath. "Are you okay?"

With a close-up view of the weeds and trash littering the trailer lot, Kelsey felt a moment's relief that she hadn't landed in a black, greasy puddle inches from her face.

"I'm fine," she insisted, even as Connor leaned down to help her up. Flames of heat licked at her. Some from the heel of her hand that had scraped across the pavement, some from the blazing heat bouncing off the black surface, but mostly from the sheer embarrassment of Connor witnessing her utter clumsiness. "Really, I—" She sucked in a quick breath as he took her hand to pull her to her feet.

Beneath his tanned skin, Connor went pale. "You're hurt."

Taking a hesitant glance down, she breathed out a sigh of

relief. "It's nothing. Only a scratch." A few thin lines of blood showed through the abraded skin on her palm, but other than the slight sting, she was fine.

Running his thumb gently across the scrape as if he could heal by touch alone, Connor said, "I never should have brought you here. It's my fault."

"It was an accident that could have happened in front of my own shop! It is *not* your fault." Gentling her voice, she added, "You're not responsible for every bad thing that happens. I don't know why you feel that way, but Connor, looking for dirt on Todd won't change things. Especially when—" she took a deep breath, reluctant to say the words but knowing she had to "—when it doesn't seem like there's anything to find."

"There is," he said flatly, refusing to consider failure. "Jake's still following a lead in St. Louis, and I'm not giving up here. I know guys like Dunworthy. He can only keep up this golden boy B.S. for so long. He's gonna slip. The closer it gets to the wedding, the more pressure there's gonna be, and he'll slip. I know it—"

"In your gut," Kelsey finished with a sigh. She turned her hand within his. Even through that light touch, she could feel the tension tightening his shoulders and arms and radiating down to the fingers she linked with hers. As gently as she could, she suggested, "Maybe it's time to stop listening to your gut."

"I can't." He gritted the words out of clenched teeth.

"Why not?"

"Because the last time I didn't listen, a woman was nearly killed."

Connor reached over and cranked the car's air conditioner to full blast, even though he doubted the frigid air would help. Sweat soaked the back of his neck, but it had little to do with the outside temperature despite the hundred-plus heat. The relentless sun, which bounced off every shiny surface to pinpoint on him as if he were a bug trapped beneath a kid's magnifying glass, had nothing on Kelsey's questioning glances.

He felt as if he was burning up from the inside out…all thanks to four little words.

You're a good man.

Kelsey had looked him straight in the eye with those words, her soft voice packing the same punch as a sonic boom. He didn't deserve that kind of faith. He'd disappointed too many women in the past: his mother, Emily, Cara Mitchell…

The more Kelsey trusted in him, the more he longed to believe in that trust, the worse it would be when he finally, irrevocably, let her down.

He sucked in a lungful of air, the heat threatening to suffocate him. He needed space—space to breathe, space to run, space that wasn't filled with Kelsey's cinnamon scent, her concerned glances, her soft voice…

"Connor…"

She was going to ask him what happened with Cara. His grip tightened on the passenger armrest, inches from the door handle and escape…even if escape meant paying the price for hitting the ground running at forty miles an hour.

No, telling truth was better. More painful, maybe, but at least Kelsey would realize he wasn't the man she thought he was.

"One of the first things I learned after opening my business was that you don't turn down work. You might not like the job, you might not like the client, but if it pays the bills, you take the job."

Kelsey slowed for a red light. Freedom beckoned, but Connor kept his hand on the armrest. "I didn't like Doug Mitchell. I didn't like the job, even though catching cheating spouses has always been part of the P.I. business. My gut told me he was bad news, but I didn't listen."

Silence filled the car, and Kelsey's gaze was as tangible as the trickle of sweat running from his temple. "What happened?" she murmured.

"I did what I was paid to do. I followed Cara Mitchell. To the grocery store, the salon, the gym… It was tedious, boring," he added, reminded of the conversation they'd had waiting for Dunworthy's meeting. "And I thought maybe Doug was wrong. That he was worried about nothing and his marriage was one of the few that would make it."

His hand cramped, and try as he might, he couldn't loosen his grip. His fingers seemed to have melded into the padded vinyl. "But then, one Tuesday, Cara drove south on the freeway. And I kept thinking it was Tuesday, and Tuesday was art class. So why was she going in the wrong direction? Before long, she ended up at a motel and when this guy opened the door, I thought here we go. I was wrong, and Doug was right."

"So she was having an affair?"

"Sure seemed that way," he said with a grimace. "Meeting some guy, staying behind closed shades, and leaving an hour later with her hair mussed and her makeup smudged… What else would you think?"

"What did *you* think?"

"I—I didn't know. It was suspicious, sure. But it wasn't proof, you know? Not one hundred percent take-it-to-the-bank proof. And in my gut I didn't believe it. Maybe I'd gotten too close. It happens, P.I.s falling for their marks, but that wasn't it. I wasn't attracted to Cara Mitchell. But I guess I—*liked* her. Respected her. She smiled at kids in the store, took the time to talk to little old ladies. She told cashiers when they gave her back too much change! I just didn't believe she was having an affair. But her husband wanted an update. He was the client, and he paid to know what I'd seen."

"But…you didn't actually *see* anything."

Connor winced at her logical protest. "And that's exactly what I told Doug. Only it didn't matter. Far as he was concerned, I'd seen enough and was off the job."

If only it had ended there…

"I couldn't get over my gut feeling that I was wrong. Wrong about Cara, wrong about what I'd seen. I thought if I followed her a few more days, I'd know for sure." Kelsey hit the gas as another red light turned green, and Connor desperately wished he was still the one driving. He'd go from zero to sixty in a split second if pure speed would give him the chance to outrun his memories.

"I was across the street watching when Doug came home from work in the middle of the day. I don't know if he hoped to catch Cara in the act, or if his rage and jealousy got to be too much. I heard her scream. I rushed into the house."

"But you stopped Doug, right?"

"Not soon enough. Cara was badly beaten and nearly unconscious by the time I got into the house and pulled Doug off her."

He could still see her, bloody and bruised, lying on the floor because of him. "The guy she went to see was a counselor. He'd rented the motel room to give her a safe place to stay, but he couldn't convince her to leave Doug, even though he'd been abusing her for years. If I'd listened to my gut—"

"But you *did* listen. You listened when you knew you didn't have the whole story. Cara Mitchell would likely be dead if not for you. You saved her life, Connor."

"If I hadn't taken the job—"

"Someone else would have. Someone who wouldn't have *cared* about a gut feeling. Once the job was over, that would have been it. They wouldn't have given Cara Mitchell a second thought."

Connor opened his mouth, ready to argue, but Kelsey's words ran deeper into his soul, soothing some of his guilt. Not that he believed he was any kind of hero. But he'd witnessed Doug's determination. He wasn't the type of guy to give up easily. Had Connor turned down the job, Doug *would* have found another P.I.

"Maybe—maybe you're right."

As Kelsey stopped for another red light, she turned to meet his gaze straight on. "I know I am," she said with the same certainty as when she'd vowed he was a good man.

Would she still think so when he told her about the money her uncle had paid him to leave town? No one had ever put the kind of faith and trust in him that Kelsey did, and every ounce of self-preservation inside him resisted the thought of telling her the truth.

Even if she gave him the chance to explain, even if she understood his reasons, the truth would change things. And yet he had to tell her. If he wanted her to believe he truly was a good man, if *he* wanted to believe that, he had to tell her.

But not tonight. There'd already been enough revelations about the past. And in case finding out about the money did change things, well, Connor selfishly wanted to hold on to Kelsey's faith in him for a little while longer.

"You know, this isn't necessary." Side by side on her couch, Kelsey watched as Connor placed the last piece of tape over the bandage on her hand. As far as a protest went, her words were pretty weak. Just like the rest of her, she thought.

Connor smoothed his thumb across her palm, his gaze intent on his task. A lock of dark hair had fallen across his forehead, shadowing his eyes and adding the slightest touch of softness to the hard planes and angles of his features.

Little shocks zapped up her arm, but it had nothing to do with pain. If she hadn't been sitting next to Connor, she probably would have melted into a puddle at his feet.

"It would have been tricky to do this on your own. Besides, it was the least I could do," he said, guilt and concern filling his expression as his hand rose to brush her hair back from her cheek.

And Kelsey couldn't resist his caring side any more than she'd been able to resist the other facets of his personality: the bad boy, the loyal friend, the protective warrior. They all combined to make up the man Connor was—the man Kelsey loved.

Her every instinct shouted in denial, but it was a useless protest. She'd been falling for him since the moment they met, a slow-motion tumble that landed her in this place, in this time, in his arms…

The intimacy of the moment pulled her closer. Her job, her family, even Connor's relationship with Emily seemed like distant, insignificant concerns. His fingers tunneled into her hair. Her amazing hair, Kelsey thought, recalling the words he'd spoken outside of Todd's office. She hadn't believed him then, but she did now. On the day she confronted him in his hotel room, he'd demanded she prove her loyalty to Emily, and she'd told him actions, not words, proved how a person truly felt. And Connor was a man of action, and he proved his feelings by trusting *her*—with his past, with his close friendship with the Delgados. How could she do anything but trust him in return?

"The last thing I'd ever want to do is hurt you, Kelsey," he vowed, that sense of responsibility carving a groove between his eyebrows.

"You didn't," she promised. "You won't."

Despite her words, doubt lingered in his gaze. Leaning forward, she brushed her lips against his, actions once again backing up words. Because whether Connor knew it or not, she *was* his. Body and soul. She shifted closer but couldn't get close enough.

Her hands charted a course her body longed to make, following a path from his shoulders to his chest, where she could feel his heart pounding a wild rhythm, and to his flat stomach and muscled thighs, which tensed beneath her hands.

Connor's hands stayed buried in her hair, but like the emotional connection moments before, the physical connection was so deep that with her every touch her own body responded. She felt the brush of his fingers trailing from her collarbones down to her breasts, to her stomach, ticklish enough to tremble at the imaginary contact.

Connor ended the kiss for a much needed breath but kept his mouth pressed to her cheek, her jaw, her throat…

A shrill buzz started them both. After the first few bars, Connor recognized his phone's ring tone, but the electronic device—one he never went anywhere without—was the last thing on his mind. He nearly groaned in frustration at the very thought of ending the kiss, of pulling away from Kelsey's embrace.

Maybe his battery would die. Maybe the signal would cut out.

His wishes went unheard as the phone rang again. Desire gradually clearing from her eyes as her breathing slowed, Kelsey pushed at his shoulders, and he had no choice but to back away.

"It's not important," he vowed, hoping his words were true as he fumbled with the phone. "I'll turn it off." He actually had his thumb on the button when he saw the number glowing on the small screen, and hesitated.

Just a split second, but the slight pause didn't get by Kelsey. "Who is it?"

The husky, passion-filled sound of her voice sent another shaft of desire straight to his gut. He could still turn the phone off. Turn it off and pretend the interruption had never taken place. The lie hovered in his thoughts, but meeting her gaze, he couldn't take the easy way out. "It's Emily."

Kelsey's eyes widened, and the warmth in them chilled even as the fire in her cheeks suddenly blazed. "Well, then, you should answer it."

"Kelsey—"

"Answer the phone, Connor."

Biting back a curse, he nearly barked into the phone, "Yeah?"

"Connor…is that you?"

"It's me. What's up?" Silence followed the brusque demand, and wouldn't it figure if the damn signal cut out *now*. "Em? You still there?"

"Yes. I'm here. What are you— Never mind. You sound like you're busy."

Forcing the slang definition of *busy* from his thoughts, he cleared his throat and asked, "What's wrong?"

"Nothing, really. Can't I call without you assuming something's wrong?"

A note of desperation had entered her voice, telling Connor it was more than an assumption. "Yeah, sure you can. So, what's up?"

"I guess I wanted to talk," she offered, uncertainty filling her voice.

Connor couldn't help glancing over at Kelsey. Her face turned away from him, she was determinedly ignoring the conversation going on only a cushion away.

Hesitation cost him for the second time in a matter of minutes when Emily said, "This was a bad idea. I shouldn't have called."

"Em—" The line went silent before he could come up with even a halfhearted protest. Flipping the phone closed, he slid the tiny device back in his pocket.

"What did she say?"

"Not much."

"She didn't say why she called?"

"No." And he didn't care. At least, not nearly as much as he cared about what was going through Kelsey's mind. "Kelsey—"

"It's okay."

"Really?" Connor asked, doubt lacing the word.

But when Kelsey met his gaze, a smile teased her lips. A little shaky around the edges, but a smile just the same. And Connor felt something in his heart catch at her remarkable strength and resiliency. He knew the call had to bring up reminders of his relationship with Emily as well as Kelsey's long-ingrained feelings of inferiority.

"Really," she insisted. "Like you said, we can't change the past, and I think it's time we both moved on."

Chapter Nine

"Kelsey, this is a surprise." Emily rose from the large oak table in her parents' kitchen, where she'd been flipping through a bridal magazine, and gave her a hug.

"I had a free morning and wanted to come by and invite you to breakfast." Kelsey mentally cringed at the half-truth. She *did* have a free morning, but the invitation was an excuse to find out what that phone call to Connor meant.

Emily wrinkled her nose. "I can't. I'll never fit into my wedding dress if I stuff myself with waffles."

So Emily was still dieting. Almost every bride thought about dieting before the big day even if they didn't stick with it. Or need to lose a single pound, Kelsey thought, as Emily walked over to the pantry—slender, graceful, and gorgeous. A powder-blue silk robe wrapped her body, and her hair was pulled back in a simple ponytail.

"You can keep me company while I have some tea and toast," her cousin suggested, a hopeful note coming to her voice.

"I'd love to. It'll give us a chance to talk."

After setting a kettle on the stove, Emily popped a piece of what looked like whole-wheat cardboard into the toaster. "What did you want to talk about?" she asked, once Kelsey declined her offer of toast in favor of fresh strawberries.

About that phone call last night, Kelsey thought. *The one you placed an hour after your oh-so-perfect fiancé met a Realtor at your dream house.*

"Uh..." Unable to jump into the conversation, her mind blanked and the last thing she expected popped out of her mouth. "I saw Matt the other night."

"No!" Looking appropriately horrified and curious, Emily sank back against the tan-and-gold-flecked granite countertops. "What happened?" Before Kelsey could answer, Emily waved off the question. "No, don't start yet."

She plopped a tea bag in a mug the size of a cereal bowl, poured the hot water and dropped her hot toast—sans butter—onto a plate. Settling eagerly onto the chair next to Kelsey, she said, "Okay, tell me everything. Did he beg you to take him back? Has he come to his senses and realized that other woman can't compare to you?"

Kelsey managed a small smile, knowing Emily didn't realize the irony of her words. Kelsey had never told her cousin *she* was the woman Matt was in love with. As blind as Kelsey had been to her ex's infatuation, Emily had missed the signs, as well. Of course, she was used to attracting male attention. Matt's shy and awkward behavior had been nothing new.

"No, he didn't beg me to come back." Though some begging had been involved, she recalled with satisfaction, thinking of Matt pleading with her to call Connor off.

But it was the look in Connor's eyes when he'd touched

her cheek that stayed in her mind, replaying like the romantic comedies she enjoyed. Last night's kiss was another memory that played over and over, and unfortunately her mind didn't come with a handy remote. The images had flickered across her eyelids for hours.

She'd talked a good game last night, declaring the past over and done for both of them, but could it be that easy? Facing Emily on a day when her cousin looked gorgeous—as usual—and Kelsey felt tired and cranky and worn by comparison, could she really believe Connor was over Emily?

Waving the desert-dry toast, Emily decreed, "You're better off without Matt."

"Yeah, that's what—that's what I think, too."

"You're an amazing woman, Kelsey. You're sweet, successful. You own your own business, and you're so totally organized."

Rolling her eyes, Kelsey ignored the heat rising in her cheeks. "I don't know about amazing."

"Do you know how impressed Daddy was when you didn't take money from him to start your business?"

"I couldn't. Your parents have already done so much for me." And Kelsey had never forgotten that her father had gotten her mother pregnant—with her—in the hope of getting his hands on the Wilson fortune. She was *not* her father's daughter, and she flat-out refused to step anywhere near the tracks he'd left behind. "I couldn't take money from them. Your mother's referrals have been the real boost the business needed."

Referrals that hinged on Emily's wedding going off without a hitch.

You're going to be a success with or without Emily's wedding. Connor's words echoed in her mind. *A single setback won't stop you.*

He was right, Kelsey realized. Weddings Amour was her

calling, her dream, one she would fight for. One wedding was not going to make or break her business.

Just like her family's approval or disapproval would not make or break *her.* She was stronger than her cousin, and if Connor was right about Todd, Kelsey needed to do what she could to look out for Emily.

With the reminder in mind, Kelsey said, "Enough about me. What's Todd up to this morning? Why aren't you two lovebirds hanging out?"

"He and Daddy went golfing."

Golf. Kelsey had never understood the sport. Especially not during the summer when tee-off times were at the break of dawn. "I'm surprised you didn't go with them."

Emily, along with looking chic in linen capris and argyle print polo shirts, was an amazing golfer. She gave a soft laugh. "You know. Gentlemen only, ladies forbidden."

"Hmm." That long-ago restriction, the acronym that gave golf its name, might have something to do with Kelsey's aversion to the sport. "You probably would have beaten them. Which might be why they didn't invite you."

"Oh, I wouldn't have—" A soft blush lit Emily's cheeks, and she turned her attention to peeling the crust from her toast.

"Wouldn't what, Em? Play to win?" Between the abbreviation of her cousin's name and the challenge she'd issued, Kelsey felt like a ventriloquist's dummy with Connor pulling the strings and his words coming out of her mouth. But as worried as she might be by his influence, her cousin's possible answer worried her more.

"Come on, Kelsey," Emily said, "you know how fragile the male ego can be."

"I can understand why you wouldn't want to show Todd up, but do you really want to live your life playing second best?"

"It's only a silly game of golf, Kelsey."

"I think it's more than that."

Emily's smile faded away, and Kelsey felt like she'd caught a glimpse of the real woman lost behind the beautiful facade. "Todd is a wonderful man. I love him. Really, I do, and I can't wait until we're married."

Kelsey had heard the words before, but this was the first time she sensed a touch of desperation underscoring the refrain. "Emily—" she began, but the opening of the kitchen door interrupted what she might have said.

"Kelsey, good morning," Charlene greeted Kelsey with raised eyebrows that seemed to ask why she wasn't keeping an eye on Connor as she'd been told. "I didn't expect to see you here."

Emily flashed a smile she'd perfected years ago, during her beautiful baby and pageant days. The slight tilt of her head, the perfect curve to her lips, the flash of white teeth. The smile was camera ready, but like an image captured on photo paper, it wasn't real. The moment and whatever else they might have said was gone.

"Kelsey came by to talk about the shower tomorrow and go over a few last-minute wedding details," she filled in, but the excuse only made Charlene frown.

"What details?"

"We're, um, we're going over the items Emily will carry down the aisle. You know, the something borrowed, something blue…"

"That's already decided, remember?" Charlene filled her own teacup and set the pot back on the stove. "You'll wear my pearls as something borrowed. I wore them at my wedding, and Aileen wore them at hers. It's tradition."

"Oh, right," Emily agreed. Kelsey knew her cousin thought pearls old-fashioned. Instead of making a fuss, though, Emily bowed to her mother's wishes. An argument built inside Kelsey like the steam building in the teapot, but what good would it do to stand up for her cousin when Emily wouldn't stand up for herself? "My bouquet will be tied with a blue ribbon, and my ring is new. So that leaves something old."

"I have a lace handkerchief that belonged to your great-grandmother." Adding a tea bag to the water, Charlene said, "Kelsey, run upstairs, would you? The handkerchief is in the bottom drawer of my dresser."

Charlene turned back to the counter to add sugar to her tea, and Kelsey wondered if her aunt was sending her on the errand because she didn't want to leave Emily and Kelsey alone. Still, she agreed. "I'll go get it."

During the years Kelsey had lived with her aunt and uncle, she rarely intruded on their sanctuary. Once she stepped inside, she saw the dresser had three bottom drawers. Which one would hold the handkerchief Charlene mentioned?

Kelsey started at the nearest drawer and found a collection of family mementos. Glancing through the items, she realized these were her uncle's belongings, not her aunt's. A packet of envelopes nestled among a worn-out glove and baseball cap. She slid the drawer halfway closed before she noticed the address on the top envelope. A Nevada location that had once been her home.

Hesitating, she reached for the letters. Kelsey flipped through one after the other, noting the changing addresses and postmark dates as well as the undeniable "return to sender" printed across the fronts.

"You can open them if you want."

Kelsey jumped at the sound of her uncle's voice. Gordon stood framed by the doorway. Dressed in tan slacks and a blue polo shirt, he looked more casual than usual. The hint of sunburn above his close-cropped beard told of the morning hours spent on the golf course, and his silver-blond hair had recently lost some of its structured style. But regardless of what he wore, her uncle was a tall, handsome man whose presence demanded attention and respect.

Clutching the letters to her chest, she said, "Aunt Charlene sent me to look for Great-grandmother's handkerchief. For the wedding. You know, something old—"

Gordon waved a hand. "The middle drawer is your aunt's."

Ignoring the errand that had sent her to the room, Kelsey held out the letters. "You wrote to my mother?"

Gordon nodded. "More times than I can count. But it was all too little, too late."

Too little. Kelsey flipped through the envelopes—years' worth of envelopes, years' worth of effort—seeing nothing little about it. "I don't understand."

"Your grandfather was a hard man. He wouldn't stand for any sign of defiance, and your mother—" Gordon shook his head with a bittersweet smile. "Your mother challenged him from the day she was born. They butted heads constantly, but when she refused to stop seeing your father, that was an impasse neither of them could cross."

Kelsey's hands tightened on the letters at the mention of her father. "Maybe she should have listened."

"She made a bad choice, and at the time I thought your grandfather handled the situation very poorly. Years later I realized how desperate he must have felt to make the ultimatum he did—forcing your mother to choose between her family and your father."

And her mother chose Donnie Mardell. She'd never talked about him, and not until her illness reached a point where there was no hope did she tell Kelsey the whole story. How she had defied her father to leave home with Donnie. How her father refused to accept that decision and paid Donnie to leave town, thinking that would force Olivia to come to heel.

But that plan backfired. Donnie left town, money burning

a hole in his pocket, but Olivia hadn't returned home. Instead, she fled even farther, cutting all contact with her family…to the point where Kelsey hadn't known she *had* any family.

Regret furrowed his forehead. "I'd hoped your mother could forgive me for what she saw as my decision to side with our father." Gordon shook his head. "So stubborn, the both of them. So unwilling to bend."

Instant denial rose up inside Kelsey. "My mother was brave and strong. She took care of herself and me without help from *anyone.*"

"And she raised you to do the same, didn't she?"

Kelsey opened her mouth to respond, only to be silenced by her mother's voice echoing in her mind. *You may not have been raised as one of the wealthy Wilsons, but you're better than they are. Hold your head high and prove to them what an amazing young woman I've raised.*

She'd done her best, trying to prove herself instead of simply *being* herself. All the judgments, all the expectations, had her aunt and uncle put them on Kelsey…or had Olivia with her dying words?

Lifting a hand, Gordon brushed his fingertips against the edges of the envelopes, flipping through fifteen years of unanswered pleas. "She was my only sibling. The last link to my childhood and my parents. I never stopped hoping we'd have the chance to overcome the differences of the past. But she was so determined to prove she didn't need anybody." He met Kelsey's gaze with a melancholy grin. "There's no doubt *you* are your mother's daughter."

She'd spent eight years trying to be exactly that. Struggling to prove herself by trying to follow step by humiliating step in her cousins' footprints rather than simply *telling* her aunt and uncle she wasn't cut out for ballet or dressage or the lead role in the school play. Insisting on taking summer jobs to pay for her clothes and books and CDs; refusing to accept her uncle's loan to get her business going.

How many other times had she pushed her aunt and uncle away in her desperation to live up to her mother's stubborn independence? Unlike Olivia, Kelsey hadn't been totally alone, but she *had* followed her mother's footsteps when it came to protecting her heart. She'd kept people at a distance, never letting anyone—even family—too close, so she could never be let down, never be disappointed. Even with Matt…Kelsey saw now she'd purposely picked someone she liked but could never love.

And what about Connor? Had she resisted because she was afraid of his lingering feelings for Emily…or simply because she was afraid? Was she using his past as an excuse the same way her mother had held Gordon's past decisions against him? A reason not to give him—not to give *anyone*—a second chance?

Wilson women against the world. The motto that had once been a battle cry of strength and independence now seemed a cowardly whimper. And an excuse not to trust, not to fall in love…

Swallowing the lump in her throat, she asked, "Why didn't you tell me? Why let me think you'd cut my mother out of your life like your father did?"

Sorrow for the sister he'd lost pulled at Gordon's features. "Olivia was gone, and I didn't want to make you choose between your memory of her—your *good* memories of her—and the truth I could have told you."

Kelsey wondered if she might have been better off knowing the truth, but how could she fault her uncle when he'd made such an unselfish decision? "I'm so sorry, Uncle Gordon."

"Don't be. I know how much your mother meant to you, and I'd never want to take that away. Besides, I'm proud of you, Kelsey. Of your determination and drive. I'm sure your mother would be, as well."

Kelsey tried to answer, but the words were blocked by the lump in her throat. Swallowing, she said, "Uncle Gordon—"

"Kelsey, can't you find the handkerchief?" Charlene entered the bedroom and stepped around her husband. She frowned at the drawer Kelsey had left open. Her heart skipped a beat as her aunt crossed the room. But Charlene merely pushed the drawer shut, opened the correct one and lifted the handkerchief without sparing the envelopes in Kelsey's hand a single glance.

"Here it is," she said with an exasperated sigh. "I might as well hold on to it."

Kelsey blinked, the past falling away as she refocused on the present. "Isn't Emily downstairs?"

"Todd invited her to brunch."

She'd missed her chance to talk to Emily about her feelings for Todd and about the wedding, but Kelsey couldn't think about anything but the letters in her hands.

"Speaking of brunch," Gordon said, "I'm starved. You wouldn't believe the calories I burned beating that future son-in-law of mine. Although I do think he might have let me win."

"Nonsense," Charlene said briskly. "Experience trumps youth every time."

"I, um, should go," Kelsey said, ducking past her aunt. She tried to slip her uncle the letters, but he squeezed her hands and mouthed, "Keep them."

After giving a brief nod, Kelsey jogged down the stairs with her uncle's written words in her hands and his voice in her head. *You are your mother's daughter.*

Connor stepped out of the shower, dropped the damp towel onto the marble floor in a limp heap and seriously considered following suit himself. He couldn't remember the last time he'd done enough reps to leave his arms and legs flopping like fish out of water.

His cell phone beeped as he pulled on a pair of well-worn jeans. The sound immediately took him back to the evening before and the reason he'd needed the killer workout. Memories of Kelsey's kiss, the feel of her curves beneath his hands, and the untimely interruption had tortured him through the night.

Only, the sound wasn't alerting him to an incoming call, but to a new message. Seeing Jake's number on the screen, he quickly dialed his voice mail.

"Come on, Jake. Tell me Sophia Pirelli gave you something on Dunworthy," he muttered while he waited for the message to play.

"Whatever happened to Sophia in Chicago still has her feeling vulnerable," Jake's message announced without preamble. "I'm getting close, though. She—she's starting to trust me. It won't be long now."

His friend said the words with an almost grim sense of finality. Once Jake found out what had made Sophia quit her job and whether or not it had anything to do with Dunworthy, Jake would be on the next plane back to L.A.

Just as Connor would be leaving Scottsdale…leaving Kelsey…

Leaving Kelsey to pick up the pieces, he thought as he snapped the phone shut and tossed it back on the dresser. If Emily called off the wedding, would it ruin Kelsey's business? He'd told her she had the strength and determination to succeed no matter what, and while he'd meant every word, he really didn't know what the hell he was talking about, did he? Could her dreams end up buried beneath a landslide of bad publicity for a wedding gone wrong?

And what about her family? The Wilsons were counting

on Kelsey. Would she see her failure as yet another time when she hadn't lived up to expectations?

But what was he supposed to do? Connor wondered. Step back and let Emily marry a guy with a narcissistic streak running like a fault line beneath his charming, sophisticated facade? Raise a glass of champagne and hope for the best?

Cara Mitchell would likely be dead if not for you. You saved her life, Connor.

He still wasn't sure he could take credit instead of blame for what happened to Cara, but he did know he couldn't have walked away. Just like he couldn't walk away from Emily.

But maybe he needed to walk away from Kelsey…

Bad enough that he'd be leaving her to deal with the professional fallout. The last thing he wanted was to leave her personal life in shambles after an affair that wouldn't—couldn't—go anywhere. It would be best to end things now, before someone got hurt.

Are you so sure it's Kelsey *you're trying to protect?* his sarcastic inner voice questioned, mocking his noble intentions for what they were—the act of a coward.

When it came right down to it, he had his own heart to protect, too. And Kelsey—with her caring, her concern, her willingness to see the best in everyone, including him—was already way too close to working her way inside.

A quiet knock on the door broke into his thoughts. He didn't bother to check the keyhole, accustomed to being able to handle anything, only to open the door and realize he could still be caught off guard.

Kelsey stood in the hallway, a lost look on her face.

"What are you doing here?" The question bordered on rude, but as he took in the uncertainty in her wide brown eyes, the sexier-than-hell freckles on her pale face, the plump lower lip she held caught between her teeth, his earlier intentions blew up in his face.

Walk away? As he caught the cinnamon scent of her skin, he couldn't even *move.*

"I went to see Emily this morning," she said as she ducked through the doorway. "I wanted to find out why she called you last night."

Last night.

The two simple words had the power to turn back time. His flesh still burned in the aftermath of her touch. He grabbed a clean T-shirt from the dresser and jerked it over his head as if he could smother the memories. Not likely. It would take much stronger fabric than simple cotton, especially with Kelsey standing mere feet from his bed.

Pushing his damp hair back with both hands, he caught Kelsey staring at him, desire and awareness swirling in her chocolate eyes. Slowly lowering his arms, he shoved his hands into the back pockets of his jeans rather than pull her into his arms. As if sensing his thoughts, Kelsey broke eye contact, her gaze skittering away as soft color lit her cheeks.

In a voice that sounded dry as the desert, he asked, "Did you?"

Blinking like waking from a dream, Kelsey asked, "Did I what?"

"Find out why Em called?"

"No. Well, maybe. It sounds like Uncle Gordon and Todd are getting pretty close. Emily says she's happy about it, but I'm not so sure."

Connor nodded. "Makes sense. Emily's always wanted her father's approval, and she's never known how to get it."

Silence followed his statement. He wasn't sure when he lost Kelsey. Her gaze was focused on the far wall, and he doubted she was captivated by the desertscape watercolor.

"Kelsey? You okay?"

"All this time, I thought I knew, but it was a lie, and I can't ask her why."

He frowned. "Ask who what?"

Shaking her head, she came back from whatever place or time had her spellbound. "Sorry. You don't even know what I'm talking about." She clutched at the oversize purse hanging from her shoulder, the lost, almost haunted look coming back.

Concern accomplished what little else could—pushing desire to the back burner. He stepped closer and watched her throat move as she swallowed—thanks to whatever she must have seen in his eyes—but he merely took her hand and led her to the couch.

"Tell me," he urged. "Maybe I can figure it out."

"If you can, you're one up on me," she said with a sound that could have been a laugh but wasn't. Still, she took a deep breath as she sank against one of the cushions and said, "Aunt Charlene walked in when I was with Emily. We told her we'd been discussing what Emily would carry down the aisle. Something old, something new…"

Kelsey seemed to expect him to fill in the rest, so Connor ventured, "Roses are red, violets are blue?"

A slight smile tweaked her lips, and she said, "Close. Something borrowed, something blue." Her smile faded as she pulled a rubber-banded stack of envelopes out of her purse. "I went looking for something old."

"And you found those?" he asked, nodding at the bundle in her hands.

"These are letters my uncle wrote to my mother. Letters I never knew about. From an uncle I never knew existed until I was sixteen."

Slowly Kelsey filled Connor in about her wrong-side-of-the-tracks father, about the demand her grandfather had made of her mother, and the money he'd paid her father to leave.

The words were a sucker punch to Connor's soul. "Your grandfather paid your father off?"

Damned if he didn't have to give the family credit. They were consistent if not original. Clearly payoffs were standard practice when it came to getting rid of unwanted boyfriends. He still remembered the look on Gordon Wilson's face when the older man handed *him* a check to stay away from Emily.

Money he still hadn't told Kelsey about…

"He took the money and never looked back. He didn't care that my mother gave up everything for him. Didn't even care that she was pregnant with me."

An old bitterness, stale and rusty, cut into Kelsey's words, and panic started to grow inside Connor. "But if he never contacted your mother, then you don't know his reasons. You don't know why he took the money—"

Kelsey gave a scoffing laugh. "Oh, believe me. I know *why*. He took the money because he was a selfish bastard. It was all he was interested in, all he wanted, and as soon as it was his, he was gone. Nothing he could say would matter, nothing he could do would ever make up for taking the money."

She might as well be talking about him, Connor thought, guilt churning inside him. There was nothing he could do to change the past. He'd known when he took the money, Emily would never understand why he'd done it, why it was so vital that he help the Delgados. Would Kelsey really be any different?

She is *different,* his conscience argued.

And, yeah, okay, he'd taken her to meet Maria with the thought that he could somehow explain. But with her past and her father's bought-and-paid-for desertion, well, she'd it said herself, hadn't she?

Nothing he could say would matter…

"I'm sorry, Kelsey," he bit out. Sorry for reasons he couldn't even tell her.

"So am I," she said as she placed the letters on the coffee table. Taking a deep breath, she seemed to come to a decision as she turned on the couch cushion to face him. "I'm sorry my mother couldn't see another choice—to let go of the past. But I've been just as guilty."

"Kelsey—"

"It's true," she insisted. "I've always kept my aunt and uncle at a distance. You saw that. I was afraid to trust them, to count on them, in case they turned their backs on me the same way I thought they'd turned their backs on my mom."

"And Gordon never told you the whole story until now?"

Kelsey shook her head. "He said he didn't want to make me choose between my loyalty to my mom and them." She caught sight of Connor's surprised look and added, "See? He's not all bad."

Surprising her, Connor said, "Yeah, I'm starting to see that." His jaw clenched. "I mean, talk about the past repeating. He looked at me and saw a guy like your father—"

"You're nothing like him," Kelsey insisted fiercely.

"Kelsey, you don't know—"

"I do. I know you're a good man."

A pained expression crossed his face. "No."

"You are," she insisted.

She thought of the way he'd taken responsibility for the women in his life: his mother, Emily, Cara Mitchell. He'd saved the woman's life, yet he held himself accountable for putting her in a dangerous situation. Then, there was the love and gratitude he showed the Delgados. And yet none of those things compared to how he made her feel. She didn't want to be a responsibility. She certainly didn't want to be family. She wanted to be the woman Connor thought she was—strong, beautiful, sexy…

She did not want to be her mother's daughter, refusing to give or take second chances. And while Connor had never actually *told* her she was sexy, he gave her the confidence to believe she was. Taking a deep breath, the emotions that had been swirling through her calmed, settled, focused on the present, on this moment, and what she wanted. "And I might be my mother's daughter, but I don't have to live my life like she did."

The confusion clouding Connor's expression dispersed as Kelsey rose to her knees and leaned closer. Crystal-clear desire and equally obvious denial filled the void. "Kelsey, wait."

Determined to wipe that denial from his eyes, Kelsey swung her knee over Connor's thighs. He caught her around the waist, the heat in his gaze burning brighter as his fingers flexed into her hips. Instead of pulling her closer, he held her steady. "Kelsey, you don't know—"

His hesitation only pushed Kelsey forward. "I know I want you to kiss me."

One kiss was all it would take to bury her doubts in a flood of need. She should have known Connor wouldn't make it that easy on her. Or on himself. A war seemed to rage inside him, the frown between his eyebrows and the lines cutting grooves in his cheeks telling the tale of the battle.

One she thought she might win when his gaze dropped to her mouth. His voice a husky rasp, he asked, "That's all you want? A kiss?"

Almost unconsciously she licked her lips, a feminine thrill rushing through her when she saw his eyes darken with desire. "It's a good place to start, don't you think?"

And she could think of only one place she wanted to finish—in Connor's arms and in his bed, with no phone calls or memories of the past to interfere. Reaching up to trace the planes and angles of his face, from the doubt still pulling at his eyebrows to the tension locking his jaw, her cousin Aileen's words rang in her head.

Connor's the kind of man who makes a woman want to live for the moment.

Maybe that was true, but all she wanted was this man, in this moment, Kelsey insisted, ignoring the greedy voice demanding more…demanding forever.

"Now," she argued with that voice, "I just want now."

"Want what?" Connor demanded, his voice a rough scrape that sent shivers down her nerve endings.

"This," she whispered as she brushed her fingertips over his mouth. "You."

Her pulse pounded so wildly in her ears, Kelsey barely heard the words, but to Connor, her response must have been loud and clear. The one word broke through his hesitation. Leaning forward, he pulled her tighter and caught her lips in the kiss she'd waited for. Just like she'd hoped, the sheer pleasure of his mouth on hers banished all doubt, erasing any worries about anything…or anyone.

His hands still on her hips, he twisted to the side, lowering her to the couch without breaking the mind-spinning kiss. She sank into the cushions, Connor's weight pressing her deeper, but even the full-body contact wasn't enough. She ran her hands down his back, breathing in his fresh-from-the-shower scent. Breaking the kiss, she trailed her lips down the column of his throat. His skin was still slightly damp, and she sipped tiny droplets of water from his skin like a woman dying of thirst in the desert.

And maybe she was, Kelsey thought, vaguely surprised by the need and desire spurring her on. After all, it had been a *long* time…

Rising on an elbow, Connor levered away from her. For a split second, Kelsey worried that something—the hotel room, the couch, *something*—had reminded him of the past, of Emily, and that he was going to pull away and leave her wanting. But neither the past nor, heaven forbid, Emily were reflected in his eyes. Instead, Kelsey saw herself as he saw her, and for the first time in her life, she felt beautiful.

"Connor." His name broke from her in a shaky whisper. She didn't think she could speak another word if she tried, but he said everything she wanted to say…everything she wanted to hear.

"A kiss is never going to be enough. I want more. I want everything."

"Okay," she breathed.

Connor's lips quirked in a half smile. "Okay?"

Nodding fiercely, she repeated, "Okay."

Taking her at her word, as limited as it might have been, Connor reclaimed her lips in a teasing, tantalizing kiss even as his fingers toyed with the buttons on her shirt. But after his determined comment, Kelsey should have known Connor wasn't playing.

Before she was even aware of what happened, Connor's hot palm laid claim to the bare skin of her stomach, stealing her breath from the outside in as Kelsey realized he'd completely unbuttoned her shirt.

"Amazing," he murmured, his eyes taking the curves rising and falling with every rapid breath.

Glancing at the off-white, no-frills bra, she gave a short laugh. She hadn't gone to Connor's hotel with seduction in mind and it showed. "Boring," she argued.

"Are you kidding?" Tracing a path across the freckles on her chest, a focused, concentrated frown on his face, Connor vowed, "I think I just found a map to the Lost Dutchman's mine."

The silly comment startled a laugh from Kelsey, and Connor's touch veered closer to hitting a different kind of gold mine. His fingers followed the map work of freckles, and her laughter faded away. Breathless anticipation took over, and she arched into his touch.

The plain material proved no match for Connor. He reached inside to cup her breast, and her nipple instantly tightened against his palm. The sheer pleasure of his touch sent her head spinning, and each gasp for breath only pressed her flesh tighter into his hand. He kissed her again, and Kelsey welcomed the exploring quest of his tongue. Her hands searched for the hem of his shirt, seeking out hidden treasure for herself. She followed the plain of his back, the valley of his spine, the rise of his shoulder blades, but none of it was enough.

Pulling her mouth away from his, she gasped, "Connor, wait."

"What's wrong?" Despite the desire pinpointing his pupils and turning his voice to gravel, Connor followed her command. Other than the rapid rise and fall of his chest, he didn't move a muscle.

And Kelsey couldn't help smiling. "You didn't want to make out in a car, and I don't want to make love on a couch. Not when the bed is only a few feet away."

Eyes dark with desire, he accused, "I told you, you make me crazy."

"The feeling's mutual."

Connor pushed off the couch and held out a hand. She linked her fingers through his and clung tight, desperate to hold onto the moment. But unlike previous interruptions that broke the mood, the walk to the bedroom, amid heated kisses and arousing touches, heightened the intensity. Her fingers clumsy with haste, Kelsey tugged at Connor's T-shirt. She stopped kissing him only long enough to push the shirt over his head and toss it aside.

In the back of her mind, she was still slightly amazed by her own actions. For the first time, need overwhelmed nerves. She could have blamed the previous interruptions or her own personal dry spell for the undeniable hunger. But the real reason was Connor. All Connor…

He pushed her shirt from her shoulders, then stripped away her bra, and Kelsey let the garments fall, too fascinated by the sheer perfection of his broad shoulders, muscular chest and flat stomach to care about the imperfection of freckles dotting her skin. Especially not when Connor seemed so fascinated by connecting the random marks and turning them into shapes: stars, triangles, hearts…

But the arousing touch was nothing compared to the intensity of his lips as they charted that same course. The damp heat of his breath against her skin was like a promise, and when his mouth made good on that promise, Kelsey's knees went weak. Connor followed her down to the mattress and reached for the waistband of her skirt. She expected him to whisk it away as quickly as he had her shirt, but instead her skirt and panties made a slow slide down the length of her legs. Inch by inch, and by the time he slipped them off, Kelsey had never been so glad to be so short.

"Connor." His name broke from her in a plea, and his green eyes glittered as he ran his hand up the inside of her thigh.

"Definitely not boring," he murmured. He stroked her skin, and waves of pleasure washed over her. She cried out his name a second time, even as he shoved aside his jeans. The well-worn denim did not make the same slow journey as her skirt. He kicked the jeans aside in a split second, then braced his body above hers.

He claimed her mouth in a kiss, his tongue plunging deep in the same moment he buried himself between her thighs. Her back arched, her body rising to meet his, and his low groan of desire escaped their kiss. And this time it was her name that broke the silence as Connor caught her hips in his hands.

That first thrust was like the striptease with her skirt: slow, seductive, measured. But then urgency took over, reckless and wild, and Kelsey had the instant thought that this must be what it was like to ride on the back of a bike—amazed, exhilarated and desperate to hold on. But unlike on a bike, the real ride began when she lost control, careening riotously, hurtling down a path that ended in a fiery explosion as she shuddered in ecstasy a second time, bringing Connor with her.

They collapsed in a heap together, both trying to catch their breath. "Definitely not boring," Connor repeated, as he brushed the hair away from her face. The look of tenderness in his gaze brought an ache to her throat, and Kelsey was glad when Connor eased away and tucked her against his side before he saw the tears burning her eyes.

With her head on his chest, Kelsey listened to his heartbeat gradually slow. But even without the weight of his body on hers, she couldn't breathe. A relentless pressure squeezed her heart, like she'd dived too deep and realized too late how far she was in over her head.

Her first impression had been wrong. Connor wasn't the type of man who made a woman want to live for the moment. He was the type of man, the *only* man, who'd made Kelsey long for forever.

Chapter Ten

Connor woke slowly, aware of two things. First it was way too early, and second, Kelsey was no longer in bed. The low murmur of her voice pulled him the rest of the way from sleep. "Everything's all set, and I'll be there to oversee the decorations and food." A slight pause followed. "Must be a bad connection. I'm—outside. I'll run out and get the cake right before the guests arrive. Yes, I'll make sure to leave plenty of time. Can I talk to Emily for a second? Oh, right. Of course. She needs her beauty sleep. I'll see you in an hour. Okay. Forty-five minutes. Bye."

A narrow shaft of light sliced through the curtains, and in the muted glow he watched Kelsey slip on her shoes. He didn't move or make a sound, but something must have given him away. She stiffened slightly and glanced his way as she straightened. "Hey," she said softly. "I was trying not to wake you."

She pushed her hair behind her ear in a nervous gesture,

and Connor felt a flicker of annoyance. What was she going to do? Slip away while he was still sleeping? And why the hell would that bother him? It wasn't as if he hadn't done the same thing before. But that was before, and those women weren't Kelsey, and he didn't want her to go.

A knot twisted in his stomach at the thought of asking her to stay. The memory of his mother's sad smile as she walked away time and time again flashed in his mind, and the words jammed in his throat. He fisted his hands against the mattress and pushed into a sitting position with a glance at the clock. "It's not even seven."

Her gaze fell from his to land on his naked chest and then cut away to search out the purse she'd left on the couch, but not before he'd seen something in her eyes that made the knot in his stomach tighten.

"I know it's early, but Emily's shower is this morning, and I have to oversee the decorations and the food and— I'm sorry."

Connor wasn't sure why she was apologizing—for the early hour, for leaving, for Emily's shower…or for the regret he'd seen in her eyes.

He'd known Kelsey would regret sleeping with him, but he'd taken her at her word when she said she wanted him. He'd believed her because—hell, because he'd wanted to believe her. But that was last night. Now, in the full light of day, with the Charlene Wilson calling the shots, everything changed.

Or, he thought grimly, everything was the same. Only this time it was Kelsey lying to the Wilsons, sneaking behind their backs to see him. It was Kelsey who pretended her relationship with him didn't exist. Familiar ground, but it hurt a hell of a lot more the second time around. And not because she'd torn open old wounds. Emily had damaged his pride, but this—this felt like something else entirely.

Tossing aside the sheet in an obvious reminder that last

night *had* happened, Connor swung his legs over the edge of the mattress and stood. Some other time, he might have teased Kelsey about the blush blooming in her face. But not this morning. Not when the heat signaled a different kind of embarrassment. He jerked on his jeans as quickly as he'd stripped them off the night before, annoyed by his body's reaction to the mere thought.

"I'm going to talk to Emily about the wedding—"

"I don't give a damn about the wedding," he said, surprised by the truth of the words. He was still worried about Emily, but as far as proving the Wilsons wrong about Dunworthy, proving them wrong about *him,* Connor no longer cared. Only Kelsey's opinion mattered, an opinion suddenly in doubt.

"I'm sorry," she repeated, before lifting distraught eyes to his.

Yeah, he got that part. She was sorry they'd slept together.

"Last night was…"

Connor's jaw clenched, waiting for the word he *knew* was coming.

"…amazing, and I'd give anything to stay in bed with you—"

"Wait? What?"

"Last night was amazing." Color flared brighter, nearly blotting out her freckles as she ducked her head. "At least I thought it was, but I'm not—"

Swallowing a curse, Connor pulled her into his arms as realization hit him like the slap upside the head he deserved. Kelsey's reactions hadn't been fueled by regret or embarrassment but by a vulnerability that played against his own insecurities. "Last night *was* amazing."

The memory combined with Kelsey's soft curves pressed against him, her warm breath feathering across his chest, was enough to remind him just *how* amazing.

"It was," Kelsey whispered. He heard the relief in her voice, felt her smile against his skin.

"This morning could be even more amazing."

"I know." Despite the apparent agreement in her words, her smile fell away, and this time, he knew he wasn't imagining the regret in her voice. Pulling out of his arms, she said, "And that's why I have to go. Because whether you give a damn or not, Emily's wedding is a week away and then you'll be going home."

She was talking about L.A., but home didn't bring to mind images of his sterile apartment. Instead, he thought of Señora Delgado's restaurant, he thought of his friendship with Javy, and he thought of every moment he'd spent with Kelsey…and he wondered what might happen if he didn't go back to L.A.

"Kelsey—"

"So, see? I have to leave," she continued despite his interruption. "Last night was an amazing moment, but it wasn't meant to last, right?"

The hope in her eyes waited for him to contradict every word she'd said, to tell her sometimes amazing moments added up to a lifetime, but he couldn't make himself say the words.

Ducking her head, Kelsey grabbed her purse off the couch and left. And even though the sound of the closing door slammed into his chest like a blow, Connor let her go. Because when it came right down to it, he was the one too afraid to ask her to stay.

Connor didn't have a destination in mind when he climbed behind the Mustang's wheel, but he couldn't stay in the hotel room any longer. Fortunately, Javy's car seemed to have a mind of its own, and he soon turned into the Delgado parking lot.

The restaurant wouldn't open for hours yet, but Connor knew Maria would already be in the kitchen, stirring giant pots of tortilla soup and prepping food. He pulled around back, the crunch of gravel beneath the tires the only sound, a sharp contrast to the night he'd brought Kelsey here when music and laughter filled the sultry air.

A metallic glint caught his eye as he climbed from the car, and he spotted a motionless wind chime made from silverware. Despite his mood, Connor smiled as a memory came to him. Furious with Javy over some scrape he'd gotten into, Maria whacked the counter with a carved spoon. The aged wood splintered on contact, adding to his mother's anger, and she'd threatened Javy with the dire prediction that if the restaurant closed, it would be all his fault; after all, how could she cook without her favorite spoon?

The statement was a meaningless heat-of-the-moment comment that had come far too close to coming true years later. Not because of a broken spoon, but due to the expenses that followed Javy's father's illness and the fire that had nearly destroyed the kitchen.

A faint humming broke into his memories, and he found Maria standing at the counter, vegetables piled high in front of her, the quick, continuous motion of the knife a steady rhythm to the song she sang beneath her breath. The rustic Delgado family recipes went back for decades, but the remodeled kitchen was completely modern with its stainless-steel counters and appliances.

Maria's face lit as he stepped inside the kitchen. "Connor! This is a surprise."

"I wanted to apologize for taking off without saying goodbye the other night."

She waved aside his apology with a flick of her knife before starting in on a jalapeno pepper, but curiosity lit her eyes as she said, "You and your Kelsey were in a hurry, no?"

Her words wiggled like bait on a hook, but Connor didn't bite. His silence wasn't enough to make the *señora* pull in her line. Watching him from the corner of her eye, she added, "That is how it is when you are in love."

Love. The word sent a flare of panic scorching through him like the grease fire that nearly destroyed the restaurant years ago. "Kelsey and I aren't in love."

Maria glared at him like she might toss him back into the water. "I was married to my Miguel for over twenty years. I know love."

Connor knew love, too. He knew the pain of losing a mother who loved him yet left him no matter how many times he asked her to stay. He knew the heartache of losing Emily, who claimed to love him but not enough to defy her parents. And Kelsey…would loving her be any different? If he told her the truth about the money he'd taken, money he'd used to save the restaurant, would love be enough to make her understand? Would it be enough for her to stand up to the family who'd taken her in when she was sixteen and scared with nowhere else to go?

"You don't understand, Maria. Kelsey's a Wilson. She's Emily's cousin—"

"And you think Kelsey is a foolish girl like Emily? Unable to think or do for herself?"

"No, she's not like that at all. She's used to taking care of herself and the people around her." He'd seen that at her shop, in her concern for her friends. Friends who had Kelsey's complete loyalty. Friends who *deserved* that loyalty.

Connor tried to picture Lisa or Trey fitting in at a Wilson family gathering and couldn't. Just as he couldn't imagine Kelsey caring what the Wilsons thought or ever, *ever* turning her back on her friends. Kelsey might not have wanted to follow in her mother's footsteps, but the path had led Kelsey to be a strong, independent woman. A woman who knew her own mind and knew what she wanted.

Suddenly it didn't matter if the Wilsons admitted they've been wrong about Dunworthy. It didn't even matter if they admitted they'd been wrong about *him.* All he cared about now was proving Kelsey *right.* She believed in him, and last night she'd wanted *him.* Now it was up to Connor to tell her the truth about the money he'd taken from her family and convince her she wanted more than a moment, that he could give her more. It was up to him to convince her that, together, they could have forever.

Kelsey struggled through the front door of her aunt and uncle's house, a huge bouquet of pink and silver helium-filled balloons trailing behind her. The carved wooden doors swung shut, catching one of the balloons in the jamb. She jumped as the loud-as-a-gunshot *pop* guaranteed her arrival wouldn't go unannounced.

"Kelsey. I expected you half an hour ago."

Okay, so she wouldn't have snuck in unnoticed anyway. "Sorry, Aunt Charlene."

"Where have you been?"

"With Connor." The truth popped out before the words even formed in her head, and she couldn't imagine what possessed her to tell the truth.

His image flashed in her mind, and she knew exactly what possessed her. She'd seen the look in his eyes when he'd caught her on the phone with her aunt. When he caught her *lying* to her aunt. If she wasn't such a coward, she would have told the truth when it mattered.

Just like she would have stayed with Connor that morning, in his hotel room, in his bed, with the courage to believe they could turn one night into something more.

Disapproval cut into Charlene's features, and Kelsey knew her aunt didn't think Connor was good enough for a Wilson—

any Wilson—but she knew the truth. She didn't deserve Connor.

"You're wrong about him," she announced, certainty backing ever word. "Connor's a good man. He isn't here to ruin Emily's life. He's here because he's worried she's marrying a man she doesn't love to please *you.*"

Her aunt didn't speak. Kelsey thought maybe her words had made a difference, at least given her aunt pause. But Charlene's gaze never wavered, and as the silence grew, Kelsey knew her aunt wasn't using the silence to consider what Kelsey said. She was using the silence to make Kelsey *reconsider* what she'd said.

But she wasn't going to back down.

It was time for both her aunt and uncle to realize Connor was a good man, not some troubled kid out to steal their daughter. And they needed to let Emily go. To let her live her own life and to stop using one youthful indiscretion to keep her in line.

"Do you really think I can't see what's going on?" her aunt questioned on a sigh. "Connor McClane is out to stop Emily's wedding, and he's using you to do it! Honestly, Kelsey, I expected you to know better."

"Connor isn't using me. He wouldn't do that. I understand why you'd have a hard time believing he cares for me after how crazy he was about Emily—"

"Oh, for goodness' sake, follow me." Without checking to see if Kelsey would obey, Charlene turned on a heel and strode down the hall into Gordon's study. Kelsey reluctantly followed. "Connor wasn't in love with Emily any more than he's…"

In love with you. Her aunt's unspoken words bounced off the darkly paneled walls, hanging in the room like the scent of Gordon's cigars.

"The only thing that man has ever worried about is

himself." Crossing the room to open a desk drawer, she pulled out a manila folder. "When your uncle kept this for proof, I always thought Emily would be the one we'd show it to."

"Proof of what?" Kelsey asked uneasily as Charlene fingered a small rectangle of paper. The letters her uncle had written her mother had been shock enough. What else did her aunt and uncle have stashed away in desks and dressers?

"Proof of the kind of man Connor McClane really is." Charlene gazed at Kelsey across the polished mahogany surface, her gaze reflecting a hint of sympathy. "He must be very convincing. Emily was sure he loved her."

Kelsey didn't have her cousin's certainty. Connor had never mentioned the word *love*. But then again, neither had she, and Kelsey could no longer deny her feelings. She was in love with Connor. For a moment, she imagined saying the words out loud and punctuating them with a bold exit. Not needing any proof of the man Connor was aside from the truth written in her heart. But she wasn't that strong.

"What is it?" she whispered.

"See for yourself." Charlene slid the paper across the table. Kelsey stepped closer. It was a check. She recognized her uncle's signature, his name and address printed on the top left, the zeros following the number in the small box off to the right. But it was the person the check had been made out to that froze her gaze. Her stomach, which had been tossing back and forth, sank.

"Why do you think Connor left all those years ago? He might not have had Emily, but believe me, he got what he wanted."

Her hand shaking, Kelsey reached out and turned the check over. Connor's name was sprawled across the endorsement line. She stared at the signature rather than meet her aunt's knowing gaze. "That was a long time ago. Connor isn't the same person anymore."

Ten thousand dollars. A lot of money, but not enough to make a dent in the family fortune. Had her father held out for more? Kelsey wondered. Even twenty-four years ago, ten thousand dollars didn't go far. Ten years ago, it wouldn't have bought a new car.

"Is that what he told you? That he's changed?" Her aunt's cultured voice didn't reflect even a hint of disparagement, but Kelsey heard it all the same.

"He was a kid back when he was seeing Emily." An orphaned kid from the wrong side of the tracks. Could she blame him for taking the money? He'd told her how he'd struggled after his mother died.

But he didn't tell you about the check, a worried voice protested. She'd told him about the money her father took to abandon her and her mother, and Connor never said a word.

"Let's look at the way he's changed. Ten years ago, he nearly ruined Emily's life by convincing her to run away from her family with him. Now he's back, and this time he's out to ruin her life by convincing her to run away from her fiancé with him."

"That's not true," Kelsey argued against the ache in her chest. "He's concerned about Emily. Just like I am. She's making a mistake by marrying Todd."

"If I were you, I wouldn't be worried about Emily *or* Todd. I'd be worried about Connor McClane."

Kelsey wasn't sure how she made it through the shower. Probably thanks to her aunt's attention to detail. By following Charlene's every instruction, Kelsey moved by rote. She arranged the flowers and decorations; she picked up the cake and double-checked the catered finger food. She walked the guests through the games—silly, irreverent, last-days-as-a-free-woman tributes—followed by opening gifts.

Even in her dazed state, Kelsey could guess what each package contained. After all, she'd helped with the bridal registry, and no one would dare step outside the approved gift list. No surprises, just as her aunt demanded.

Charlene planned for every contingency. Even Connor McClane, Kelsey thought, her heart catching as his signature seemed to flash in front of her eyes, written by an unseen hand.

"Thank you, Kelsey! It's beautiful." Emily held up a snow globe. Strains of the wedding march filled the room as sparkling "snow" fell on the bride and groom waltzing through a wedding wonderland.

Kelsey offered a weak smile. She'd bought the gift B.C.—Before Connor. She couldn't *not* give her cousin a gift, but she felt as uncertain about Emily and Todd as she now did about Connor.

Kelsey had started to believe him, to trust his gut, as he called it, but now she didn't know what to believe, and her own gut was pitifully silent. "You're welcome, Emily. I just want you to be happy."

Emily masked the flicker of doubt with a wedding-portrait smile. "I am happy, Kelsey. I'm getting married!"

A half an hour later, as the guests were leaving, Kelsey started collecting the plates and utensils, her movements automatic and unthinking. She blinked in surprise when her aunt laid a hand on her arm.

"The maid can get that, Kelsey."

"It's my job—"

"And we're your family." Her expression softened to a degree Kelsey had never witnessed. "You're a beautiful woman in your own right, Kelsey, and I'm sorry if I've made you feel less than my own daughters. But there's only one thing Connor McClane is interested in, and it's not true love."

* * *

Kelsey debated calling Connor, but the conversation wasn't one she wanted to have over the phone. Stopping by his hotel room was out of the question. She'd come alive in Connor's arms the night before, letting go of the past and all her insecurities. But seeing proof of the money he'd taken, the past was in painful jeopardy of repeating. The insecurities Connor lifted with his seductive words and intoxicating touch crashed back down, hitting harder than ever. Making her question if last night had been as amazing as she'd thought…

Kelsey hit the brakes a good twenty feet shy of her driveway. The black Mustang was parked at the sidewalk, the right front tire bumped up on the curb. Mirrored glasses shielding his eyes, Connor leaned against the hood.

Ready or not, she was going to have to confront him about the money he'd taken. It wasn't something *she* could pretend hadn't happened. Nerves jerked in her stomach, and she carefully eased her foot back on the gas, her car crawling the last block.

Connor grinned as she stepped out of the car, and aching or not, her heart still sped up as he approached. Maybe he had a reason, an explanation for taking the money.

And a reason for keeping the truth from her?

Kelsey could forgive something that happened ten years ago, but why hadn't he told her? Why did she have to face the shock of another family secret?

"Hey, I went by to see Señora Delgado. You have an open invitation, and she made me promise that next time, I'd actually let you stay and eat." Connor stuck his hands in the pockets of his jeans, a hint of uncertainty in his stride weakening her resolve as she wondered what else he'd talked to the older woman about.

"Connor—"

"She likes you," he added with a crooked smile, "but then, who wouldn't?" His smile fell away when she didn't respond, and he stripped off his glasses. Worry shone in his emerald eyes. "What's wrong?"

"Wrong?" Kelsey echoed with a broken laugh, the word far too simple to describe everything that had happened. Her decision to trust him, to *sleep* with him, to defend him to her aunt…only to find out he was just like her father.

It was a long time ago, her heart argued. *Maybe he had a good reason. Maybe—*

"Why didn't you tell me?"

"Tell you what?"

"The real reason you left all those years ago. Why didn't you tell me about the money?"

A muscle in Connor's jaw flinched as if she'd slapped him. Kelsey wasn't sure what she'd expected—excuses, denials—but she hadn't counted on the dead silence that followed her words. The sun beat down on them, magnifying the pain in her head. Cicadas in a neighbor's tree started to buzz, a low pitch that soon revved louder and louder, building like the hurt and anger inside Kelsey until she couldn't keep from lashing out.

"I *told* you about my father—about the money he took to leave my mother, and you never said a word! I trusted you, I believed in you, I—"

Love you, she thought, her heart breaking as Connor stoically withstood her verbal attack. If not for that very first flinch, she wouldn't have even known he was listening.

Surely if he had some reason, some justification for taking the money beyond pure and simple greed, he would tell her. He would say…*something, anything!* But silence—*guilty* silence—was Connor's only response.

"My aunt and uncle were right about you all along," she

whispered. Just as her grandfather had been right about her father. "They were right about everything."

At her words, Connor finally reacted. A cruel, calculating smile curved his mouth, and though Kelsey never would have thought green eyes could be cold, a chill touched her as his gaze iced over. He looked every inch the bad boy her aunt had warned her about less than two weeks ago. If only she'd listened.

"Congratulations, Kelsey. Your family must be so proud. Seems like you're a real Wilson after all."

Muttering a curse beneath his breath, Connor stalked over to the car. Despite the weight of restrained sobs pressing on her chest, Kelsey let him go. She might have lived her life under the misconception of her and her mom against the world, but Connor was just as deluded, believing it was always him against the Wilsons. This wasn't about her family; it was all on Connor and the secret he'd kept.

"Mama's right. You look like hell."

Ignoring his friend's voice, Connor didn't look away from the production of sliced limes, saltshaker and shot glass he'd filled with tequila. He'd taken over the small outdoor bar at the back of the Delgados' restaurant, where they'd installed patio seating for times when the weather was nice. In the middle of June, even at eight o'clock at night, it wasn't.

He barely noticed the oppressive heat, the way his T-shirt clung damply to his skin, or the bugs that hovered around the string of multicolored lights. After shaking out salt on the back of his hand like it was rocket science, he reached for the shot glass.

Catching Connor's wrist, Javy asked, "How many of those have you had?"

Connor glared at his friend from the corner of his eye. "Counting this one? Two."

His friend barked out a laugh that ended in a curse as he let go. "You're in worse shape than I thought. Wanna tell me what happened?"

Wincing at the strong burn of the tequila, Connor replied, "You said it yourself when I brought Kelsey here. Some people never learn."

"Sorry, man."

Javy didn't say more, and the two of them sat without speaking. Mariachi music, the din of the diners, and the occasional shout from the kitchen were the only sounds.

Finally Connor shoved the shot glass aside. "It was Emily all over again. I was stupid enough to think things would be different this time. But when push came to shove, she sided with her family."

He'd seen the disappointment in Kelsey's eyes. Forget all she'd said about how he'd changed. Forget all they'd shared. She'd been waiting all along for him to show his true colors, and she'd jumped back to her own side of the tracks the minute his character came into question.

You should have told her sooner, his conscience berated him. If she hadn't found out the truth from Charlene… But would that have made a difference? Or would Kelsey's reaction have been the same?

He should have known he and Kelsey didn't have any chance at a future. Her family's disapproval would eat like acid, weakening Kelsey's feelings until they were worn clean away. He was lucky it had happened sooner rather than later. He couldn't stand to live life with Kelsey the way he had with his mother, always knowing she had one foot out the door and it was only a matter of time before she left and didn't come back.

"Wanna tell me what happened?"

"Her aunt told her I took money to leave town, to leave Emily."

"And she believed it?" his friend demanded, slumping back against the bar stool in disbelief. "Just like that? With no proof, no—"

"The Wilsons had all the proof they needed. I took the ten thousand dollars."

Shock straightened his friend's spine. "You what? But why would you—" Realization slowly spread across his features, along with a large dose of guilt. Javy swore. "Is that where you got the money you gave my mother for the restaurant?"

"Like you said, this place means everything to Maria. I couldn't let her lose it." Eyeing his friend closely, Connor said, "You never asked where I got the money."

"No, I never did." Javy let out a deep breath, reached for the bottle of tequila and poured himself a shot. For a long moment he stared into the glass before looking Connor in the eye. "I didn't want to know."

"What? In case I'd broken the law? Done something illegal?" Connor pressed. Well, why wouldn't Javy believe that? It was just the kind of thing Connor McClane would have done.

Once.

"You think *I* didn't consider it?" Javy shot back. "It's *my* restaurant! My responsibility. My family—"

"Mine, too."

"Yeah," his friend agreed, frustration and anger draining away. "But I should have been the one to come up with a solution. And you shouldn't be the one paying for it now."

"I made my choice, and I would do the same thing again. In a heartbeat. So, tell me, you gonna drink that?" Connor asked, pointing at the shot glass sitting untouched between them.

Javy slid it across the bar without spilling a drop. "Look, man, I've been trying to pay you back for years. You've gotta let me—"

"Forget it. After all your family did for me, it was the least I could do."

"Then we'll draw something up. Make you a partner in the restaurant. And I'll talk to Kelsey."

Connor shook his head. "No."

"What do you mean 'no'?" Javy demanded. "Why don't you want to tell her the truth?"

"She knows the truth. I took the money."

"Oh, come on, Connor! That's not the whole truth, and you damn well know it! If you told her *why,* Kelsey would understand."

Yeah, maybe she would…this time. But what about the next time she had to choose between him and her family?

Chapter Eleven

It had been three days since Kelsey had seen Connor. Three heartbreaking, regret-filled, uneventful days.

At first she'd been too hurt to do more than curl up on her sofa and cry. But Kelsey never believed self-pity helped anyone, so by the second day she had thrown herself into working on her shop, finishing up the details that transformed the place from a simple suite into the office of her dreams.

She'd had photographs from previous weddings enlarged and wrapped in gilded frames: an elegant wedding cake with a single piece missing; a bridal bouquet in midair with ribbons streaming; a close-up of an unseen couple's hands, fingers entwined, showing off sparkling wedding rings.

She'd hung sheer curtains and floral drapes at the windows and found a bargain on a secondhand wicker coffee table, which displayed a crystal vase and fresh flowers from Lisa's shop. She'd brought a CD player from home to fill the air with soft, lilting music.

And if her heart broke a little more with every romantic touch she added, not once did Kelsey let that slow her down.

If she had any doubts about her hard work paying off, she'd received encouragement from an unlikely source. When Charlene called earlier, the talk had centered around the rehearsal dinner that night, but nearing the end of the conversation, Charlene had fallen silent before saying, "If I haven't told you before now, Kelsey, I appreciate all you've done for Emily's wedding. We never would have been able to pull this off so quickly if not for you."

After saying goodbye to her aunt, Kelsey hung up the phone and looked around her shop. She had everything she wanted: her shop was up and running, Emily's wedding was only days away and her hard work had gained her aunt's approval.

Congratulations, Kelsey. Your family must be so proud. Seems like you're a real Wilson after all.

Guilt wormed its way through her stomach, but Kelsey pushed it away with a burst of anger as she grabbed her purse and keys. She had no cause to feel guilty, she decided as she locked the front door behind her with a definitive twist of the key. None at all. Connor was the one who'd kept secrets, told lies of omission.

And yet maybe he had a reason. After all, hadn't he encouraged her to consider that her father might have had his reasons for taking the money? At the time, Kelsey thought Connor was talking only about her father. But could Connor have been talking about himself? Hoping that she might understand why he'd taken the ten thousand dollars? And what had she told him?

Nothing he could say would matter, nothing he could do would ever make up for taking the money.

Little wonder, then, that he hadn't bothered with explanations!

She had to talk to Connor, Kelsey decided as she climbed into her car and turned the air on full blast. If she expected him to tell her the truth, she owed it to him to listen without making judgments based on her own past.

Her phone rang, reminding Kelsey that she couldn't drop everything to go see Connor. After the rehearsal, she vowed as she pulled out her cell and flipped it open.

"Kelsey?"

Startled by the unexpected male voice, Kelsey asked, "Yes?"

"It's Javy Delgado. Connor's friend."

"Javy?" She couldn't imagine why he'd call her unless… "Is Connor okay? Has something happened?"

He paused long enough to strip a few years off Kelsey's life before he said, "Do you still care about him?"

"Of course I care about him! I—" *Love him,* Kelsey thought.

"I wasn't sure after the way you treated him."

"The way *I* treated *him?* I know you're Connor's friend, but—"

"Not as good a friend as he's been to me," he interrupted. "And that's why I called even though he asked me not to."

So Connor didn't want to talk to her. He didn't even want his friend talking to her. That didn't give her much hope. "Why wouldn't he want you to talk to me?"

"He doesn't want me to tell you the truth. He's afraid it won't matter. I hope he's wrong about that. About you. Just like you've been wrong about him." Javy sighed. "The money he took, the money your uncle paid him—Connor gave it to my family. He used it to save our restaurant."

* * *

"I have what you need."

Even though Connor had been waiting for the damn call for days, it took him a moment to recognize the voice on the other end. He pushed away from the small table in his hotel room, pent-up energy surging through his veins.

"Jake, it's about time you called. Tell me what you've got is good. I can't wait to get out of this town."

The words were the biggest lie he'd told in the past five minutes. Which was about how long it'd been since he'd last tried to convince himself Kelsey Wilson wasn't worth the effort, and he'd forget all about her the second he got back to California.

"Good? No, I wouldn't call it good," Jake ground out.

Jake sounded nothing like his normal self, and although he and Connor were close, their relationship didn't include a lot of heart-to-heart talks. Still, he had to say, "You sound like hell, man."

"Doesn't matter. I got the job done. I found what I was looking for."

A garbled voice over a loudspeaker sounded in the background. "I have to go. They're calling my flight. I'm e-mailing everything you need right now. Just do me one favor."

"What is it?"

"Use it to nail that guy."

"I will."

"Good. It's about time he gets what he deserves."

As Connor flipped the cell phone closed, his friend's voice rang in his ears. Connor supposed most people would say he was getting what he deserved, too. That Kelsey turning her back on him was just desserts for the way he had taken the money and left Emily years ago.

Except maybe Kelsey's anger wasn't about his relationship

with Emily or the past he couldn't change. Maybe it was about *their* relationship right now, and the truth he'd kept from her.

Okay, yeah, she'd told him nothing could excuse what her father had done when he'd taken money to leave her mother, but maybe if Connor had explained about the Delgados' restaurant…maybe if he'd told her about the money up front so she wouldn't have had to hear about it from *Charlene,* of all people…

Could he really blame Kelsey for reacting the way she had? Between the money her father had taken and the secrets her mother had kept, she had every right to be wary.

Sure, it would have been nice if she'd learned about the money and had still been willing to believe the best about him. But he hadn't placed all his faith in Kelsey, either. He'd been afraid to tell her about the money because he'd feared his reasons—his love and loyalty to the Delgados—wouldn't matter. He'd been holding on to his own past and his own fears that *he* wouldn't matter. He should have trusted her more than that.

His computer e-mail alert sounded, letting him know Jake's report had arrived. A few taps on the keyboard, and Connor understood his friend's anger. "Don't worry, Jake. We've nailed the guy."

After Javy's call, Kelsey longed to turn the car around to go immediately to Connor's hotel, but she couldn't skip the rehearsal, not as Emily's wedding coordinator and not as a member of the Wilson family.

When her phone rang again, her heart skipped a beat as Connor's number flashed across the screen. Still, she hesitated a split second. She wanted to be able to look into his eyes when she apologized. To see that he believed her when she told him she understood why he took the money and she wouldn't expect any less of him than the sacrifice he'd made for his friends.

But after the way she'd treated him, she offered a quick whisper of thanks that he wanted to talk to her at all. Flipping the cell open with one hand, she turned into a nearby parking lot. She immediately sucked in a quick breath, but Connor interrupted any greeting or apology she might have made. "Kelsey, it's Connor. Don't hang up."

She pressed the phone tighter to her ear as if that might somehow bring her closer to Connor. "I'm not. I won't."

"Look, I can explain about the money, I swear—"

"You don't have to—"

"But not now—"

"I talked to Javy—"

"Jake called—"

"What?"

"Jake called. He found Sophia, the Dunworthy's former maid."

Trying to switch gears while her thoughts were going one hundred miles at hour, Kelsey said, "Did he find out why she quit?"

"Turns out she was fired after Dunworthy Senior caught her and Junior together."

"Caught them?"

"From what Sophia says, he'd been hitting on her for months before she finally gave in. Only to lose her job because of it."

"But didn't you say she stopped working for the Dunworthys only a few months ago?" Kelsey asked, mentally going over the timing and coming to an unbelievable conclusion. "Todd and Emily started dating six months ago. They were *engaged* two months ago!"

"Yeah, they were. Evidently sleeping with the maid was the last straw. The way I figure it, Todd proposed to Emily as a way to try to win back his family's approval."

"I can't believe he would do that to Emily!" Anger for her

cousin's sake started to boil inside Kelsey, along with a disgust at the way Todd had smiled and charmed his way into her aunt and uncle's good graces.

"It gets worse."

"Worse! How can it possibly get any worse! Is there someone else?"

"In a way." Connor paused. "Sophia's pregnant."

"Preg—Are you sure the child is Todd's? Considering the money his family has, and after the way Sophia lost her job—"

"Jake is sure of it. He believes her, and I believe him. Judging from his family's reactions, I'd say that the Dunworthys believe it, too. The family doesn't want anything to do with Todd. That's why they aren't here for the wedding." He hesitated. "You were right, Kelsey, and I should have listened to you."

"It doesn't matter now. You did it, Connor. You found the proof you needed."

"Yeah, I've got everything I need," he agreed, his voice sounding hollow. "Look, Kelsey—"

She waited, her heart pounding for everything she wanted to hear, everything she wanted to say. But the silence stretched on, the words unspoken. Finally she said, "The wedding rehearsal is tonight. I'm already on my way to the chapel."

"I'm at the hotel now. I can be there in fifteen minutes."

"Fifteen minutes," Kelsey echoed quietly, before hanging up the phone.

She had fallen in love with the small chapel the first time she saw the cottage-style building, with its cobblestone walls and stained-glass windows. The close proximity to the hotel made it an ideal location. Right now Kelsey wished the chapel were a world away, anything to delay the inevitable end. Once Connor stopped the wedding, he'd have no reason to stick around...and if he did, Kelsey feared it wouldn't be for her.

* * *

Minutes later Kelsey stood inside the empty chapel. It was as beautiful now as when she'd first laid eyes on it. She'd immediately known the perfect arrangement of flowers and candles for alongside the carved pews. Just the right placement of the wedding party on the steps leading to the altar. Exactly where the video and photographer should stand to best capture the light streaming through the windows. She'd known all of that months before Emily had gotten engaged. When Emily had bowed so easily to her suggestions, Kelsey had set in motion the wedding of her own dreams.

She was as guilty as Charlene in pushing her own ideas on Emily. It was *her* dream location for the wedding and reception. All of *her* friends were working side by side to make the day memorable. Maybe if she hadn't been so focused on what she wanted, she would have stopped a long time ago to ask if any of it was what *Emily* wanted.

But she hadn't, and now all their dreams were going down the drain—the perfect wedding to make her business, Emily's dream of marrying the perfect man, Gordon and Charlene's perfect son-in-law. Only Connor had succeeded. He was stopping the wedding as he'd said he would.

He was a man of his word, a good man, and she should have trusted him. Kelsey knew how much it must have hurt when she turned her back on him, just as much as regret and heartache were hurting her now.

A door squeaked behind her, letting in a rush of summer air, and Kelsey took a deep breath. Turning to face her aunt and uncle, she said, "Aunt Charlene, Uncle Gordon, I need to talk to you…" Her voice trailed away when she saw Emily and Todd following a few steps behind.

The one time Kelsey had counted on them being late.

"What is it, Kelsey?" Gordon asked.

"I—" She'd hoped to have a chance to talk to her aunt and uncle alone, to prepare them for what Connor had discovered, so together they could find a way to tell Emily. "I was wondering if I could speak to the two of you in private."

She tried to make the suggestion as casually as possible, but there was nothing casual about the way Charlene's eyebrows arched toward her hairline. "What's wrong? Is it the flowers? The music?"

"Relax, Char," Gordon interjected. "Weren't you saying this morning that Kelsey has everything under control?"

Her uncle's reminder and confident smile sent a sick feeling through Kelsey's stomach. How was she supposed to tell them about Todd?

Taking note of her watching him, Todd crossed his arms over his chest, a not-so-subtle challenge in his expression. "You have something to say, Kelsey?"

She took a deep breath, but before she had chance to speak, the chapel door swung open again. She heard Connor's voice a second before he stepped through the doorway. "Actually, I'm the one with something to say."

"McClane! What are you doing here?" Gordon demanded, a lightning bolt of wrinkles cutting across his thunderous expression.

Todd draped a proprietary arm over Emily's shoulders. "I told Emily inviting him was a mistake. He's still in love with her, and he's probably here because he thinks he can stop the wedding."

"I'm not in love with Emily," Connor insisted.

I'm in love with Kelsey. His heart pounded out the words he never thought he'd say, but damned if he'd say them for the first time with the Wilsons and Todd Dunworthy as witnesses.

He felt the irresistible pull of Kelsey's gaze and he couldn't help meeting her gaze any more than he could resist the earth's gravity. *Not now. Not like this,* he mentally pleaded as he looked into her eyes, willing her to understand.

"Then maybe you'd like to explain *exactly* what is going on here?" Gordon repeated.

This was his moment, Connor thought. His chance to prove he was right and the Wilsons were wrong. Wrong about Todd. Wrong about him. But his triumph rang hollow. He didn't need the Wilsons' approval. He wasn't sure why he'd ever thought he did. All he needed was Kelsey. Her faith. Her trust. Had his past and his secret destroyed that?

"Connor?" Kelsey's voice called to him.

Dressed in a blue-green print dress that hugged her curves, her hair free to curl around her face, she looked absolutely beautiful—strong and vulnerable at the same time, and he couldn't look away.

Whatever Gordon and Charlene saw in his expression had them quickly closing ranks around Kelsey. Surrounded by her aunt and uncle, the Wilson misfit suddenly looked at home within the golden circle, and Connor was alone on the outside.

Tearing his gaze away, he focused on Gordon and pulled the information he'd printed from his back pocket. "Your golden boy has a history of using women. His blue-blood family, who mean so much to you, has completely cut him off after he got one of their maids pregnant." He slapped the pages into Gordon Wilson's reluctantly outstretched hand.

Charlene gasped, color leaching from her face, but doubt pulled Gordon's silver eyebrows together.

"Todd, what is Connor talking about?" Emily asked, her eyes wide as she stared at her fiancé.

"He's lying," Todd scoffed. But instead of trying to console Emily, he looked to Gordon with a can-you-believe-the-nerve-of-this-guy expression. "You know you can't trust anything McClane says."

"But you can trust me, Uncle Gordon," Kelsey insisted as she stepped closer.

"What do you know about this?" her uncle asked, taking a look at the papers.

"I know Connor is a good man." She spoke the words to her uncle, but her gaze never broke from Connor's. "He's here because he's worried about Emily. That information is true."

"Don't listen to her," Todd issued sharply. When Gordon's steely gaze cut his way, filled with the same distrust he'd pinned on Connor's seconds earlier, he quickly backed down. Relaxing his features into a more conciliatory expression, he said, "I'm afraid Kelsey has fallen for McClane's lies, but it's all a smear campaign to stop the wedding."

"How exactly is Connor McClane behind the significant amount of money your family paid this Sophia Pirelli?"

Todd's confident look faded, clay showing through the once-golden facade, but he still didn't give up. "My family let her go, so she went after us for money, claiming the kid she's carrying is mine. The money was a way to keep her quiet."

"A simple paternity test would have done the same thing and been *much* cheaper," Connor pointed out. "The kind of money your family paid… That's not hush money. It's guilt money."

Connor watched with satisfaction as the truth spread across Dunworthy's face and disgust and disappointment over the Wilsons'. Realization hit Emily last, leaving her pale and shaken as she looked from Todd to her parents. Finally her gaze locked with Connor's, and she burst into tears before rushing into his arms.

Seated in Gordon Wilson's study a half hour later, Connor nodded when the older man held up the bottle of scotch. Gordon poured two glasses, handed one to Connor and took a swallow from his own glass before claiming his spot behind the large mahogany desk.

Connor took a sip of his own scotch while he waited for the older man to speak.

"We owe you our thanks," Gordon said after a minute of silence. "When I think of my little girl married to that liar—"

At the chapel Gordon had made it clear to Dunworthy that the engagement was over and the wedding off, and that he'd live to regret it if he ever went near Emily again. Gordon and Charlene had reluctantly agreed to Emily's request that Connor drive her home after Charlene immediately tried to take charge. Emily had surprised them all, demanding some time alone. Connor thought—hoped—that she was learning to stand up for herself.

"I'm glad I found the proof I needed. I only wish I had found it sooner."

"And I wish you had come to me with your suspicions sooner."

Connor couldn't choke back a disbelieving laugh as he set the glass of scotch aside. "I'm not sure how you think that conversation would have played out, but I don't see you taking my side over your handpicked future son-in-law."

"I did not *handpick* Todd. You make it sound like some kind of arranged marriage."

"Wasn't it?"

A flush rising in his face, Gordon struggled for a calming breath. "Look, I'm trying to say that I appreciate what you've done. I don't know how we can repay you."

Pay him...

Shoving to his feet, Connor ground out, "I don't want your money."

"I wasn't offering any," Gordon shot back. He rose to glare at Connor from across the expanse of his desk.

The silent stalemate lasted several tense seconds before Gordon sighed. The tension drained from his body, leaving his shoulders a bit stooped and signs of age lining his face. "Sit back down." He gestured to the leather chair Connor had abandoned. "I've had enough drama for one night."

Hesitating, Connor glanced at the study doorway.

"Expecting someone?"

"I thought Kelsey would be here by now."

In the aftermath of the argument with Dunworthy and Emily's collapse into tears, Connor hadn't had a chance to talk to Kelsey. He'd expected her to head back to the Wilsons' with the rest of her family, where he'd been counting on the chance to talk to her.

But maybe he'd misunderstood what she'd said during the phone call. He should have known Javy wouldn't keep his mouth shut just because he'd told him to, but the more time Connor had to think, the more worried he became. Did her absence mean that Javy's explanation hadn't made a difference? That she still couldn't forgive Connor for the money he'd taken?

Gordon sucked in a deep breath as if preparing for a painful blow and admitted, "I was wrong about Todd."

They were the words Connor had come to Arizona to hear. The perfect lead-in to tell Gordon he hadn't been wrong just about Todd Dunworthy; he'd been wrong about Connor, too. But as he'd already figured out, it no longer mattered. Only Kelsey…

When he stayed silent, the older man repeated, "I was wrong about Todd. I realize now you came back to help Emily, and you have. But you still have some work to do to convince me you're good enough for this family."

"Good enough—" Connor's words broke off when he caught sight of what almost looked like respect gleaming in the older man's blue eyes. Shaking his head and wondering how a single sip of scotch could so seriously impair his judgment, he said, "You don't have to worry about me being good enough. Emily and I are friends. That's all."

As if the night hadn't already been surreal, Gordon Wilson circled his desk to clap a hand on Connor's shoulder. "Who said anything about Emily?" At Connor's surprised glance, Gordon said, "At the chapel I saw the way you were looking at my niece. You never looked at Emily like that. So don't you think it's time for you to go find Kelsey?"

Sitting in her car outside her shop, Kelsey stared at the freshly painted window. Weddings Amour scrolled across the glass in a flowing, curlicued font. The script matched the business cards and letterhead she'd had made—by the thousands, since it was cheaper to buy in bulk.

Kelsey sighed. She should have gone with the rest of her family—and Connor—back to her aunt and uncle's house. But this was Connor's moment. His moment of triumph…of success. And her moment of failure.

Not that Kelsey had expected her cousin to go through with the wedding once she realized Connor was right about Todd. Still, she felt sick with disappointment. She'd worked so hard on the wedding. Her friends had worked so hard! Lisa and Sara… Like her, they had been counting on Emily's wedding, and Kelsey hated letting them down. She dreaded calling them with the news, but that, too, was part of her job. Along with canceling the reservation at the chapel and the hotel reception, phoning all the guests, arranging for gifts to be returned. The mental list went on and on, with Kelsey's hopes and dreams sinking deeper beneath the crushing weight.

But it had to be done, and sitting in her car wouldn't accomplish any of it. Grabbing her purse off the passenger seat, she climbed from the car. As she opened the door to her shop, she tried—and failed miserably—to forget her excitement and gratitude only days earlier as her friends had pitched in to help decorate. The smell of peach potpourri drifted toward her the moment she stepped inside, but it was the memory of Connor's aftershave that filled her senses, playing games with her mind and her heart.

No matter how many unpleasant tasks lay ahead of her, Kelsey would gladly face the professional failure head-on as long as she could turn a blind eye to the personal heartbreak tearing her up inside.

"You should be happy for him," Kelsey whispered as she sank behind her desk and grabbed the box of tissues. She'd placed it there with the idea that a bride might be overcome with emotion and shed some tears of joy. She hadn't anticipated that she'd be sitting alone in her shop, tempted to put her head down and cry.

Connor had done what he'd set out to do. He'd listened to his gut, proved her aunt and uncle wrong, saved the damsel in distress. If life were a Hollywood movie, now would be the time for him to once again ride off into the sunset…this time with Emily.

He said he didn't love her.

But his lack of feeling for Emily wasn't exactly an undying declaration of love for Kelsey. Especially now that Todd was out of the picture and Emily was back in Connor's arms.

She heard the front door swing open and fought back a groan. The sign in the front window still read Closed, but she hadn't remembered to lock the door behind her. She couldn't afford to turn away potential clients, but she'd never felt less like talking about weddings with a head-over-heels-in-love couple.

Pasting on a smile, she pushed away from her desk and walked to the front of the shop. "Can I help…" her voice trailed away as she caught sight of Connor standing in the doorway "*...you?*"

"I hope so." He wore his sunglasses, as he had the first time Kelsey saw him, but the reflective shades didn't offer the protection they once had. She knew now, behind the polished lenses, his eyes were a vivid, vibrant green. Just as she could read the uncertainty behind his cocky smile and the nerves his confident stance—his legs braced wide and arms loose at his sides—couldn't disguise.

Her heart was pounding so hard, Kelsey half expected the shop's glass windows to shake from the force of the vibrations, but only her entire body trembled in reaction. "What are you doing here? I thought you were—"

"With Emily?" he filled in, taking a step farther into the shop.

"She *is* the reason you came back. To stop her from getting married."

"To stop her from getting married to the *wrong* man," he clarified. He took another step forward, and it was all Kelsey could do to hold her ground.

"Are you—" Kelsey licked dry lips and forced the words out, even though they scraped like sandpaper against her throat. "Are you the right man?"

"I like to think so. But not for Emily."

No longer holding her ground, Kelsey was frozen in place as Connor drew closer. His movements slow and deliberate, he stripped off his sunglasses and set them on the wicker coffee table amid the bowl of potpourri and a dozen bridal magazines. Without the glasses, she could see not only his gorgeous green eyes, but the vulnerability and doubt she'd caused with her lack of faith.

"I like to think I'm the right man for you."

Kelsey opened her mouth to agree he was the *only* man for her, but her voice broke on his name and she surprised them both by bursting into tears. Panic crossed Connor's features for a split second before he pulled her into his arms. "It's okay, sweetheart."

Clinging to the warm cotton of his T-shirt and breathing in the sea-breeze scent of his aftershave, Kelsey swallowed against the tears scraping her throat. "I am so sorry, Connor. I should have given you the chance to explain why you took the money. I should have known you would have a good reason, an *honorable* reason."

"I took an easy way out. Don't make it into something it wasn't."

"You were looking out for the Delgados—for your family. I shouldn't have expected anything less."

"And your family was looking out for Emily. I get that now," he said, running a comforting hand up and down her spine. "Besides, I think Gordon and I have an understanding, even if it is going to take a while for your aunt to get used to the idea."

Lifting her head from the comfort of Connor's chest, Kelsey asked, "Wh-what idea?"

"The idea of me and you." His eyes steadily searching her face, he added, "The idea of me loving you."

They were the words Kelsey longed to hear, words she'd thought she would never hear, and she had trouble believing her ears. Surely her imagination had to be playing tricks. Maybe this was nothing but a dream and she'd wake up in her bed—alone—any minute.

"Kelsey?" Connor prompted.

"In my dreams, you're wearing a tuxedo."

Glancing down at his usual jeans and a T-shirt, he swore beneath his breath. "Leave it me to mess this up. Your aunt told me—"

"No, you didn't mess up at all!" Kelsey insisted.

Connor wasn't some fantasy groom who could spout

poetry and had a picture-perfect smile. He wasn't perfect at all. He was real. Loyal and determined, and she loved everything about him—including his bad-boy past. A past that had shaped him into the good man he was now.

"It's perfect and— You talked to my aunt?"

"To your aunt and uncle both. When I asked them for permission to marry you."

Heart pounding crazily in her chest, Kelsey saved wondering about *that* conversation for another time. For now, she could only focus on one thing. "You want to marry me?"

"I love you, Kelsey. I want to spend the rest of my life with you."

"But what about what you said? About love and marriage being nothing but a lie?" she babbled over the voice in her head all but screaming, *Say yes, you idiot!*

"Yeah, well." Looking a little sheepish, he admitted, "I let my parents' relationship color the way I looked at marriage. Of course, my job didn't paint a rosy picture, either. It's one of the things that makes you perfect for me. I'll have you to remind me that sometimes happily-ever-after does come true. That is, if you say yes."

The screaming voice in her head could no longer be silenced, and Kelsey burst out, "Yes, of course. Yes! I love you, Connor. I think I loved you from the minute my aunt showed me your picture and told me it was my job to keep an eye on you. You've been on my mind and in my heart ever since."

The slow smile he gave her was vintage Connor McClane, but the love and tenderness and emotion Kelsey tasted in his kiss…that was brand-new. She clung to his shoulders, never wanting to let him go, and knowing now that she wouldn't have to. He wasn't a man of the moment; he was the man she would love forever.

As Connor slowly eased away, his breath still warming

her lips, his fingers still buried in her hair, he asked, "About your shop… How much damage will Emily canceling the wedding cause?"

It took a second for Kelsey to focus on anything outside the joined circle of their arms. "Well, um, people will understand her calling off the wedding when they find out about Todd. I don't think they'll hold *that* against me. But the chance to show all the guests an amazing wedding and the word-of-mouth publicity the ceremony and reception would have generated, that's a lost opportunity. For me and my friends. I hate disappointing them," she said, a small touch of sadness dimming her joy.

"What if you don't have to?" Connor asked, a familiar gleam in his eyes. The same look he'd had before he suggested they pair up as a team. The kind of look that told Kelsey he was about to offer some crazy solution that just might work.

"What do you mean?"

"I love you, Kelsey. And while I've never thought about it before, I suspect long engagements aren't my style. I want to marry you, and I have it on good authority that the best wedding coordinator in town has the perfect wedding already planned."

"You mean—*Emily's* wedding?" A startled laugh burst from her lips. "You cannot be serious!"

"No?"

"No! I mean, sure, everything's all planned, but it was done for Emily."

"Was it?" he challenged with a knowing lift to his eyebrows. "Was it Emily who insisted on hiring all her friends? Emily who ran around with a hundred lists to make sure every last detail was exactly the way she wanted it?"

How could Kelsey argue when Connor was right? Along the way, the lines had blurred and Kelsey had planned the kind of wedding she'd dreamed about as a starry-eyed, hope-filled little girl, not the kind of wedding she'd dreamed about as a professional career woman.

"Hey, it's just a thought," Connor said. "For all I care, we can go to Vegas or a justice of the peace—"

"Stop!" Kelsey protested in mock horror, even as excitement bubbled inside her like champagne. "A Vegas wedding? If word got out, my career would be over for sure!"

"But what about switching places with the bride? Think your career can withstand that scandal?"

"Well, as long as it's just this once..."

Her words ended in a laugh as Connor spun her around the room. "Oh, I can guarantee we'll only need to do this once," he vowed, love and commitment shining in his eyes.

"You'd really be okay with a big—and I mean, *big*—wedding, with all the Wilson family and friends in attendance?"

Lifting a hand, he traced a pattern on her cheek—the five-point star he'd confessed drove him crazy. But there was only tenderness in his touch as he knowingly said, "They're your friends and family, too."

Kelsey smiled. "You're right. They are." And now that she no longer felt she had to live up to her mother's motto of Wilson women against the world, she knew they would only grow even closer. "And soon they'll be yours, too," she teased with a laugh when Connor groaned. "Are you ready for that and all the happily-ever-after, love-of-a-lifetime, till-death-do-us-part stuff?"

Kelsey could read the answer in Connor's eyes—the promise of a future filled with happily-ever-after.

"With you?" he vowed. "I can't wait."

* * * * *

ACCIDENTAL PRINCESS

BY

NANCY ROBARDS THOMPSON

Nancy Robards Thompson is a sister, wife and mother who has lived the majority of her life south of the Mason-Dixon line. As the oldest sibling, she revelled in her ability to make her brother laugh at inappropriate moments and she soon learned she could get away with it by proclaiming, "What? I wasn't doing anything." It's no wonder that upon graduating from college with a degree in journalism, she discovered that reporting "just the facts" bored her silly. Since hanging up her press pass to write novels full-time, critics have deemed her books "funny, smart and observant." She loves chocolate, champagne, cats and art (though not necessarily in that order). When she's not writing, she enjoys spending time with her family, reading, hiking and doing yoga.

This book is dedicated to Jennifer.
Never forget you're a princess.

Prologue

Once upon a time in the days of old (1975), in a kingdom far, far away (an independent island off the coast of France), there was a very naughty teenage *princesse* who had a penchant for very bad boys. She fell in love with a wild rock star and became pregnant out of wedlock. Before the *princesse* told the rock star of her situation, she entrusted the news to her chambermaid, who promptly informed the queen, who in turn informed the king.

The king was furious because he did not think the rock star suitable for his royal daughter. To avoid a scandal, the king sent the *princesse* away against her will to have the baby in secret. Immediately after the birth, the baby was secreted away. Only the king knew the whereabouts of the child.

Something inside the *princesse* changed after giving birth. Haunted by the baby girl she'd never held, she determined that she would get her baby back. When she was free of her father's imprisonment, she got in touch with her beloved rock star, who had been devastated by her disappearance. During the time without her he, too, had changed his wild ways because he knew that the *princesse* was his one true love. He was overcome with a mixture of joy and sadness when he learned of the baby and how the child was taken from his beloved. He immediately dropped down on one knee and vowed to make the young *princesse* his bride and reunite their small family.

However, on the dark and stormy night when the *princesse* and the rock star set out to start their life together, there was a terrible accident. The plane in which they were flying crashed, and much to everyone's sadness, the *princesse* and the rock star perished in the disaster before they could reclaim their child.

Chapter One

"Is everything in place?" Luc Lejardin rose from his antique desk and paced the length of the wooden floor to the arched office window. Expecting an affirmative, he watched the setting sun cast an impressionistic glow over the Mediterranean Sea, reflecting the colored lights of St. Michel as brightly as the crown jewels.

The American on the other end of the line hesitated a split-second too long. "Not quite. I'm close, though."

Lejardin frowned. Most wouldn't have picked up on the nearly imperceptible uncertainty in the speaker's voice. But Luc had. That was his job. To detect lies, disloyalty, duplicity. A human polygraph, as he liked to think of himself.

He trusted no one. Especially now when, for the sake of national security, everything must go without a hitch. There was no room for error on this mission. Not in the wake of the tragedy.

A tragedy he'd failed to prevent.

"I'm not pleased, *monsieur,*" Lejardin snapped. "We arrive stateside in less than ten hours. I trust you will have completed your job before we board the plane. If there is a problem, I will assign someone more capable."

"There is no problem," the deep voice assured him. "I'll e-mail the last of the photos to you within the hour."

Luc terminated the call and tucked his Blackberry into the breast pocket of his Armani suit. Underneath the fine fabric, his heart felt heavy. He leaned against the wooden window frame and closed his eyes out of respect for the grieving king and those who'd lost their lives.

The tragic fire that killed Prince Antoine and his family had happened under Luc's watch. Not directly, as Prince Antoine had his own team of Royal Service Agents—agents who worked for Lejardin.

Those men had perished in the fire, too.

As minister of protocol, the blood of those who died would forever remain on Luc's hands. It was something for which he would never forgive himself, despite how King Bertrand insisted there was no way Lejardin could've prevented it.

Refusing to believe that someone was responsible for the tragedy that had stolen what remained of his family, the king clung hard and fast to the belief that the House of Founteneau was cursed. Sometimes Lejardin's most challenging job was protecting the king from himself.

Then the curse had struck again.

Ah, but Luc knew better. He was too much of a realist to believe in curses or anything so far beyond his control. A murderer was behind this tragedy—and most certainly the other deaths that had happened one by one over the past thirty-three years. Each carefully orchestrated to look like an accident. Someone had taken enough care so that even the Crown Council and Luc's own father, who had been minister of protocol until the day he died three years ago and Luc stepped up to the post, had ruled each of the tragedies an accident.

With this "accident," every one of King Bertrand's children, every known Founteneau heir to the St. Michel throne was dead—each perishing in separate, but equally tragic, "accidents."

That one family would endure so much loss was almost unfathomable. Whether he had the king and the Crown Council behind him or not, Luc would not rest until the responsible parties paid for the innocent lives they'd taken.

In the meantime, though, he had other pressing business: ensuring the safety of the only remaining heir to the St. Michel throne. An heir who until yesterday nobody except King Bertrand knew existed.

Sophie Baldwin could've lied to herself and claimed the dress in the window of Tina's boutique was what stopped her dead in her tracks on that cold, gray late-November morning.

Right. As if she'd window shop in downtown Trevard, North Carolina, when she was late for work—again. Not to mention freezing due to the arctic temperatures.

No. It wasn't the dress that had stopped her.

As she walked, she'd glanced enticingly at her reflection, expecting to see the slim, attractive, young woman who lived in her mind's eye, but instead what smiled back at her made her stop and bite back a startled oath—

"What the h…?" She moved closer for a better look. But it was no optical illusion. Bundled up in her big, canary-yellow wool coat, she really did resemble a life-sized squeeze bottle of FRENCH'S Classic Yellow Mustard.

It was startling, really, seeing herself like that. As she assessed the grotesque image, she realized it wasn't just the coat that made her look dumpy. Her brown hair was flat and lank, her green eyes were bloodshot and puffy. She looked haggard, worried and miserable. Much too old and tired for thirty-three.

As people flowed by on the sidewalk, she reached out and touched the weary reflection in the glass. Standing palm to cold palm with this alien, she tried to pinpoint when this dramatic shift had happened and why, until now, she hadn't seen it.

Of course she'd been so busy trying to stay afloat since the divorce that she didn't have time for spa day at the Red Door. Not that she went to the spa regularly predivorce. Come to think of it, Trevard didn't even have a Red Door…unless you counted the one at the entrance to Cheap Tilly's Bargain Barn, but that was about as far away from the Red Door as you could get.

Still, spa or no spa, once upon a time, Sophie Baldwin had been quite a catch. And then she'd turned to mustard. Because don't they say that the outside is simply a reflection of what you are on the inside? Obviously she wasn't even the exotic, spicy variety of mustard. Nope. Just plain-old bland water and vinegar with a few generic spices thrown in to make it palatable. Barely.

Sophie sighed. Yeah, once upon a time men noticed her. Really, they did. It didn't seem so long ago, either. She was a different person then—someone who wouldn't have been caught dead in the hideous mustard coat; someone who laid on the floor to zip herself into skin-tight jeans; someone who would've danced the night away in painfully high stilettos.

Because they would've been sexy stilettos.

And men would've noticed.

But that was when she'd been young and in love and sure that Frank was her Prince Charming and their next stop was happily ever after.

She hadn't fathomed that after fifteen years of marriage and one child together Frank would take a detour to the land of pert, perfect eighteen-year-old bodies.

Shallow idiot, that ex-husband of hers. Ditching his family and shirking his responsibilities to date girls who were just a few years older than his fourteen-year-old daughter.

A gust of cold, wet wind cut through the coat, chilling Sophie to the bone. It was snowing. First flakes of the season. Sophie turned up the yellow collar and held it shut with her gloved hand.

Never mind Frank's midlife crisis. What was going through *her* head when she'd sworn off black and its slimming goodness for *brighter, cheerier* clothes she'd fancied were more representative of her *brighter, cheerier* postdivorce life?

As she tore herself away from the mirror image, she nearly bumped into a woman pushing a toddler in a stroller.

"Oh. I'm sorry," she murmured, realizing the baby was crying. *Screaming.* Tears streaming and snot stringing from her tiny red nose.

For a split second Sophie locked gazes with the young mother, who looked to be in her early twenties. What she saw was both complicated and familiar. On the one hand, she was young and beautiful, the picture of Madonna and child (if the Madonna pushed a stroller); on the other hand, she looked frantic in a how-did-I-lose-control-of-my-life sort of way.

Sophie wanted to tell her, Yes, I was you once. Young and beautiful, owned by a fussy baby, too tired to have sex with my husband…and look at me now.

FRENCH'S mustard on two legs.

By that time the woman had moved on.

Sophie turned off Main Street onto Broad Avenue, quickening her steps toward the social services building. As she walked the remaining two blocks to work, she made a mental note to ban from her wardrobe all colors that resembled condiments…well, except for the coat.

She couldn't do anything rash like dumping it at Goodwill. Not unless she wanted to walk to work in her shirtsleeves in the bone-numbing cold.

She couldn't afford to replace it right now. In fact, she couldn't afford much outside her tight budget, which was one of the reasons she'd chosen to walk the mile and a half to work. Every penny counted right now, and if she could save even a tiny bit by walking, that was an easy sacrifice.

It's just that it had turned so cold.

She snuggled deeper into the ugly coat. At least there were no hotdog vendors in the park in the winter. The chances of someone actually mistaking her for a tubby vat of mustard were slim.

She smiled at the pun, and as she passed the diner, she breathed in the tantalizing scent of bacon, toast and coffee. Her stomach reminded her that she'd been too rushed—again—to eat breakfast. Someday when money wasn't such an issue, she was going to treat herself to a nice, leisurely breakfast before work.

But not today.

As she pulled open the big wooden door of the social services building, it dawned on her that this practical person she'd become must signal that she was in a new life phase.

Being a single mother did tend to push one toward practicality. Gone were the whims and flights of fancy. She'd traded them in for grounding and sensibility because that's what it took to give her daughter, Savannah, the best life possible.

That's what kept Sophie from telling Savannah the ugly truth about the divorce. Despite how Savannah blamed her mother, all Sophie would say was that the matter was a grown-up issue. No matter how much Savannah pushed and needled, Sophie refused to expose the child-support-dodging, two-timing louse who could do no wrong in his little girl's eyes.

Maybe someday when Savannah was grown they'd have that conversation, but not now.

Even if he wasn't forthright in supporting his daughter monetarily because he'd spent the better part of the year "between jobs," he did spend time with Savannah, and the girl needed to cling to that rock when he was in town. She had suffered enough during the divorce.

One of the things that surprised Sophie the most about the ordeal was that she thought working as a social worker would've prepared her for divorce. She'd helped numerous women get back on their feet after their marriages dissolved. Still she'd felt just as alone and scared as the best of them.

At least she had a good job and benefits—that was one of the main reasons she'd decided not to pack up and move to Florida with her parents after Frank left.

The elevator *dinged,* and Sophie waited for three people aboard to exit. Once they did, she stepped inside and gave a cursory glance around the lobby to see if there were others rushing to catch the elevator, too. Nope, she was the only one. She glanced at her watch to see just how late she was and her heart quickened: 8:20.

Twenty minutes. Yikes. Her first appointment wasn't until 8:30. Maybe she'd still be able to slide into her office unnoticed.

She jabbed the third-floor button a few times, as if that would shift the ancient machine into express mode. But the doors stayed open, like a big mouth indulging in a long, lazy yawn.

"Come on." She gave the button another impatient tap. This time the doors slid shut. She hated being late, but sometimes she just couldn't help it. Sometimes she was operating on only three or four hours of sleep after working her second job waiting tables at Bob's Steak House. This was one of those mornings, and it had turned into a comedy of errors that began with a scavenger hunt for a homework assignment Savannah swore she'd left on the table the night before. That prompted Sophie to issue the usual "you need to get everything ready the night before" speech. Which, in turn, elicited eye rolls and sullen *harrumphs* from her daughter.

That she was forced to be the "bad cop" rankled her on so many levels. She was the disciplinarian, while Frank got to ride in on a figurative white horse, like Prince Valiant to the rescue. The cool dad who'd moved to California, gotten a tattoo and had his ears pierced, when Sophie had just vetoed her daughter's request for a belly-button ring.

When the elevator finally reached the third floor and the

doors slid open, Sophie's heart lurched at the sight of her boss, Mary Matthews, standing at the front desk talking to Lindsay Bingham, the receptionist and Sophie's best friend.

Mary, wispy, thin and city chic, stopped midsentence and leveled Sophie with a look, before glancing pointedly at her watch.

"Nice of you to join us." She tucked a strand of sleek, black bob behind an ear. "Sleeping in?"

Luc sipped a glass of sparkling water and opened the thick file on the tray table in front of him. He leafed through the stack of photos he'd received a mere forty-five minutes before boarding the plane. Cutting it a little too close for his liking, but at least the investigator had come through.

He paused at a close-up of Sophie Baldwin's face. There was no denying the woman was attractive, with her engaging smile, shoulder-length dark hair and light green eyes. Though, she wasn't exactly what he'd expected. *Très naturelle.*

Naturally she hadn't been groomed for the role that was about to be thrust upon her. So, really, should there be any expectations?

A little voice inside him that knew far too much piped up, *Oh, but everyone will have expectations. Lofty, unfair ideals that no mere mortal should ever be held to. But she will be. Just as has each of those who've come before her.*

He flipped to the next photo of Sophie on the porch of a modest clapboard house. Then to another of her bundled up in a hideous bright yellow coat, with a large purse slung over her shoulder and a satchel in hand as she walked along a quaint downtown sidewalk; then to yet another shot of her in a market—or grocery store as they called it in the States—

reaching for something on a shelf. In this photo, she wasn't wearing the coat. Her clothes were neat but ordinary, except for how they clung to her voluptuous body, making her curves look rather sexy—

Luc dropped the thought like hot coal. He closed the thick case file with a sharp flick of his wrist, irritated with himself for letting his thoughts stray.

Closing his eyes, he rubbed his throbbing temples.

It was fatigue talking. Yes, that was the reason. He'd barely slept since the accident.

How long had it been now? He'd lost count in the midst of the madness, but it had to have been more than seventy-two hours.

Seventy-two of the worst *damn* hours of his life.

Just three short days ago everything had been normal. Then the world upended and in the blink of an eye everyone in St. Michel was plunged into the nightmare of yet another royal death. The most recent in a long tragic line that began with the loss of Princess Sylvie, who died in 1975 in a plane crash; then Princess Celine lost her life in a car accident eight years later; next Prince Thibault drowned in a 1994 diving disaster; now Prince Antoine and his entire family…wiped out in one fatal blow.

Luc drew in a sharp breath, trying to work through the pain that was as real as if a strong hand twisted his gut.

He hadn't even had a chance to say goodbye.

Antoine was more than the youngest son of his employer. The prince had also been Luc's friend and confidant.

Growing up in the St. Michel palace, he'd played with Antoine as a kid; they'd gone to school together as adolescents and caused their share of heartache with the ladies while away at university. Luc had been with Antoine the night he met Leanna, and stood up with them when they took their marriage vows.

This loss went deeper than anyone could ever understand. Especially since his gut screamed that this—like the other senseless deaths—was no accident.

Luc closed his eyes against the pain—against the fury. The realization came over him in waves that in the midst of the chaos he hadn't had a chance to slow down long enough to grieve the loss of his friend.

The plane dipped through a patch of turbulence. The jolt yanked him back to the present, a safe distance from his despair. Glancing around the cabin at the five dark-suited security agents who'd accompanied him on the mission—each sleeping or reading or otherwise occupied—Luc steeled his resolve and reminded himself of his duty.

He was the minister of protocol.

He set the tone for the mission.

Despite how this loss, this assault on his king and country—on his *best friend*—devastated him, there was no time to let emotion cloud his judgment.

A corner of one of the Sophie Baldwin photos had worked itself out of the folder, as if challenging him to take another look. Luc drew it out and analyzed it with professional eyes.

She looked like a nice woman.

Too bad she'd be dragged into the midst of this mess.

He tucked the photo back into the folder, straightened it so that the contents were aligned and glanced at his watch.

The plane would land stateside in approximately one hour. He and his team would hit the ground running. Luc wanted to be *damn* sure that everyone involved understood the importance of their roles.

Especially Sophie Baldwin.

Mary Matthews drummed her French-manicured nails on the reception desk. Her hardened gaze meandered the length of Sophie's yellow coat.

Under the scrutiny, Sophie shifted her briefcase from one hand to the other. Her mind raced to find a plausible excuse for her tardiness, but she came up at a loss for anything but the truth.

"I'm sorry. I worked at the restaurant last night, and Savannah and I got off to a rough start this morning."

Mary's lip curled.

"Right. Rough starts seem to be part of your morning routine. They happen so frequently."

Sophie took a deep breath, tempted to list all the times that she'd worked late.

"It's just that—"

"Clock in and meet me in my office. Five minutes."

Mary had been Sophie's boss less than a year, joining the Trevard Social Services team just after Sophie filed for divorce. Needless to say Sophie hadn't been herself since she'd met Mary, despite every effort to put her best foot forward. She tried. God knows she tried, but sometimes on mornings like this it seemed next to impossible to get out of her own way, much less get an eighth-grader out the door and to the bus stop on time. Even so, Sophie had a feeling even if everything in her life had been perfect, she and Mary Matthews wouldn't have mixed.

Even though Mary had been a punctuality stickler when she first arrived, she seemed to have lightened up on clock watching over the past few months. Or so Sophie thought.

As she got to her cubicle and stashed her purse in the bottom desk drawer, she wracked her brain, trying to guestimate how many times she'd been tardy lately. Of course all Mary would have to do is pull the time sheets to see when Sophie had punched in.

When Sophie got to Mary's office, she discovered that was exactly what she'd done. The woman nudged a piece of paper with a neat row of dates and numbers running the length of the page.

September 3—fifteen minutes late.

September 5—twenty-five minutes late.

September 10—seventeen minutes late.

And so on…each infraction highlighted in bold fluorescent yellow.

Sophie's cheeks burned. For God's sake, the woman hadn't just printed out a report; she combed through the past year and tallied up each infraction.

How much time had *that* project taken?

"I've warned you, Sophie." Mary sat sunken cheeked and ramrod straight in her chair, her hands folded neatly on the spotless desk blotter. "Time and time again, I've warned you, but you're not taking me seriously, are you?"

"I—"

A simple flutter of Mary's hand silenced Sophie.

"Since you've chosen to ignore me, you leave me no choice but to write you up."

The words slapped Sophie speechless. It was as if her voice had been encapsulated in a soundproof bubble that was lodged in her throat…

Then the bubble popped.

"Mary, I'm sorry if it seems that I've blatantly disregarded your wishes. That certainly wasn't my intention. But I'm sure if you poll my clients and look at my caseload, you'll see my work hasn't suffered even if on occasion I don't punch the clock at eight on the dot. I mean, come on, when I'm late I stay after to make up the time."

Mary's stonewall expression remained impervious.

"Office hours are from 8:00 a.m. until 5:00 p.m. Those are the hours of operation. If I make an exception for you, I have to make exceptions for everyone else. In fact just the other day one of your coworkers asked if she could telecommute for a portion of the day." Mary rolled her eyes. "Of course I had to say no. It would be unfair to refuse her request and then turn around and tolerate your habitual tardiness."

Once again Sophie was speechless, exasperated by her boss's twisted logic.

The rasp of Mary opening her center drawer broke the silence. She pulled out yet another piece of paper and a black pen and slid them across the desk toward Sophie.

"If you'll sign this document acknowledging that I counseled you, we can both get to work."

Sophie stared at the paper as if it would scald her if she touched it. If she didn't, maybe it would self-destruct.

Fat chance.

Then as if someone turned up the heat on the resentment that had been simmering inside her, anger flared. She'd had it up to her eyebrows with documents that demanded her signature. Since the divorce she'd signed so many papers against her will she'd lost count. People telling her what to do, when to do it. That she deserved *nothing* from a divorce she didn't even want. When actually what she wanted was quite simple: She wanted to wake up from this nightmare. She wanted to sit up in her bed, foggy with sleep, breathing a sigh of relief that Frank was beside her. The divorce had all been a bad dream. Her husband wasn't a cheat—he valued their marriage and family as much as she did.

It was a nightmare all right. Only it wasn't anything she could escape.

She looked up at Mary, mustering her best poker face. "And what if I don't sign?"

Mary blinked, sucked in a deep breath as if she was taking a long drink of patience.

"Then I will be forced to note that you…that you *refused.*"

Feeling a little dizzy from flirting with defiance, Sophie glanced around Mary's office trying to get her bearings. Her boss had no personal photos in her office. In fact the only things that remotely warmed up the cold, white institutional space were a couple of cheap-looking floral prints slapped on the sterile walls. How could she expect a woman like Mary Matthews to understand? It suddenly washed over Sophie that no matter how bad life seemed right now, at least she *had* a life. She had photos on her desk of a teenage girl who sometimes needed her in the morning and, yes, sometimes caused her to be late and if that was such a crime, well—

Mary's intercom buzzed. "Excuse me, Ms. Matthews?" Lindsay's voice sounded through the speaker. "I'm sorry to bother you, but Sophie has two clients out here waiting to see her. Mr. Carlo, her *first* appointment and um, Laura Hastings, who doesn't have an appointment but says it's important."

Sophie felt vindicated by the way Lindsay had emphasized *first* appointment. She'd obviously made it to work in plenty of time for her clients—and even had a few extra minutes to debate the finer points of punctuality with Mary.

She forced a smile that didn't make it to her eyes. "Well, I'd love to sit and chat all day, but I need to get to work. My 8:30's here."

Sophie stood to go.

"The document," Mary said. "Sign it before you go."

Sophie snatched the paper off the desk and returned Mary's stone-cold gaze. "I never sign anything until I read it."

"Fine. Take it with you, but I expect it on my desk by the end of the day."

As she walked out of Mary's office, Sophie resisted the urge to crumple the unsigned form into a ball. Instead she took a deep breath and did her best to cope with the adrenaline rush, pumped by the argument with Mary.

There was no time for stewing. She had back-to-back client meetings with Laura Hastings added to the mix. She was already behind. She'd get to Mary's form when she could. It might even be this weekend.

As she rounded the corner into the crowded waiting room, Laura stood to greet her. An ambivalent smile pulled at the corners of her lips, but didn't quite reach her sad eyes. The fragile-looking redhead was one of Sophie's favorite clients and proudest success story. This single mother of four had fled an abusive marriage, and with Sophie's help, she'd managed to cross the rickety bridge from welfare checks to being gainfully employed and enrolled at the community college part-time, working toward a nursing degree.

It was a full load, but Laura was the poster child of why Sophie loved her job. Helping people better themselves was the reason she went into social work in the first place. *To make a difference in the world.*

"Laura, good morning." She gave the woman a quick hug. "How are the kids?"

Laura cleared her throat. "Well, that's what I wanted to talk to you about—"

"Excuse me, I have an 8:30 appointment and it's already 8:35." A short, round man who resembled Danny DeVito sidled up to them. "I'm going to be late for work. Can we get this show on the road?"

Sophie looked from Mr. Carlo to Laura, who ducked her head and cleared her throat again.

"Of course," she whispered apologetically, taking a step backward as if retreating into her shell. "I'm sorry. Go right ahead."

"Can you wait?" Sophie asked Laura.

She nodded.

"Sophie there's a call for you on line one," Lindsay said. "Do you want to take it or should I put it through to your voice mail?"

Mr. Carlo threw up his hands. "What's the point of an appointment if everyone else waltzes right in ahead of you?"

At that moment, Mary rounded the corner with her purse on her arm. "Is there a problem?"

Voice mail, please, Sophie mouthed to Lindsay, who in turn mouthed, *Sorry.*

"Yes," said Mr. Carlo, his voice raising several decibels. "I booked an appointment for 8:30 this morning so I'd get right in. Now it's nearly quarter till. I'm going to be late for work because you guys can't get your act together."

Mary arched a brow and shot Sophie a knowing look.

Oh, for God's sake.

"Sophie, take care of the gentleman. Lindsay, I have an appointment at the county building. I'll be out for a couple of hours."

With that, she left.

Yeah, thanks for the help, Mary.

"Mr. Carlo, please have a seat in my office—first door on the left. I'll be right there."

The man didn't budge. "Oh, no, no, no. If I go in there and leave you two out here, you'll yak about the kids all day long. I'll wait right here and walk back with you."

He crossed his arms over his barrel chest and drummed his fingers on his beefy arm.

"I'll…I'll…I can come back," Laura stuttered, edging toward the door. Something was wrong. She only stuttered when she was upset, and Sophie had a feeling she wasn't simply flustered by Mr. Carlo's blustering.

"I won't be long, Laura. Please wait."

But the woman waved her off with an unsteady hand and slipped out the door.

Chapter Two

Sophie's office phone rang as she swallowed the last bite of tuna sandwich. Before the divorce, she used to treat herself to lunch out on Fridays. Sometimes with Lindsay, sometimes by herself. It was always something she looked forward to.

Someday she'd enjoy that indulgence again, she reminded herself as she tossed a piece of used plastic wrap into the trash and answered the call.

"This is Sophie Baldwin."

"Hmm…Mom?"

She glanced at her watch—12:30. The school day wasn't over yet.

"Hi, honey. What's wrong?"

Sophie's mind raced to what she'd say to Mary if she had to leave to pick up a sick child after being late today.

"Oh. My. God. Mom, you need to come home. Right now."

Sophie's heart quickened at the sound of Savannah's panic-laced voice.

"Home? Are you at home?"

Savannah hesitated for a moment.

"Grandma and Grandpa are here. Did you know they were coming? And that they were bringing six creepy men with them?"

"What? Grandma and Grandpa are here? In town? What's going on? Where are you?"

"I said I'm at home, and I have no idea what's going on. That's why I'm calling *you.*"

Ah, there it was—the sarcasm that seemed to penetrate every conversation with her daughter these days.

"Did Grandma and Grandpa pick you up from school?"

Silence.

"Savannah, are you there?"

"Yeah."

"Put your grandmother on the phone."

"Well…*hmm*…I can't."

Oh, for heaven's sake. "Why not?"

Another stretch of silence. Sophie wondered if this might be another of Savannah's cries for attention. She'd been pulling stunts since her father left. Nothing horrendously bad, just pushing Sophie's buttons with out-of-character antics such as cutting class and befriending a goth girl—er—*emo* girl, as Savannah had pointedly corrected her. Because goth was so five minutes ago.

Whatever happened to Elmo—the little, lovable, red, fuzzy monster on *Sesame Street* Savannah used to love so much not *that many* years ago?

These emo kids were a far cry from Elmo—they were dark

and scary. Or as Savannah explained, emos were all about *emotion.* That's why Emo Jess had tattooed her boyfriend's name, Tick, across her neck in bold, three-inch letters.

"Savannah, put your grandmother on the phone right now."

The girl sighed—as if all the problems in the world rested on her shoulders. "Grandma asked me not to call you. She said we could talk about this—whatever *this* is—after you got home from work. But something's going on and it's really creeping me out. Will you *please* come home?"

All the fight and sarcasm had left her daughter's voice. She sounded like the sweet predivorce kid Sophie so desperately missed. If her daughter *wanted* her there—

"Okay, sweetie, I'm on my way."

When Sophie got home, the first thought that crossed her mind was the man who met her at the door—the one with the French accent who'd introduced himself as Luc Le-something-or-the-other and maintained eye contact even as he *bowed*—yes, he actually bowed—was the spitting image of the actor Olivier Martinez.

His disarmingly handsome face had the same chiseled cheeks, intense dark eyes that crinkled at the corners when he smiled and a similar aquiline nose above the most gorgeous full lips.

The resemblance was uncanny, and it knocked her for a loop.

For about two seconds.

"What the heck is going on, Mr. Le…?" she demanded. "Why are you in my house?"

Several possibilities crossed her mind: This guy was a repo man concerned about her ex-husband's bad debts or a flimflam man who was trying to take advantage of her elderly parents.

"Luc Lejardin," he repeated, his accent as smooth as butter. "I am here with your parents to discuss with you a matter of great importance."

Knowing her parents, it was more likely to be an Amway sales pitch than a home invasion. Still, a single mother couldn't be too careful.

Sophie clutched the cell phone in her coat pocket. The situation didn't seem dangerous, but if anything changed, all she had to do was call 911. Her index finger traced the numbers as she pushed past Olivier—er Luc, or whatever his name was—through the foyer and into the living room.

There were five more men in there dressed in somber dark suits, looking like they'd stepped out of a scene from *Men in Black.* And there were her parents, Rose and John Jones, perched sheepishly on the edge of the chintz sofa, looking not the least bit frightened, but definitely a tad surprised to see her.

"Sophie, *ma chérie.*" Her mother stood, and her father, a man of few words, followed stiffly. "Are you home for lunch?"

Sophie narrowed her eyes.

"No, I was eating my lunch when Savannah called to tell me you and your…*friends* had dropped by. *All the way from Florida, no less.*"

Her mother shook her head and scowled. "I told her not to bother you at work." Her French accent was more pronounced than usual. That always happened when she was flustered. "This really could have waited until you got home." She hugged Sophie and gave her a quick kiss on each cheek.

"By the way, why was Savannah home from school today?" Rose wagged her finger. "If she was sick, she shouldn't have friends over. She especially shouldn't be alone in the house with a boy."

What?

"Savannah didn't stay home sick today." Sophie narrowed her eyes at her mother. "You and Dad didn't pick her up from school on your way in?"

They did that sometimes.

But her parents shook their heads.

The slow burn simmered in her belly and she felt like maybe she'd caught *someone* trying to pull a fast one.

"Where is Savannah?" she asked.

"In her room."

She'd deal with her daughter later. "Good. While she's in there, you can tell me what's going on."

A deer-in-headlights expression swept over Rose's face. "Well, *ma chérie,* it's a long, complicated story."

Rose lowered herself onto the couch. John did the same. Her parents looked at each other as if deciding who would speak first.

"I don't even know where to begin." Rose shot Luc a pleading look.

"Madame, allow me." Luc turned to Sophie. "I'm sure you have heard of the unfortunate tragedy that has befallen the nation of St. Michel?"

What? What does this have to do with the situation? Sophie nodded guardedly. Who didn't know about it? The accident had commanded the headlines for the past three days. Her mother was a huge fan of the St. Michel royal family and had called, in tears, the moment she'd heard about it. For as far back as Sophie could remember, Rose had kept a scrapbook on the House of Founteneau. But that wasn't the reason the tragedy had touched Sophie so deeply.

It was kind of silly…but she felt bad for the king of St. Michel. It was crazy and almost a little celebrity obsessive, and she wasn't infatuated with the St. Michel royals—she just knew about them by virtue of her mother's fixation. Still, that a father should outlive all his children was more than any parent should bear. Savannah was her life. She couldn't bear to think of losing her.

Sophie whispered a silent prayer for the king—one parent to another.

"Because of the sad turn of events, I have come to seek your assistance," said Luc

Assistance?

Virtual warning lights flashed in Sophie's head. *Wait a minute, buster.* She glanced at her parents for some indication of what this was about, but neither would make eye contact.

"How on earth could I help you with anything having to do with St. Michel?"

"It's a very complicated story," Luc said. "But you are the only one who can help King Bertrand. Would you care to sit down while I explain?" He looked her square in the eyes and flashed that smile of his—a smile that could probably talk the pants off any woman…or talk all the money right out of someone's bank account. But Luc Lejardin had no idea whom he was dealing with. She was on to him and his rat scheme.

Weren't tricks like this mostly confined to e-mails where the scammer, safely cloaked in the anonymity of cyberspace, *humbly begs your pardon, but has chosen you out of all the people in the world to help transfer millions of dollars out of a fictitious Ivory Coast bank?*

"So con artists are making house calls?" she said.

Luc looked confused. *Oh,* he was cute *and* he was a good actor. The guy had skills. Yeah, and using the Founteneau tragedy to scam others—and her mother would be the perfect target—was lower than low.

"Get out now. All of you." Sophie pointed toward the door. "Or I'll call the police."

"Oh, Sophie, no," said Rose.

"I don't mean you, Mom. You and Dad stay right there. I want *them* out. Now."

She pulled out her cell phone and started punching in 911.

"No, don't. Please." Luc held up his hands in surrender. "I know this sounds incredible, but please hear me out. Please allow me to explain."

"Sophie, hear him out," her father demanded.

Dear God, did Luc have her father snowed, too? Still, there was something in her dad's expression that preempted Sophie from completing the call.

For one very short moment.

Holding her finger over the dial button, she said, "Mr. Lejardin, you have exactly ten seconds to explain. Starting now."

He nodded.

"Your Highness, forgive me for speaking so plainly, but you are the granddaughter of King Bertrand. He requests that you come to St. Michel so that he might talk to you about assuming your rightful place as heiress to the throne of St. Michel."

Your Highness? For a moment, Sophie's knees threatened to buckle, but then a wave of anger so strong she thought she'd breathed fire coursed through her. To keep from screaming at the ridiculous man, she controlled her voice, letting the rage bleed through loud and clear.

"What kind of fool do you take me for? What do you want? Money? Well, I don't have any. Neither do my parents. And you'd better stay the hell away from my daughter because if you lay one finger on her, I will rip you apart with my bare hands—"

All of a sudden her father's arms were around her. "*Mon Dieu,* my love," he soothed. "*Shh.* Don't talk like that."

Only then did Sophie realize that she'd been shouting.

"Listen to me," John pleaded, looking down at her as tears misted his eyes. "Come. Sit. Listen to what we have to say."

Sophie looked from him to her mother trying to make sense out of the absurd assertions.

"It's true," Rose said, bowing her head. "Monsieur Lejardin speaks the truth."

Sophie glanced back at Luc, hoping beyond hope that he wouldn't be there. If he disappeared, that would mean this was one of those bizarre dreams where you wake up and laugh about how ridiculous it was—*Ha ha! Imagine that. Me, the princess of St. Michel. What a hoot.*

But Luc Lejardin was there. Handsome as ever. Standing in her living room, gazing at her with those eyes and looking way too polished and sophisticated amidst her shabby chic furnishings.

She allowed her father to lead her to the couch.

As she settled between her parents, Luc motioned for his men to leave the room.

"Mom? What's going on?" Savannah's voice cut through the surreal haze. The girl stood in the hall that led to the bedrooms. Emo Jess's tattooed boyfriend was with her, looking pale and dangerous with his spiky black hair and pierced bottom lip.

Sophie didn't quite know how to answer her daughter's question. She certainly didn't want to get into it in front of Flea—or Tick—she couldn't remember his name without the benefit of reading the tattoo on Jess's neck.

In fact, as motherly concern vied with the confusion over the royal revelation, she wanted to ask her daughter the same question.

What is *going on, Savannah? Why is that boy here?*

But she couldn't form the words. Even so, she could do the math in her head: Emo Jess was absent. Her daughter looked rumpled and pink-cheeked and totally wrong with Emo Jess's boyfriend's arm slung casually around her shoulder, his limp hand dangling dangerously close to her daughter's right breast.

That's what her mother meant about having a boy over.... Had they skipped school and been here alone in this house all morning?

Oh, dear God.

Had the whole world turned inside out? Because everything seemed to be upside down today and sliding toward a big black hole that used to be the center of their lives.

Somehow, miraculously, Sophie found her voice.

"We're having a family meeting, Savannah. Your friend needs to leave."

The boy didn't say a word, but he remained, looking scuzzy in his low-slung, skinny jeans and ripped black T-shirt.

Expressionless. And still *touching* her daughter.

Savannah reached up and took his hand. "Tick doesn't

want to leave. If this has something to do with me, he can stay. We have no secrets from each other."

Rose gasped.

"No, he needs to leave," Sophie insisted.

The boy still didn't budge.

At a loss, Sophie glanced from her daughter to her parents, to Luc, whose piercing dark gaze snared and held hers.

The next thing she knew, Luc was hulking over the kid. Then, without touching him, he was showing Tick the door.

"Oh my *Gaaaawd,*" Savannah whined. "I cannot believe he just did that. How could you let him do that to me, Mom?"

It was all too much.

Too. Much.

All crashing down on her at once.

"Go to your room. We'll talk about this later."

Savannah stomped off.

A door slammed.

Sophie bristled.

"Are you going to let her get away with talking to you like that?" Rose asked.

Sophie turned to her mother. "I don't let her *get away with* anything. However, right now, I think I have another situation I need to deal with first."

Her mother seemed to shrink back in her seat.

Luc was in her line of vision, wearing an expression that ranged somewhere between disbelief and disgust. She wanted to say, "Well, Mr. Armani Suit, you've obviously never lived with a teenager. Try it sometime, then we'll talk."

She could feel her left eyelid twitch as she forced a smile. "So, where were we?"

The four of them sat in silence until finally her mother

cleared her throat and spoke. "Many years ago your father and I worked for King Bertrand of St. Michel. In order to avoid a scandal that would have potentially destroyed the House of Founteneau, he sent his daughter into top-secret confinement before anyone even knew the girl was pregnant. Then when the child was born, he secretly adopted her out. Princesse Sylvie was only seventeen years old, after all. She thought she was madly in love with that rock star Nick Morrison. You've probably heard of him. The king would have no part of it and did what he thought was best for his daughter and his country."

Sophie shuddered inwardly as she thought of Savannah coming to the same pregnant fate after spending the day alone with that boy.

"Don't you understand where this is leading?" Rose beseeched.

Sophie blinked at her mother. Feeling as if she'd missed something, she shook her head. "Oh, this just keeps getting better and better. I can't imagine where it's going."

Rose silenced her with a wave.

Sophie shrugged and traced the floral pattern on the sofa cushion with her finger.

"Sweetheart, *we* were the couple who adopted the *princesse's* baby. We named her Sophie and raised her and loved her as our own. *You* were that baby."

As her mother's words became clear, the edges of Sophie's vision closed in. She heard her father's voice now, as if it were streaming through a long tunnel.

"We never told you because we pledged secrecy to the king," he said, as if that were supposed to make everything all right. "We were his humble servants. We were honored he would entrust his granddaughter to us and felt duty-bound to keep our word."

Sophie stood up fast—too fast—and Luc caught her by the elbow as she wavered. His touch was sure and strong, and she was positive he could see right through her to her shaky, scared inner child. A child who'd been suddenly stripped of the only life she'd ever known, orphaned by the revelation of a well-guarded secret.

"Excuse me." She pulled away and walked over to the window, needing space, needing to see something familiar to help her make sense of this bombshell.

The first things she saw were the three *Men in Black* sitting on her porch in the freezing cold…which reinforced the fact that her parents weren't her parents. She was the daughter of a dead princess and a rock legend whose CDs were in her collection.

It was incomprehensible. Totally and completely absurd. Like some sort of bad joke—

Wait a minute.

She whirled around. "This is a *joke,* right? Like *Candid Camera* or *Punked?* Well, if it is, it's not funny. In fact, it's really pathetic given what's happened in St. Michel."

Nobody said a word. They didn't have to. Their grave faces told her everything she needed to know.

"Oh, my good God." Her voice trembled and seemed to come from somewhere outside her body. "I have to get out of here."

It was Luc's job to stay one step ahead of the situation. He was good at reading people and circumstances. As Sophie grabbed her purse and keys, Luc anticipated her next move and headed her off at the front door.

"Get out of my way." Her green eyes blazed and threatened that she might hit him if he didn't move. It wouldn't be the first time a woman's hand had smarted his face.

"*Pardonnez-moi,* Your Highness, but I cannot allow you to go out unattended."

Her pale cheeks flushed, and she stubbornly tilted her chin. "You've got to be kidding me. You can't hold me prisoner in my own house."

Strange, though, he hadn't expected the protective empathy he'd feel for her. Usually, he had no problem compartmentalizing his feelings—a must for someone in his position—so that he could keep a clear head and get a proper read on situations as they presented themselves.

For some reason, perhaps because of Antoine, this case felt different. Hit a tad too close to home.

"Your Highness—"

"Stop calling me that."

"Very well then, *Madame,* given what just happened to the prince—your uncle," Luc bowed his head out of respect, "I cannot allow you to leave alone."

"It's Sophie."

"I beg your pardon, *Madame?*"

"Stop with the *Your Highness* and *Madame.* My name is Sophie, and I'd appreciate it if you stick to that."

The photos didn't do her justice. Her eyes were nearly the shade of emeralds. Paired with her dark hair they really made a striking contrast.

"If you insist, *Sophie.*" It felt improper—too intimate—to call her by her given name. "I have no intention of holding you prisoner. If you would like to leave, there is a car outside and I would be happy to escort you anywhere you would care to go."

"So you're saying if I walk out of this house, you'll follow me?"

Luc nodded.

Following her would not be so unpalatable.

He blinked away the inappropriate thought and focused on the reality of the situation: As a servant of the royal family he couldn't *force* her to do anything against her will. He could only make strong suggestions and, if all else failed, he'd resort to charm.

Whatever it took. Because he had less than twenty-four hours to convince her to come back to St. Michel, or they'd be forced to switch to Plan B, which involved King Bertrand coming to Trevard to close the deal himself.

Luc really didn't want it to come to that.

"What if I call the police?" Sophie threatened.

"I cannot stop you from doing so, but I ask you to consider the consequences. If you involve the authorities, the media will most likely get wind of this. Once the story breaks, the security threat for you and your family will increase one hundredfold. You won't even be able to get out of your front door because media from all over the world will be camping on your lawn."

Sophie's eyes widened, looking pure and green and innocent. Clearly she hadn't considered this possibility.

"If you won't think of your own safety," Rose called from the living room, "consider Savannah's."

"I'm not talking to you and Dad right now," Sophie answered back, then immediately squeezed her eyes shut as if she regretted her words.

Neither Rose nor John responded. Gauging Sophie's expression, Luc couldn't tell if that made things better or worse.

She sighed.

"Come on," she said, her voice a hissed whisper. "You and I are going somewhere private where we can talk. I want the whole story and I want you to give it to me straight."

After Luc instructed his men to keep close watch on the place, Sophie softened her tone and asked her parents to tell Savannah she'd be back before bedtime.

Two minutes later, she and Luc were in the back of his rented Lincoln Town Car, heading toward the highway.

"Where would you like to go?" the driver asked.

She shrugged. "Just drive for a while. I need to get away from here so I can think."

They rode in silence for about forty-five minutes. Sophie sat next to Luc staring out of the passenger window. Luc could see her profile in three-quarter view.

She looked like Princesse Sylvie, he thought. The spitting image of her, or what he imagined she would've looked like had she lived. Those who died young were forever immortalized in perpetual youth. Never aging, the patina of youth growing more beautiful with each passing year.

"Has anyone ever told you how much you look like your mother?"

"Which one?" she asked, with a sardonic quirk of her brow.

"Princesse Sylvie, of course."

Sophie laughed, though there wasn't much humor in the dry sound. "The funny thing is people used to tell me all the time how much Rose and I looked alike.... I never saw it. Now I know why."

"It is a bit unnerving how much you resembled the late *princesse*. A tad—" Luc searched for the right word "—*stupéfiant*."

"Stupefying, huh?" The right side of her mouth twitched, but the humor gave way to a softer expression. "What was she like?"

Now they were getting somewhere.

"She had quite a zest for life. *La joie* is how we call it. That love of life seemed to radiate from her every pore. She gave your grandfather quite a challenge, though. The press loved to photograph her—dancing the nights away in Paris and sunbathing on the deck of some baron's yacht on the Côte d'Azur. Always with that devil-may-care gleam in her eyes. You have her eyes, you know? Many thought of her as the ideal woman. Yet, those who knew her best said she was a very kind person."

Sophie didn't look impressed.

"Did you have crush on Princesse Sylvie, Monsieur Lejardin?"

He flinched. "I beg your pardon?"

Sophie laughed. "A *crush,* you know, to be intrigued with, to have the hots for. A crush."

She was toying with him. Even so, it was good to see her lighten up a bit.

"I have always held the late *princesse* in the highest esteem."

"Well, I would expect nothing less from you," she conceded as they approached a quaint restaurant fashioned to look like a log cabin. "Stop here, please. I need some coffee."

Luc assessed the place as the driver steered the car off the road into the gravel driveway. It looked harmless enough, out here in the middle of nowhere. Two cars dotted the parking lot. Not busy. If they had to stop, this was probably as good a place as any.

When they walked in, he was relieved to see that indeed the place was nearly empty, except for a flannel-clad couple sitting on red and silver swivel stools at the Formica counter, having pie and coffee.

He'd never seen anything like this place. It was a regular Norman Rockwell depiction of middle America. Like a quaint foreign country he was visiting for the first time.

"Y'all grab a seat anywhere ya like," the waitress drawled from behind the counter.

They settled into a back-corner booth.

He picked up a menu—mostly out of curiosity, to see what type of food one found in a place like this. Standard American fare: burgers, French fries, milk shakes. Some of the items he wasn't familiar with: grits? hash browns? red-eye gravy?

After the waitress served the coffee—if you could call the thin, caramel-colored water she poured into the cups coffee—Sophie asked wearily, "So, what happens next?"

Luc stirred a packet of sugar into the hot liquid.

"I would like to take you and your daughter back to St. Michel to meet King Bertrand."

She looked at him as if he'd suggested she re-create Sylvie's nude sunbathing escapades.

Again, he found himself blinking away the image of her lounging, cat-like on the bow of an expensive cigarette boat.

"I don't think so," she said.

"Why not?" he asked. "Aren't you at all curious about your country?"

"You just don't get it, do you?"

He shrugged.

"I suppose not. Would you care to explain?"

She put her palms flat on the table and leaned toward him.

"I have two jobs. Savannah has school. We can't just drop everything because King Grandpa beckons."

King Grandpa? For some reason, the phrase struck him as funny and he had to purse his lips to keep from smiling because this was not a time to make light.

Except that the more he talked to Sophie, the more she proved to be like her mother. Strong-willed, irreverent… smart, funny.

He dragged a hand over his jaw in an effort to control the deluge of awareness that coursed through him. An awareness the likes of which he hadn't felt in a very long time.

Why her? Well, that was easy enough to answer. She was *magnifique.* But why did she have to be the king's granddaughter?

That made the situation hopeless.

His family name had nearly come to ruin because of indiscretion and it had taken all he and his two brothers had to rebuild it. He would not lose everything they had worked so hard to reconstruct by developing a schoolboy crush on the king's granddaughter.

He took a long, slow sip of coffee and mentally packaged up the remnants of those thoughts, tucking them away where they would be a nonissue.

He shrugged. "If you refuse to go, King Bertrand will simply come to you."

She looked exasperated.

"I'm not ready to talk to him. He has to understand that this has all come out of left field. I haven't had a chance to digest it yet."

Luc sipped his coffee again, buying himself time. It wasn't his place to offer advice to Sophie. However, it was his job to ensure she would listen and ultimately agree to what the king proposed.

"If I may be so bold as to offer you something to consider." He returned his cup to the saucer. "As Princesse Sylvie's illegitimate daughter, you would've lived a life wracked with scandal. You would've paid for your mother's mistake."

Her jaw dropped and her right brow arched.

"So that's all I am to the king? A mistake?"

"Don't twist my words. Even though it might not appear so on the surface, the king did the right thing by sending you away. He gave you a better life."

She grimaced. "Right. While Gramps lived the high life in his ivory tower, I've been working two jobs to put food on the table for my daughter. Yeah, that's a much better life than he's lived, I'm sure."

"You've only struggled since your divorce last year."

She set her cup down hard and coffee sloshed over the rim. "How do you know this? It freaks me out more than just a little that you know so much about me. Especially given that until a few hours ago I had no idea you even existed. You know about my divorce; how to contact my parents; where I live; where I work, I'm sure. Is that right? Do you know that?"

He wanted to tell her that he even knew what kind of underwear she'd recently purchased—the value five-pack of white Hanes cotton briefs, and that he thought she deserved more than that—but thought better of it. "It's my job to know these things."

She curled her lip. "Do you have any idea how sickening it feels to know that your life is an open book that everyone but you has read?"

Luc considered this for a moment. Yes, he did. If not the world, at least all of St. Michel. He knew how it felt to watch the intimate details that ruined his father play out in a very public arena. He'd watched his stepmother's improprieties take such a toll on his father that they eventually took his life.

At least Sophie's divorce had been private. However, that did not diminish the hurt she obviously suffered at the indiscretions of her ex-husband.

And what kind of a moron would let this woman go?

The empathy that had clouded his judgment threatened again, and he knew he'd better steer back to solid ground.

"You have been struggling since your divorce. That's a very real concern, but financial woes can be a thing of the past if you take your rightful place as the heiress to the throne of St. Michel. You'll never have to worry about money again."

Sophie bristled.

"I don't want the king's money. I'm simply making a point that my grandfather didn't do me any favors by shipping me off. Let's not pretend it was a noble deed."

Luc stifled a sigh. Yes, she absolutely had the tenacity of the late *princesse*. And it was just that dogged stubbornness that would make her a good candidate to succeed her grandfather.

"It was a difficult decision for your grandfather to make. It wasn't easy for John and Rose to keep the secret all these years, but they did so not only out of duty, but also out of compassion. They did it out of love for you. Couldn't you at least hear what the king has to say?"

"Excuse me? I'm not going to drop everything and jump just because King Bertrand snaps his royal fingers. If life as

Princess Sylvie's mistake would've been so hard to endure back then, what's going to make it any different now?"

"Times have changed. People are more open-minded. Plus, you would be welcomed with open arms because...." He couldn't bring himself to say it out loud...that all of the Founteneau heirs were...dead. "Let's just say you'd be welcomed with open arms by a country that loves its royal family."

Sophie squeezed her eyes shut and leaned her head back against the booth wall, as if trying to block him out. From that angle, her lips looked soft and sensual. Luc felt another surprising stir of desire.

He gave himself a mental shake. His job was to ensure the safety of Princesse Sophie and her family, not contemplate the taste of her lips.

Merde. This was no time to blur the lines of...protocol.

He'd been immersed in work since rising to the post of minister of protocol three years ago. In his position, with his proximity to the king, he had to be careful, especially when it came to matters of the heart. He'd witnessed firsthand the fallout from getting involved with the wrong person. That's why it had been so long since he'd been serious about a woman.

She opened her eyes and said, "If the king wants to talk to me he'll have to come here. I don't have time to jet off to Europe right now."

Luc nodded. "I will let him know and he will probably arrive tomorrow."

When they arrived at Sophie's home, Rose and John were asleep, fully dressed, in the recliners in the living room. The TV was turned to half-mute, playing an infomercial for a food chopper.

Luc walked Sophie inside and started the interior perimeter check, ensuring everything was locked and secure.

But he wasn't prepared for the shattering sound of Sophie Baldwin's scream.

Chapter Three

When Sophie opened the door to Savannah's dark bedroom to kiss her good-night, the last thing she expected to see was a figure launch itself off her daughter's bed, in one swift cat-like motion.

That image, and the echoes of Luc's security warnings, elicited a scream so loud it could've woken up the whole of western North Carolina.

She flipped on the lights. Tick stood there. Although they were both fully clothed, Savannah groped to pull her shirt into place. Sophie's fear morphed into mother-tiger–like rage.

"What the hell do you think you're doing?" she demanded.

By that time Luc's men were in the room and they had Tick's left arm yanked so far behind his back it was a wonder she didn't hear the pop of his shoulder dislocating.

"Get him out of here," Luc ordered.

"Don't hurt him!" Savannah jumped from the bed and started beating on the security agent who had Tick pinned.

Before Sophie could pull Savannah away, the guys had Tick out of the room. Luc strategically headed off Savannah so she couldn't follow. Sophie watched the scene unfold as if in slow motion, feeling more than ever as if her life was totally beyond her control.

"Let me go!" Savannah screamed. "You can't do this to us!"

"Savannah, you are fourteen years old," Sophie said. "You have no business allowing a boy in your room, much less in your bed."

The girl quit struggling.

"I love him and he loves me. He told me so."

Oh, baby, you don't know what love is. Even though you think you do, it won't last. It never does.

But she knew better than to spew her jaded views of the heart on her daughter. She had to focus on what was important. The boy had been in Savannah's bed. Even if her daughter had no intention of having sex, she put herself in a very bad position.

"Of course he's going to tell you he loves you." She softened her voice. "He might really mean it, although it's hard to believe since just last week he was slobbering all over Jess."

Savannah rolled her eyes.

"What would you know about love? You couldn't even stay married to Daddy."

Sophie flinched. If Savannah was looking for the best poison arrow to shoot, that was the one.

It pierced Sophie right through the heart.

She must not have been able to disguise the pain because Luc grimaced and gave her a sign over the girl's head that said *I'll leave you two alone.* He slipped out of the room, leaving her to face her daughter on her own.

Savannah didn't seem to notice his exit—or maybe she was ignoring it. She walked back over to her bed and flopped down.

Sophie stared at her, wondering what had happened to her daughter who was once so sweet. The obvious answer was this creature who called himself Tick, but Sophie couldn't follow that thought through. Besides, this change had been coming on slowly since Frank left. Maybe Sophie had been too soft on her. If so, it was born of good intentions. She thought she was doing the right thing, protecting her daughter, letting the moodiness and flippant quips slide, being her daughter's punching bag to soften the blow this divorce had had on Savannah.

It hit her all at once that rather than helping her daughter, she'd created a monster.

"I know things have been hard since your dad left, but that doesn't give you a license to be disrespectful." Her voice was soft but firm. "You've been disrespectful to me a lot lately and I'm tired of it. As much as I hate to have to do this, I'm going to have to ground you for that and for skipping school and having that boy in your room."

"How could your men let him in?" Standing in the living room, Sophie glared at Luc with burning reproachful eyes.

It was true. While he and the *princesse* were out, the boy simply knocked on the door, asked to see Savannah, and was allowed to enter.

Tick hadn't been identified as a security threat or otherwise been named as a person who should be barred. So when the boy followed the proper procedure for admittance—that is, knocking on the front door—the agent let him in.

This explanation didn't do a thing to appease Sophie.

"Common sense should scream that you don't leave a teenage boy and girl alone in a bedroom." She sputtered with indignation. "Come on, you were a teenager once. Think about it."

She had a point.

Still, if there was one thing Luc didn't understand, it was teenage girls. Princesse Sophie had her hands full with that one.

Luc was in a precarious position. While he was responsible for the young *princesse,* he and his men weren't at liberty to correct her behavior without express orders from the royal family.

"And Mom, where were you and Dad?"

At least she was still calling Rose and John Mom and Dad.

The older woman shrugged and stared at her hands. "We were in the kitchen. We didn't even hear him arrive.

"Sophie, I know you're upset with us right now and what I'm about to suggest will possibly aggravate the situation, but this behavior isn't like Savannah. Do you suppose it's her way of crying for help? I know she's been upset since her dad left and you've been out of the house more working. Even though it's unfortunate what happened to Prince Antoine, God rest his soul," Rose looked up to the heavens and crossed herself, "going to St. Michel might be an opportunity for you to reconnect with your daughter."

John nodded. "Take that girl to St. Michel. Get her away

from here, from all this confusion and that boy who seems to have cast such a spell on her."

Sophie gaped at her parents as if they spoke a foreign language.

"I just don't know if moving is the best thing for my daughter."

The first fingers of early morning light reached through the blinds and shook Sophie awake. She'd spent a restless night tossing and turning. Now it was time to get up and face another day. Yesterday seemed like a strange dream and what lay in store for today seemed so big it was almost overwhelming.

Especially the parts that involved Savannah.

Sophie hated to go to bed when she and Savannah were mad at each other, but last night she knew it was for the best that they let their emotions cool. She wasn't so much mad at her daughter as she was disappointed.

There was a time not so long ago when Sophie's being disappointed in her would've mattered to Savannah; when disappointment would've been worse than any punishment Sophie could've dished out. Then again, that was when Savannah loved Elmo and thought boys were yucky.

It was okay that boys weren't the enemy anymore—especially in light of the divorce. But finding a boy in Savannah's bedroom—Sophie shuddered and sat up and hugged her knees.

Straight off this morning, not only did she have to discuss boys with her daughter, she also had to break the news—*Oh, by the way, you're a princess and the great-grandfather you never knew—who also happens to be the king of St. Michel is stopping by for a visit this afternoon.*

The thought made her flop back down onto the bed, as if

the enormity of the situation physically weighed her down. Was going back to bed and pulling the covers over her head an option today?

It wasn't.

She had to get up and face this day head-on.

Even though yesterday Savannah had been too self-absorbed to be concerned about anything that was happening outside the orbit of her teenage world, she was bound to ask why the *Men in Black* were still hanging around today.

Sophie wasn't sure how Savannah would react to the news. Because she wasn't quite sure she even knew her daughter these days.

She partially blamed herself for this change in Savannah's behavior—for not being around enough. But darn it, she was doing the best she could.

The only thing that was certain was that she wouldn't get anything done lying in bed. She sat up, put her feet on the floor and prepared for battle.

It was already nine o'clock, but Sophie decided to shower and dress before waking Savannah. And a half-hour later she stood outside her daughter's room in her bathrobe with her hair in a towel and no idea what she was going to say. She took a deep breath. Muffled voices and cooking sounds came from the direction of the kitchen, along with the smell of coffee. She could certainly do with a good strong cup before she met Savannah head-on, but she needed to talk to her daughter alone without her parents listening in and mostly without the distraction of Luc Lejardin.

She let herself into Savannah's dark room, opened the blind so that soft light filtered into the room and sat down on the edge of her daughter's bed.

"Savannah, honey, wake up. We need to talk."

* * *

Part one of Sophie's heart-to-heart with Savannah went surprisingly well. It started off a little rocky with plenty of pleas such as "Mom, you've just got to give Tick a chance" and "We're in love."

Still, as Sophie held her ground, eventually Savannah softened and even ended up apologizing and admitted that letting the boy into her room was a mistake. Sitting there on the bed next to each other, they talked a little about how their relationship had changed since the divorce. Savannah opened up and acknowledged that she knew she shouldn't blame her mother.

"Dad was the one who left." She stared at her hands for a moment, then with tears in her eyes, she reached out and hugged Sophie and said, "I love you so much, Mom. I'm sorry I've been treating you so bad. I don't know why I do it."

"Maybe because it feels safe to be mad at me?" She whispered into her daughter's ear.

Because you know I'll always be here.

She thought about Rose and wondered if that wasn't exactly why she felt free enough to be so angry at her own mother?

A mother who wasn't really her mother.

A mother who'd kept this secret of who they really were tucked away all these years.

Panic blossomed in her chest, and Sophie hugged Savannah tighter to block out the hurt and confusion. Instead she concentrated on keeping her relationship with her own daughter on track.

Ugh, she hated to spoil it with the *princess revelation,* but she had no choice. According to Luc, the king was due to arrive that afternoon and it would be far worse if Savannah were blindsided by his appearance.

It was almost as if fate was in her corner, because as Sophie was weighing her words, figuring out how to broach the subject, Savannah pulled out of the embrace and said, "So are you ever going to tell me why those men were here with Grandma and Grandpa yesterday?"

Sophie forced a smile. "Well, I thought you'd never ask."

Her voice sounded a little too bright, as if she were going to follow it up with, *They're here to escort us to Disney World, for a private, behind-the-scenes tour.*

Obviously Savannah caught the false note. She furrowed her brow and said, "Okay, what gives, Mom?"

Luc paced the length of the living room, feeling like a caged animal—or worse yet, a man with a job to do held hostage by an ambivalent *princesse.*

He still didn't know whether Sophie would agree to the king's proposal. He should've clinched that deal yesterday. That was his job, after all.

Everything hinged on Savannah.

He and Sophie had agreed that she would break the news to her daughter. But he didn't understand why, against his advisement, she'd waited until the very last minute to do so.

Sure there was the unfortunate incident of discovering that boy in the girl's room last night, but he didn't understand why Sophie didn't just take charge of the girl and lay down the law. Tell her how things would be and be done with it.

Lord knew the woman was stubborn enough. He couldn't figure out why she didn't make this easier on everyone and use some of that will on her daughter.

In his mind's eye he could see her lifting her lovely chin and meeting his gaze with an icy, defiant stare. Much to his dismay, he found that strength appealing—in an exasperating, irksome way he didn't quite understand. Or maybe it was more apt to say it irked him because he didn't want to find anything about Sophie Baldwin appealing.

Restless and irritable, Luc sat on the chintz sofa and went over the morning's plan one more time: He was due to leave within the hour to make sure the airfield was secure for King Bertrand's arrival late that afternoon. This was a particularly challenging task because he had to ensure the usual level of security for the king, while at the same time not drawing any unnecessary attention to them.

It would be disastrous if word got out prematurely, as they hadn't yet advised the St. Michel Crown Council of Sophie's existence.

As much as he hated to work clandestinely, there were too many variables, namely Sophie and Savannah's safety and whether Sophie would cooperate.

Much to Luc's dismay, her cooperation remained the number one variable. Was he losing his touch? When it came to matters of state security, he never had a problem getting the job done. Especially when it involved members of the opposite sex.

But *princesse* or not, Sophie was not typical. As experience had taught him, most women would trade their soul for the chance to don a title and the crown jewels. His stepmother was an embarrassing case in point. She'd all but ruined the Lejardin name in her quest to get ahead.

All of this and more was being handed to Sophie on a royal cushion. Yet she wasn't sure she wanted any part of it.

That's what made her so maddeningly interesting—and Luc's job so much harder.

If she refused, it was best to keep her blood ties to the royal family quiet.

To that end, they'd taken all possible precautions to prevent the media from getting wind of King Bertrand's trip to Trevard—the king and his entourage would fly into Washington, D.C., ostensibly to visit the St. Michel Embassy. Then he and a pared-down staff consisting of his personal secretary and three security agents would fly in, landing at a rural airstrip just outside of Trevard. Luc would meet them there and escort them to Sophie's house.

The flight crew was on the king's payroll, and the king's personal secretary, Marci, understood the delicate nature of the king's business—even if she didn't know the details. So there was no worry about the press getting wind of the king's arrival. Luc would be there to ensure that everything went according to plan.

He checked his watch.

Sophie and Savannah still hadn't emerged from their bedchambers. It was enough to make him get up and start pacing again.

"I just brewed a fresh pot of coffee, Luc," Rose called from the kitchen. "Why don't you come in and pour yourself a cup?"

Rose kept insisting that everything would be fine, that Sophie would cooperate. But she hardly seemed clearheaded about it. One moment she was busily cooking and bustling about readying the place for the king. The next minute she was fretting over Sophie, about how she never dreamed things would turn out this way; then in the next breath, she was encouraging Luc to have faith that Sophie would do the right thing, that he should just give her some space.

He wondered if the pep talk wasn't as much for Rose's own benefit, because she was obviously worried about the damage that had been done to their mother–daughter relationship.

He poured himself a cup of coffee and sat at the small, round kitchen table, which was covered with fresh brioche and other confections that Rose had been baking for the king.

"King Bertrand always was crazy about my brioche," she said with pride. "He always told me that none could top mine. And of course there's no place in Trevard to purchase it. So I thought I'd make some for him."

"I'm sure he will be deeply appreciative." He sipped his coffee. "She doesn't strike me as the type to hold a grudge."

Rose looked a little startled as she glanced over the top of her wire-rimmed glasses. She was pouring chocolate cake batter into round pans, and scraped the sides of the mixing bowl a little faster.

"*Non,* she usually doesn't," she said. "Probably because usually we don't fight. We've always had a close, loving relationship. Maybe that's why this feels like the end of the world to me."

Luc sipped his coffee. "Just like you said, give her time and she'll come around. She'll realize that a parent is more than just a flesh and blood relation."

Rose put down the mixing bowl and wiped her hands on a dish towel. "You're a good man, Luc. I know in my heart Sophie will do the right thing. When she does, I will count on you to keep my girls safe."

Luc nodded as he walked to the sink to rinse his cup. "That's my mission."

"And there's no doubt you do it well. It's just that she and Savannah are everything to John and me. You know I am loyal to King Bertrand and St. Michel, but the girls are our life."

"Then I give you my pledge I will guard them with my life."

He set his cup in the sink and went to find Sophie himself.

He felt like a trespasser in the hall that led to the bedrooms and even worse when he strained to listen to what the female voices coming from the last door on the left were saying. As he made his way toward the voices, he glanced inside an open door.

Sophie's room.

It was unfamiliar and grippingly female territory.

Feeling like a voyeur, he drank in every detail of her private quarters: the unmade bed in which *she* slept; the rumpled white sheets twisted amidst the powder-blue eyelet duvet cover; her nightgown draped across the foot of the bed. The scent of her hung in the air—floral and spice and something maddeningly feminine.

Tension tightened in his belly as he fought a sudden urge to step inside the room and press the silky nightdress to his face and savor the essence of her.

But the murmur of conversation from the room down the hall rose in pitch, then fell back into the same indecipherable hum, and he blinked away irrational thoughts of that gown and nothing else on Sophie's naked skin.

He turned away from the room and made his way down the hall and knocked. The voices stopped for a moment before Sophie opened the door.

Her wet hair softly framed her face. She looked freshly scrubbed, standing there barefoot in a soft pink terry robe that revealed just a hint of cleavage that kept tempting his eyes to fall.

"Good morning." Luc looked her squarely in the eyes.

The look on Sophie's face was anything but welcoming. "Good morning. Don't tell me *he's* here already."

Behind Sophie, Savannah glared at him from the bed where she sat clutching a pillow. The mood barometer registered dangerous thunderstorms.

"No, King Bertrand has not arrived as of yet. He'll be here late this afternoon. But I will be leaving in a few moments to take care of some matters before he comes, and I wanted to brief you and your daughter before I left."

From the look on Sophie's face, you would've thought he'd asked her go and pick up King Bertrand herself.

"I'm sort of in the middle of something here."

Sophie glanced back at her daughter, then stepped into the hall, brushing against Luc as she closed the door behind her. They stood so close, he recognized hints of the same intoxicating scent he'd smelled in her bedroom. To his relief, she gathered the lapel of her robe and held it closed.

"I was telling her about the situation and she's a little confused," Sophie whispered. "She's just started high school and she thinks she's in love—although I'd move to St. Michel just to get her away from that boy."

Was it her shampoo or perfume…?

Whatever it was, it tempted him to lean in closer.

"Plus she has this crazy notion that her father and I will get back together again someday. She thinks if we leave, that won't happen."

This suggestion caught him off guard and instantly sobered him.

"If you stay will it happen?"

Sophie blinked at him.

"Of course not."

He found himself exhaling a breath he hadn't realized he'd been holding. At least she didn't seem to be pining over her ex-husband. Thank God. A woman like Sophie deserved better than the jerk he had read about in her file. "Look, I think it's best if you brief me and let me relay any instructions to my daughter. Like me, she needs a little time to digest the situation."

The briefing. Right. The job he'd come to do. He was irritated with himself for getting sidetracked in such a foolish way.

He glanced at his watch. "I hope she will be able to—how do you say—*digest* the situation soon, because the king will expect her cooperation as well as yours."

Sophie glared at him.

She looked weary and fragile and beautiful. He felt guilty for continuing to press the matter.

"I understand that he is the king of St. Michel," she said. "But in my house he's a guest. *An uninvited guest.* So don't climb up on your high horse and expect me to fall on my knees. If my daughter isn't ready to meet him when he gets here, he'll have to accept it. I'm not even sure *I* want to meet him."

Chapter Four

When King Bertrand arrived at Sophie's house at 5:30, Rose and John fell to their knees in reverence.

Even Sophie, who'd vowed to hold tight to her you-put-your-pants-on-one-leg-at-a-time-just-like-the-rest-of-us resolve, was a little taken aback by the sight of him. It was weird seeing the king of St. Michel in his fine suit, a little grayer and a bit smaller than he looked in the media; so out of context standing in the middle of her living room.

Out of the corner of her eye, she caught a glimpse of her mother, who was still on her knees, glaring at her. Sophie glared back. Rose redoubled her glower and motioned toward the ground with her head, obviously insisting that Sophie should join her in this show of subservience.

But by that time, King Bertrand, who appeared oblivious to Sophie's lapse of etiquette—actually, he seemed to not even notice Sophie at all—said, "Please rise. Rose, John, it's been far too long."

He hugged the couple one at a time, greeting them like old friends he was genuinely happy to see.

Tears streamed down her mother's face, and she couldn't recall another time when her father stood so tall and beamed with such pride.

She felt a little bad for being so mutinous.

"You have served St. Michel well," said the king, "and you will be duly rewarded once we return."

Hmm...once who returns?

The king turned to Sophie. "The tragic loss of my son and his family is not only cause for great personal sadness, but it is also cause for concern for the entire country. Without someone with Founteneau blood running through *her* veins, the 750-year-old Founteneau dynasty will end upon my death. If that happens, a collateral heir will be chosen by St. Michel's Crown Council, the administrative body that advises me on domestic and international affairs."

"Yes, I understand what the Crown Council does," Sophie said. "Luc has been very good about filling me in."

"Yes, well...there is no way I will allow the Founteneau dynasty to fall. That's why you must immediately come back to St. Michel and accept your rightful place as heir to the throne and eventually become the queen."

Sophie nearly snorted her coffee. "*Me?* A *queen?* You've got to be kidding me?"

It was all she could do to make it to work on time and manage her client load. How in the world was she supposed to run an entire country?

"Don't get ahead of yourself. As of now you're only a

princesse, but yes, because of the bloodline, eventually you will be queen. That's the point of this. Don't make it any more tedious than it needs to be."

He looked her up and down appraisingly, leaving her with the impression that she didn't measure up.

She bristled.

"You come crawling out of the woodwork and expect me to welcome you with open arms after you've sat up there on your royal high horse ignoring me all these years? Do you really expect me to drop my entire life, pack up my daughter and move to St. Michel because you beckon? What happened to my being the national embarrassment? When did I suddenly become fit to be queen?"

"Granted, Madame Baldwin, you're not ideal," he said. "But you're all we have."

Sophie wasn't sure if it was the use of her married name or the king's icy, formal tone that bothered her more. Maybe it was both heaped on top of this absurd rock-and-a-hard-spot circumstance.

A bad situation she intended to put an end to once and for all.

"You know what?" Sophie set down her coffee cup and stood. "Since the good people of St. Michel aren't any the wiser about me, let's not disappoint them. Why don't we just go ahead and let me remain the family's dirty little secret?"

Rose gasped. "Sophie, you don't mean that. Your Majesty, she doesn't mean it."

The king looked stunned.

"Oh, yes, I do. It's clear he doesn't believe I'm suited for the job. So let's all forget this ever happened."

She started toward the door.

"Goodbye, Your Majesty. I'm sure under other circumstances it would've been a pleasure."

She stopped in the foyer. The once-so-majestic king looked downright panicked.

"Sophie, wait," Luc called after her. From this vantage point, she couldn't see his face but could imagine him. "This is awkward for everyone. Perhaps we should start over."

Feeling like a naughty child, Sophie avoided eye contact with the king as she shook her head. "I don't think so."

Luc stepped into the foyer. He was putting words in the king's mouth and it struck Sophie that at the moment, Luc seemed more regal than the man who held the royal title. But wasn't that always how it was? The real power always lay behind the throne. As a general rule, Sophie had never been drawn to powerful men, but there was something about Luc looking so confident and self-possessed in that dark suit that was downright sexy.

And that made her want to squirm.

"Perhaps we've underestimated you?" His sultry, unwavering gaze held hers.

Something about the way Luc was looking at her made her feel naked. Not the sensual, I'm-imagining-you-without-clothes-let's-get-it-on sort of naked—*au contraire.* It was the stripped-bare, see-right-through-you-to-the-center-of-your-very-being kind of naked.

It made her feel exposed and classless. As if this sophisticated Frenchman were humoring an insufferable hick who had no idea how to behave in the presence of royalty.

He put an arm around her and gently led her back into the living room, where the king and her parents silently waited.

After she was seated again, the king cleared his throat.

"You're not the Founteneaus'—how did you say?—dirty little secret." He pursed his lips—so very French, Sophie thought—and glanced at Luc, who picked up without missing a beat.

"Times have changed, Sophie. As I have told you, I am confident the wonderful people of St. Michel would see you as a saint and savior. However, in the 1970s in St. Michel, news of a seventeen-year-old princess getting knocked up by an unsavory rock-and-roll musician would've caused a great scandal. His Royal Majesty was just trying to save his daughter from a grave mistake."

There was that word again: mistake.

The king must have read her mind. His expression softened and she could see true contrition in his watery green eyes. Eyes that were nearly the same color as hers.

"Perhaps I was the one who made the mistake all those years ago." His voice cracked on the last word.

Again, Luc stepped in. "If the royal house spins the announcement of *the return of Princesse Sophie* just right, you could become a national heroine at a time when the people desperately need someone to love. You could make a real difference."

Everyone was quiet, apparently waiting for her to say something—anything. All she could think of was how once making a *real difference* was what mattered to her the most. That's why she'd gotten into social work. But somewhere along the way, that fight to change the world had become an uphill battle. Not that she was giving up. She wasn't, and she certainly didn't expect life to be a smooth, bump-free ride. What she hadn't counted on were the Marys of the world fighting her every step of the way, turning things that should be common-sense simple into obstacle courses that were harder and harder to navigate.

Ha! If she had a hard time circumventing Mary to get the job done, imagine what it must be like running a kingdom.

Besides, she liked her job. It was people like Laura who made Sophie know her work did make a difference.

"This is all well and good, but I'll need to think about it."

Everyone gaped at her as if they couldn't believe she'd have the audacity to *think about it.*

"What?" she said. "You can't expect me to just jump when you say so. I need some time to think about things."

For once it seemed as if King Bertrand understood better than the others. He stood and said, "Very well then. We'll be in touch tomorrow morning to see what you've decided. I'd also like to meet Savannah."

That was iffy. And there was a good possibility that she wouldn't have answers for him tomorrow, but because he was making his way to the door, she knew better than to say that and start the whole vicious debate over again.

Luc, Rose and John stood. This time, Sophie did, too. She wasn't feeling quite so defiant now. It was more like a jumbled ache that haunted her now. One minute it was insisting *there's no way.* Then the next, it was saying, *why not...?* But she could list at least ten quick reasons why not.

Luc escorted the king to the door, raising Sophie's hopes that he would leave with him. At least she'd be able to relax and try to remember what life was like before madness descended.

"I just don't see how you can refuse, lovey," Rose said as she started gathering cups and places onto a wooden tray.

I don't see how you could keep this from me my entire life. The words were on the tip of her tongue when the phone rang.

"I'll get it," Sophie said, relieved at the distraction. Maybe it would be someone who would give her an excuse to take the handset into her room and shut herself in for an hour or two. If not, then she was definitely checking out for a nap of the same duration.

"Hello, Baldwin Residence," she said in her most melodic voice.

There was a pause and Sophie was just about to repeat herself when the voice on the other end of the line said, "Sophie? This is Mary Matthews."

Sophie tensed. *What now?* If she's calling to chew me out for leaving early yesterday without signing the reprimand—

"I'm calling with bad news. Your client Laura Hastings died last night."

Rose, John and Louis Dupré, one of Luc's men, took Savannah for an "outing" to give Sophie time to pull herself together. Initially, Rose didn't want to leave with her daughter so upset, but Sophie insisted, saying Savannah would be worried, too, and Rose should comfort her. Under duress, Rose finally agreed with the stipulation that Luc would keep a constant eye on her.

He fully expected Sophie to close herself up in her room, but to his surprise, she seemed to want to talk about it.

"The authorities can't tell if it was an accident or suicide." Sophie blotted her puffy eyes and stared off into the distance. "There's no note. But that morning, she put her kids on a plane to stay with her parents in California. Then last night, she crashed her car into a wall near her apartment.

"Mary thinks Laura committed suicide. I just can't imagine her taking her own life. She was doing so well. My

God, Luc, she came to see me yesterday morning, but I was so busy I didn't have time for her. Maybe I could've prevented it."

She succumbed to another bout of tears, buried her face in her hands and sobbed. Luc sat next to her on the bed and put an arm around her.

"Sophie, I don't think there was anything you could've done. Don't do this to yourself."

She didn't respond.

"Sophie, listen to me. I know how upsetting this is for you. I've never even met the woman and I find it very sad, but you can't blame yourself. That's not doing anyone any good."

She looked up at him, the color of her green eyes intensified through the tears.

"You don't understand, she came to me for help, but I was so busy that I couldn't talk to her. Now she's dead. Maybe if I'd made the time to talk to her things would've turned out differently. Maybe Mary's right. Maybe I'm not cut out for this type of work. Maybe I should do something else where I won't lead anyone else to suicide."

"I highly doubt that you led her to suicide. Did you consider that perhaps the best type of social work would be for you to save St. Michel—and the Founteneau dynasty? Don't think of it as doing a favor for the king, but consider it the ultimate act of paying forward a good deed—to the entire nation. At least consider visiting before you rule it out."

She shrugged.

"Nothing makes sense anymore," she whispered. "My parents aren't my parents. They're strangers who've kept a huge secret from me my entire life. Now my own grandfather wants me to come back because I can do something for him.

And don't forget Savannah and this…this Tick. And Laura…."

Her face crumpled and she was crying again. He felt like a heel, pushing too hard. He reached out and rubbed her back and gently swept a strand of hair off her tear-stained face.

Luc had no idea how it happened, but the next thing he knew, Sophie was in his arms, sobbing on his shoulder.

One minute she was turning toward him and the next, his right arm was around her.

He tilted his chin so that it rested on top of her head and stroked her hair in a soothing gesture. Her hair smelled like springtime and sunshine…lavender with a exquisite hint of something else that was entirely Sophie.

She smelled wonderful.

And he felt like a heel for pushing so hard. It wasn't an ideal time to bring up a visit to St. Michel. But for some reason—probably because he was intoxicated by her scent—he thought the idea of helping St. Michel would comfort her.

He found himself holding her tighter, relishing the scent of her, his heart aching for her and all that she'd been through.

As he searched for the right words to comfort her, he reminded himself that he was a pair of arms to comfort her, a shoulder on which she could lean. If he just focused on that—and not on how right she felt in his arms they'd both get through this.

He wished more than anything he could think of something that would make all the pain she was feeling disappear. He wanted to see that spitfire spark return to her eyes, that expression—so uniquely hers—that brought her face to life.

She nuzzled closer and he could feel her warm breath on his neck. The sensation sent waves of fire coursing through him. Then she looked up at him, her eyes impossibly green and her lips too full to resist. And for a fleeting moment he wanted nothing more than to taste her lips, but he caught himself.

If she hadn't been so fragile, he just might've given into that urge for just one taste of those lips. But he pulled back, putting some distance between them.

Early the next morning, before the rest of the house stirred, Sophie worked at her potting bench in the mudroom.

The cozy area was one of the reasons she'd rented the house after the divorce.

She'd envisioned a morning like this when snow frosted the windowpanes and it was too cold to go outside and putter in the yard. Here, she could ground herself by putting her hands in the earth, but be inside where the ground wasn't frozen and the windchill factor didn't threaten hypothermia.

The only thing was, her initial vision hadn't included the sickening feeling induced by the recent trio of disasters: catching Savannah in a compromising position with that boy, the revelation of the great family secret and losing Laura.

Her heart ached as she steeped a cup of Earl Grey and lit a fire in the fireplace. The dazed aftershock of the three blows tangled and sat heavy in the pit of her stomach.

How would anything ever be the same?

Her mind skittered back to how being in Luc's arms yesterday felt like a safe haven. But that wasn't real. Death was real; the possibility of Savannah ruining her life was real; the visit from King Bertrand was real.

Luc was just doing his job, and she shouldn't read anything more into it. She set down her tea and prepared to get her hands dirty.

As she coaxed a philodendron out of its terra-cotta pot onto her workbench's newspaper-covered surface, she tried to sort out her jumbled emotions, gently tending to the plant that was dangerously close to dying from its root-bound condition.

Hmm, maybe she was suffering from the same problem as the plant. She'd inextricably rooted herself to this life in Trevard that seemed to keep going from bad to worse.

Laura's sad face, the way she'd looked as she disappeared out the door on Friday flashed in her mind.

Sophie squeezed her eyes shut, trying to block out the image, but all she managed to do was remind herself how tired she was. The kind of tired that weighed you down but wouldn't let you sleep.

She'd tossed and turned again last night, awaking intermittently wondering if she'd only done things differently, if she'd seen to Laura rather than sending her away maybe the woman would still be alive.

But she hadn't, and there was no going back to correct this mistake. Tears burned her eyes, but her hands were covered.

As she thought about Laura, the problems with Savannah and St. Michel loomed in the back of her mind, like ghosts whispering a foreboding warning not to put off dealing with the problems or, as with Laura, they would come to a bad end.

Do something.

Act.

Make things right. Now.

She had two choices: sending Luc away and going back to work tomorrow, back to Mary's berating and a dead-end job. Savannah would go back to school, back to Tick and plenty of unsupervised time for God knew what; or she could take a leave of absence (if Mary would grant her one) and she could go to St. Michel for a *visit.*

Nothing said she and Savannah had to stay.

"Good morning."

Luc stood in the doorway, holding a foam cup, and looking so delicious it set off a strange tingling in the pit of her stomach.

She inhaled sharply against the sensation.

"Good morning." She focused on her hands and brushed the dirt off, a little embarrassed that the potting soil was caked under her nails. She curled her fingers inward to hide the mess. "You didn't have to buy coffee out. We have plenty here."

He took a sip and shrugged. "It was early and I didn't want to make noise in the kitchen. Are you feeling better this morning?"

She could feel his gaze on her, and she didn't even have to look up to know that he was looking at her in that way that made her think of things she hadn't contemplated in a very long time. If she let her thoughts run away with her, she imagined he was thinking the very same things.

She turned back to her potting bench and chose a bigger pot for the philodendron.

"Somewhat."

Or maybe it was the grief and exhaustion making her delirious? Making her imagine one minute that a maddeningly handsome and sophisticated European dignitary who worked for her grandfather was on a mission to seduce her.

Was she nuts?

Of course he'd do anything—including using the power of seduction—to convince her that returning to St. Michel was the right thing to do.

She shouldn't take it personally, especially not in the personal direction her newly awakened libido was leading her. Thank goodness her better judgment had been intact last night when, at the last minute, she'd pulled out of his arms and excused herself. She'd actually thought for a delusional moment that he might kiss her.

She glanced at his lips and was suddenly warm again. Given the way everything had been crashing and burning around her, she knew better than to go…there.

"I had a thought," he said. "What if you set up a trust fund for Laura's children?"

She poured potting soil into the terra-cotta pot.

"It's a nice thought," she said. "I could spare a little each month, but I can barely make ends meet as it is. It certainly wouldn't be anything grand enough to call a trust fund, but it really is a good idea."

He smiled, and her stomach dipped. She didn't want to like him. Not like *that.* She was fine when he kept his distance and didn't hold her when she was upset or try to do nice things, but darn it, she was struggling here. She had enough to worry about without his making her want something else she couldn't have. In her life, she'd built too many castles on shifting sand.

She dug a little hole in the soil, put the plant in it and covered the roots with the dirt.

"I have my resources," he said. "As the future queen of St. Michel, so will you. You could make sure those boys were well cared for, if you so chose."

"Is this a bribe? So you can get your way and get me to agree to come back to St. Michel? If so, you're not playing fair."

He pursed his lips and shrugged in that way of his that made her feel so unsophisticated, as if he were humoring her and at any moment would burst out laughing at her lack of social grace. Then again, if he did that, he wouldn't exactly be exhibiting social grace, either.

Why did she let him make her so nervous?

To get back on solid footing, she thought of Laura's four little boys. They were so young to be without a mother, relying on the charity of relatives who may not be any better off than Laura was.

She narrowed her eyes and studied Luc's expression to see if he was joking. But why would he joke about something like that?

Here she was in a real position to help. How could she just turn her back on them?

"I think it would be wonderful if we could do that," she said.

He nodded.

"How soon can we do it?" she asked.

"How soon can you be ready to leave?"

"Don't answer my question with a question."

"Well, that's part of it," he said.

"So you are trying to blackmail me."

"It would be a despicable thing to do."

"Yes, it would."

"Would it be any better for you to turn your back on a nation?"

"That's not fair. It's hardly the same thing. St. Michel will not cease to exist if I refuse to become the heir to the throne. No one there will go hungry or be homeless or mistreated without me. In fact, seeing that I know nothing about running a country, the nation might be better off without me."

"How much did you want to put in the trust?"

"What?" The non sequitur threw her.

"For the boys—how much?"

She decided to call his bluff. "I want those little guys to be well taken care of for the rest of their lives."

"Done."

She blinked. "Excuse me?"

"I'll need contact information and the name of a bank in which to set up the trust."

"Are you—are you joking?"

His face was serious now. "Absolutely not. I want you to see the great things you are capable of doing as the future queen of St. Michel. As for the nation being better off without you, I don't think so. You will have time to work with your grandfather, to learn his ways and means. It's in your blood, Sophie Baldwin. After yesterday, I just hope that you recognize that life is too short to waste, especially once your destiny comes calling."

He smiled at her and his gaze lingered in an intense way that made her knees weaken and her belly flutter.

Then he turned and walked away, leaving her speechless. Literally. Standing there with dirty hands and her mouth agape.

A trust fund for Laura's boys. Done. With a virtual wave of her hand. Well, that certainly put a new spin on everything.

Her knees were a little weak and her head was spinning, not in a way that made her feel as if she might pass out, but with possibilities.

Maybe she could make a difference.

A real difference.

She steadied herself with a deep breath. High on possibility, she made her way to the kitchen to wash her hands.

Rose was in there making a pot of coffee and taking things out of the refrigerator for breakfast. She set a carton of eggs on the table and looked at Sophie with a sorrowful expression that seemed to add years to the woman's already advanced age.

Sophie didn't say anything as she washed the grime from her hands. She only thought about this woman who had raised her so well, with so much love that Sophie never had an inkling she was adopted.

Life was short.

Luc's parting words echoed in her heart.

Yes, life *was* short.

She dried her hands and went over to Rose and put her arms around the woman.

"I'm sorry for getting so angry."

The woman gasped, a gentle intake of air that spoke more of relief than surprise, and clung tight to Sophie. "I'm so sorry," she said, hanging on to her daughter for dear life. "I'm so very sorry."

"*Shh,* you're not to blame. No one is to blame."

Her parents might have kept the truth from her, but that didn't take away from the good life they'd given her. They would *always* be her parents—her family—no matter the circumstances. She shouldn't be angry with her parents for their loyalty to the king.

They'd always showered her with unconditional love and they deserved her unconditional love in return.

As she held her mother, it all snapped into focus….

King Bertrand's talking about a dynasty coming to an end when he died; Sophie hanging on to a job where even taking the smallest steps felt like an uphill climb…

Life was short.

The move would be hard on Savannah, but it was the best chance she had of giving her daughter a good life.

Chapter Five

The fire felt nice. It warmed the living room, making it a sanctuary against the bitter cold.

Luc handed Sophie a mug of coffee and settled into a chair next to the hearth, warming his hands on his cup.

She'd asked him in here so they could talk privately, away from Rose and John, who, he was sure, would still find a way to listen.

He was certain Sophie wanted to discuss establishing the trust for the Hastings boys, but she suddenly had a different air about her. She'd washed away the potting soil grime and donned a smart pair of wool trousers and a pink cashmere sweater that brought out the pretty blush in her cheeks. She seemed stronger, more serious and pulled together than she'd been since he arrived.

She settled on the couch across from him and lifted the mug to her full lips and blew to cool the hot liquid.

Off-limits, he reminded himself. The princess of St. Michel, his boss's granddaughter, was one hundred percent off-limits. Good thing he hadn't lost control yesterday when he was tempted to kiss her.

How in the world would he have explained himself? A moment of weakness? That inappropriate relations ran in the family?

He blinked away the thought.

"How do you tolerate such inclement weather?" he asked, searching for a lighter note. "On the coldest day in St. Michel, temperatures rarely fall below fifty degrees. When that happens, it's deep winter for us."

She arched a brow.

"This isn't typical. It gets cold, but usually not this bad. Maybe it would be a good time to get away from all this snow and ice and see if winters in St. Michel really are as nice as you claim."

He studied her for a moment, trying to determine what she meant. If, in fact, this conversation was leading where he hoped.

"Are you considering a visit?" he kept his voice even, not allowing emotion to color his words.

She smiled. "How soon can we leave?"

"Tomorrow if you wish. I'll make arrangements."

"I hope you're happy," Savannah wailed. "My life is ruined. This is my last year of middle school and you're taking away everything I've worked for these seven years."

"We're just going for a visit," Sophie offered.

The girl scowled.

"Can I stay with Dad while you go, so I won't miss school?" she added, an obvious afterthought.

"Your dad is in California. What would be the difference of your going there or to St. Michel? You'd still miss school."

"In Cali, at least they'd speak the same language I do. Dad will come here. Watch, I'll call him."

It was against her better judgment to let Savannah make the call. There was no way Frank would drop everything to come back to Trevard. But the girl was already dialing.

"Savannah, please, you can't tell him about King Bertrand's visit. We're not ready for anyone to know about what's happened—about my real business in St. Michel. I may not even stay and if that's the case *no one* can ever find out that we're related to the royal family. It would just be chaos. Just tell Dad that Grandma and Grandpa are taking me there to reconnect with relatives."

She wasn't sure her daughter was listening. "Savannah, did you hear me?"

The girl turned her back on Sophie. "Daddy? Hi! It's me, Savannah."

Sophie held her breath, resisting the urge to yank the phone out of her daughter's hand until she promised to keep the secret—or at least acknowledged that Sophie had spoken to her.

"I'm fine! How are you? Oh my God, I miss you so much!" The smile in the girl's voice brought Sophie's anger down a peg. But still, this was important—

She walked around so that she and Savannah faced each other. Tried to look at her eye to eye, but she couldn't connect with her daughter's gaze. "Savannah," she stage-whispered. "Please. You don't understand how important it is that you not tell your father why we're going. I'm not asking you to lie to him, just—"

Savannah waved her mother away and stuck her finger in her ear.

Arrrrrrrrggh! Sophie wanted to scream—

"Well, the reason I'm calling is because Grandma and Grandpa want to take Mom on this really boring vacation to St. Michel." She rolled her eyes. "You know, that little place where they're from. There's like relatives there or something. Well, it sounds so-o totally boring. I was wondering if you'd come and stay with me here in Trevard while she's gone so that I don't have to go and, you know, miss all that school. You and I could like hang out. 'Cause I really miss you—"

Sophie blew out the breath she'd been holding as she realized Savannah had heard her and was doing exactly as she'd asked. Since the divorce decree stated neither she nor Frank could take their daughter out of the country without permission from the other, the call had to be made before they left. Better now than later, in case Frank caused a stink—despite how he most likely wouldn't come to stay with Savannah.

Still, Sophie was torn between hugging the girl and sitting her down to talk about respect. A simple "Okay, Mom. I'll do as you asked" would've gone a long way toward fostering mother-daughter relations. At least they were getting the call to Frank over with.

"She'll be gone three months," Savannah said into the phone. "Daddy, I really, really miss you and it'll be just like old times with your staying here. Of course Mom will be gone, but—oh. Yeah. Okay, she's right here."

Looking hopeful, Savannah held out the phone to Sophie. "Dad wants to talk to you."

As Sophie took the handset, a sense of foreboding swooped down on her.

"Hello, Frank," she said, doing her best to keep her voice neutral.

"Sophie, what the hell is going on?" She could envision Frank gritting his teeth. "You know I can't pick up and leave for three months to come babysit while you go gallivanting in Europe. Why'd you even let the kid call and get her hopes up?"

Sophie glanced at Savannah who watched her with wide, eager eyes. She hightailed it into her bedroom and shut the door to spare her daughter from what was sure to come.

"Hello? Sophie, are you there?" Frank asked, sounding even more annoyed.

"Yes, Frank, I'm here. For your information, I didn't put Savannah up to calling you. Because I knew you'd find some way to break her heart."

"Oh, give me a break. You can't expect me to come all the way across the country—"

"No, Frank, I don't expect anything out of you. But since you won't come and stay, then that means I'll have to take her with me."

She cringed at the way the words sounded. But she knew that if she asked his permission—rather than pretending that taking their daughter with her was a hardship—he'd put up a stink about Savannah going to St. Michel. If she made him think it inconvenienced her, he'd fall right into step with her plan. What an idiot.

"I don't give a damn what you do, Sophie. Just leave me out of it. I can't believe you put her up to calling me to ask if you could pawn her off while you do your *thing*."

Oh! How was it that he could make everything sound so dirty? She'd said she was going to St. Michel with her parents. Yet he'd managed to imply—with one sentence—that she was going off on some tryst. "That's not why we called. Your daughter just wanted to know if for once you were willing to step up to the plate and be a man or at least be a father to her."

"I don't have to listen to this crap. It's five o'clock in the damn morning here and you wake me up to insult me. That's low, Soph, really classless."

Yeah, this from the mouth of Mr. Manners himself, but Sophie knew arguing with him would only leave her beating her head against the wall.

"Look, just tell her you can't do it and we don't even have to talk to each other. Unless you'd care to discuss child support."

The other end of the line went dead.

He'd hung up on her. The no-good, lousy son of a—

The bedroom door opened and Savannah stood there looking pale and deflated.

"I heard," she murmured.

"Oh, baby, I'm sorry."

Once again she was left holding the bag. She could either clean up Frank's mess and make excuses or devastate her daughter by telling her the truth. She just hoped Savannah hadn't heard the part where she tried to make Frank think it was a burden to take her. Because it wasn't.

"We're going to have so much fun in St. Michel. We'll get to stay in a real castle. Haven't you always wanted to stay in a *real* castle?"

Savannah looked at Sophie as if she was spouting nonsense.

"Not since I was like five years old, Mom. Look, I'm going over to Jess's house."

Sophie wanted to tell her she couldn't go. "But what about Flea? Isn't Jess mad at you for stealing her boyfriend?"

There was that look again.

"God, Mom! His name is Tick. Why can't you remember that?"

Flea? Tick? What's the difference? Weren't both blood-sucking parasites?

"She's over him," Savannah said as if Sophie should've known. "God, did you think I'd actually try to steal my best friend's boyfriend? What kind of person do you think I am?"

I don't know anymore. That's the problem. Sophie had the sensation of swimming upstream desperately trying to keep ahold of Savannah's hand, but little by little she kept slipping….

At least one of the security agents would go with her. That wouldn't even be something she could fight with Sophie about.

"Well, don't stay long. We're leaving tomorrow. I'll have to talk to Luc to find the exact itinerary. But you need to pack. Three months is a long time to be gone."

"Exactly. That's why I want to say goodbye to my friends."

Ten minutes later, the front door slammed.

"Savannah?" Sophie called from her bedroom where she'd been putting away the clean laundry Rose had folded.

The girl appeared in her room, looking flushed and breathing hard.

"What's wrong?" Sophie asked.

Savannah folded her arms and paced the length of the room before turning to Sophie and sputtering, "Jess and Tick. That's what's wrong. I showed up at Jess's and guess who was there? Tick, that's who. They're back together. Can you believe that? I can't believe I ever liked that loser or thought Jess was my friend."

Sophie tried to think of some words to comfort her.

"How soon can we leave on this trip?"

Chapter Six

The plane landed in St. Michel at nine-thirty Tuesday evening. The second Sophie set foot on land, she noticed two things: the temperature, which the pilot had informed them, was a balmy sixty-seven degrees even though it was November; and the island smelled like paradise.

Luc gestured at a black stretch limousine on the airfield. Sophie marveled as the uniformed driver bowed and opened the car door. Savannah—who was punching the buttons on her cell phone—and Sophie's parents piled in. They took the seat that faced backward.

"After you," Luc cupped her elbow to steady her as she climbed in the car. In somewhat of a daze, Sophie found herself in the seat facing her parents. Luc slid into the vacant space next to her, popped the cork on a bottle of Krug Clos du Mesnil champagne and poured some sparkling cider for Savannah.

When everyone had a glass, Luc raised his for a toast.

"Welcome, Sophie and Savannah. Welcome back, John and Rose."

It had been more than thirty-three years since Rose and John had set foot on the island, and Sophie was torn between watching them toast each other and savoring her first glimpse of this place she might very well rule one day.

The enormity of the thought made her shudder.

Thank goodness Luc began pointing out sights of interest and spouting off facts such as "St. Michel covers an area of 197 hectares."

Hectares?

"Which would be approximately 487 acres."

Oh.

And "The *Palais de St. Michel* was built in the thirteenth century. The exterior of the castle still resembles the original thirteenth-century fortress, but the inside has been renovated and updated with the most modern of security and conveniences," he said. "It has ninety-five offices, seventy-five bathrooms and two hundred and ten bedrooms. And employs four hundred and fifty people.

"The state rooms are open for public viewing during the summer, and since 1920, the palace courtyard has been the setting for concerts given by the St. Michel National Orchestra."

"A lot of people must visit each year," Sophie said.

"True. However the *Palais de St. Michel* isn't simply a tourist attraction and museum. It is a fully working palace and our governmental headquarters. The king is involved with the day-to-day running of St. Michel and treats the nation as a business as well as a country."

Sophie's head spun.

"Will there be a pop quiz tomorrow?" she asked, only half joking.

Luc smiled, which made his eyes crinkle at the corners in a way that caused Sophie's gaze to linger and her belly to flutter.

"Look out there." He touched her arm and his shoulder pressed into her as he leaned forward and gestured toward a harbor brimming with yachts. "That's the famous St. Michel Marina. And that large boat right there—you see? That's the *Poseidon V,* which once belonged to Stavros Andros, the Greek shipping magnate. You have heard of him?"

Sophie nodded.

"Andros was a frequent visitor to our little country. The boat was sold after his death and is currently chartered by Yves De Vaugirard, the son of Pascal De Vaugirard, St. Michel's minister of finance."

"That's a big boat," Sophie said, completely and utterly aware of the heat of Luc's arm, which, even though he'd settled back into his seat, still touched hers.

"When Andros owned the *Poseidon,* he used to display Van Goghs, Renoirs and a treasure of other Impressionist paintings on board. The boat was a virtual museum afloat on the Côte d'Azur."

"Nice."

It must have been a European trait, that tendency Luc had of invading her personal space.

The car turned right and Sophie, lost in the masculine feel of his hard muscles, didn't fight the gravity that made her body lean into him a little bit more.

When the car straightened, neither of them reclaimed

their personal space. And for just a moment she wondered what the rest of his body would feel like pressed against hers—flesh to flesh…

"Are there any specific places you would like to visit?" he asked.

Oh, you have no idea.

She nodded, but she couldn't look at him because her cheeks were flaming. "The beach and the National Gallery."

"We'll come back so you can become intimately acquainted with each of them."

Intimately acquainted…that's the best idea I've heard since—

"My phone doesn't work here." Savannah's grousing pulled Sophie back, out of the world of van Goghs, Renoirs and world-class yachts, reminding her of the whirlwind it had been getting to St. Michel."

"I'm sorry there wasn't time to switch the service before we left," Sophie said, suddenly wondering what else she'd left undone.

"I'll have that taken care of in short order." Luc's words were for Sophie. "I'm at your service."

He seemed at home here. The master of this very expensive universe. As if he'd be able to make just about anything possible. And he probably could. Whereas Sophie didn't even know the location of the closest bathroom or where to buy a toothbrush if she'd forgotten to pack hers.

She racked her brain to remember if she had.

Leaving early Tuesday morning hadn't left time to take care of much but the essentials before they departed. Sunday was a blur of packing and battening down the house for three months of what was proving to be a harsh winter.

Monday at work, Sophie had to explain to Mary that she needed a leave of absence without telling her the *real* reason. All she could say was, "It's a family emergency."

And it was.

She certainly couldn't confide that the balance of the House of Founteneau rested on her shoulders. Even if she had, knowing Mary, that probably wouldn't have been reason enough to justify a leave of absence.

When they talked, Sophie's justification for the leave sounded hedgy even to her own ears. Mary asked if a family member was sick or dying and Sophie said no because she didn't want to lie.

In the end, of course, Mary, irritated and harried, turned down her request and leveled an ultimatum; "Be in the office tomorrow at eight o'clock sharp or you're fired."

Fired?

She'd never been fired from anything. Unless you counted her marriage…

Mary left Sophie no option but to spend the rest of Monday composing her letter of resignation (which Mary accepted with near glee that she didn't even try to disguise) and contacting her clients to say goodbye, assuring them they'd be in good hands.

Dear God, she hoped they'd be well taken care of, that whoever Mary hired would look out for their best interests rather than the bottom line.

Better than Sophie had done with Laura in the end.

Laura's family wasn't having a memorial service for her in Trevard. They were having her cremated and flown to California where they'd "take care of things," as Mary had so bluntly put it.

It was over.

Finished.

Not our problem anymore, Mary had said so matter-of-factly.

Exhaustion seemed to seep into her bones, and Sophie leaned against the limo window—away from Luc and his hard body, and all that talk of shipping magnates and floating museums and getting intimately acquainted—and watched the city whiz by in a blur of golden and white lights set against the indigo sky.

St. Michel looked like an exquisite Fabergé egg.

Oh, she was so out of her league.

When they reached the back security gates of the *Palais de St. Michel,* the sentries waved them through. It wasn't the first glimpse of the castle that Luc wished for Sophie. In fact, they were inside the understated back entrance and secured in the bowels of the castle so fast, she probably didn't get a proper look.

The amber half light cast shadows on her face, accentuating her cheekbones and full lips. How beautiful, he thought. Classic, unadulterated beauty.

She was just what St. Michel needed.

He wasted no time ushering Sophie and his other three charges out of the limo and unceremoniously into an elevator, which carried them directly to the living quarters—a wing of the house never open to the public.

The staff had been told only that four important guests would arrive but were given no details of who they were or their business at the castle.

He turned to Sophie to tell her as much and saw the utter exhaustion on her face and decided to spare her further briefing—at least for tonight.

Soothing classical music filtered into the lift, filling the silence as the car carried them up to the third floor. Even after the long flight, she still looked beautiful, he thought.

When the elevator doors opened, two women in gray maid's uniforms stood at the ready. "Monsieur, Madame, this is your floor," Luc said to John and Rose. "Beatrice and Rochelle will show you to your room."

Rose and John exchanged good-nights with Sophie and Savannah, hugging them and promising they'd be in good hands with Luc. As the doors closed and the lift climbed one more floor to the royal family's quarters, Sophie looked vulnerable standing there, and a little taken aback when she saw the staff of twelve that lined the elevators in two rows of six, when they finally reached her floor.

As they stepped off the elevator, Sophie looked first at Luc, then at the staff, then around at the expansive hallway. Savannah hung back slightly clinging to her mother's arm.

"This is Sophie Baldwin and her daughter, Savannah," he said. "They are very special guests of King Bertrand. I trust you will make them feel at home and treat them with the same respect as any other person who has ever occupied these quarters."

Luc found Sophie's wide-eyed expression endearing. He gave the reception area a cursory glance—from the ornate crystal chandeliers that hung from the thirty-foot ceiling, down the white and gold walls, to the marble floors—trying to see it through Sophie's eyes. The statues, mirrors and gilding must have looked extraordinary.

And quite daunting to someone who wasn't used to it. It was nice to notice it again through fresh eyes.

"Thank you," he said to the staff. "For now, I shall escort Madame Baldwin and Savannah to their apartment."

He dismissed the crew with a nod.

"This way." He led Sophie and her daughter down the hall to a set of large guilded double doors. The two hung back.

"This is where you will stay," he said. "I took the liberty of putting the two of you in the same apartment. I figured you'd be more comfortable that way. But if you'd prefer, Savannah can have her own quarters."

"No!" they both said simultaneously.

"I mean, thank you," Sophie said. "But I'd prefer that Savannah stay here with me."

The girl nodded.

"Very well, the apartment contains six bedrooms, so you should have plenty of room."

"Six bedrooms?" Savannah asked. "Are you kidding me?"

"No, I'm not," Luc said. "All for your mother and you. You may choose three for you and three for your mother."

"Whoa!" With that, the girl took off down the hall, calling something about *dibs.*

Sophie laughed and crossed her arms over the front of her. "You'll have to excuse her—well, both of us actually. This is a little overwhelming for both of us. This *apartment,* as you call it, is twice the size of my house."

Her humility was touching, a breath of fresh air in this climate of women who would stop at nothing to get what they wanted.

"Only the best for the *princesses* of St. Michel."

Sophie dipped her head, but not before he noticed the color that bloomed in her cheeks.

"I know you're tired," she said, glancing up at him without raising her chin. "But will you come in? Please?"

The request seemed more of a plea than an initiation. A protective impulse unfurled inside him.

"Of course. I was hoping you'd give me the honor of giving you the grand tour. It's a special place. This is where Princess Sylvie lived."

She looked up at him with large, astonished eyes.

"The apartment has been closed off for many years, but King Bertrand decided to open it for you and Savannah—you are his family," Luc said. "I'm sure you're eager to see your mother's room."

Silently they walked side by side, through the expansive hallway, stopping at a set of double doors nearly as large as the ones in the front entryway. Luc snared Sophie's wide gaze before opening them, revealing a room that continued the gilded and white theme of the apartment, but with added touches of pink velvet and ceilings that rivaled the Sistine Chapel.

Sophie stood at the door as if she was afraid to enter. Luc cupped her elbow and led her inside.

"This was her room, and if you think you'll be comfortable here, it can be yours. Please, have a look around."

He stepped out into the hallway, leaving Sophie alone to explore. A few moments later she joined him.

"Okay, I take back what I said before. The *bathroom* in there is bigger than my house. The rest of this is just…"

She shook her head and ran a hand through her hair.

"A little overwhelming?" he asked.

She nodded.

He understood how he felt. It was overwhelming to him in a different sort of way. He'd spent much of his youth in this apartment, when Antoine and the royal family lived here. In fact, he hadn't been inside since the king had moved his family to the apartment he was in now.

"Where do you live?" she asked. "Are we neighbors? Do you have your own mansion inside this castle down the hall?"

She made a fluttering gesture with her hand and smiled. A dimple in her right cheek that he'd never noticed before winked at him. How had he missed that?

"I have a house about two kilometers from the palace. If you need me, no matter what time of day or night, I insist you call."

In a flash of irrational thought, he hoped she would somehow need him…

Savannah trotted up alongside her mother. "Oh. My. God. Mom, can you believe this place? I mean it…it's like Cinderella's castle."

Subdued by the random intimacies that kept permeating his thoughts, he knew it was time to leave.

"I'm sure you and Savannah would like to get settled in and get a good night's sleep. King Bertrand plans to present you to the Crown Council tomorrow."

Sophie's throat worked.

"Really?" she asked. "I don't know if that's such a good idea, because I'm still not sure we'll be able to stay…permanently."

She was exhausted, he thought, and that's what was contributing to her hesitancy.

"Perhaps I can convince the king to delay the meeting a day or so. To give you time to adjust."

He hoped it was exhaustion talking, because now that she was here, he couldn't imagine this place without her. Sophie Baldwin was exactly what St. Michel needed.

Chapter Seven

Miraculously Sophie slept through the night.

It wasn't exactly restful, more like a strange dream-filled sleep, of swirling images of Luc leading her through a labyrinthine castle. In the dream, she couldn't find her daughter, but the king kept insisting that she *move forward, that she keep going.*

Sophie sat up and blinked at the sunlight streaming in through the French doors on the wall and saw Savannah snuggled down under the pink satin duvet next to her in the expansive four-poster bed.

She sighed with tender relief and fell back onto the pillows.

Sometime in the middle of the night, Savannah must have crawled into bed with her. Maybe she'd had the same unsettling dreams?

Probably not. They were far away from home in this

strange old castle. That could be sort of unsettling for a girl…of any age. She reached out and smoothed a lock of dark brown hair off her daughter's forehead.

Savannah stirred but didn't awaken.

Sophie carefully removed her hand, returning it to the cool of the buttery soft, white cotton sheets.

The events of the past week seemed almost as unreal as the bizarre images she'd dreamed of last night.

But here they were. This castle, this bedroom in this sprawling apartment were as real as could be.

What was it like for Princess Sylvie to grow up in this *Palais de St. Michel?* She tried to picture her in this very room.

Had this been Sylvie's bed? She ran her hands over the sheets—obviously new or at least not thirty-three years old. The place smelled like furniture polish and old money. Sophie's gaze scanned the gilded room. On the bedside table sat a black-and-white photo of the young princess.

This was her *birth mother…*a woman she knew next to nothing about aside from the glorified wild-child legends spun by the paparazzi. It was the most incongruent feeling looking at a picture of a young woman who was familiar, yet nearly as two-dimensional and far removed as one of the goddesses painted on the ceiling above her bed.

Sophie stared at the photo and tried to imagine Sylvie as a living, breathing girl sitting at the Louis XIV dressing table getting ready for…for…a night out with Nick Morrison, the celebrated bad-boy rocker?

Nick Morrison?

Sophie let her arm fall over her eyes and tried to see Sylvie and Nick as parents. *Her* parents. But it just didn't fit.

She could almost see it, but it was absolutely, positively too much for her to wrap her head around.

Her mind kept superimposing a famous shot of Sylvie—one of her in a 1970s Paris disco, smoking a cigarette with her long, straight dark hair framing her face, her dramatic eyes done up in Cleopatra-like fashion. The shot was so overused by the media it had become the defining image of the young woman who had been just three years older than Savannah when she died.

Sophie's heart pinched at the thought.

She sat up and hugged her knees to her chest. Then as she reached out to pick up the framed photo off the nightstand, someone knocked on the door. Sophie's hand flinched away. She half expected museum security to burst in and demand she not touch the *objets d'art*.

Instead, a slight woman dressed in a gray maid's uniform hesitantly pushed open the door.

"*Excusez-moi, s'il vous plaît,* Madame Baldwin. Monsieur Lejardin is here to see you."

Sophie's heart hammered.

"Just a moment," she whispered. "Don't let him in just yet." She got out of bed carefully so as not to wake Savannah, raked her hands through her hair and swiped at the sleep in her eyes. The thought of Luc catching her drowsy and sleep-rumpled was far worse than museum security bursting in.

"He is waiting in the dining room and would very much appreciate a word with you as you enjoy your breakfast. After you make yourself ready."

"Oh. Of course."

Sophie stood awkwardly in bare feet and the borrowed silk

nightgown someone had laid out for her the night before, unsure of how to dismiss the woman.

"Hmm…*merci beaucoup.*"

The maid nodded and left.

Right. As if he'd be standing outside her bedroom. They weren't in Trevard any longer. They were in the *Palais de St. Michel.* Things were more formal here.

It was just that she'd gotten used to Luc always being there—right over her shoulder. Right next to her, as he'd been in the limo last night. Now that she had so much more…breathing room in this place, it was ludicrous to think Luc would continue to be a constant presence in her life. Because if he did, that would mean it was by his choice rather than out of duty.

She snuffed out the vague sense of disappointment at the thought of their going their separate ways and left Savannah to enjoy the sweet sleep of the innocent. As she headed toward the bathroom, she noticed someone had set her suitcase inside her room.

Hmm…she thought she and Savannah had been alone in the apartment last night. Although it was harmless, the thought of an unknown person creeping in as they slept gave her the heebie-jeebies.

Maybe they weren't alone, she thought as she turned on the faucet in the huge marble shower and peeled off her nightgown. The best staff was supposed to be all but invisible except when needed.

She covered herself and glanced around the bathroom. Okay, now she was just being ridiculous. Surely some things were sacred.

Still, there must be thousands of places to hide in this

castle. As a child, Sylvie must have played some marvelous games of hide-and-seek in this maze of a mansion.

Right about now Sophie wished she could discover some of those hiding places and render herself invisible while she decided whether she had it in her to accept full responsibility for what lay on the horizon.

Luc stood and bowed when Sophie entered the dining room. She looked gorgeous in classic gray tweed slacks and a black sweater that hugged those curves he found so enticing.

"Good morning," he said. "Happy Thanksgiving."

She stopped for a moment and blinked, as if she'd forgotten something.

"Good morning." She shook her head as if clearing a haze. "In all this excitement, I didn't realize today was Turkey Day. I guess I'm still messed up on time."

The room seemed to light up in her presence, he thought as he pulled out a chair for her at the dining table. As she sat, he caught a whiff of her freshly washed hair and resisted the urge to lean in closer.

Unfortunately that smile in her eyes was certain to vanish when he delivered the news that the meeting with the Crown Council was firmly set for noon.

As Luc took a seat to Sophie's right, he strengthened his resolve to lead with his head rather than falling prey to the intoxicating scent of black sweaters and shampoo.

"Did you sleep well?" he asked.

She nodded, then shrugged. "Jet lag, I guess. My inner clock's a little off. Obviously my calendar's off, too."

She laughed, a sound like fine crystal.

"I have something for you," Luc said. "Phones for you and Savannah."

He took them out of his jacket pocket and laid them on the table next to her.

She knit her brow. "There must be a mistake. These aren't our phones. We had the old Nokias—not very fashionable, I'm sure. But they do the job."

It was wonderful to be able to do this for her. Because she didn't expect it. She wasn't about flash and glamour, although her natural beauty was far more attractive than most of the women he'd met who tried so hard. Too hard.

"This a new phone that isn't even on the market yet. A friend is marketing them and he gave me a few to try. They will target iPhone customers. I figured Savannah might think it was—how do you say…cool? To be the first to own one."

Sophie looked a little taken aback. She opened her mouth to say something, stopped, then started again. "Thank you, Luc, but…" She bit her lip. "*Hmm,* this is a little embarrassing, but they are expensive."

He nodded. "I'm sure they are. Isn't it ridiculous what people will pay for a telephone? But yours is gratis. Of course the *Palais de St. Michel* has its own network. So there's no cost for service."

She looked as if she'd become instantly wide-awake. He picked up the phone with the tag that read *Sophie* and handed it to her. She slanted him a glance and hesitantly accepted it.

"I had our technology director transfer the numbers stored in your former phone. I took the liberty of having him program my number into speed dial. Please, never hesitate to call me. I am at your service."

As she bit her bottom lip, he hoped she would call, because

outside of taking care of her phones and informing her of the Crown Council meeting—which really wasn't his job; it would be her assistant's once she was set—he shouldn't call her. Not for the reasons he wanted to.

"Thank you. Savannah will be so excited."

A server entered the room and placed two large platters on the center of the table—one heaped with breakfast meats and eggs cooked in every fashion imaginable; the other held bread and pastries. The servants filled coffee cups and crystal goblets with juice—a choice of orange, grapefruit, pomegranate and tomato.

Sophie chose the freshly squeezed orange juice, but waited until Luc said, "Please, help yourself to some breakfast," to serve herself a modest helping of scrambled eggs and bacon.

He followed suit, serving himself as he weighed the best way to break the news.

"I met with King Bertrand early this morning," Luc said. "He's very glad you're here."

Sophie swallowed a bite of egg and smiled.

"This morning you've already gotten us new phones *and* had a meeting. Before breakfast. Do you ever sleep?"

That was the beauty of being organized and unencumbered. The reason he needed to focus on work and not on the scent of the *princesse's* shampoo. That's how he got things done.

"Sleep is highly overrated."

"When will I have the pleasure of seeing my dear grandfather?"

"How about today for lunch, in honor of your Thanksgiving holiday? We don't celebrate it here in St. Michel, but he thought it might be a nice way to welcome you."

"He's in luck. I just happened to have an opening in my schedule."

Her eyes twinkled and he hated to say anything that would change that, but it wouldn't be fair for her to expect an intimate lunch with her grandfather and walk into a council luncheon meeting. "Great. How about if the Crown Council and I join you?"

She frowned and set down her fork with a loud clank.

"Well, in that case, I'm busy. I mean, you're welcome to join us, but I'm not ready to meet the Crown Council."

"The king thinks it best that you're introduced today. The longer we delay, the greater the chance of word leaking. If anyone learns of this before the council has been informed, we will have a mutiny on our hands. Of course, the king is right."

And even if he wasn't, this wasn't a battle Luc wanted to fight. The meeting was inevitable. Better sooner than later.

She glared at him.

"And what if I don't come?"

"That wouldn't be a good idea."

She stared at her hands for a moment.

"Sounds like you're not giving me a choice, doesn't it?"

"We certainly won't force you to do anything against your will. However, the king is concerned that—"

He paused and glanced at the footman who stood innocuously against the wall.

"We require privacy, *s'il vous plaît.* Please leave us and close off the dining room."

The servant nodded and indicated the bell affixed to the underside of the table. "Monsieur, madame, please ring if we may serve you."

With that he disappeared.

Luc waited for him to close the doors before continuing to speak. The walls had ears, especially in a case like this, where the royal apartment had been opened and readied for *guests* for the first time since 1983 when the king had vacated the place after the loss of his wife and second daughter.

The queen had suffered a stroke and never recovered. Then just four months later, Princess Celine had died in an automobile accident. It was almost too much for the king to bear. Thus he moved himself and Prince Thibault and Prince Antoine to smaller quarters in the east wing of the palace.

Was it any wonder that opening the apartment after all these years to two Americans had caused speculation amongst the staff to run rampant?

All the more reason to introduce Sophie to the council. All the more reason to speak cautiously, even though they were supposedly alone.

He scooted his chair closer to Sophie and leaned in.

"Pardonnez-moi," he whispered, fully aware that his proximity was making her uncomfortable. She tried to scoot back, but he took her arm and refused to let her reclaim her space. "I know this is not comfortable, but this is the perfect example as to why we must not waste any time informing the Crown Council. The servants have eyes and ears. They listen and see. Even overhearing a simple conversation such as this could spell disaster if someone were to leak matters to the press before we inform the council."

She jerked her head away and he noticed her cheeks were flushed. "Yes, but—"

Luc pressed a finger to her lips. She glared up at him with a look that registered somewhere between anger and defiance.

A vaguely sensuous current passed between them. She was so close and again he was tempted to lean in and kiss those enticing lips. The tips of his fingers brushed her jawline as he removed his finger. An action that could've been interpreted as unintentional…or not.

"Meeting the council doesn't mean you must stay, although I truly hope you will."

She blinked as if surprised to hear him utter that confession. Perhaps he'd surprised himself, but this was no time to backpedal, not when he needed her to cooperate.

It was his job to ensure she cooperated, he reminded himself, determined to ignore the vibrant chord those green eyes plucked deep down in his solar plexus.

"Oh. My. God. I can't believe the new phone Luc gave me. It makes an iPhone seem like a dinosaur." Savannah flopped down next to Sophie on the brocade couch in the living room of their apartment. "I didn't know they gave presents on Thanksgiving here in St. Michel. But it's pretty cool that they do! Look, Mom, it gets Internet and television. It's got all kinds of movies and songs already loaded—oh my God! It has the new Panic at the Disco CD. It hasn't even been released."

The girl squealed, shoved an earbud in her right ear and handed Sophie the other one. Obligingly, Sophie listened to a few strains of the loud music, feeling both grateful to Luc for giving them the phones and resentful at his pushing her to meet the council before she was ready. And more than a little confused by the undeniable attraction that zinged through her every time she looked at him.

"Savannah, turn it down a little, sweetie. You're going to

ruin your hearing. Please don't turn up the volume past the halfway mark."

Much to Sophie's amazement, the girl minded her without so much as an eye roll. Maybe this getaway would do them both some good. If Sophie could just make it past the Crown Council…and the magnetic pull of Luc Lejardin.

After breakfast she'd halfheartedly agreed to attend the luncheon on the stipulation that Savannah didn't have to go.

Not yet.

Luc reluctantly agreed, asserting, however, that they'd want to meet the girl sooner or later, and it might as well be sooner.

The Crown Council just sounded so…formal and *unfriendly.* There was no reason to subject Savannah to that. What was the point of subjecting a fourteen-year-old girl to the board if they ended up going back to Trevard?

Which might happen.

She'd come to St. Michel on a fact-finding mission…for a look-see to determine if it was the right move. But this quick meeting was starting to feel like a bait and switch: *Now that we have you captive—sit here, wear this…. Ooooh, doesn't she look perfect on the throne with the crown on her head?*

"Look, Mom, I can even take pictures and record things on it. Here—" she held out the phone. "Say something."

Sophie touched her daughter's hand.

"I'm glad you're happy. Don't forget to say thank-you to Luc. He'll be here any minute."

"You bet I'll say thanks," Savannah said. "I want to hug him."

Yeah, so do I, sweetie.

* * *

Since that wasn't possible, Sophie vaguely wished for something just as exciting to look forward to—something to distract her from the ominous meeting.

What were they looking for in her?

Shouldn't experience outtrump bloodlines in the qualifications for running a country?

Right. Just as her decision to pack up and move to the other side of the Atlantic should be based on wanting to do the job, not because every time Luc's gaze met hers her heart turned over.

She'd learned her lesson the hard way with Frank, and she wouldn't make the same mistake again. Although Luc, with his Armani suits and sexy smile, was worlds different from Frank.

"Oh my God, I have voice mails—look!"

With a pale pink painted thumbnail, the girl held down the key that retrieved messages.

"One from Jess and one from…Tick? *Ugh.* Can you believe Tick had the nerve to call me after he hooked up with her again? He's an idiot if he thinks we're getting back together. I'm going to my room to call Jess. She's going to die when she hears I have the new Panic CD." Savannah stood as she dialed her phone. "Let me know when Luc gets here. Oh—Hey, Jess…It's me, Savannah. Oh. My. God. You'll never believe what's going on…."

Her voice trailed off as she walked down the hall and was finally muted by the closed bedroom door.

Sophie sat alone in the living room listening to the ticking of the antique grandfather clock, relieved that there was an ocean between her daughter and Emo Jess…and Tick. Yes, especially Tick.

When Sophie was a teenager, she and her friends had a "sisters before misters" pact, meaning they'd never date each other's exes and they'd never let a guy come between their friendship. When they left Trevard, she'd thought that Jess and Savannah's Tick tug-of-war had been such a breach of this principle that the dubious friendship was over. Then again, maybe that's where the "sisters before misters" rule applied. Tick was out. Their friendship was in.

*Hmm…*perhaps that was one point in favor of staying in St. Michel. Although keeping her daughter locked away in a castle, like Rapunzel, certainly wasn't the solution, either.

"Who is Savannah talking to?" Sophie started at the sound of Rose's voice.

"Hi, Mom. I didn't realize you were here."

"I just arrived." Rose sat on the wingback chair across from Sophie and crossed her ankles. "Claude let me in."

Claude? Oh, the butler, or whatever the French called a man who slipped around like a ghost—not really there, yet always there.

Sophie thought about what Luc had said at breakfast about the walls having ears and it gave her the creeps. Could she ever get used to never being alone again?

"Happy Thanksgiving, *ma chérie.*" Rose kissed Sophie on the cheek.

"Happy Thanksgiving, Mom."

"Where's my granddaughter this fine morning?"

"Luc activated her phone, and she's returning calls."

Rose glanced at her watch. "She does realize there's a

seven-hour time difference between St. Michel and home, doesn't she?"

Sophie shrugged.

"It's not that early at home—well, six o'clock. If she wakes someone up, I'm sure that'll make her more conscious of the time change than anything I could say."

Rose nodded and fidgeted. She uncrossed her ankles, then recrossed them the other direction, smoothed her skirt and seemed generally restless.

"You look awfully nice," she said. "That's a beautiful outfit. What are your plans this afternoon? I was hoping you and Savannah would want a traditional Thanksgiving dinner tonight."

Sophie glanced down at the conservative navy-blue Chanel suit her maid, Adèle, had laid out for her to wear to the luncheon. Surprisingly, it fit as if it had been custom-made for her. Amazing, seeing how she'd never had a fitting. Her mother's handy work or another page from the open book of details about her life?

"What, Luc hasn't given you my itinerary? In fact, I'm surprised he didn't send you here to make sure I hadn't defected."

Actually, now that she'd voiced the thought, it held more truth than she'd initially intended.

"Did he?" Sophie asked.

"Ma chérie." Rose laid her hands in her lap, ladylike, one over the other. "I wish you would trust us."

Sophie had to bite the inside of her cheeks to keep from reminding Rose that she had trusted her. All her life. And given the circumstances she thought she was doing pretty well to have come this far.

Rose cleared her throat. "I know what you're thinking,

Sophie. I can only pray that you'll find it in your heart to truly forgive me for keeping the truth from you all these years. Please, you must know that I couldn't love you more if I had given birth to you. You are my daughter."

Sophie felt the dam start to weaken as tears threatened. After Laura's accident, she'd decided to forgive, but she and Rose hadn't had time to sit down and discuss it. "Mom, I know that and I love you, too. It's just…It's just so much, so fast. But I wonder about…"

She couldn't bring herself to say the words…to wonder aloud about Sylvie, her birth mother. It was crazy. If anyone would know, it would be Rose.

"About Sylvie?" she asked, as if reading her mind. "It's perfectly natural for you to be curious about her."

Sophie nodded and a rush of relief flooded over her.

"She was such a young, beautiful girl," Rose said. "A handful, yes, but a good girl at heart. You favor her. Have you noticed from the pictures?"

Sophie nodded and the grandfather clock struck twelve-forty-five.

"Are you ready?" Luc's voice sounded from behind her, jolting her with awareness before she even had a chance to turn around.

Rose smiled. "We will talk more later, my love. We'll have a fabulous feast tonight. Luc, you will join us, *non?*"

Sophie felt strangely shy and rooted to the sofa, but then Luc appeared at her side. He was getting awfully good at being there—in the right place. At just the right time. Just when she needed him.

"Are you ready?" He smiled and offered his hand. There was something reassuring in his steadfast strength.

She put her hand in his and stood, savoring the delicious rush.

For the first time since she'd arrived in St. Michel, Sophie felt as if she might be okay.

Because everything would be okay. She had to believe that.

Really, feeling like this, what was the worst that could happen?

Chapter Eight

She looked like a painter's study of light and shadow, Luc thought, as he led Sophie down a series of corridors toward King Bertrand's chambers.

Neither of them spoke, and it gave his mind plenty of opportunity to ponder the contrast of dark hair against creamy skin and startlingly green eyes.

She was reminiscent of a Renoir come to life.

Beautiful.

Simply stunning.

He wrenched his mind from the landscape of her beauty, opened the door to the anteroom and waited for her to enter. As she did, he noticed her earlier confidence seemed to have melted into guarded apprehension.

The door closed behind him and they were alone in the

room. He touched her shoulder. Perhaps not a professional gesture, but he wanted to reassure her.

It was his job to reassure her, to make sure she was of the state of mind to put her best foot forward to the council, but this felt more personal.

He wanted her to succeed. His hand slid down to her arm and the firm, feminine feel of her sent a jolt right down to his toes, especially when she turned toward him and they stood face-to-face.

"Everything will be fine," he reassured, taking her hands in his. "Simply be yourself."

She lowered her gaze, holding on to his hands. He was suddenly overcome with the urge to lift her hands to his lips. But when she looked back up at him, ready to say something, she gazed past him, pulling her hands from his.

"*Bonjour,* Monsieur Lejardin," said a voice from behind them—Marci, a petite brunette who served as assistant to the king's personal secretary. "King Bertrand is expecting you."

Luc stepped back. It wasn't like him to allow himself to get caught up in the moment.

As Marci walked toward an antique writing table, her gaze swept a cool, head-to-toe assessment of Sophie.

Marci picked up the telephone. "Monsieur Lejardin is here," she said into the receiver, then showed them into the room.

"Good, you're early." King Bertrand sat behind his desk writing in a journal. "I want a word with Sophie before we head to lunch."

Sophie shot Luc a panicked glance, as if he were her lifeline. Perhaps he should've better prepared her, but given the short notice, it had seemed better to verbally brief her on the various personalities of the seven-member council rather than inundate her with policies and political leanings.

Not that she couldn't have handled it, but too much, too fast would've been counterproductive.

She'd be fine, and he'd come to her aid if she needed him.

The king stood, walked over and extended his hand.

Seeing them together, the king with his granddaughter—the first woman in ages to threaten his good sense—reminded Luc of his place: he was here to serve. He was to assist Sophie, to steer her in the direction of what was right for St. Michel.

Falling for her wasn't part of that assignment. She was of royal blood and he was what amounted to the hired help.

Emotionally, he forced himself to take a big step back, distancing himself from Sophie and doing his best to ignore the ensuing pang of regret.

The moment Sophie, the king and Luc walked into the royal dining room, which vaguely resembled a scaled-down version of *Hogwarts's* great hall, seven pairs of curious eyes sized her up, then dismissed her.

She wanted nothing more than to hide under the lavishly dressed luncheon table. If it wouldn't have been so utterly undignified, she just might have done it.

Better yet, she wanted to make a run for it—grab Savannah, leave the *Palais de St. Michel* and never return.

Except that she had no idea how to find her way back to the apartment through this maze of a monstrous place, much less how to get out of this fortress. If she tried, she'd probably end up having to call Luc to come find her.

Hmm—maybe that wasn't such a bad idea…

Alas, because Luc's hand was firmly on the small of her back propelling her forward, and her legs felt like sun-warmed chocolate, it was probably in her best interest to stay. Too bad the two of them couldn't escape back into Marci's office. The way he'd held her hands as they waited had felt nice. Perhaps she was just imagining it, but she could've sworn that a current of—something—passed between them. Maybe it was wishful thinking. Or perhaps nerves. Not to mention, she hadn't yet adjusted to the seven-hour time difference.

A server appeared with a tray of champagne flutes. The king helped himself and turned to address two men who were standing near. Luc lifted two glasses off the tray, handed one to Sophie and raised his glass to her.

"Santé!"

Whatever had or hadn't passed between them, his presence was reassuring and she focused on him rather than the fact that she was the only woman amidst this group of downright grumpy-looking old men. Well, Luc wasn't old, and really neither was the guy to the king's left, the one who looked as if he smelled something foul.

She glanced around the room taking in the aristocratic opulence—the dark polished wood, the intricate tapestries that adorned the walls, the lavishly set luncheon table. It was like something from a dream—or Hearst Castle, where you were supposed stay behind the velvet ropes.

Yet here she was on the inside; heiress to…all this?

At least Luc was close by. That made her feel better. He was proving to be the one constant in this ever-shifting sea of change.

How strange that he was part of this exclusive inner circle, yet worlds different. And it wasn't simply the age difference. The others had a completely different vibe—a stuffy self-importance that smacked of calculation and hidden agendas.

Maybe it wasn't right to peg them before she'd even been introduced, but it didn't take a genius to know that a person didn't get a seat on the Crown Council without some political clout.

"Sophie," said the king. "I would like you to meet my godson and fellow council member, Vicomte Yves De Vaugirard."

He gestured to the thin man on his left, the one who looked as if he smelled poo.

"Yves, allow me to introduce Sophie Baldwin."

Now that they'd been formally introduced, it appeared as though the stench he smelled had worsened. The *vicomte*—no less—was probably in his early- to mid-fifties, Sophie guessed, or maybe not even. Maybe it was his pinched look that aged him.

"Comte De Vaugirard, Yves's father and the senior member of the council, is over there." The king gestured with his head at a man across the room. "They are from one of St. Michel's oldest and most respected families.

"Yves, I trust you will entertain Sophie with anecdotes about our great nation," the king prompted.

"But of course. I welcome any opportunity to brag about my beloved St. Michel." After her grandfather disengaged and wandered off to join another conversation, Yves measured Sophie over the top of his champagne flute, as if weighing whether he should divulge inside information on an exclusive club in which she didn't stand a chance of joining.

Yves took a long, bored draw of his aperitif before he began. "Of course we are one of the best examples of a nation benefiting by betting on the rich rather than the poor. The proletariat make up but a minute segment of the population. Because of that, we have very little poverty—and what little we do have is so small it's hardly an issue. It has been so for centuries."

Okay. And what was she supposed to say to that?

Oh, bravo. The poor are such nuisances.

"Ah, but Yves, did you mention the high literacy rate and the emphasis on education?" Luc pressed. "That's a contributing factor to the high standard of living. You make it sound like we're an elitist society."

She loved how Luc didn't simply go along with the *vicomte's* party line. That he challenged what sounded exactly like elitist propaganda.

Yves sniffed, then turned to say something in French to the man standing next to him. Sophie might have worried that he was talking about her, but really there was no chance of that.

She wasn't even on the Vicomte De Vaugirard's radar.

Luc leaned in and whispered, "A regular humanitarian, isn't he? My brother, Henri, is the minister of art, culture and education and he takes pride in our country's high literacy rate. I like to remind the Crown Council of the good job he does every chance I get."

He winked and their gazes snared. Something about the Mr. Darcy-esque look combined with the velvet of his French accent caused the jumble of butterflies in her stomach to swoop in one big spiraling loop.

And for a moment she feared she was in trouble, but in the nick of time the king made his way to the table and everyone followed.

"Take the seat to the king's right," Luc whispered, as if

nothing had transpired between them. Maybe nothing had—not now or earlier in Marci's office. At least not on Luc's part. Maybe it was just her imagination. And if so, it was probably best left at that.

Still, she was relieved when he claimed the empty place next to her. With his prompting, she might not make a total fool of herself.

Or so she thought until a server rushed up and yanked Sophie's napkin off her plate with a flourish, and placed it in her lap. Should she have done that immediately after she sat down?

But other liveried servants gave the council members the same treatment. Sophie relaxed a little, remembering a trick she'd learned in a high school etiquette class where you put your hands in your lap and discreetly touched the thumb and forefingers to make the "okay" sign on each hand. If you looked more closely, the fingers on the left hand formed a lowercase *b,* indicating your *bread plate* was on the left; the fingers on the right hand formed a lowercase *d,* indicating your *drink* was on the right.

Okay, so it worked best at crowded round luncheon tables where the place settings tended to bump one into the next. Here—at this expansive rectangular table—each person had plenty of room. It was obvious which components of the place setting were hers.

Too bad she didn't have more Miss Manners tricks up her sleeve. She'd just have to make do with the basics, like not talking with her mouth full, which probably wouldn't be a temptation, because no one but Luc seemed the least bit interested in what she had to say.

That was fine with her.

Too bad they couldn't take the bottle of champagne and get out of here....

She stole a glance at Luc, who'd been ensnared in conversation by the man to his right.

She smiled to herself. Contemplating the places she and Luc could go was a thought that just might sustain her through what was otherwise proving to be a torturous afternoon.

*Okay...*obviously she'd had enough bubbly.

"Madame Baldwin has experience working in social services for her county in North Carolina," Luc said in an attempt to draw her into the conversation with the council member to his right—*Oh, what was his name? The introductions had been fast, the accents thick and the champagne flowing freely. Geesh, if this was a working lunch, how the heck did anyone get any work done around here?*

The councilman nodded and engaged in another conversation with the bald man across the table. Still, social services was something familiar, something she could discuss intelligently, and because Luc had mentioned it, she said, "Earlier, the *vicomte* mentioned that a small segment of the population lived in poverty? Who are these people and does the government do anything to help them?"

The bald man across the table surprised her by answering, "It's a sad fact, but most of our country's poorest are employees of the *Palais de St. Michel.* Still, I suppose that one could view it as the government helping them by giving them work, no matter how meager."

She was so startled by the quip that for a moment she was speechless. Then the king raised his glass in a toast.

"I'm very happy that we are all together today," he said. "I've called this *Thanksgiving* luncheon rather than a regular meeting in chambers because it's a very special occasion. One, in fact, that will give each of us a reason to be thankful. Before I get to that, I would like to introduce you to Madame Sophie Baldwin. As I requested in the bulletin you received, we will conduct this meeting in English for Madame Baldwin's benefit. Later, I will tell you more about her and why she's here today. But first we shall eat."

A legion of servers appeared with covered trays and did a synchronized revealing of the first course: *foie gras.*

Eat? Oh, sure.

How could she eat this lavish meal when the person serving her might be living in poverty? She felt like Marie Antoinette.

Even if Sophie had no stomach for lunch, King Bertrand ate with enough zeal for both of them, quickly polishing off his duck liver and knocking back two glasses of Beaujolais.

All around her she heard snippets of conversation: a world leader's name mentioned here, quips about foreign policy and alternative energy sources over there. She wanted to revisit the question of St. Michel's poor—did they have enough to eat? Adequate health care?

As she glanced around—at the king, who seemed lost in his own culinary nirvana, and the other men who comprised the counil—it suddenly hit her that *they* were the power behind the throne.

They weren't looking to her, as heir to the throne, to "run" the country—oh no, that was their job. They needed a figurehead. Someone to sit on the float and wave while the council steered.

Of course.

She wasn't sure if that realization made it better or worse.

Could she ever be content to sit passively, while the rich and powerful did the work and *turned a blind eye* to a small, yet *très* undesirable segment of the population whose only crime was that they were poor?

The thought weighed heavy as the entrée (read: appetizer) gave way to the *plat principal* (read: entrée) of terrine de saumon aux épinards (salmon and spinach terrine)—not exactly traditional Thanksgiving fare, but it was fine since they were having turkey and the trimmings that night. The salmon was followed by a salad, which was cleared for the cheese course and finally a delicious crème caramel and café. But for some strange reason, they didn't serve the café with the dessert; it came afterward.

"And how is it that French women don't get fat?" Sophie murmured as she sipped her coffee.

"Fat?" Luc looked confused. "You have nothing to worry about. You look fabulous."

"Thank you." She hadn't meant to say it out loud. "I wasn't fishing for a compliment. I was just referencing the book…." She was suddenly drowsy from the food and wine and weary from always trying to explain herself. If one thing had become clear today it was that Luc was on her side. And she couldn't think of anyone she'd rather have in her corner.

"You know what? Never mind. Thank you for the compliment. I'll take it."

He smiled, that sexy, lazy smile of his. "As you should."

He looked as if he wanted to say more, but King Bertrand was tapping his dessert spoon against his champagne flute, calling his council to order. In a matter of moments her secret would be revealed.

Chapter Nine

After Sophie's introduction, the Crown Council meeting disbanded abruptly. Good thing, Luc thought, because Sophie did not need to hear the inevitable fallout sung by a chorus of bruised egos.

He escorted her back to her apartment and returned to the council chambers for a meeting Pascal and Yves De Vaugirard had demanded with the king. He hadn't been invited, but because he was already deeply involved, he thought King Bertrand could use some backup. As minister of protocol, he wouldn't be entirely out of place.

When Luc walked in, Yves stopped midtirade and turned his venom on him.

"What the hell are you doing here? This is a private meeting between Crown Council members and the king. Get out."

King Bertrand slammed his fist down on the table. "Nobody gives orders in this office but me. Monsieur Lejardin will stay."

The elder De Vaugirard stiffened and the younger glared at Luc like a cobra poised to strike. Seated in the two chairs in front of the king's desk, both emanated an aura of mutinous revulsion. The only difference was that the father was better at disguising his than the son was. Nonetheless, Luc still picked up on it.

"If you think you can pull that commoner out of the woodwork and install her as heiress to the throne, you're more senile that I thought."

"Yves, that will do." Pascal didn't flinch as he reprimanded his son. "You must remember with whom you are speaking. He is the king of St. Michel and you will treat him with due respect."

Yves leaned forward and spat through gritted teeth, "I don't care if you are the king, you're in violation of the St. Michel constitution. Even *you* cannot get away with that."

A bad feeling urged Luc to slip his hand inside his jacket pocket to his holstered gun, ready to draw if need be.

King Bertrand stood, fire blazing in his dark, watery eyes. He pointed toward the door. "Get out or I'll see you impeached from the council."

Yves did not move, but Pascal was on his feet in an instant, trying to smooth the king's ruffled feathers.

"Here, here, we've behaved irrationally, Your Majesty. Please, forgive us. We're just a bit…overwhelmed by the news you've bestowed upon us today."

"Would you like me to escort Vicomte De Vaugirard to the door?" Luc offered, itching for the opportunity to throw him out on his ass.

"You lay one hand on me and I'll—"

"Yves!" Comte De Vaugirard glowered at his son, who'd redirected his venomous anger at Luc.

Luc knew he was playing dirty, but he moved his arm back just a bit, keeping his hand on the butt of his gun, knowing the move gave the *vicomte* a peek at the weapon. As minister of protocol, Luc was licensed to carry a gun. Even though he didn't relish the thought of shooting anyone, he was ready to protect the king he'd vowed to defend and serve.

The move had the desired effect. Yves's eyes flashed a barely perceptible start of surprise and he settled down, leaving the talking to his father.

For a man in his fifties, Yves was more child than adult with that hair-trigger temper, Luc thought. The only reason he'd gained a seat on the council was because Pascal was first cousin to the king and the king was Yves's godfather.

The nepotism was so deep that Luc was always afraid he would drown in it. It almost brought down his family when the Patrice scandal broke. Yet, in the end, the De Vaugirard strength had merely bent him. It did not break him.

They would never break him. And he would personally ensure that they didn't get the best of Sophie, either.

"Now that we all have our wits about us," said Pascal, "if I may point out something with all due respect, Your Majesty?"

The king sighed. "What?"

Pascal arched a brow, but remained as smooth and unmovable as a river stone. "Your Highness, one thing you must consider before you introduce your granddaughter to society is that Sophie is the daughter of your Sylvie, God rest her soul."

The *comte* crossed himself. The ostentatious show made

Luc want to spit. That man was no more a devout Catholic than the dog that begged for scraps at the kitchen door. And his grief for the late *princesse* was equally contrived. Luc had a sixth sense for this type of deceit, and his BS radar was buzzing.

"Yes, make your point, Pascal," the king snapped impatiently.

Sudden anger lit the *comte's* eyes, but disappeared as fast as it flashed. "The constitution clearly states that the heir to the throne must be of legitimate birth." His voice was not as patronizing as it had been a moment ago.

In fact, it held a slight edge. Luc did not like where this was going.

"The king and the Crown Council can change the constitution if they so choose." The words leaped out before he could stop them. Three pair of eyes pinned him to the spot.

King Bertrand smiled. "Yes, that is exactly what I intended."

"Ah, but I must remind you, to do that requires the unanimous agreement of the council," said Pascal.

"But of course," said the king as if it were a given.

"I dare say you will be shy at least two votes," said Yves. "Therefore a change will be impossible."

King Bertrand looked crushed.

"Why would you do that without even giving Princess Sophie a chance?" Luc spat out the words. "Because regardless of what the constitution says, she remains your *princesse*."

"When did this become your business?" hissed Pascal.

"He does seem to have gotten awfully cozy with Madame Baldwin," said Yves. "In fact, if I didn't know better, I'd venture to say that it looks as if he were trying to further his own interests through the king's granddaughter."

The *vicomte* shrugged. "After all, social climbing does run in his family."

The king slammed both hands down on the table. "Get out, both of you. Get out *now!*"

As anger surged, something else clicked in Luc's gut. Something to the tune of the *vicomte doth protest too much.* It wasn't anything concrete—other than the assertions of social climbing and that it was a classic pot-and-kettle situation. The De Vaugirards were the first to *further their own interests.* Still, something in the exchange had set off the alarms.... It smacked of how those who have something to hide often make a stink about the very infraction of which they're guilty—like a man who is having an affair suddenly accusing his wife of flirting, to deflect his own guilt.

Luc did his best to separate personal dislike of the De Vaugirards so that he could be objective, but it was getting harder to find unbiased ground.

How much of the loathing he felt came from wanting to see his enemy taken down and how much was legitimate?

That answer remained to be seen.

However, two things were certain: He wouldn't stop until he could clearly answer that question; and until he did, he needed to distance himself from Sophie, for her own good.

She was the *princesse,* and when he was around her he tended to lose his head—to linger in thoughts of the sublime way she smelled, to stand much too near her, and give in to the temptation to touch her.

He would always be her loyal servant.

One who would never forget his place.

* * *

Sophie walked through the state dining room, feeling displaced, like a child in the way as the adults rushed around getting the place ready for a special occasion.

The table looked beautiful—set with the finest crystal, china and silver. The centerpiece with its harvest-colored flowers, wispy wheat stalks and mini pumpkins looked like something out of a *Better Homes and Gardens* editorial. And the smells of turkey, sage and spices made her stomach rumble.

It was the perfect Thanksgiving, and she didn't have to lift a finger. As nice as it sounded, it really did feel odd.

She and Frank were still together this time last year. It was their last holiday as a family. As usual, he had been no help.

She'd worked the day before Thanksgiving, did the shopping on the fly the night before. He'd yelled because she'd paid too much for a fresh turkey since there wasn't enough time to thaw a frozen bird, complained that she should've been more organized like his mother used to be.

Then she dragged herself out of bed at four-thirty in the morning to begin preparing the dinner. By the time the three of them sat down to eat, Sophie was ready to fall asleep sitting up.

Her parents couldn't join them last year because her dad had been sick. At least they were together this year, even if she felt removed and everything was a little topsy-turvy—especially the way she anticipated spending the evening with Luc.

Something had shifted today. She had awakened this morning unsure whether duty or something more personal kept bringing him back. Yet after he'd walked her back to the apartment after the Crown Council meeting—after the way he'd touched her, almost possessively, in Marci's office; after the feel of his hand on her back and the way he'd looked at her made her feel both protected and vulnerable…vulnerable to opening herself to him—she sensed it was edging toward the personal.

And getting personal with Luc Lejardin suited her just fine.

Sophie walked into the living room so that she could greet him when he arrived. She couldn't recall a single moment in her life before now when she'd been at a loss for something to do. Usually it felt as if she were trying to cram ten pounds of life into a three-pound bag. She was constantly juggling and praying that she didn't drop one of the fragile balls. There was always an after-school activity for Savannah, clients' files to update, bills to pay, clothes to wash, dishes to scrub….

The list went on and on.

Too much to do, too little time.

And here she sat, the *princesse* of St. Michel, with nothing to do—except attend luncheons and dinners and go girly over a man. For someone who'd gotten on her nerves the way he initially did, he'd really become important to her. She hadn't wanted to like him at first, but never in her life was she so glad to be wrong.

Her maid, Adèle, entered the room holding a lone crystal champagne flute.

"Madame, I thought you might care for some champagne."

"How very nice of you, Adèle."

Sophie accepted the glass, feeling a little guilty drinking fine champagne, which seemed to flow like water in the *Palais de St. Michel.* If they had a moat around this place, it would probably be full of the stuff.

Adèle stood there, looking hesitant, as if she had a question.

"Is everything all right?" Sophie asked. *Do you have enough to eat? Does your family have shelter?* The woman looked clean, well and rested. But if not her, then who? Who was it that the fine people of St. Michel overlooked with their collective blind eye?

"Well, Madame, I was told that you didn't need my services past seven this evening? That I was to have the night off?"

The woman looked wary, as if someone were playing a joke on her.

Sophie nodded. "It's Thanksgiving, Adèle. You should be home with your family."

Her guarded look morphed into one of confusion.

"Madame, with all due respect, we don't celebrate Thanksgiving in St. Michel."

Sophie smiled. "I know, but as hard as you work, you could still use a night off. Don't forget to take the meal I had the kitchen staff package for you. Maybe just this once, you and your family could celebrate Thanksgiving, too. It never hurts to count your blessings."

The confusion faded into gratitude. "Oh, it is very kind of you to think of me. It just happens that it is my son's birthday and he will be so surprised when I get home."

Her son's birthday? And she was working?

"Happy birthday to him. How old is he?"

"Six years old."

"Well, then, he definitely needs his mother. You may leave now and you will receive full pay. Go celebrate."

Adèle hadn't been gone ten minutes when one of the footmen entered the room with a note on a silver tray.

"A message for you, Madame."

Sophie took the note off the tray, feeling like a character in a Jane Austen novel—well, if Jane Austen had written a book set in a castle off the coast of France.

She ran her hand over the cream-colored linen envelope admiring the fine quality of the stationery before she pulled out the note:

Dear Madame Baldwin,
Thank you for the dinner invitation. I deeply regret that I will not be able to attend.
I remain your humble servant,
Luc Lejardin

Chapter Ten

So much for edging toward the personal.

Two weeks had passed and Sophie hadn't seen even a shadow of Luc. She thought about calling him since he'd programmed his number into her cell phone and told her to use it.

A couple of times, she'd even gone so far as to hold the phone in her hand and contemplate pushing the speed-dial button he'd programmed to call his number, but she couldn't bring herself to do it.

Please, never hesitate to call me. I am at your service, he'd said that day he delivered the phones. *I remain your humble servant…*he'd written in the note excusing himself from dinner.

Well, then where was he?

Luc was a busy man. His mission to bring her to St. Michel

was complete. He was probably enmeshed in another assignment and didn't have time for her because he just wasn't interested.

It was just that she thought he was a friend.... He certainly was a bright spot in this strange turn of events. She understood that he had a job to do, that he wasn't hired for her amusement. But she missed him. Couldn't he spare a few minutes?

She should call him...just to say hi...

And she would've if she hadn't been so busy overseeing the Christmas decorating, attending etiquette lessons and fittings, and organizing a toy-drive for the underprivileged that the Comte De Vaugirard had so cavalierly brushed off at the Crown Council luncheon two weeks ago.

Even in the midst of the rush, she missed him.

Was that such a bad thing?

Sophie was thinking about that as she went to join her grandfather for tea. They'd been having short, informal get-togethers all week. Sophie was touched by the effort he was making to get to know her.

"Are the Christmas decorations in your quarters to your liking?" He sat in the wingback chair next to Sophie, a sterling pot of Earl Grey and a selection of cakes on a tiered tray between them. He seemed more relaxed than ever, which in turn allowed her to relax.

"They're beautiful," she said. "The apartment looks like a wonderland."

It truly did. In addition to the wreaths and garlands, there were three Christmas trees: a small one in the foyer adorned with nutcracker ornaments; a massive regal Fraser fir in the living room decorated in white and gold; and a more traditionally trimmed blue spruce in the dining room decked out in an eclectic mix of ornaments in various shapes, sizes and colors.

"It was amazing," Sophie marveled. "Adèle asked me how I wanted the house decorated and within two days it was done."

King Bertrand smiled. "I'm glad you're pleased. And the deportment lessons? Are they going well?"

"Yes, fine."

It was the cotillion lessons she'd never received as a child. All week, she and Savannah had been working with teams of French teachers, etiquette and public relations specialists whose task it was to make them *princesse* perfect and put just the right spin on why Princess Sophie had been hiding all these years.

Their identity was still top secret, of course. She had a feeling that once the professionals were finished with them, they wouldn't even recognize themselves.

She glanced around her grandfather's office, at the antiques and gilded finery. From what she'd seen, not a corner of the palace had been left undecorated. It was beautiful, but expensive and foreign and so contrary to the life she was used to. The investment the king was making in her and her daughter would make it harder to walk away at the end of three months. But she needed more of a sense of purpose than seasonal decorating and an endless stream of fittings to make a life here.

An elegant porcelain nativity scene displayed on the credenza caught her gaze.

God, I'm so confused. Please send me a sign that will help me make the right decision for my daughter and myself.

She wasn't a religious woman, but somehow the universal familiarity of the manger was comforting. A sign of hope that transcended all languages.

And speaking of hope, it was on the tip of her tongue to ask about Luc—if her grandmother had seen him; if so, what he had been up to—when Marci knocked and opened the door hesitantly.

"*Pardonnez-moi,* Your Majesty, but the Vicomte De Vaugirard is here to see you. He says it's urgent."

Sophie's heart sank. Not exactly the sign she'd hoped for. She set down her cup ready to make an exit at the first opportunity.

"Send him in, please," said the king. "And please bring us another cup in case the *vicomte* would care for some tea."

Marci bowed and disappeared.

A moment later De Vaugirard entered and bowed. "Your Majesty."

"Yves, come in. Have a seat." The king gestured to the sofa across from him and smiled broadly.

Tall and slight with a delicate air about him, De Vaugirard wasn't quite *effeminate,* but just up to the line. With his graying hair and expensive clothes, he was handsome in a well-heeled, aristocratic sort of way. If Sophie didn't know better, she would've never have guessed he and her grandfather had been at bitter odds since her arrival. Well, except for traces of the same I-smell-something-rank expression she'd spied on his face that first day.

Yves's gaze shifted to Sophie, then back to the king.

"Perhaps I should come back another time," said Yves, "when you're not busy."

"Nonsense, Sophie and I were just enjoying some tea. Join us."

As if on cue, Marci entered with a fresh cup and saucer. She poured some tea for the *vicomte.* "Cream, sugar or lemon, *monsieur?*"

Yves sighed as if the situation pained him, and said, "Plain will do."

He seated himself on the sofa across from Sophie and the king and accepted the cup that Marci offered him.

Is this guy for real?

He was probably in his early fifties, yet his affected mannerisms made him seem much older. He was like a caricature, Sophie decided. The poster boy of spoiled privilege forced to slum with someone he deemed far beneath him.

The king made small talk. With an air that hovered somewhere between bored and downright disgusted, Yves mostly ignored Sophie. It seemed as if her grandfather was grasping at straws when he said, "It's ironic that you dropped by when you did, Yves. I was planning to call upon you today for a favor. I was wondering if you would be so good as to show Sophie around St. Michel? Give her the grand tour. She has been cooped up inside since she got here, and I know she'd like to get out. Since you know the delicacy of the *situation* until she has been formally presented to the public, I know I can trust you to use the utmost discretion in public."

The following Monday, Sophie sat in the apartment study at a gorgeous Louis XIV desk working on details of the toy-drive, which was shaping up nicely. They were set to deliver three hundred wrapped gifts to the St. Michel Community Center on Christmas Eve. She jotted a note to herself to ask her grandfather to appeal to the De Vaugirards, one more time to help deliver the toys as a goodwill gesture. They and council member Norbert Guillou were the only three who refused to participate. Sophie could read between the lines. They also happened to be the three dissenting council members who were against her succeeding her grandfather. Couldn't they rise above petty political differences one day of the year? Especially when it involved children?

Adèle knocked on the door and announced that she had a visitor in the living room. Sophie's heartbeat upped its tempo.

Luc?

She ran her fingers through her hair and wished she could slip into her bedroom to reapply her lipstick, but because the study was off the living room, she couldn't.

When she stepped out to greet the visitor and saw Yves De Vaugirard waiting, her spirits took a nosedive and her guard went up like a wall of steel bars.

No. Not him.

When her grandfather had suggested that he give Sophie the grand tour, the sourpuss could do nothing more than grunt. *Why was it that the wealthy could act inappropriately and it was called eccentric?* Seems like Yves could stand a deportment refresher. All the more reason to show him how it should be done.

"Vicomte De Vaugirard, to what do I owe this pleasure?" She didn't even sound like herself. She crossed the parquet floor and extended her hand, just like Daphne, her coach, had taught her, even though it felt awkward and insincere.

Yves bowed stiffly and straightened.

He made her feel uneasy the way he watched her with those small ice-blue eyes of his. They seemed to bore right through her. Did the guy not even blink?

"Thank you for receiving me without an appointment, Your Highness."

Your Highness?

Wait a minute. This from the guy who was so adamantly opposed to her very presence?

In the spirit of good manners, she decided to talk to him for a few moments and then feign an appointment.

"I hope you don't mind, but I took the liberty of checking your schedule with the king's secretary and since you had a free afternoon—"

Or not...

"I would be very honored if I might spend some time with you this afternoon," he said, "and show you the beauty of St. Michel as your grandfather suggested."

She must have looked utterly flummoxed because he added, "You are a matter of...great importance to our country. I would be remiss if I didn't make an effort to get to know you...personally."

What? Well...this was certainly an unexpected change of heart, but definitely a step in the right direction. Her grandfather would be so pleased.

"Please, have a seat." She gave him her best *princesse* smile, and started to order some coffee, but he interrupted.

"Excuse me, *Your Highness.*" He gave an affected bow of the head with the words. "If I may be so bold, I know a lovely place that overlooks the water where we might enjoy tapas and wine. It would be my honor if you will allow me the privilege of spending the afternoon with you."

A chance to leave the palace? After being cooped up inside for two weeks? The place was starting to feel like a prison.

Savannah was at school and would be occupied for the day.

Sophie was afraid her daughter would get behind in her studies and had insisted that her daughter go to a real school with kids her own age before they drove each other crazy. Under strict orders not to spill the *princesse's* beans, Savannah was enrolled in the best private school in the area.

Going with Yves was the perfect opportunity to do a little internal PR, a chance to win him over and prove that she wasn't simply the poor North Carolina hick he and his father had made her out to be.

Maybe it was the principle of the matter, but for some reason she was more determined than ever to make friends with Yves De Vaugirard.

This grand tour might be the perfect way to do it.

Her mind skittered back to the night she first arrived and how Luc, leaning into her, invading her space, had promised to show her the island. But where was he? He'd disappeared without so much as a goodbye.

"A tour and lunch would be wonderful," Sophie said, ignoring the disappointment that she would tour the island for the first time without Luc.

Fifteen minutes later, they were in Yves's car negotiating the serpentine turns and hills along the narrow coastal road that led away from the castle. Looking down the steep, rocky embankment into the sea below, Sophie grasped for conversation to distract herself from the mean case of vertigo that threatened each time she looked down.

"What kind of car is this?" she asked for lack of another neutral topic.

It was probably a gauche question—though Daphne hadn't specifically spelled out asking the brand of car to be among the many taboos to be avoided during polite St. Michelian conversation. Plus she'd never seen anything like the black and cherry two-seater. The way it slanted down in the back, swelled up in the middle, yielding to a curved nose, it looked almost reptilian.

To her relief Yves smiled warmly and purred, "A Bugatti Veyron. You like?"

She almost expected him to reach out and stroke the dash.

"It's very nice."

The admiration of his *baby* seemed to break the ice. As they made their way down the rocky mountain that housed the palace, she was surprised by how warm and personable Yves proved to be. He pointed out various spots of interest and shared fascinating bits of trivia such as the stretch of road where a James Bond movie had been filmed.

Around the next bend, Yves abruptly pulled the car over onto the shoulder. For a panicked instant, Sophie feared they might slide off the road. She reached out for the dash to brace herself as Yves stopped the car. She slanted him an alarmed glance and thought she caught the barest trace of a smirk curving up his thin lips. Was he trying to scare her?

"What's wrong?" she asked. "Why are we stopping?"

His face was somber again. He rolled down the car windows, then stretched his right arm across the back of her seat and leaned in to point toward the passenger-side window with his left hand, nearly surrounding her with his body.

It gave her the creeps, especially when he turned his head and looked at her at such close range. His face was much too near; the mingled scent of his musky cologne and warm, stale breath nearly overwhelmed her.

There was nothing romantic in the gesture. The way he studied her was calculated, almost a bit passive aggressive.

"This is the unfortunate place where Princesse Celine lost control of her car and plunged to her death."

His words were matter-of-fact, devoid of emotion.

Sophie shuddered as a sudden cold chill swept over her. She turned away from Yves, moving closer to the window, gazing intently down the steep incline, more to escape him than to see the morbid site.

It was a gray day. The temperature had dropped probably ten degrees since she had arrived in St. Michel—since that night in the limo when Luc sat so close and she'd fought the overwhelming urge to move toward him. Not like this with Yves, who conjured up a strange mixture of sadness and unease.

She struggled with a ridiculous sense of loss but couldn't quite define it. The loss of Celine and Sylvie who'd died before their time? The fact that Luc had all but disappeared. It seemed inappropriate to even think about him right now.

Finally, after another clumsy moment, Yves shifted back into his seat. They rode silently until he steered the car into the valet parking line of a busy restaurant that fronted a rocky stretch of beach. She was tempted to ask him to take her back to the palace, but didn't want to chance offending him and worsening relations. After all, he really hadn't crossed the line of inappropriateness. Though he'd edged right up to it. Nothing Luc hadn't done. The only difference was, with Luc, she'd walked right up to that line with him and was just about to drag him over. Until he stopped calling.

She needed to stop thinking about Luc.

"I thought you might enjoy a light bite to eat and some champagne." Yves sat with his left elbow resting on the open window frame, his right wrist draped over the steering wheel, as blasé as if the awkwardness at the top of the hill had never happened.

A cold wind off the water blew in through the open windows, biting through Sophie's silk blouse. She rubbed her arms trying to warm herself.

"You are chilly?" Yves asked. "Allow me."

He unbuckled his seat belt, removed his navy blue wool sports coat, and leaned over to place it around Sophie's shoulders.

Sitting there in that expensive sports car, parked in front of the Côte d'Azur, the strangest thought washed over her: She'd come a long, long way from that hideous mustard-colored coat. Shouldn't that feel good, rather than so unsettling?

Ah, well....

She was just about to thank him for the nice gesture when he leaned in closer, and this time, she thought he actually might try to kiss her.

What the heck?

Panic seized her and she fought the urge to push him away. Instead, she turned her head to the right and pretended to brush something off the jacket's shoulder.

Was this what he was pathetically fumbling for up at the site of Celine's crash? Only now they were in public. In full view of the valets and people coming and going.

This was worse than any bad date she'd ever been on. And it wasn't even a date. It was a reconnaissance mission, a goodwill attempt to make peace with the enemy. All for her grandfather. For St. Michel...Because of that, if she didn't do something to allow him to save face, this little outing might end up doing more damage than good.

"Thank you, Yves." She wouldn't look at him, but she kept her voice light. "I really should've brought a jacket."

At that moment, thank God, the valet appeared at his door. Still playing the gentleman, Yves got out and walked around to the passenger side, helped Sophie out of the car and into an embrace, kissing full and deep.

Then it was as if everything moved in slow motion. One moment she was struggling to get out of Yves's arms, the next she was staring down the lens of a camera as a photographer documented the sordid exchange, then Luc and three *Men in Black* appeared from out of nowhere. As two of Luc's men shielded her from the fray, the other went after the photographer, while Luc whisked her to a waiting car, away from the press and the Vicomte de Vaugirard.

"What the hell were you doing with Yves De Vaugirard?" Luc spat the words as he slammed his Audi into fifth gear, unsure if he was more outraged at the *vicomte* for putting his hands on Sophie or mad at himself for leaving her alone with the snake.

"What was I *doing?*" She sounded just as angry as he felt. "I wasn't *doing* anything. My grandfather asked the *vicomte* to show me St. Michel. I have no idea why he kissed me like that. God knows I didn't lead him on."

Luc slanted a glance at her in time to see a rogue tear meander down her cheek as she scrubbed the back of her hand over her lips.

Thank God she'd followed protocol and informed the king's secretary where she was going. Marci had immediately phoned Luc. Something about it smelled funny. Following his instincts, Luc decided to tail De Vaugirard on this unlikely outing. And he was damn glad he did.

Now two of his men were in a separate car, making sure

no one followed Luc as he drove Sophie to safety. He was still awaiting word from Dupré as to whether he was successful in wrangling the camera away from the photographer.

Sophie was shaking. He wanted nothing more than to stop the car and hold her, but he couldn't. Even though he'd effectively ditched the media, it was only a matter of minutes before they caught up.

The last thing they needed was for the paparazzi to come upon Sophie and him parked along the side of the road.

But Luc had a better idea. He steered the car off the highway and onto a back road.

"Where are you going?" Sophie asked swiping at a tear.

"I live about a half-mile from here. I'm taking you to my house so that you can compose yourself before we go back to the castle."

He made a right turn, then a quick left and his phone rang. "Did you catch him?" he barked.

"The photographer handed off the camera to a waiting car," said Dupré. "This looked like a pretty tight operation. Someone tipped them off. I wonder who they're working for?"

Luc growled under his breath. "Yeah, I wonder."

He snapped the phone shut.

The minute Yves had Sophie in his arms, the scumbag paparazzo swooped in, got the shots and threw the camera to the driver, who took off in the car while the photographer took off on foot.

The plan had worked too damn perfectly. And it smacked of De Vaugirard.

The photos discrediting the newfound heir to the throne were sure to run in the paper the next day.

But what the De Vaugirards didn't realize was that in their desperation, they were getting sloppy. They were tipping their hand and it was just a matter of time before Luc had the concrete evidence he needed to nail them.

This war had been a long time coming—vengeance for his father's death and the king's lost family. For his friend Antoine.

It was a war Luc was hell-bent on winning.

"What the heck just happened back there, Luc?"

"I hate to tell you this, but you were set up."

"Set up? What do you mean?"

Luc glanced in his rearview mirror to make sure they hadn't been followed before he pressed a button that opened the wrought-iron gates surrounding his house.

"Since news of the *vicomte* hitting the town with yet another woman is hardly fodder for the paparazzi, I'm afraid that possibly someone has leaked your story," he said as the gates closed behind them. "Tomorrow it is likely that all of St. Michel will know about its new heiress."

"Oh, my God." She pressed her hands over her beautiful mouth.

Luc drove into the garage, closing the door so that it might serve as a second layer of privacy and protection.

"Can't you stop them?" she asked. "I mean, come on, my grandfather is the *king*. Doesn't he have any power?"

Luc opened the car door. "Unfortunately, not over the press. Especially when they're working for the De Vaugirards."

The car's engine ticked in the quiet garage.

"They sound like mafia," she said.

He opened the car door. "Let me assure you, the mafia has nothing on the *comte*."

Luc turned off the security system and held the door for her, fighting the urge to pull her into his arms and promise he would do everything in his power to protect her. Even after two weeks of keeping his distance, the woman still affected him. What in the world was he going to do?

They entered the kitchen, which opened onto a large living room that had a breathtaking view of the sea.

As Luc removed his shoulder holster and set it on the kitchen counter, Sophie moved, transfixed, into the living room and stared out the large plateglass windows.

Luc drew some water in a kettle and put it on to boil.

"How can he get away with this?" she murmured, her back still to him as she gazed out at the ocean. "Better question is, why would he do this? He has to know how much it will hurt my grandfather. Why would an old friend fight so vehemently against another over something that should be a celebration? My grandfather thought every member of his family was dead, but he still has me. Shouldn't his *oldest friend* be happy for him?"

The look on her face was heartbreaking. She moistened her lips, and the simple action reminded him that even though he'd removed himself from temptation, even distance couldn't tame his craving for her.

"One would think," he murmured.

Luc had his theories, but he couldn't tell her. Not until he was absolutely certain. In the meantime, it was imperative that she and Savannah not be left unattended. He couldn't take that chance.

Luc walked up behind her with a small cashmere throw and draped it around her, resisting the urge to run his hands down her arms and taste the ivory skin where her neck met her shoulders.

"Did he hurt you?"

She shook her head and turned to face him as she pulled the blanket tighter. "Only my pride. I feel like such an idiot. I actually thought I was making headway by going with him today. I should've known better."

She looked up at him with fresh tears glimmering in her eyes.

"No," he said. "There was no way to know without someone warning you about him. I should never have left you alone."

She bit her lip. He saw her throat work, and his heart turned over in response.

"Luc, where have you been?" Her voice was barely a whisper. "I've missed you."

His mouth went dry. As he searched for the words, she reached out and ran a gentle finger along his jawline.

His head tilted into her touch and his arms went around her, gently pulling her close. He wanted to keep her here. Safe and away from barracudas like de Vaugirard. Her mouth was just a breath from his. Those lips…so tempting…would taste so sweet. A rush of desire urged him to give in, to sample the taste and feel of her while the rest of the world melted away. There were so many reasons he shouldn't…but at the moment, he couldn't seem to remember any of them—

The teakettle whistled, sounding an alarm, warning him to back away.

"I need to get that." He stepped back, away from her touch, away from temptation as reality rushed in and common sense chastised him.

The *princesse* was vulnerable after her ordeal with the *vicomte.* How could he even think the things he had contemplated?

"Let's have some coffee and then we need to get you back to the castle and begin damage control."

When Sophie and Luc returned to the castle, he took Sophie back to her apartment to freshen up. He needed to clear his head and focus on the De Vaugirard situation before he went to the king's chambers. After giving the situation some thought, Luc decided it was his duty to share his theory—though unfounded—with the king. So much of his job revolved around gut instinct. The big problem was if he waited to test these theories, by the time he had solid proof, sometimes it was too late. In the wake of what happened with Antoine and his family, he couldn't afford to chance waiting.

When Luc told the king of Yves's very odd and very public display of affection and the ensuing photography, King Bertrand was furious and visibly shaken.

"It makes no sense," King Bertrand insisted. "The paparazzi are always milling about down by the water. It had to be a fluke, a case of Yves being in the wrong place at the wrong time."

"Unless," Luc asserted, "Yves intended for the incident to be photographed."

The king's eyes flashed.

"Absolutely not. Why would he do that? He knows better than anyone what a disaster it would be for word to get out before we're ready to present Sophie."

"Exactly," Luc said. "What I am about to suggest will not be easy for you to hear, Your Majesty, but it is my duty as minister of protocol to alert you to potential problems. Since the loss of the prince and his family, I must remind you that the Vicomte De Vaugirard's name has been mentioned as a likely successor."

He paused to give the king a chance to digest what he was suggesting. But the man simply stared back at him with uncomprehending bewilderment.

"Your Majesty, you upset the plan by adding your long-lost granddaughter into the equation just when the *vicomte* thought he was home free. Can you think of a better way for him to discredit Sophie than by marring her introduction to the people of St. Michel?"

The king's mouth fell open. Then he found his words. "Watch what you're saying, Lejardin. This is my *godson* you are defaming. The son of my lifelong friend. You seem to forget he would have been putting his own reputation on the line if he'd staged a setup with these photographs."

"Your Majesty, I humbly beg your pardon, but the *vicomte* has delighted in building just that sort of reputation. He thrives on that type of publicity. So much so that the *vicomte* out with a new woman ceases to be news. Unless the press had been tipped off that his latest conquest wasn't just any woman."

The king flinched.

"Do not be crass, Monsieur Lejardin."

He expected this reaction and knew it wasn't easy for the king to hear.

"I humbly beg your pardon, I hate having to bring you this news. But this was a very well choreographed operation. One of my men went after the photographer to try to retrieve the camera, but there was a getaway car waiting. The media had been tipped off and I will work to find out who informed them."

The look of doubt that washed over the king was heartbreaking. This was the part of Luc's job he hated the most—exposing lies, shattering trust. Yet it was either that or expose the king and his family to unnecessary risk. Too much death had already happened under his command. His heart ached at the thought of Antoine, whose memory was already seeming to dim in the month he'd been gone.

There had already been too many innocent lives lost. There would be no more. Especially not Sophie. He couldn't fathom the thought of losing her and, if forced, he would fight to the death to protect her.

"With whom have you shared your theory?" the king asked.

"No one else, Your Majesty. It is much too sensitive a matter to carelessly bandy about."

The king stroked his beard and nodded, a faraway look in his eyes.

"However," Luc continued, "given the circumstances, it is my duty to inform you of any potential threats. To that end, I have heightened security measures concerning Princess Sophie and Princess Savannah. If there is need for them to leave the palace, I will personally escort them. It is also prudent for you to use the utmost caution as you go about your business, Your Majesty."

"You make it sound as if we are preparing for an imminent attack."

The older man looked weary, as if all the fight had been zapped out of him. Although Luc was betting against himself by hoping he was wrong, the alternative was unthinkable.

"Your Majesty, I hope to God we aren't. However, we can't take any chances."

The intercom interrupted them. Marci announced Sophie, the Vicomte De Vaugirard, and Pierre Benzanet, the chief of palace communications, who had been summoned to formulate a crisis PR plan that would somehow turn this mess in their favor.

It seemed that everyone was arriving at once. Luc was curious to see how De Vaugirard would treat Sophie now that they were holding in the eye of the storm.

The *vicomte* was a good actor. He feigned concern for Sophie, he even manages a bit of stiff praise for Luc for miraculously being in the right place at the right time.

"Lejardin, it seems you are everywhere these days."

Luc couldn't put his finger on it, but something was off. Maybe it was the way Yves chose to perch on the wingback chair rather than claiming the empty space on the couch next to Sophie, as Luc longed to do.

In fact, when Luc did just that, De Vaugirard didn't seem to notice. There wasn't an ounce of territorial concern or other indication of the attraction that might inspire a man to spontaneously pull a woman into a passionate, very public kiss. No, every ounce of Yves's focus was trained upon Benzanet.

"The press office phone will ring nonstop once the paper is released," said the communications chief. "The media will surely demand an audience with Princesse Sophie and the *vicomte.* It is imperative that we agree on a plan for a morning press conference before we leave this office tonight. Because the obvious question on everyone's mind will be, who is Sophie Baldwin and what exactly is the nature of her relationship with the Vicomte De Vaugirard?"

Chapter Eleven

Relationship with the Vicomte De Vaugirard?

The thought and ensuing mental flash of what a relationship with Yves would entail made Sophie feel vaguely ill.

There was no way.

Absolutely no way she could even pretend to play the part when she didn't feel that way about him. Because when she was in love it consumed her, it radiated from the inside out like a light she had no intention of veiling.

Reflexively she glanced at Luc. As if he sensed her, his gazed flicked to her and a knowing look passed between them. The single glance said that he, too, thought this was a crock of PR crap. A private conversation between them in the midst of a crowded room.

That alone made Sophie feel better.

Benzanet excused himself to get to work on the crisis PR

plan, after suggesting that they go with the idea of a brief and very innocent *relationship* between the *princesse* and the *vicomte.* The two could amicably "part ways" over the next few days. They could be seen out to dinner together, perhaps be photographed out for a cruise on the *vicomte's* yacht. Given the *vicomte's* social standing, it might even be a good way to introduce her. A sophisticated royal romance was always a surefire way to raise the monarchy's approval rating.

If Sophie felt vaguely ill before, now she was downright queasy.

After the door shut, the *vicomte* sighed. "Well, this is quite a little mess we've gotten ourselves into, isn't it, now?"

We? He made it sound as if they'd sneaked off together for an afternoon tryst. The only *we* she could come up with was that that must have been a mouse she felt in his pocket when he pulled her into that sloppy kiss.

"If only I had known I was putting her at risk," Yves said to the king, "I would have never heeded *your* suggestion and gone through with the outing."

Oh, so now it was the king's fault for suggesting the outing. The vicomte *certainly didn't like to take responsibility, did he?*

Yves looked nonplussed and much too effeminate as he crossed his right leg over his left knee. He seemed to be avoiding looking at Sophie. But as he pursed his little mouth, the expression made Sophie remember how he'd pecked at her with those thin lips and an angry bubble burst inside her.

"Why did you kiss me?" She hadn't meant to say the words aloud. They just sort of popped out like an errant hiccup.

At least the *vicomte* had the decency to look embarrassed. He studied his shoes. Then his gaze slanted toward the king and back to the floor before he cleared his throat.

Still not looking at her.

"*Pardonnez-moi,* Your Highness. I couldn't seem to help myself." He gave an awkward little shrug.

What…?

She should've been flattered that she'd inspired so much passion in a man that he'd be so moved as to lose control of his wits and lay a big passionate kiss on her in public…but *puh-lease.* Did he really expect her to believe he was so overcome by passion that he *couldn't seem to help himself.*

There was one important element missing from the equation—passion.

So…why did he do it?

"I assure you, madame, I meant no harm." The *vicomte* lifted his chin regally. "And I would very much like to see you again."

Sophie wanted to squirm. Or maybe laugh. She wanted to call him on this contrived, robotic request for a second date and ask him *why?* She wasn't buying it…. Was anyone else? She glanced at Luc and her grandfather. They both wore poker faces, but something in Luc's eyes told her to be quiet. To wait and talk to him.

That he had the answers she was looking for.

"Well," said the king, "I suggest we call it a night. It's best that we get some rest before tomorrow's press conference."

With a hasty bow to the king, the *vicomte* mumbled pleasantries to Sophie and Luc and made his retreat.

Right. He was so eager to see me again he didn't even offer to walk me home.

Thank God. Because she didn't know what she would've done if he tried to kiss her again. This time when no one was looking. Imagine that.

In the awkward moment before she left, she tried to somehow reassure her grandfather that everything would be okay…but the words escaped her. All she could say was, "I'm sorry."

All he could offer was a weary smile and a valiant "I'm sure everything will be fine. Get your rest, because tomorrow will be a trying day."

By the time Sophie and Luc left, the corridor was eerily silent except for the echoing cadence of their shoes on the marble floor.

With every step the echo seemed to sing: *mistake, mistake, mistake, mistake.*

Coming to St. Michel was a mistake of colossal proportions.

"What was I thinking?" she murmured.

"I don't know," Luc said. "Tell me what you're thinking."

Sophie shook her head. "Maybe the Crown Council's right? Maybe it's time for a new era? Because I'm certainly in way over my head."

"So you are saying that you're better suited for gray cubicles and endless stacks of case files?"

"At least in my job with the county, I knew what I was doing. It was something worthwhile. I was helping people rather than destroying a dynasty."

Her heart grew heavy with memories of Laura. She hoped her boys were doing okay after losing their mother, wished there was something more she could do for them, but she was so far away.

"I can tell you that as the heiress to the throne of St. Michel, you will have many opportunities to make a difference. As the *princesse,* you have carte blanche. The only way you will bring down the Founteneau dynasty is if you quit. You don't strike me as a quitter, Sophie."

Oh. Well, thanks. I think.

How did he do that? How was it that he had that uncanny ability to disarm her? To make her feel as if anything was possible. Anything in the world…especially between them.

They walked side by side, neither of them speaking again until they reached the front door of Sophie's apartment.

Claude met them in the entryway with a polite bow. "*Bonsoir,* Madame Baldwin, Monsieur Lejardin. I trust you had a good day?"

Oh, if he only knew.

"It was fine, thank you, Claude. And you?"

The butler looked a bit taken aback by the question, as if he weren't used to people asking. "Yes, madame, it was a quiet day. When would you care for your dinner and will Monsieur Lejardin join you?"

"Please stay, Luc," she said. "I could use the moral support when I prepare Savannah for tomorrow." She dreaded the thought, but she had to do it. Before Savannah saw a picture of her mother kissing the *vicomte* plastered all over the paper. Worse yet, she had no idea the angle the paper would take with the story or what they'd say. Savannah needed to be prepared. And so did her parents. The task almost overwhelmed her.

Until Luc said, "Of course. I'd love to."

The way Luc looked at her made Sophie's stomach roll over. To pry her thoughts loose from the pull of his dark, enigmatic gaze, she said, "And Claude, speaking of Savannah, where is she?"

The clock in the hall showed it was after seven. Sophie was surprised her daughter hadn't already called looking for her.

"Mademoiselle Savannah asked a school friend to stay for dinner. They have already eaten and are in her room doing homework."

Homework? Without my having to threaten to ground her? At least something went right today.

Savannah had been talking about the friends she'd made in school. For the first time since the divorce, her daughter actually seemed happy. Sophie's heart weighed heavy with the thought that one news story might change that.

"I guess it will just be the two of us for dinner. Please let us know when it's ready."

The butler gave a little bow. *"Très bien, madame."*

"Thank you, Claude."

As Sophie led Luc into the living room she suddenly became aware that they were alone. Aside from the few staff who remained after hours, Savannah and her friend, it was just them. No cameras, no *vicomte.* It was an enemy-free zone. It felt safe to be tucked away with Luc, insulated from the real world.

It was hard to believe that not even a month ago he had been a stranger delivering a message that totally changed her world. Now it seemed as if he was one of the only people in the world—or at least in this strange world of St. Michel—whom she could trust. One of the only people in the world she wanted to spend time with. Balm for her weary soul.

There was a fire in the fireplace. That and the glow from the Christmas tree was the only lighting in the room. If her heart hadn't been so weighed down by the baggage of today's fiasco, it might have seemed romantic.

She was beginning to feel like the queen of bad timing.

"Have a seat, I'm going to tell Savannah I'm back."

As she walked out of the room, she wished she could go

back and undo the moment she'd agreed to go out with the Vicomte De Vaugirard. But this was not a fairy tale where she could look into a magic mirror and wish away the bad. Oh no, this mess was her introduction to the people of St. Michel and the only thing she could do was deal with it, and pray that somehow she could turn it around in her favor. As if.

She could hear laughter when she reached her daughter's door. It was like music to hear Savannah so happy, and Sophie stood there for a moment savoring the sound. When she knocked on the door, Savannah called "Come in." Sophie opened the door and saw Savannah and her friend lying on their stomachs on the Persian carpet in front of the fireplace. Their books were open and they were sharing a bowl of popcorn. They seemed to be having the time of their lives—as fourteen-year-olds should. The girl wasn't pierced (beyond the ears) or tattooed (that she could see…*nah,* not on this one). She didn't even know her name, but she could tell the girl wasn't the type.

They were just two teenagers having fun—*doing their homework.*

"Mom! Hi, this is my friend Camille." She said the name with the proper French inflection—*Ca-mee*—and the girls giggled again. "Camille, this is my mom."

She smiled and greeted Sophie politely. And she didn't even have a sullen, pierced pout. How refreshing.

"I invited her to stay for dinner, I didn't think you'd mind," Savannah said. "Can she sleep over?"

Oh, how Sophie wished she could say yes. But she couldn't.

"Nice to meet you, Camille. You two certainly sound like you're having fun. How about a sleepover this weekend, okay?"

Collectively the girls groaned, "No, tonight!" But it wasn't the typical *battle call* that usually followed Sophie's shooting down one of Savannah's spur-of-the-moment ideas. Seconds later they were giggling again.

"I'm having dinner with Luc. But just holler if you all need anything."

They were too busy making plans for Friday night to hear her. But that was okay. That was the way it should be. Savannah happy and laughing, having fun doing the things that normal fourteen-year-olds do.

As Sophie stood outside Savannah's closed door, the strangest feeling washed over her. Yes, *this* was the way it *should* be. She didn't want to take this away from her daughter. This was her birthright. Hers, too. Was she going to let a greedy *vicomte* rob them of it?

A strange, shaky feeling washed over her. Like an adrenalin rush. Akin to what it must be like to contemplate jumping out of an airplane. Something she would never do. But sometimes you have to step out of your comfort zone to really find yourself.

Taking chances was exactly what she was thinking about when she stepped back into the living room and saw Luc sitting on the couch in the half-light of the fire, holding a flute of champagne. He stood when she entered the room.

"Claude thought we might like an aperitif." Luc lifted the other crystal glass off the coffee table and held it out to her. She took it and scooted a little closer to him on the couch. And he didn't seem to mind. They clinked glasses and sipped the golden liquid.

"Savannah's having such a good time with her friend. She seems so happy here. That alone could convince me to stay."

Luc smiled. "Well, then, I shall do everything in my power to ensure that your daughter remains in a constant state of bliss."

He reached out and toyed with a lock of Sophie's hair. There was something intimate about the gesture and she shifted closer to him. The fire warmed the room—or maybe it was the unspoken that lingered between them. Words that needed to be said.

"Have you been avoiding me?" The words escaped in a rush, before she had the good sense to think about what she was asking.

He let her hair fall, sipped his drink as if thoughtfully searching for what he wanted to say.

"Because if you have been staying away on purpose, I think you should know there hasn't been a day that's gone by that I didn't long to see you."

Then he simply nodded.

She squeezed her eyes shut. "Why, Luc? Why have you been avoiding me?"

He exhaled, and the breath sounded heavy and jagged, full of the same longing that was about to make her burst. The way he looked at her was devastating.

"Because of wanting to do this," he murmured as he ran his thumb slowly over her bottom lip. "And this." He softly traced the plane of her cheek. "And this." His hands were in her hair now, pulling her toward him.

It wasn't the first time she'd wondered what he'd taste like. No, that question had bloomed the very moment he'd appeared at her front door that very first day. The longing had never subsided. It lurked in the back of her mind as strongly as he'd stood by her—just as he was doing now—being her friend, her protector, her rock.

And then those lips she'd been dying to taste closed over hers, finishing what had almost begun at his house earlier that day. His kiss was surprisingly gentle. He tasted her, but didn't take her. He was so tender, tasting like a hint of champagne and something else, something uniquely Luc. As her lips opened under his, passion overtook her and for just a moment she wanted him to take her—right here, right now—in a hard, punishing kiss that would block out all the ugliness of the day.... He was nothing like Yves. He was the man she wanted to kiss...but Savannah could walk in...and Claude was due to call them to dinner any moment...and tomorrow the photo of her and Yves would be plastered all over town—

Breathless, she pulled away.

Luc blinked, looking a little dazed. "I'm sorry," he said. "I shouldn't have—I should go."

He stood, but she grabbed his hand.

"No, Luc. Please don't go. That was..." She searched his eyes as he stared down at her, uncertainty clouding his face. "That was wonderful, and something I've wanted for a long time. It's just that I can't masquerade as the girlfriend of one man when I'm involved with another."

God, one kiss didn't mean they were involved. But she didn't want this to end with one kiss. There was a lot more she wanted to explore with him. But first—

"I need to tell my grandfather in no uncertain terms that I won't pretend to be involved with Yves. I don't care if it is the easy way out."

Luc's expression shifted. When he sat back down, Sophie moved her hand from his arm to his hand.

"It was Yves's scheme that landed us in this position. As far as I'm concerned, he can lie in the bed he's made." She knew she was rambling, but she couldn't stop. "The only thing I will tell the press is I have no idea why he kissed me. If he goes off about how he *couldn't help* himself, he'll have to deal with my saying I do not return his feelings. I know it's harsh, but I know he's not telling the truth. He set me up to look like an idiot in front of the entire nation of St. Michel, so he's going to get himself out of the mess."

Sophie wanted to memorize the look on Luc's face. It was something between awe and admiration. There wasn't a hint of fear in reaction to the suggestion they might be "involved." No one had ever looked at her that way and it made her giddy…then breathless as she leaned in to taste his lips one more time.

"The king needs to know how I feel," she said, their lips a whisper apart.

As they sat there forehead to forehead, he gently stroked her cheek. "I think it is very important that your grandfather know how you feel. I would like to tell him that I feel very passionate about…you…doing what you feel is right. May I come with you to talk to him?"

Chapter Twelve

The cat was out of the bag.

She didn't even have to see the newspaper to know. It was evident in the reverent way the staff bowed when Sophie walked into the room. The former "Madame Baldwin" address was replaced with respectful murmurings of "Your Highness."

They knew.

Dressed in yet another Chanel suit that had appeared in her closet compliments of the couture fairy, Sophie resisted the urge to explain, because she hadn't talked to her grandfather this morning.

Last night, he flinched at Sophie wanting to deny any feelings for the *vicomte*. He wasn't convinced that leaving Yves to explain his actions to the media was the best way out of this.

"It will make it appear that there is infighting among the

Crown Council," he said. "It is imperative that we present a united front on all counts, especially since we will be digging ourselves out of the hole trying to explain why we hid you away all these years."

"What was wrong with the truth?" she'd asked.

He looked sad as he tried to explain, "Sometimes when it comes to matters of state, the truth isn't always as clear cut as one might like it to be."

That sounded like a load of political hogwash. She hated to level an ultimatum, but if being the heir to the throne and ultimately the queen of St. Michel meant compromising her integrity, meant pretending to be interested in a man like the Vicomte De Vaugirard…well then, she'd be on a plane back to Trevard quicker than Yves would have a new woman on his arm.

Luc stood by her the entire way, his professional opinion as minister of protocol and as a close personal friend never wavered under the political guilt trip her grandfather kept heaping on them.

The king finally agreed to discuss the situation with Pierre Benzanet so that he could factor it into his recommendations. They would meet early tomorrow morning before the scheduled pre-press conference briefing.

So, with everything pending, Sophie thought it best to resist explaining herself to the staff until after the briefing. Especially because she hadn't yet seen the paper.

As Sophie sat at her dressing table, a knock sounded on the bedroom door.

"Come in," she said, finishing the final stroke of mascara.

Adèle opened the door. "*Pardonnez-moi,* Your Highness." She curtsied. "I thought you might like some coffee and toast as you get ready this morning?"

"That's very nice of you, Adèle. Thank you."

The maid wheeled in a cart with a covered plate, a china cup and saucer, and a silver coffee pot. She poured the coffee, stirring in the perfect amount of cream, exactly the way Sophie liked it.

"Here you are." She set the cup and a plate of wheat toast on the left side of the dressing table.

"Thank you, Adèle. I appreciate your bringing this to me. I won't have time for breakfast this morning."

The maid made a polite bow and offered a shy smile as she pushed the cart toward the door. Sophie watched in the mirror as the woman paused in the threshold, turning back as if she wanted to say something.

"Your Highness?" she said hesitantly.

Sophie swiveled around on the round vanity stool to face her. "Yes?"

"Forgive me for being so bold." The maid wrung her hands. Sophie hoped she wouldn't ask questions, but if she did, she'd do her best to answer them honestly. That's all she could do.

"My *maman* had the great privilege of serving the Princesse Sylvie, God rest her soul." Adèle cast her eyes heavenward and crossed herself. "It is an honor and a privilege to have the opportunity to carry on that tradition by serving you."

The maid bobbed a quick curtsy and turned back to her cart.

Her mother knew Sylvie—my mother?

"Oh, Adèle, really? Does your mother still live in St. Michel?"

With hopeful eyes, Adèle turned back, nodding vigorously. "I have told her about you—how kind you are. Even before we knew you were—" Again, she gave a slight reverent bow and bit her lip as if remembering her place. "*Pardonnez-moi,* but you have always been so very kind, and I speak for the entire staff and many others when I say we believe you will serve St. Michel well."

Oh—the unexpected show of support stole Sophie's breath.

The maid bowed her head again and turned to go.

What a very sweet thing to say…

"Adèle, I would love to have tea with you and your mother. If you would care to and she would agree to come? I would love to ask her about my…my mother."

The maid gasped and her face lit up. "Oh, *mon Dieu,* yes, Your Highness." She curtsied again. "It would be the highest honor. We shall come whenever you summon us."

She knew my mother….

Of course Sophie had to wait to see what the press conference brought before she could extend an invitation to tea. Even so, her breath caught again. This was someone who *knew* Sylvie, someone who might be able to shed some light on the real person….

"Adèle, what is your mother's name?"

"Her name is Marie, Your Highness."

"Well, please tell Marie I look forward to meeting her soon."

Soon Luc arrived with a rolled copy of the *St. Michel Report* and the day took off as if she'd stepped on a roller skate.

"How bad is it?" she asked, knowing the answer from his solemn expression.

As he handed her the paper, she searched his eyes for traces of regret after last night. The news story should be the only thing on her mind right now, but Luc mattered. Besides her grandfather, he was her only political ally—not just that, he was more…. She couldn't imagine staying in St. Michel without him.

Luc met her gaze unflinchingly, and she gleaned silent reassurance from the way he looked her in the eyes.

Slowly, she unrolled the paper, her stomach churning as she did. The headline above the fold read: "The Secret Royal **Heiress—King Bertrand kept Princesse Sylvie's illegitimate daughter a secret.**"

The story below the fold questioned: "St. Michel's Future Ruling Royals?" It speculated that Sophie might *marry* Yves as a way to get around the issue of her illegitimacy. That perhaps marriage to the king's likely successor was the only way the conservative Crown Council would acknowledge her as the heiress to the throne.

"Nice." If Yves De Vaugirard would've been near she would've boxed his ears.

The photos that accompanied the *Report's* exposé made it look as if the two had been making out all over town. Not only did it feature a photo of the lip lock in front of the restaurant—with a caption asking if Sophie was a wild child, following in the footsteps of Princesse Sylvie—but also shots of Yves and Sophie stopped at the site of Celine's accident; the way Yves had leaned in created the perfect angle for the editors to retouch the photos to look as though the two were kissing. The same for when he had leaned over her with his jacket as they waited for the valet at the restaurant—another contrived smooch shot.

Lovely. Just lovely. She wanted to scream. She wanted to tear the paper into shreds.

"Well, I think this is all the proof that we need that the *vicomte* set me up. Nobody can be in that many *wrong places* at the wrong time. Let's go talk to my grandfather. Now. Because there is no way I am going along with this so he can save face."

Luc didn't blame Sophie one bit for being angry. Frankly he wanted to deck the son of a bitch. He was just as eager as she was to talk to the king, to get a jump on figuring out how they were going to make De Vaugirard confess. *Yeah, right. As if the* vicomte *would do that.*

Still, if Sophie threatened to tell the press that the *vicomte's* kiss was both unexpected and *err,* that under no circumstance were they a couple, De Vaugirard would be forced into the uncomfortable corner of being publicly scorned by a suitor. This would be a new role for him given the legions of women who would give away their firstborn to date the man, who was billed as the king's likely successor.

Luc got a perverse thrill from the possibility of the *vicomte* being publicly humiliated.

It served him right for underestimating Sophie.

Luc and Sophie arrived at the king's chambers a full forty-five minutes before the scheduled briefing. They stepped inside the antechamber only to discover they were alone. Marci wasn't there.

Despite all that lay ahead of them, it was nice to have a moment alone together to catch their breath.

Sophie looked nervous. He hated what this was doing to her. Hated that Yves had snared her in his sticky web of self-importance. He'd walk on hot coals if that meant he could somehow make this situation go away. He reached out and ran a finger along her jaw.

He wanted to take her in his arms, but this wasn't the time or the place. Not when they were preparing to go to do internal battle over a kiss. The last thing they needed was another publicized display of affection. Even if this one was the real thing.

His hands claimed hers. He gave them a reassuring squeeze. "Everything is going to be all right. Don't forget that, okay?"

Sophie smiled and squeezed his hands in return.

Then suddenly the sound of an angry voice alerted them that someone was in the king's chambers—

"Need I remind you that we *must* secure a viable successor to ensure a smooth transition when the day comes that you are no longer 'leading' our country?"

The door leading from the antechamber into the king's office was cracked. Immediately, Luc's antenna signaled high alert.

It was Pascal De Vaugirard's voice. Luc held his index finger up to his lips. Sophie nodded her understanding.

The king's response was too low to hear what he was saying. Luc walked over to the door to better assess the situation.

"Once you are dead, the council will get its majority vote by default," the *comte* said. "Yves's ascent to power *will* happen. You can either graciously agree or die appearing to not have your country's best interest at heart."

He slowly eased open the door a fraction, just enough to allow him to peer inside without being seen.

He discovered that he and Sophie weren't the only ones who had planned an early meeting with the king. It seemed that Pascal and Yves De Vaugirard had the same idea.

King Bertrand didn't seem to be in immediate danger, so Luc kept his secret watch. A moment later he was glad he'd remained in the shadows because Yves De Vaugirard all but handed him the next piece of evidence he needed when he said, "If I were you, I'd take the proposal to heart. Or you just might find that we will get that majority vote sooner than you'd care to imagine, Your Majesty."

Luc pushed open the door. "Was that a threat, *vicomte?*"

All three turned to gape at him.

King Bertrand looked positively ashen, too stunned to speak. Arresting De Vaugirard was certainly one way to prevent him from putting his hands on Sophie. Luc was itching for a reason to put the conniving weasel away where he wouldn't cause any more harm.

"I beg your pardon, this is a private meeting," said Pascal. "You seem to make a habit of barging in where you don't belong."

Yves glared at Luc with a look that echoed his father's contempt.

"It is my duty to protect the king, and I am not comfortable with the threat I heard you issue." He kept his voice steady and low, putting his hand on his hip so that his jacket opened the slightest bit, exposing his holstered gun.

The king finally found his voice. "I'm sure you misunderstood the *vicomte,* Monsieur Lejardin. Yves is like a son to me and he would never endeavor to threaten me. Isn't that right, Yves?" He looked pointedly at the younger De Vaugirard, who did not answer. "Come, let us all begin again so that we may present a united front at the press conference."

* * *

It was no wonder that Pierre Benzanet was the chief of palace communications. He was a genius.

His plan for cleaning up the Yves scandal was to pin the onus on the *St. Michel Report.* The statement he penned claimed that the tabloid newspaper misrepresented the situation by manipulating the photos.

It wasn't a total lie—they had doctored two of the three to make it look as if Yves and Sophie had been hot and heavy all over town. The third? Well, even though it would've been more to Sophie's liking if Yves had faced public rejection—because he wouldn't admit he'd set her up for a humiliating introduction to the good people of St. Michel—this way everyone saved face. Plus if she was looking for a silver lining, the press conference gave Sophie a chance to plug her Christmas Eve toy-drive, broadening the scope from corporate and palace donations to pleas for public contributions.

Of course in between the photo controversy and the toy-drive announcement, there was the simple matter of where Princesse Sophie had been hiding all these years.

This was the crowning jewel, one for which Sophie could excuse the slight stretching of the truth with the photos. Because her grandfather told the truth.

In response to the question, he said, plain and simple, that upon learning of unwed Princesse Sylvie's pregnancy, he sent his newborn granddaughter to be raised in the United States because he thought he was giving her a better life rather than being raised with the stigma of being illegitimate.

"Hindsight is always clear," he said. "If I had the chance to go back and do it over again, I probably would have done some things differently—such as having contact with her as she was growing up. But she is here now, my heir when we thought the House of Founteneau had reached an end. A bright spot to light the darkness. I ask that you forgive my all-too-human mistakes, as Princesse Sophie has found it in her heart to do, and embrace her and my great-granddaughter, Savannah, as a new life for the Founteneau family and the citizens of St. Michel. The two will be formally presented at the annual St. Michel New Year's Eve state ball, which will celebrate its one hundredth year in just over two weeks."

As reporters from newspapers from all over the world began bombarding Sophie and the king with questions about the past, present and future, Sophie couldn't help but think that this was the very best revenge.

The Yves De Vaugirard PR nightmare was old news. Did he really think he could bring her down so easily?

A voice in the far reaches of her consciousness warned that the battle was just beginning.

Chapter Thirteen

"Oh. My. God. Sophie, is it really you?"

It was so good to hear Lindsay's voice. It had been nearly a month since she'd talked to her friend. Sophie settled into the deck chair on the terrace off her bedroom.

"It's really me, Linds. Merry Christmas Eve. I'm sorry to call so early, but I wanted to wish you a good holiday before the day got away from me." It was seven in the morning in Trevard, but Lindsay sounded wide-awake. "I wanted to call sooner, but…well, things have been a little crazy around here. How are you?"

"Are you kidding? I'm fine. I'm flabbergasted. You're a princess? I can't even comprehend it."

It was a beautiful day. In the low seventies, it was warmer than it had been, and compared to North Carolina in December, it was like spring. The sky was impossibly blue and the air smelled like a mix of herbs and sea salt. Sophie inhaled the delectable scent and reveled in the sound of her friend's voice.

"Yeah, you and me both. It's still a little surreal."

"It's been all over the papers and TV," Lindsay said. "I have to tell you that Mary nearly flipped when she heard the news. She's been acting like the two of you were tight. It's all I can do to keep from snorting. So you can see not much has changed. I have to get out of here. Know of any other countries looking for a princess?"

"Come for New Year's Eve, Linds. The king throws a big ball every year and this is our hundred-year anniversary. It would be fun. Plus I could really use some girl time right about now. I'll send you a plane ticket."

"I would if I could, but I just don't see how I can get away. But soon, okay?"

"I'm going to hold you to that. I've met someone and I want you to meet him."

She couldn't believe she was saying that. It was still too soon and with all the change that was swirling around her, there was no way to know where it was leading. Still, every time she doubted the relationship, Luc managed to prove her wrong. If anyone understood the crazy life that she'd fallen into, he did.

And frankly, she didn't want anyone else.

"Okay, so you get to be a princess and you get the hot guy. Not fair."

"Well, would it entice you if I told you that St. Michel is full of hot men?"

"Maybe…"

"Well, you'll just have to come and see for yourself. I'm not going to give up until I get you here."

They talked for a few more minutes about holiday plans, about how the issue of her illegitimacy could keep her from becoming queen—and how Luc had set his youngest brother Alex, who was an attorney, to comb the constitution for any sort of loophole that might help them change the law without unanimous approval of the Crown Council; and finally, Lindsay told her about how the police had finally ruled Laura's death an accident.

"A mechanical inspection they did showed that the accelerator on that old heap she drove stuck. That's what caused the crash. I thought you'd want to know."

Tears welled in Sophie's eyes and suddenly she wanted to bawl. On the one hand, Laura didn't commit suicide. It was a relief to know that after all that hard work and determination she didn't just toss in the towel. But on the other hand, it was heartbreaking that after Laura had come so far it all ended before she even had a chance to really spread her wings. The boys should've received the Christmas presents she sent them, alhough she knew all the money and gifts in the world wouldn't fill the void losing Laura left in their young lives.

"Linds, thanks for letting me know. I promise to call to wish you a happy New Year, okay?"

Then it was time to go. Adèle and her mother were coming for tea and then she and a delegation, which included Savannah, Luc, her grandfather, a few council members and Luc's brother, Henri, were going to deliver the toys to the St. Michel Community Center. Then they were all coming back to the apartment for a Christmas Eve supper. It was going to be a full day.

She was still sitting in the deck chair, holding her phone, when it rang again.

"What did you forget to tell me?" she asked, fully expecting it to be Lindsay calling back with a forgotten morsel of gossip.

"A better question is what did *you* forget to tell *me?*" The deep voice on the other end jolted her.

"Frank?"

"Hello, *princesse.* Why didn't you tell me your little secret before you took our daughter out of the country?"

The sarcasm in her ex-husband's voice set her teeth on edge. She did not have the time or patience to deal with him right now. She stood and walked back into the bedroom.

"I don't owe you any explanations. I followed the rules when I called and asked if you minded if Savannah came with me. You said you didn't mind. So it's all good. But I'm sure that's not the real reason you called. What do you want, Frank? Make it fast. I'm running late for an appointment."

"On Christmas Eve?" His tone was a bit gentler.

"Yes, on Christmas Eve. What is it?"

"Well, uh, I was just calling to say Merry Christmas."

Oh. She sat down on the bed.

"Well, Merry Christmas to you, too. How's Amber?"

Silence stretched over the line.

"You know with it being the holidays and all, I was just sort of missing you and that kid of mine. Where is she?"

Sophie hated herself for it, but she felt kind of bad for him. Not being able to see his daughter on Christmas. Even if it was his own choice to leave his family and move to the other side of the country for a woman who was closer to his daughter's age than his own. Sophie would've died if she had to wake up on Christmas morning and not see Savannah.

"She's not here right now." She was with a friend.

"Oh. Well, I guess I could call her cell. Is it working all the way over there in Europe?"

"Yes, it is. I think she'd really love to hear from you."

More silence. She got up and pulled the towel from her hair, then walked over to her dressing table and sat down.

"Uhh… I've been thinking about you, Soph. You know, missing you. Do you still think about me and what we had together?"

No. Now his melancholy was starting to make her squirm.

"Uhh…how would you feel about me coming out there for a few days? You know, maybe we could ring in the New Year together? You know, talk about being a family again?"

Okay. Now it was starting to make sense. Now that she was the *princesse* of St. Michel, she was attractive again. Or maybe he saw an opportunity to live the high life and wanted a piece of the action.

"No, Frank. I don't think that's possible. I've had a hard year. When you first left, I thought I'd never be whole again. But you know what? I healed. I've moved on."

She thought of Luc and how it felt to be in his arms, and a spiral of white-hot longing unfurled inside her.

"You can't keep my kid from me, Sophie." His voice was angry again.

"I don't intend to keep her from you. You can come and see her anytime you'd like."

"No. I want her to come home. She lives in the States and this is where she needs to be. Not in some backward foreign country."

"Frank, you didn't want her when she called to ask if you could come stay with her while I visited St. Michel. Do you expect me to believe you want her now?"

"Yeah, I do. I'll take legal action to get her back."

* * *

The staff had prepared a beautiful tea—scones, tea sandwiches, cookies and an array of fresh fruit. The spread was set out on the sideboard in the dining room. Sophie had given Adèle the day off—and Christmas Day, too. The staff who worked she'd made sure received double pay in addition to another paid day off—so that they could spend some quality time with their families. She hated to ask the woman to come in on her day off, but Adèle had heartily agreed to the Christmas Eve tea.

Sophie was eager to meet Marie, eager to glean the private bits and pieces about her mother that nobody except one who'd been there in the capacity that Marie had would know.

Marie did not speak English and Sophie's French wasn't good enough to communicate in St. Michel's native tongue. So Adèle had to act as a translator for her. This made her more determined to become fluent in the language.

"My mother was the one who informed the queen, God rest her soul, of Sylvie's pregnancy. She thought she was doing the right thing when she told. Though, now she wishes she had kept her mouth shut. That's why until now she remained quiet about the *princesse's* nuptials.

"Nuptials?" Sophie was so startled, she repeated the word to make sure she'd heard correctly. "As in marriage?"

Adèle nodded. "She didn't mention the *princesse's* marriage to the king after her death because he had made it clear that the *princesse's* relationship with Nick Morrison was a taboo subject. He was grieving and she couldn't bear to add to his torment. However, it saddens my mother to hear the press call Your Highness illegitimate, and she wants you to know that your parents were, in fact, married, even if it was after your birth."

Oh. It was *after* her birth. For a moment she'd thought she'd discovered the key to getting around the Crown Council. If she were legitimate, then their argument would be a moot point. Still…

"Thank you for sharing this with me, Adèle. It's not that I doubt your mother, but how is it that she knows they were married, when no one else does?"

Adèle repeated the question in French to her mother, and Marie talked animatedly, gesticulating as she spoke.

"She was with them. She accompanied Princesse Sylvie the night she and your father, Monsieur Morrison, ran away to St. Ezra. It is a *village perché,* er, a perched village." With her finger she traced a hill in the air. "You understand? An old medieval village, perched high upon a rocky hill."

"Yes, I know what you're talking about."

"St. Ezra is still very old-fashioned. Because of its location, it is virtually cut off from the rest of the world, and because of that, its people are usually cut off from news and those who might be celebrities. It was a place where the *princesse* and Monsieur Morrison would not be recognized. Because of that they went there to the *maire*—the village mayor—and exchanged vows in secret before boarding that ill-fated plane for Bora Bora that crashed and took their lives.

"My mother helped the *princesse* get ready for her wedding, but they wanted to go on their wedding trip alone. Thus her life was saved."

Marie had tears in her eyes as Adèle relayed the story to Sophie.

"She says, that time she decided not to tell the queen

because the last time she did, they sent the *princesse* away and she returned without her baby."

Marie gestured to Sophie and shook her head in a display of sorrowful regret before she resumed talking. Adèle said, "Although she often wishes she'd done something to stop the *princesse* from going on the plane that night. You see, my mother was to return to the castle before anyone got suspicious. She was not to go on the honeymoon to Bora Bora with your mother and Nick. Had she stopped her, maybe Sylvie would still be alive. She told once and it was wrong. She didn't tell a second time and it turned out tragically. She says many people admire you and the charity work you are doing. In your short time here, you have made a difference in the lives of many people."

The words took Sophie's breath, and she was moved nearly to tears. "Please tell your mother it's not her fault that things turned out the way they did. And I appreciate her sharing this information with me."

After Adèle translated Sophie's words for her mother, the older woman reached out and took Sophie's hand. Adèle's eyes widened, and Sophie understood enough of Adèle's words to know that she was admonishing her mother for touching the *princesse* like that.

"It's okay," Sophie said, holding on to Marie's hand.

A tear meandered down Marie's cheek, and she seemed visibly absolved of her guilt.

It was good to see Henri. His brother was one of the few men in the world with whom Luc could relax and let down his guard.

He'd convinced his brother to help distribute the toys

Sophie had collected, though it hadn't been a hard sell. With their busy schedules, it seemed there was never enough time to catch up. This drive to the castle, where they would meet Sophie, Savannah and King Bertrand, was one of those rare opportunities.

Henri shook his head at his brother's recap of what had gone on behind the scenes prior to the press conference—about the threats he'd heard the De Vaugirards tossing about and how the *vicomte* had set up Sophie.

"Ah, the political minefield you are forced to navigate," Henri said. "I'm glad the artifacts and antiquities I deal with don't involve the curmudgeons of the council."

"Right, except when you procure the loan of a priceless Monet—" Luc smiled "—and remind the council your job has some significance."

Henri shrugged. "I suppose getting my hands on a priceless painting pales in comparison to your bringing home a new *princesse*. But I'll have you know I had to cancel a mistletoe date with Raquel so that I could attend this soiree for your *princesse*."

Henri was the ladies' man of the family. Happily single, he had a long list of women he kept in constant rotation, each more beautiful than the next. He was a master at juggling and somehow managing to keep each of them happy yet at arm's length.

"I'm sure Raquel will forgive you, since it's an official invitation from the king."

"Forgive me? I'll have to pay dearly." A wicked smile tugged at the corners of Henri's mouth. "Ah, but with Raquel, making up is always the best part. Even so, I would be remiss in my duty to state and family had I turned down the king's invitation."

From the castle, they would ride in the limousine with Sophie, Savannah and King Bertrand to the community center, where four of the seven members of the Crown Council had agreed to join them. The two De Vaugirards and Councilman Norbert Guillou had declined under the sour pretense of being otherwise engaged on this Christmas Eve—although it was perfectly clear their refusal was simply passive-aggressive backlash to the *princesse's* rising popularity.

"Besides, based on the photos I saw in the paper, I'm dying to meet Princesse Sophie," said Henri. "She sounds like my idea of the ideal—"

"Do not even venture where I think you are about to go," Luc warned.

"Oh, I see," said Henri. "Calling dibs, are we?"

You bet.

Luc slanted a quick glance Henri and steered his Audi A4 Cabriolet into a straightaway out of a serpentine turn.

"Your propensity for the inappropriate never ceases to amaze me."

"So what's going on with you, big bro?" Henri pressed.

What was going on? That was the million-dollar question. This time last month, he was just a man doing his job. Then he met a woman who turned him inside out.

Mon Dieu, what *had* happened to him? All he knew was he'd never felt this way about anyone. From that first day when he'd seen her standing there on the front porch of her modest little North Carolina house in that hideous big yellow coat, he'd fallen for her—it was her spunk, her tenacity and most of all her tendency to go against the grain of all things royal. She was authentic and sincere and just plain fabulous.

The perfect *anti-princesse.* He was so far gone it was becoming clear that he should simply stop fighting it.

"Okay, then... So..." Henri said as if he were reading his thoughts. "I approve, because all work and no play was beginning to make Luc a very dull boy. I can't remember the last time I saw you smile like that."

He hadn't even realized he was smiling. He raked a hand over his mouth, as if he could wipe the grin off his face. But it was hopeless. She did make him smile. She made him laugh and dream and feel things he thought he could never feel. Still, even as close as he and Henri were, he didn't feel like sharing the intimate details with him.

Fortunately for Henri, their stepmother's disgrace on the family didn't seem to have taken as big an emotional toll on him as it had on Luc. Henri dated frequently and always managed to keep his head above water and his public and private lives separate.

Luc had been cut a little deeper than his two brothers. Or maybe it was simply that he and his brothers were built differently. The three of them were as different as could be. Yet they'd always been close, and had grown even tighter since their father's death.

In the tumultuous sea of St. Michel politics, his brothers were a steadfast constant he knew he could count on, even if he didn't feel like kissing and telling.

The toy delivery couldn't have turned out better. They gave away five hundred wrapped presents to the children of the *Palais de St. Michel* staff and other families that needed help. Sophie was already contemplating how she could expand the holiday drive next year and provide festive food for families who might not have a traditional meal on their Christmas table.

Her grandfather assured her no one would go hungry. Still, if she and the Crown Council could enjoy an endless supply of expensive champagne throughout the year, the least she could do was to ensure that the people who served her were well fed and cared for.

After the issue of her legitimacy was settled, she planned to challenge the council to review staff wages. It was exhilarating to realize that she potentially held the power to create so much change. Nothing like the red tape and hurdles she had to maneuver when she worked for the county. That and the fact that Savannah was happy were reason enough to make her want to stay in St. Michel. Okay, so she had to count Luc in that list, too. The thought made her smile.

All that and she'd had the great opportunity to meet Henri, Luc's brother she'd heard so much about. While they were at the community center, and Sophie and Henri were working alone together giving out the toys, he mentioned that their youngest brother, Alex, was arriving later to surprise Luc for the holidays.

"It's the first Christmas we'll spend together since we lost our father," Henri said. "Alex just found out yesterday that he could get away and he decided to surprise Luc."

"Please join us for dinner tonight," Sophie insisted. "It's going to be informal. But I can guarantee that the food will be out of this world and the company will be divine."

"We would be delighted," he said.

She could tell that Henri was the charmer of the family. He just had a certain way about him, a perpetual spark of mischief twinkling in his brown eyes. He and Luc were alike in so many ways, yet so different.

She couldn't wait to meet Alex, to see the three brothers together. She'd grown up in a loving but small family. Because of that she always wondered what she'd missed as an only child and had always been fascinated by the dynamics of sibling relationships. The chance to glimpse the special bond Luc shared with his brothers made her giddy.

Once they were back at the apartment and everyone was busy toasting and sampling the hors d'oeuvres, she and Luc grabbed two flutes of champagne and stole away, alone out on the terrace.

"Carol of the Bells" played softly in the background, as the sun set over the Mediterranean Sea. A cool breeze swept in from the water blowing her hair across her cheek. Luc reached up and brushed the errant strand out of her eyes, then leaned in and dusted her lips with a whisper of a kiss. It felt like the world had shifted—her world had anyway. He just had that effect on her.

They were both careful about not being too physical in public. Nobody knew about them yet. Sophie didn't even fully know where they stood; they hadn't discussed it, but really there didn't seem to be a need. Everything felt…right. Everything from his voice, to his lips to the way his body felt against hers when he held her.

Theirs was a private slow burn rather than a flashing blaze. Even though the fire that smoldered between them was hot—so hot that sometimes it was hard to keep their hands off each other. Still, they wanted to be careful—in light of the near scandal with Yves.

The thought was a downner, and it made her recall the legitimacy issue, which made her think of the two things she needed to tell Luc—the conversation with Marie, and the phone call from Frank. She decided to start with the good news first.

"My chambermaid Adèle and her mother, Marie, gave me one of the best Christmas presents I could hope for," she said. "Stories about Princesse Sylvie."

She recounted how Marie used to be Sylvie's chambermaid, and she told Luc how Marie swore that her parents were married the day that they died in the plane crash.

"I was already born, so it doesn't help with the Crown Council battle. Too bad legitimacy isn't retroactive when the parents marry after the child's birth."

Luc's brows knit and a strange look passed over his face.

"What's wrong?" she asked.

"Nothing. Just realized something I need to check into. So, it must have been nice to hear firsthand from someone who knew your mother."

Sophie nodded, suddenly flooded with a warmth and a feeling of contented well-being, but it was short-lived as she remembered the other thing she needed to tell him.

"I also had a not-so-great experience today. My ex-husband called."

Luc's right brow shot up. "He did?"

"I don't really want to talk about him right now, because I don't want to spoil the festivities, but I thought you should know he's heard the *news.* I probably should've told him before I left. But there's usually no talking to the man. Today was no exception. He's threatening to cause trouble over Savannah living here. The perverse thing is he didn't have time for her when we were all in Trevard. Then it was next to impossible when he moved to California. I hate to sound cynical, but I think he's thinking in terms of child support. I get the feeling that he's thinking that now that my circumstances have changed, he'll sue for primary custody and get a hefty child-support check for his efforts."

She hated to sound so jaded, but after living with the man for fifteen years, sadly she knew that was how he operated. Always the opportunist.

"Don't worry about it," Luc said. "Especially not on Christmas Eve. Just know that I'll make sure he doesn't bother you."

"I don't want to keep Savannah from seeing her father. I wanted to warn you…just in case."

He pressed his forefinger to her lips.

"Don't worry. I will ensure that both you and Savannah are happy."

His words caused a lump to form in her throat. As if all the emotion she was feeling was lodged right there.

How did she get so lucky? Luc was clearly a huge part of the reason she wanted to stay in St. Michel. For once, everything seemed to be lining up and her heart was finally recognizing that he might be the one.

The one. For a perfect moment she stopped and savored the thought as Luc took her hand in his.

"Here he is." They flinched apart at the sound of the male voice behind them.

The look on Luc's face was priceless when he turned and saw Alex standing with Henri.

"Surprise, bro. Merry Christmas."

Alex was cut from the same dark, gorgeous Lejardin mold as his older brothers. Yet, as with Henri, she could immediately sense the differences. Maybe it was the contrast of his jeans, casual sweater and loafers next to the more formal attire of his older brothers or maybe it was the hint of a tan and the sun-bleached highlights that glinted in his longish mop of hair (no amount of money could buy hair color that perfect and Sophie's immediate impression of Alex Lejardin was that he was much too laid back to even contemplate hair color.)

"I don't believe it," Luc said as he enfolded Alex in a back-slapping man hug. "When did you get here? How did you know to come here?" Luc glanced from Sophie to Henri. "Wait a minute, I sense a conspiracy. Ah, but it doesn't matter. I'm so glad you're here."

Watching the three brothers together filled her with a bottomless sense of peace and satisfaction that carried her through the dinner and merriment.

After all the guests had gone home, Savannah went to bed anticipating a visit from "St. Nick." Even though Luc should've gone home to spend time with his brothers, he stayed to help her fill stockings for the staff and set out Savannah's Santa gifts. So Sophie and Luc set to work in front of the fire.

After they finished, he said, "I can't stay long, but I want a moment alone with you. It seems jolly old St. Nicholas entrusted me to give you a little something on this fine Christmas Eve night."

He produced a small, square box wrapped in gold paper out of his jacket pocket and handed it to her. Sophie's stomach flip-flopped as he handed it to her.

"He asked me to have you open it tonight." Luc winked at her.

She leaned in and kissed him.

"What a coincidence. He left something with me for you."

Sophie set the box on the coffee table and got up to retrieve a festively wrapped box from under the tree.

With another man, it might have been difficult to find just the right present or awkward to give it to him because their relationship was so new. And still so uncertain.

She sat down and handed it to him.

"Open yours first," he said.

She felt suddenly shy as she gently tore the paper from the box. "It's so beautiful, I almost don't want to ruin it."

Wasn't that the truth.

The phone call from Frank reminded her that they had married so young and been together so long. She'd had a few dates since they'd divorced, mostly with men she'd met waiting tables at the steak house, but she'd been so busy she hadn't had the time or desire to think of starting anything serious. Or maybe it was because no one had seemed worth the effort. Until now. Luc was a rare mix of sexy and sophisticated and he was just plain easy to be with. The first man to make her stop and think…maybe this could work…that maybe he could be the one. Even so, Frank was the only man she'd ever been with, and contemplating Luc as a lover was a bit overwhelming.

Frank had taken a lot from her when he'd left—literally and figuratively. He'd made her believe that love was a fairy tale that existed only in storybooks. But Luc made her want to believe in white knights and castles and happily ever afters.

As she lifted the lid of the box, the beautiful strand of gray pearls inside took away her breath. "Oh, Luc, they're beautiful."

"I'm glad you like them."

She slipped the pearls around her neck so that the clasp was in front and held up her hair so he could help her fasten them. "Do you mind?" she asked.

"My pleasure."

As he leaned in, his lips were a fraction away from hers. He was close enough for her to breathe in his breath and the intoxicating scent of him. After he slid the clasp into place, his fingers found their way around to the back of her neck, into her hair and he closed the distance between them.

Tender and soft, the feel of Luc's lips on hers sent heat shimmering through her body. His touch, the simple feel of his mouth on hers swept her away into a world that was theirs alone. Tonight things were different, deeper, impossibly right. And for the first time in a long time, her heart opened.

He shifted to deepen the kiss, the essence of him infusing itself in her senses, going to her head like rare and expensive wine. She was drunk on his taste, his scent, the feel of him so close to her. Her hands explored the expanse of his shoulders, trailed down the hard muscles of his back, and the shimmer of heat in her belly sparked and her yearning flamed, burning deep and hot.

"Luc, we have to stop," she murmured breathlessly as he trailed kisses down her neck. "We can't do this here. You warned me once that the walls have eyes."

"Your bedroom is totally blind," he whispered.

She wanted him. So badly. But right now it wasn't a good idea. Her life was taking so many twists and turns, she couldn't quite tell if making love to him would be a wrong turn. If it was, she might lose him forever, and she'd rather wait—as hard as that might be—than risk it.

Even though common sense screamed that the last thing

she needed was Luc in her bedroom, her heart answered that maybe that was exactly what she needed.

As if he sensed her dilemma, he stood and offered his hand. "Dance with me."

She laughed a shy laugh. "We don't have any music."

He held up a finger. *"Un moment, s'il vous plaît."*

He walked over to the stereo, which was still housed in the same antique armoire it had been all those years ago when Antoine lived here as a boy and Luc used to come over and hang out. Granted, the system had been upgraded with the latest state-of-the-art equipment in preparation for Sophie's visit, but everything was still in its original place, like an old friend in his corner.

"You seem to know your way around this place pretty well," Sophie said.

He scanned the impressive selection of CDs. "I spent a lot of time here, way back when. Prince Antoine was my friend and we spent many hours in this very room talking, laughing, listening to music."

"I didn't realize you were close with the prince." Her voice was soft and held a note of sorrow.

Luc nodded as he chose a Nat King Cole disc, set the CD to Play and pulled Sophie to her feet and into his arms. He didn't want to talk about Antoine. Not now—and he knew that's exactly how his friend would want it. He would've said go for the girl. Even if she was his niece, because he would've known Luc's intentions were pure.

As strains of "Unforgettable" emanated softly from the stereo, Luc decided he didn't want to talk, period. Not with words. He wanted to hold this woman in his arms and show her how he felt—connect with her, feel her body moving with his, lose himself in the feel of her and revel in the way she was responding to him.

It would be torture watching her dance with other men at the ball. He would be working, of course, and would have no time for dancing. Not when there was so much at stake. He pulled her closer, as if he could protect her with his body—surrounding her, coveting her, needing to make her his own. He savored the way she seemed to melt into him, fitting perfectly into the space he'd created for her, as if she belonged there. And she did. He knew that without a doubt.

She gazed up at him, her eyes dark and full of emotion, their lips a breath apart as they swayed together—not in a formal dance that moved them around the room, but in a slow, private dance of desire that moved through them, joining them, making them one.

When she'd entered his life, the moment he'd first set eyes on her, something had shifted. Life as he knew it had ceased to exist. It had gone from automatic gray, going-through-the-motions to something bright and shiny, filled with purpose and breathtaking possibility.

He hadn't looked back since that first day, and now that she was in his arms, he intended to keep moving forward—as fast as she would comfortably let him.

Chapter Fourteen

After Yves De Vaugirard threatened King Bertrand the morning of the press conference, Luc was successful in planting informants among the wait staff in the de Vaugirard households. From those plants, he obtained information that they were, indeed, plotting an attempt on the king's life. The plan was to be carried out at the New Year's Eve ball.

With this information, Luc tried to dissuade the king from holding the ball.

Granted, the party was only two days away, but this was a code-red security concern. It could cost the king his life, not to mention the danger it put Sophie and Savannah in. Informing King Bertrand of the traitorous information he'd uncovered involving his godson and good friend was one of the worst moments of Luc's life—ranking right up there with his father's death. The look of betrayal was heart wrenching. But it finally hardened into a stance of challenge

The king leaned back in his desk chair. "I will not cancel a hundred-year tradition. If I do it, it will appear as if I'm running scared. I refuse to live that way. I want them to understand I am the king and I will not buckle to pressure even if it costs me my life."

A silent understanding passed between them and at that very moment, Luc had never respected any man more in his life—nor had he known one so maddeningly stubborn.

"It is one thing to arrest the De Vaugirards for plotting to kill me," the king said. "But they are slippery and rich and short of your catching them with a smoking gun in their greedy hands, the likelihood that they will wriggle out of the plotting charges is great. But if we catch them in the act, it will be quite another matter."

Luc ran his hands over his tired eyes. The weight of the matter had been keeping him up nights. When he did manage to sleep, nightmares of assassination attempts plagued his dreams. He wasn't able to stop the monsters from killing Prince Antoine, but he'd be damned if anything happened to the king or Savannah or Sophie.

No. He would take the bullet before he lost Sophie or anyone close to her.

"What you must understand, Your Majesty, is that in all likelihood, they're not going to be the triggermen. They will place themselves in obvious places so that there's no doubt of their alibis."

However, the information he'd obtained from the informants coupled with an actual assassination attempt would, in all likelihood, present enough evidence for a sound conviction. It was a huge risk, one that he was not at all comfortable with, but because the king was hell-bent on holding the ball, this could be his opportunity to put the De Vaugirards away for good. One thing they had in their favor was that the two were getting anxious—and that's when people slipped up. They'd waited patiently all these years, biding their time, spacing out the murders and executing them carefully so that they looked like accidents. Just when they thought they were nearly home free, the king pulled his long-lost granddaughter out of the woodwork.

Oh, to have been a fly on their wall after the luncheon when Sophie was introduced.

"The important thing is that you guard Sophie and Savannah with your life," said the king. "My life is secondary to theirs."

It was a touching display of grandfatherly love, but, "Your Majesty, with all due respect, if you're assassinated before Sophie's position is secured, there will be more lost than a hundred-year-old New Year's Eve tradition. The entire Founteneau dynasty will come to an end."

"That is why I have complete faith in you, Luc."

The king's use of Luc's given name caught him off guard.

"I know you have my granddaughter's best interest at heart." The king stroked his chin and regarded Luc contemplatively. "I've noticed you two seem to have developed an affinity for each other."

The blood in Luc's veins ran cold and he could hear it rushing in his ears. In an instant all sorts of possibilities flashed in his mind—ranging from how he would react if the king forbade him to be involved with Sophie to what he would say if the king brought up Patrices's inappropriate behavior and asked if he hadn't learned a lesson—but this was different. It was true that Sophie outranked him by virtue of royal blood. He was a commoner. A simple man. But St. Michel law did not prohibit monarchs from marrying out of the royal gene pool and that was the one glimmer of hope that he'd clung to.

"In case you were wondering," the king said with a certain look in his eye, "I think the two of you would do a world of good for each other. And if you were ever planning on asking, I would certainly give my blessing."

Luc was on his way to see Sophie when his phone rang.

"Lejardin."

"Lejardin here, too." It was Alex. "I have some news that I think will make you very happy—and could very well make me a national hero, too. It's that good."

Luc stopped and scanned the empty hallway to assure he was alone. He was.

"What is it?" he asked cautiously.

"Are you absolutely sure that Princesse Sylvie and Nick Morrison were married before they perished in that plane crash?"

His heart lurched. On Christmas Eve, when Sophie had told Luc of the conversation with Princesse Sylvie's former chambermaid, he'd thought he remembered something about illegitimate children being legitimized after their parents' marriage, but he hadn't know where to look it up. Since Alex was the lawyer, and was helping them comb the constitution, he'd asked him to check into it. Could it be…

"It's the word of a chambermaid, who says she was with Princesse Sylvie on the day she married. I don't have the documents, but I know where to look for them."

"Well, you'd better get your hands on them fast. That's her ticket to the throne. Article 222 of the St. Michel Civil Code states in part: children born outside marriage are legitimated by the subsequent marriage of their father and mother."

She wasn't expecting Luc tonight. Savannah was at a sleepover—with a security guard in tow, much to her dismay, but she was learning that along with the cool wardrobe and great shoe collection, the life of a princess came with excess security baggage, too.

Sophie had a date with a good book and a nice hot bubble bath. Because Luc had been working overtime with security concerns about the New Year's Eve ball, she'd resigned herself to seeing him in fits and snatches until their January 2 date to go to St. Ezra.

She was soaking in a hot sea of bubbles when Adèle knocked on the bathroom door. "*Pardonnez-moi,* Your Highness, I hate to disturb you, but Monsieur Lejardin is here to see you and I thought you'd want to know."

Luc? Here? A rush of adrenaline pumped through her at the unexpectedness of his visit.

"Thank you, Adèle. Please tell him I'll be right out."

She scrambled out of the tub hastily swiping a plush towel at the water and bubbles dripping from her skin. Nervous energy coursed through her and she dressed hurriedly in a pink cashmere sweater and black slacks.

The sight of her made him catch his breath. He loved her best with no makeup. Just the way she looked right now, with wet hair and bare feet looking oh so touchable in the dim glow of the lit Christmas tree she insisted on leaving up until after the new year.

"Hello," he said. "I probably should have called before I stopped by, but I need to talk to you."

"No." She ran a hand through her damp hair as she walked toward him. "I'm glad you're here. Is everything okay?"

He blew out a breath, pacing himself.

"I have news and lots of it. Do you want the good news, the even better news or the best news first?"

She stepped back and shook her head, looking bewildered and impossibly gorgeous. "Start with the just plain old good news and work your way up from there, okay?"

"Okay. Now that I think of it, I hope you consider this good news," he said, backtracking. "I think it's good because—"

"What? Just tell me."

"Your ex-husband won't be bothering you anymore. We offered him a reasonable sum of money and we will pay for his flights and accommodations for him to visit your daughter four times a year. He seemed to think it was a fair settlement. In exchange, he is not to challenge you for custody. Does that sound okay with you?"

She nodded, her brows knit. "That was easy." She shrugged. "Yes, I guess that is good news. I just hope he'll keep up his end of the bargain and come visit his daughter. What's the *even better* news?"

"Come on, let's sit down." Luc took her by the hand and led her to the couch.

She looked at him skeptically. "You're sure this is good news?"

He smiled. "You be the judge. Alex called with the answer we've been looking for."

Her eyes grew large. "Are you saying what I think you're saying?"

He nodded and relayed the conversation he'd had with his brother. The only problem was that the offices of the St. Ezra *maire* were closed until January 2. He'd made a couple of phone calls and discovered the delay. "That means we have four days before we can put our hands on solid proof. I think it's best that we don't tell a soul until we have that document in our hands. With all due respect, I think it's best that we hold off mentioning it to His Majesty, too. I would hate to disappoint him if for some reason this turns out to be a wild-goose chase." As the reality set in, Sophie was stunned speechless.

That was fine. He couldn't talk, either, could only answer her with a kiss, drawing her into his arms, savoring the taste of her and the warmth of her body pressed against his. As he held her, the world melted away. The emotions that had awakened that first day made a final shift into place, as if the right key had finally been inserted into the lock that had held him stoically captive all these years. He wanted her. Needed her. There was no more denying, no more pretending or trying to contain his feelings.

The journey to her bedroom seemed the longest path he'd ever traveled, starting and stopping again and again to savor the feel and taste of her, unable to quench his desire for this woman who had captured his soul. When they finally reached her room, they stumbled through the doorway, pulling at each other's clothes, driven only by the burning need to get closer, closer, until their bodies joined as one.

His touch was possessive. She wanted him to possess her. Every inch of her. She pulled his shirt over his head, wanting skin on skin. Wanting to touch and be touched. Wanting his hands on her body in places that had ached for him for far too long. A little moan of pleasure escaped her as he removed her sweater. His hands slid down her bare back and cupped her bottom through her pants, pulling her in so that her body begged her to let the hardness of him find its way home.

It had been a long time since she'd allowed herself to fully want, to fully trust, but that was over now and all that mattered was how she needed this man. His need for her made her feel powerful and beautiful. Strong and desirable. As no one had ever made her feel before.

The rest of their clothes fell away and he walked her backward to the bed and laid her down, covering her with his massive body.

"I love you," he whispered. "That was the other thing I came to say."

At that moment she knew that not only had she fallen in love with St. Michel, but somewhere along the way she'd fallen in love with Luc, too.

She looked as if she'd stepped from a dream. Luc's stomach constricted with renewed desire as he gazed across the ballroom at Sophie in that ruby-red gown that so perfectly hugged those curves he'd taken to dreaming about on the nights he wasn't able to possess them. Too bad she was proving to be as stubborn as her grandfather when it came to matters of security.

From his post on the east balcony, he watched her as she stood alongside her grandfather, receiving guests, as regal as if she'd been raised in a Grand Ballroom. All around her women in designer gowns and fabulous jewels mixed with men in tuxedos. Yet Sophie stood out among the rest, outshone every woman in the room, and Luc's gaze kept tracking back to her.

Sophie Baldwin was born to be a *princesse.*

He remembered how she felt in his arms last night. How their bodies had fit together as if they were made for each other, how they'd moved together so perfectly. A rush of longing coursed through him and he knew he was in trouble. Tonight of all nights he had to keep his mind on the job.

It was crucial.

Just as he had tried to dissuade King Bertrand, he all but begged Sophie to bow out of the New Year's Eve ball. He'd leveled with her, told her it was just too dangerous. But like her grandfather, she refused to run and hide.

Luc didn't know if she was brave or foolish—either way, he loved her and couldn't stand the thought of losing her when they'd just found each other.

According to the informant, the assassin would strike at the stroke of midnight. Luc and Dupré had revised the security plan for the evening. As far as the Crown Council was concerned—specifically the de Vaugirards—the plan Luc had detailed at the meeting two days ago was the only plan: the king would ring in the new year on the east balcony, as was tradition. But in reality, King Bertrand and Sophie would leave the party just before midnight. The revelers would think they were on their way up to the gossamer-draped, gilded balcony, where at the very last minute, Dupré would discreetly roll out a lifelike mannequin into the king's spot and place another in a red dress identical to Sophie's toward the back of the box. The king's decoy was the one they used to divert the media. From a distance it looked quite realistic.

The only other change to the plan was that they'd kept Savannah at home and planned to reply that the child was under the weather if anyone inquired after her.

The evening was half over. The dinner had gone smoothly and Luc was fairly comfortable that if the assassin stuck to the plan the informant had detailed, they would be okay. What worried him were the remaining hours leading up to midnight when there would be so much movement on the dance floor. His entire security force was on high alert, stationed inconspicuously, watching for anything out of the ordinary.

Because somewhere out there in the sea of silk and jewels lurked a killer, and if that killer attempted to strike tonight it was the end of the road for the de Vaugirards.

But Luc vowed that the royal family would not suffer another tragedy.

As if the New Year's Eve ball—the final exam of her deportment lessons—wasn't enough to rattle her nerves, just toss in a few nasty rumors about an assassination and it was enough to make Sophie a wreck.

Not to mention, she wouldn't be able to dance with Luc tonight. As the Baron von Something-or-other—one of her many dance partners tonight—twirled and dipped her around the wooden dance floor, he just didn't compare. Luc was the only one she wanted to dance with, and she didn't want to be here if she couldn't be with him. Reflexively she scanned the room to see if she could catch a glimpse of him, but he was nowhere to be found. Invisible.

Still, she had no choice but to make the best of this. Since her grandfather insisted that the show go on—and he had made such a big deal that the ball was the time when he would present her and Savannah—who was she to disappoint him?

She was the heir to the throne, so dancing with men who smelled of mothballs and bad breath, making inane small talk with smug, privileged women, and shrugging off the occasional death threat were going to be a hazard of the job, right?

Perhaps. But she didn't have to like it, she thought as the music ended. She curtsied to the baron and exited the dance floor, politely declining invitations to dance the next waltz.

Still, she had to draw the line somewhere.

Actually she already had. She refused to endanger her daughter, who was just as happy to stay in when she found out there wouldn't be any kids her age at the party.

Tomorrow, Sophie decided as she took a seat at the table that was reserved for the king and his party, she would draw the next line—she would sit down with her grandfather and have a serious talk with him about this pissing match he was having with the De Vaugirards. Enough was enough. The men were killers, plain and simple, and they needed to be put in their place. If Luc had enough evidence to arrest them for plotting to kill the king, she was all for running with it. Even if they managed to wiggle out of the charges, wouldn't their mission be exposed and wouldn't that in itself be enough to keep them from making any future attempts?

It seemed like a no-brainer, but who was she to say—and why didn't anyone else see it except her, and possibly Luc? She was just tired—and it was not quite eleven o'clock. She still had a good forty-five minutes to go before she could leave.

Maybe she could fake a headache, which wouldn't be a total lie. These people wanted to talk to her only because she was the king's granddaughter. All they wanted to do was gossip about her legitimacy—or lack thereof—or who was wearing which designer, and whose jewels were borrowed or, better yet, fake. Her feet hurt and she didn't want to dance anymore.

She just wanted to find Luc and go home and take a nice long bubble bath and talk about their trip to St. Ezra—

Two gunshots and a chorus of screams rang out in the ballroom. In a flash, Luc appeared from out of nowhere, shielding her with his body.

As he hustled her off to safety, through the crowd she saw her grandfather sprawled on the parquet floor.

Thank God for bulletproof vests.

The king had worn one under his tuxedo, and it had saved his life. The force of the bullet hitting the vest was what knocked the frail old man off his feet. He escaped with only a mild concussion from hitting his head on the wooden dance floor.

The second bullet had most likely been meant for her. But Luc had saved her.

Two days later, as Luc drove Sophie to the village of St. Ezra, she shuddered at the thought of how tragically things would have turned out if the killer had chosen to aim for her grandfather's temple rather than his heart. From this perspective, it seemed reckless to have gone through with the ball—when they knew good and well that there was a valid safety concern—just so her grandfather could prove he wasn't a man who was easily intimidated. Yeah, he'd come very close to being a dead man.

As she watched the hilly farmland of southern France roll by out the window of Luc's Audi, it seemed a miracle that innocent bystanders weren't hurt in the fray, that someone else hadn't been shot or that people hadn't been trampled in the frenzy to get out of harm's way.

Only now did she realize that on the day of the ball, she

hadn't truly believed they'd been in danger—that someone would actually hire an *assassin* to shoot another human being for his own personal gain. Only now did the magnitude of the situation sink in.

This accidental princess role she'd been playing wasn't make-believe. It was serious business and she was in it—she'd dragged her daughter into it—up to her eyebrows.

The only consolation—if it could be called a consolation—was that the authorities had arrested the gunmen and the Comte De Vaugirard at the ball. As far as Sophie was concerned, he could rot in hell, because that's where he belonged.

The bad news was his son, the *vicomte,* had escaped—throwing his father to the lions. With him loose, it was like a horror movie come to life, not knowing when the monster was going to pop up. She hated horror movies. She just wanted to go home. She wanted to wrap herself in that hideous mustard-yellow coat and disappear into the anonymous life she'd been plucked from just a month ago.

Luc reached out and rubbed her thigh. "Are you okay?"

"I don't know if I am or not, Luc. They actually tried to kill my grandfather, and I don't know if this is the kind of life I want to live."

"Everything is going to be okay. You're just a little shell-shocked by what happened."

Anger bubbled up inside her. *Shell-shocked?* As if it was something natural she'd get over. That made her *so* mad.

"How can you say that?" Her voice had an edge.

He slanted her a glance and returned his gaze to the road without answering her.

And *that* made her furious. Furious at him for being a part of this self-absorbed royal society. Furious at him for bowing to the whims of her grandfather when he knew the safety concerns—furious at him for…for…. She looked at his profile and her heart turned over in her chest. It wasn't because he was so devastatingly gorgeous.

It was because he was involved in all the things that made her so mad, yet he was so removed from them. Her common sense screamed at her that he didn't have a choice but to go along with the party, that he was just doing his job—and he did it well.

She and her grandfather were alive, weren't they?

Off in the distance, the *village perché* of St. Ezra rose like a giant specter on the horizon. Up there was the key to her future, although she might not need it once the Crown Council had a chance to reconvene and decide how to move forward without the De Vaugirards. But that didn't seem to matter anymore.

"Luc, come back to North Carolina with me."

This time he didn't look at her—he kept staring straight ahead at the road. "I'm not cut out for this life. Let's just stop. I don't want to go to St. Ezra. I just want to get Savannah and go home."

He pulled the car over along the shoulder of the road and sat there for a couple of beats before he looked at her. His eyes, his expression were devastating. "You're upset and that's understandable, but people are counting on you. I am counting on you. If you run away, you will be running from the truth, and taking away all that right and good and just from the people of St. Michel and essentially turning it over to those like the Vicomte De Vaugirard. If you don't stand up to evil, it will win."

Oh, God. Wasn't that, in so many words, what she used to

tell her clients? If they didn't face the hard times head-on, they'd never get to the good on the other side.

They drove the rest of the way to St. Ezra in silence.

They parked at the base of the hill and prepared to make the big climb up the steep incline to the top of this perched village—the place where her mother had run off to all those years ago to risk everything, to marry the man she loved so that she could get her baby back. So that they could be a family.

Didn't she owe it to her mother—and her daughter—to stand up and fight for what was right?

Gazing up at the village walls, she realized the situation was so much bigger than her, the only way she could approach it was to not think about making it to the top. She just needed to take the next step. And then the next. Tears welled in her eyes. She reached out and took Luc's hand and they took that first step together. Until they rounded about halfway up the hill and stood face-to-face with the Vicomte De Vaugirard, who was pointing a gun at Sophie's forehead.

In the off-season, no one but the locals came to St. Ezra. It was inland and just far enough north that the bitter winter winds left their biting mark on those who ventured up the hill. Luc knew he had to think fast to find a way to get the gun away from De Vaugirard before the homicidal maniac decided to use it on Sophie. The thought of that made him burn with anger, made him want to rip the gun right out of the bastard's hand and turn it on him.

The *vicomte* yanked Sophie toward him, pulled her in front of him and pointed the gun at her temple. She let out a scared squeak.

"If you scream, I swear I will blow your head off right now. Not that anyone would hear you, they're so far up there." Yves gestured upward with his head. Luc could tell by the crazed look in his glassy eyes that the *vicomte* would shoot. He said a silent prayer that Sophie didn't try to play the heroine. "Lejardin, turn around and start walking down the steps. Go on! Do it. *Vite!*"

Luc's heart hammered in his chest as he complied. Keeping his head forward, he scanned the area with his eyes, but all he could see was brown rock wall to his left and the long stretch of highway they'd traveled, which was visible over the low portion of the winding wall on his right. He didn't have much time to think of something and he'd have to act fast once he did. Because he was walking in front of Yves and Sophie, the madman could easily shoot him in the back of the head and leave him for dead.

"Why are you doing this, *vicomte?*"

"Don't talk, just keep walking."

He was taking a big chance of annoying him if he continued to talk, but right now, it looked as if that might be his only way out. The guy wasn't in his right mind—if he ever had a *right mind.* Getting him to talk was the best way to distract him so that he could knock the gun out of his hand.

But he'd only get one chance at it....

"I just don't understand why a man like you, someone who has everything would do something like this. Especially when Sophie was just telling me she has no desire to succeed her grandfather."

Silence.

Good. That meant Yves was thinking.

"She was saying she misses North Carolina and wants to

go back. Can't imagine herself here. So why don't you just let us go? You can go back to St. Michel, the Crown Council will carry on with their plan to name you as the king's successor and life will resume as planned."

Luc's mouth was so dry, he could barely form the words. "Right, are you kidding me? They've put my father in jail."

"Then he needs you to set him free. As the future king, you have that power."

"I've worked long and hard waiting to become king."

Yes, there it was. Luc didn't say anything, in hopes that Yves would keep talking.

"There were so many of you in my way. But after Sylvie died, I got the idea, why not help them along. Celine and Thibault's accidents were a breeze." Yves made a sound as if he was blowing out a candle and white-hot anger from the injustice of the killing gripped Luc. So he'd been mostly right about the deaths, and the murderer had a gun to the head of the woman he loved. He had to steel himself to keep from acting irrationally. As they rounded the bends on the spiral, Luc could see Yves in his peripheral vision. He was getting lost in the story. The gun was not always at Sophie's temple. His hand was unsteady and on the steps down, it bounced up a little. It would take only another moment....

"Prince Antoine and his family, that was another story. So many of them. Like rats. And what's the best way to get rid of rats? You burn them all—"

As they rounded the next bend and Yves started to step down, the gun wavered a bit. In one swift motion Luc reached back and grabbed Yves's wrist.

"Run!" he screamed channeling all the crushing rage he

felt at the murder of his friend and the danger Sophie had been in into the vice grip he had on De Vaugirard.

Sophie tried to run back up the steps—it was the only way she could go since Luc, as he struggled with the gun, blocked the downward passage. Plus help was up toward the village. But before she could get away, Yves caught a fistful of her hair and held on as he continued to fight with Luc for the gun. She yanked backward. Yves lost his footing, stumbled on the steps and let go. Just as she started to run, the gun went off and Luc dropped to the steps in a puddle of blood.

It was the shock of seeing the man she loved lying in a crumpled heap that made her do it. Her loathing of the Vicomte De Vaugirard fueled the force. She turned around and head-butted the *vicomte* so hard that he fell backward over the low portion of the winding wall, into the mucky retaining pond. That's where the police found him when they arrived a few moments later responding to a report of gunshots.

Epilogue

Once upon a time, in a kingdom far, far away, there was a *princesse* who fell in love with a very brave man. It wasn't just his good looks that attracted the *princesse*—nor the fact that he resembled Olivier Martinez, only better. No, it was his knack for rescuing her that did it. And after she got used to the idea, she found it kind of sexy.

The king also thought his granddaughter *princesse's* love was a very brave man and he named him a national hero and knighted him a Chevalier of the Order of St. Michel.

The knight was never afraid to step up when it mattered. He stood by the *princesse* and her family through the best and worst of times. The brave knight even took a gunshot to the shoulder for his beloved *princesse* and survived to tell about the scar.

If that wasn't love, the *princesse* knew there surely wasn't such a thing.

Once the bad guys were tried and convicted of a slew of charges—including murder, attempted murder and treason, among other crimes—it became clear that the brave knight might not have to rescue his *princesse* that often—not from danger, anyway.

So the brave knight took her back to the *maire* of St. Ezra to complete the task of finding the papers that legitimized her birth. Being such a noble knight—and a very romantic soul—he proposed to the *princesse* in the same place where her parents had exchanged their wedding vows.

The *princesse* accepted the proposal with great joy, for she knew all along that he was more than just a brave knight. He was her prince.

And together they started planning their happily ever after. Because there's nothing like a royal wedding to raise the monarchy's approval rating.

* * * * *

Mills & Boon® Special Moments™
brings you a sneak preview.

In Their Second-Chance Child *Tony Herrera must have been crazy to hire his ex-wife Rebecca to oversee his vocational bakery for foster kids! But Becca was best for the job…and his four-year-old daughter fell for Becca instantly. Were Tony and Becca heading down the road to renewed heartache or was this the second chance they never dreamed possible?*

Turn the page for a peek at this fantastic new story from Karen Sandler, available next month in Mills & Boon® Special Moments™!

Don't forget you can still find all your favourite Superromance and Special Edition stories every month in Special Moments™!

Their Second-Chance Child
by Karen Sandler

Rebecca had anticipated a difficult reunion with Tony. She'd expected that storm cloud of anger in his face, the hardness in his usually soft brown eyes. As much as she wished otherwise, she'd come here knowing she might be escorted from the property the moment Tony realized that Rebecca Tipton was actually Becca Stiles.

But she hadn't been prepared for the heat that sizzled inside her, the throbbing low in her body. It had been more than eleven years since they'd last made love, since they'd been man and wife, but her body remembered his touch, his scent, every intimate word whispered in her ear.

His dark brown hair was shorter, but just as thick. His shoulders were broader, almost too wide for the Hawaiian shirt he wore, his arms more muscular. His hands were the same, blunt-fingered and strong, but like everything else about him, they spoke of power and competence. During their marriage, their lives had been filled with unknowns. Now it looked as if he'd found some answers.

As she gazed up at him, he leaned toward her, still angry but maybe pulled by the same memories. He almost reached for her; she could see his fingertips stretching toward her. Then he strode past her and put his desk between them.

"Sit," he said sharply, then bit out, "please."

Was he going to give her a hearing after all? Rebecca lowered herself back into the secondhand office chair.

"You remarried," he said.

"I hear you did as well."

Something dark flickered in his face. "I can't possibly offer you this position."

Rebecca dug in. "You know as well as I do that I'm perfect for the job."

"You're married. This is a live-in position, and I don't have accommodations for a couple."

"I'm divorced."

A long, silent beat as he took that in. Then his gaze narrowed on her. "Estelle didn't say a word when she recommended you."

"You wouldn't have even considered me if you knew. Even if no one else with my qualifications has applied."

"I may have named the program after Estelle, but she isn't the one that hires and fires here. I am." His gaze fixed on her, his dark eyes opaque.

She shivered, blaming the chill fingering down her spine on the gust of cool air spit out by the window air conditioner. Wrapping her arms around herself in self-defense, she considered the arguments she'd prepared, knowing in advance she'd have to fight for this job.

But did she really want to? Maybe he was right—she ought to return to her car. Head back down Highway 50, don those same imaginary blinders she'd worn on her way here as she passed the off-ramp to West Hills Cemetery. Take Interstate 5 south and drive back down to L.A.

Except what waited for her there was just more despair. In the two months since Rebecca's foster daughter, Vanessa, had been returned to her mother, Rebecca had been hollowed out with grief. One moment social services was dotting the i's and crossing the t's on Rebecca's adoption of Vanessa, the next they were calling to notify her that Vanessa's mother had regained custody. Now the five-year-old girl was lost to Rebecca forever. Just as her son was.

She had to at least plead her case with Tony. Hands linked in her lap, she tipped up her chin in challenge.

"You won't find anyone to match what I can offer. You

know from my résumé I have impeccable credentials as a baker. I've volunteered teaching cooking classes for two years at a local Boys and Girls Club. And you know as well as I do that my understanding of what these kids have been through in the foster system isn't just academic."

She'd spent a year in foster care when her parents were badly injured in a freak accident and required extensive rehab to get back on their feet. Estelle had lavished loving care on the frightened nine-year-old that Rebecca had been, becoming a second mother to her in that short time.

Tony's hands curled around the arms of his chair, the skin over his knuckles taut. "You'd be living here full-time. We'd be in each other's faces practically twenty-four/seven."

"It's been eleven years. We can put the past behind us."

"Some pasts shouldn't be forgotten."

That stung, although she probably deserved it. "I know I'd do a good job."

He almost seemed to consider it, then shook his head. "I have to think of the kids. They've all just been emancipated from foster care, and they're anxious enough about their futures. I can't increase their tension by adding you into the mix."

"Don't you think I deserve a chance?"

He shoved his chair back and pushed to his feet. "Damn it, Becca, these kids need some constancy in their lives. They need someone who will commit their heart and soul to them for the entire five months of the session. I can't let you get involved with them and then have you leave them in the lurch if the going gets tough."

He might as well have punched her in the gut. "I was nineteen years old, Tony. Young and confused. I'm not about to walk out on these kids the way I…"

The way I walked out on you. The silent words seemed to echo in the small space. On their heels came the harsher indictment—*The way I walked away from our lost son.*

He started past her, moving toward the door. Rising, she put her hand on his arm to stop him.

A mistake. Her palm fell on his biceps, just below where the wildly colored sleeve of his shirt ended. His skin was hot, the musculature under it rock hard. She yearned to move her hand along the length of his arm, from biceps to forearm to wrist, then lock her fingers in his.

His dark gaze burned into her, the visual connection sending a honeyed warmth through her. Her heart thundered in her ears, so loud she thought he must hear it, would know her self-control was slipping away.

Then he covered her hand with his. To break the contact, she thought, to get free of her. But his fingers lingered, his thumb stroking lightly across the back of her hand.

He pulled his hand back with a jolt, putting space between them at the same time. "You should go." His voice scraped across her nerves like rough silk.